On the Frontier of a Fading Empire

On the Frontier of a Fading Empire

J Leslie Evenden

Philadelphia, Pennsylvania, November 2023

ISBN 979-8-218-31936-6

FICTION/Historical/Ancient
Keywords: Britannia, Roman Empire, Dark Ages

Published by WiltonLogic LLC
Philadelphia, Pennsylvania, USA

Map 1: Part of Britannia

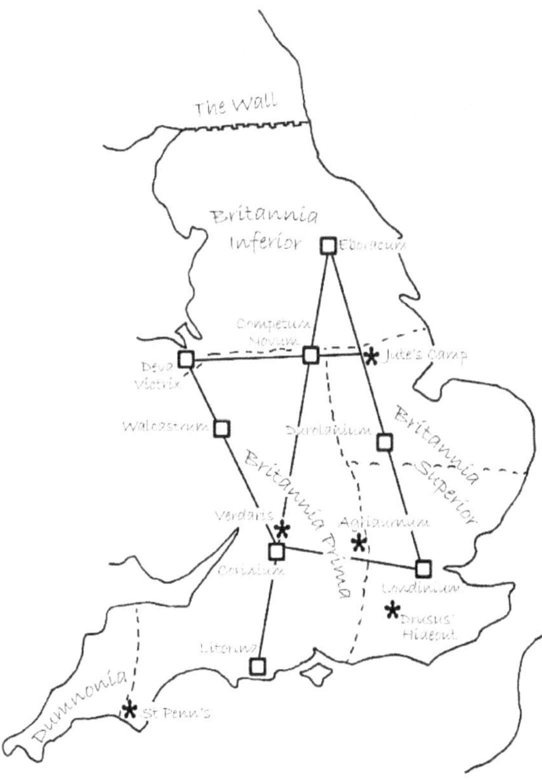

There seems to be disagreement among experts on where the exact boundaries between the four provinces of late Roman Britannia lay. However, in post-Roman Britain there would probably not have been hard-and-fast boundaries at this level. More important would have been the boundaries between the lands of different chiefs, their inter-relationships and their loyalties. Some of the towns on this map have pseudonyms. Even if these correspond to actual towns in Roman Britain, the descriptions in this story are entirely fictitious.

Map 2: Sketch of Town of Corinium as Described to the Author

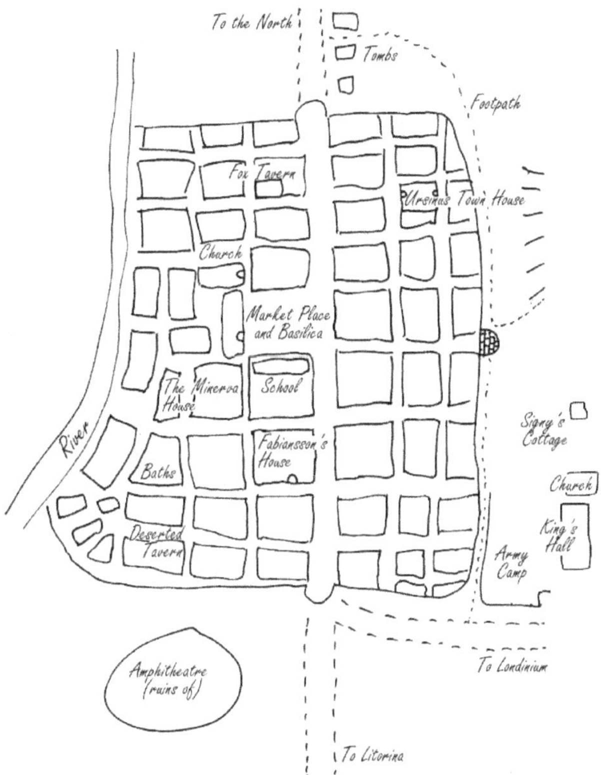

This map is of an imaginary town in the location of Corinium (today's Cirencester). An imaginary map is necessary because not enough is known about the layout of the real Roman city to provide the background for a story such as this. I ask readers to imagine that this map was drawn by an author unfamiliar with the actual city, based on tales heard while sitting in the shade of a tree a long way from the scene of the events.

Characters

Principal Characters

Signy..Saxon captive
Marcus Lucullus Ursinus/Silvanus
....Military magistrate of West Britain
Megana Fabiansdaughter....................Merchant Fabiansson's daughter
Thorgill...Jute chief
Bryna Apollinaria....................................Marcus Ursinus' second wife
Constantinus.......................Vitellus Astrebanus' son, Drusus' nephew
Drusus Astrebanus...........Former landowner, rival to Marcus Ursinus
Fabiansson....................................Merchant and friend of Marcus
Irmengaard....................................Priestess and wise woman in Juteland
Laurentius..Sea captain and trader
(Prince) Merwyn............Marcus' daughter Silva's husband, from Wales
(Chief) Oswulf....................................Jute chieftain and bandit leader

Minor Characters

Alexander...........................Fabiansson's son, Megana's half-brother
Alwynn, Liutmann........Frisian warriors, retainers of Drusus Astrebanus
Amalric..Germanic bandit
Amanda, Silva..Marcus' daughters
Apostoles, Patronus....................................Wealthy southern landowners
Atle, Maglorius, Notius.....................................Northern notables
Aurelius, Flavius, Pacius, Theo............Administrators of West Britain
Barnulf....................................Steward of the Verdaris Estate
(Deacon) Baxter...Signy's tutor
Beltrice....................................Captain of Marcus' bodyguards
Berthold, Fonberga....................................Staff of Minerva House
Borno Atlesson....................................Son of Chief Atle
Carassus..Pontius' son
Colfax..Fabiansson's clerk
Cull....................................Marcus' friend from his youth
Delia..Megana's servant
Edwulf Gislasson
................Chief Gisla's son, Marcus' daughter Amanda's husband
Einar..Marcus and Signy's son
Father Felix....................................Christian priest in Corinium

Ferland, Hrasmus, Asser, Bjornfot ...... Jute warriors
Fulvia ...... British noblewoman
Gallum, Quallius ...... Farmers near Corinium
(Chief) Gisla ...... Saxon ally of Marcus Ursinus
Grunwald ...... Jute warrior, member of Marcus' bodyguard
Gudrun ...... Helga's maid
Gunhilde ...... Servant in brothel
Helga ...... Thorgill's primary wife
Henrik ...... Fabiansson's stable master
Horvath ...... Saxon warrior in Gisla's retinue
Hypatia Ursina ...... Marcus' first wife (deceased)
Jarmi ...... Stable hand at Verdaris
Julia ...... Bryna's maid
Icauna ...... Alexander's wife
Lanius of Burdigala ...... Fabiansson's business partner
Lanric, Walfrith ...... Ship captains
Lucius ...... Marcus' son
Malcolm ...... Cull's son
Maria ...... Signy's maid in Britannia
Martha, Leema ...... British slave women
Mathilda ...... Father Felix's friend
Maud ...... Barnulf's wife
Meri ...... Dairy maid at Verdaris
Milesia Cornelia/Astrebana
...... Widow of Marcus' enemy, Vitellus Astrebanus
Ornfrid, Neema ...... Priestesses, Sisters of Freya
Pacius ...... Lawyer, deputy to Aurelius
Pontius ...... Trader, Fabiansson's cousin
Priscilla ...... Fabiansson's wife
(Chief) Sigg ...... Oswulf's father
Silke ...... Housekeeper of the Ursinus townhouse
Skalgrim, Radwulf, Ravnberg, Ulvholm ...... Jute chiefs, Oswulf's allies
Sophia ...... Megana's daughter
Soraya ...... Fabiansson's mistress, Megana's mother
Surik Carl, Qusi ...... Members of Laurentius' crew
(Factor) Titus ...... Trader in Juteland
Vitellus (Vito) Astrebanus
...... Drusus' brother, Milesia's husband (deceased)
Wulfthere ...... Master carpenter

❦ Prologue ❦
The Baltic Sea, around 435 CE

How long would it continue, Laurentius wondered, for himself, for Surik Carl and Qusi the boatman, the insatiable desire for luxury goods from the Empire, for amber, for furs and for slaves? Not that slaves were luxury goods. They were the motive power of industry, agricultural labour and service inside and outside the home. They were the muscle that pulled his own boat when the wind dropped, physical effort in return for food and shelter, and there were plenty of men who were glad enough of that exchange in these difficult times.

It was a hard life, trading along these shores, he admitted, but he loved it, loved the freedom, loved the challenge, the camaraderie, the clink of coins at the end of the journey. It was a better life than sitting in a house, stuffed up in a town, seeing the same people every day, the same perpetual routine, no matter what Fabiansson claimed. He, Laurentius, would continue trading until he died. But what would be left for his sons now the Empire seemed to be fading away, leaving men like Flavius Aetius and Marcus Ursinus struggling to maintain order in the north-west provinces?

Laurentius' eyes travelled the length of the boat, over the crew who were resting while the wind was astern, taking in the barrels and crates and sacks that filled the centre, until they came to rest on two girls, dark-haired, dark-eyed, tawny-skinned, sitting huddled, wrapped in woollen blankets, just below his feet. He had been compelled to truss them up to prevent them from throwing themselves over the side. He was not an unnecessarily cruel man, so he hoped they might find good masters. Life had turned out well for Soraya, after all. Fabiansson always said he had never had to beat her even once. And as for their daughter…to think it was only last summer that she had been here in this boat, on this very same voyage. The crew had objected to begin with. *No women on board*, they had said. Slave girls didn't count; they were cargo. But the girl had been with them to learn the business, so there was nothing much the men could do about it. After all, she could be their master one day.

He shook his head and chuckled to himself. The little minx! He had known her since she was an infant, but even he had been surprised at what she had got up to in Puttby. Fond memories. Fond memories which would have to remain a secret between them, their little secret.

A burst of spray flew into his face, returning him to the present. The water on this side of Juteland was sweeter, did not sting in the same way, but was still unpleasant to have dribbling into your eyes and down your cheeks, soaking your beard. He rubbed a hand across his face to remove the worst.

He glanced down at the girls once again, and their frightened eyes met his. In the end, it wasn't his business what happened to them. His responsibility was to convey them to the next port alive and in as good health as could be expected. After that, he thought, shrugging, it's in the hands of the gods, but he would expect a couple of blonde-haired, blue-eyed beauties in exchange. They were cheap enough on these shores, but in Arelate or Mediolanum, or even Rome itself, some trader would get a good price. So long as he got his share.

The boat plunged forward with a regular thump as each wave struck the prow. Surik Carl was balancing against the motion, his eyes scanning the horizon, the long, low, green line of land, looking for the shift in shade that signalled the first farms and the outskirts of the occupied area around the Danborg.

"Ahead!" shouted the lookout.

"Gyre," called Qusi.

The boatman leaned on the steering oar, and the ship slowly swung in towards the coast. Laurentius braced himself as the angle of the vessel shifted, as the blows from the waves struck from a different quarter. The crew adjusted the ropes and prepared for a stint of hard rowing.

"The Danborg!" confirmed Surik Carl. His sharp eyes must have picked out the distinctive outline of their destination.

It would have been a horrible miscalculation if it wasn't, thought Laurentius. Impossible…beneath his dignity…though it happened now and then if the weather conditions were deceptive. Now they would slice a diagonal course towards the coast, towards the river mouth, where they could be beached before sunset.

What would be waiting for him when he reached the port? Bags of amber scavenged along the eastern shores, passed from hand to hand until they were collected together in the Danborg? Bundles of furs, black and brown and white, ready to be made into cloaks or hats or baubles for the rich men and women of the Empire? Those were the goods he was hoping for – small in bulk and worth a great deal. If he was out of luck, there might just be bags of grain, stacks of hides or a cluster of surly captives from the interior, to be fed and watered until they reached Puttby and he could pass them on to a dealer. And, of course, whatever he could bargain in return for the two shivering parcels by his feet.

He glanced over his shoulder at the position of the sun. Still plenty of time remained to skim across the placid East Sea and arrive safely before nightfall. Tomorrow would reveal whether there were treasures or bulk cargo awaiting him on this visit.

☙ Chapter 1 ❧

Summer was just shifting to autumn, and the first leaves on the birch trees were beginning to turn yellow. The girl sat in the courtyard, milking the cow. Soon the cow would stop giving milk, and it would be time to start preparing for the winter. She sat alone on a low stool, with her back to the river. Her mother had gone to a neighbour who was expected to give birth any day. Her father and brothers had taken the path through the low woods bordering the river to fields in the clearing beyond. Soon the harvest would be ready, and there would be days of work bringing it in to store for the lean months.

The little farm had only three buildings. The main house, a wooden hall with space for the family at one end and the animals at the other; a storehouse, square in shape and raised on stone footings in the shape of mushrooms to discourage the rats and mice; and a workshop, well away from the other buildings as a precaution against fire. A bare courtyard stretched from the three buildings down to the flat, wide river. A boat passed by, quite close to the bank, and the girl turned and glanced at it. It was nothing unusual – four men, drifting with the stream. Many boats passed up and down the river, trading from one village to another, collecting the farm produce, cloth like her mother wove and simple wooden goods like the ones her father made in the workshop. And bringing with them salt for preserving the meat, metal tools that could not be made on the farm and treats for feast times.

The girl had lived on this farm all her life. She knew all the paths, all the places where birds laid eggs, the wild fruit trees, and where snares could be set for animals. Recently, her mother had started showing her where the special plants grew, the ones that were needed for the medicines she used to treat the family, and which she took with her on her visits to the neighbours when they were sick, became old, or, like today, when it was time to give birth. Often a woman would appear along the track to the house and sit for a while with her mother. Then her mother would search through her stores, mix some herbs, and there would be extra meat at the evening meal or another cheese in the storehouse.

The last of the milk was spurting into the bucket when the cow gave a little start. The girl reached out and patted it on the flank to calm it down. In the next moment, a rough hand covered her mouth, and another grabbed her arm. She felt herself falling backwards off the stool. Other hands grabbed her ankles. She tried to scream, but the hand blocked her voice, and a moment later it was a replaced by a cloth, quickly wrapped tightly over her mouth and her eyes. She felt someone tying her arms behind her back, and another rope was coiled around her ankles. Men's rough voices spoke quietly. One of them put his arms under her shoulders, a second lifted her feet from the ground. She tried to struggle, wriggling back and forth, but their grip was too strong. She could not see where the men were heading, but her sense of place told her they were taking the path behind the storehouse and into the woods. Soon they would reach the small creek where the willows hung low over the water and ducks swam in the summer.

As she was being carried away, she realised that they must have tied up their boat in the creek. The three of them must have crept round the farm, carefully checking to make sure she was alone. Then they had swooped in. As she was bundled into the boat, she felt how a fourth man untied the rope that was preventing the vessel from drifting away from the bank, and then, with a quick push of an oar, sent it out of the creek mouth and into the big river, where it started to drift away downstream. The girl lay in the bottom of the boat. She could not move. She could hardly breath through the stifling cloth. She thought of her mother coming back and finding her gone, not knowing where she was. She thought of her father and brothers returning from the fields to find her mother in tears, and how desperately they would search high and low, until they found the footprints in the mud, and would know that she had been taken, taken away who knows where. And as these thoughts came into her mind, tears welled in her own eyes, and she began to sob, sob for the feelings of her parents, and sob for fear of what would become of her. As she lay tied up, she remembered the animals, young pigs and bull calves, that her family had bound just like the men had bound her. They had thrown them into boats like this one, and how the pigs had squealed, and the calves had bellowed, and nobody thought anything of it. It was just the way life was. They were animals, and they were going to slaughter, as they did every autumn, every year. So where was she going? Her tears dried up as she tried to imagine. Surely they wouldn't kill her and eat her. People didn't do such things, but she had heard stories of girls who were kidnapped and disappeared, boys too sometimes, and even men and women could vanish from one day to another in the vast expanse of the forest. Some simple people said that the fairies had taken them. The men who had travelled, the few men who came back from the warbands, knew better, but they kept silent.

Presently, one of the kidnappers stooped over her. She could hear his breathing and the rustle of his clothes. He undid the cloth that was covering her face. She took a couple of deep breaths and blinked in the light of the sun directly overhead. How nice it was to feel fresh air flowing into her lungs! She tried to sit up, but with her arms still tied behind her back, she could not. She thought about screaming, screaming for help, but what good would that do? They would just gag her again to stifle her cries. How long had they been drifting? She looked up towards the sky, trying to judge how much of the day had passed from the angle of the sun. Would her mother have come back to the house yet? Would her father and brothers have started searching for her? The sun was still too high. The baby wouldn't be out, and her mother wouldn't leave until she was sure it was healthy, that the birth mother was well and the baby suckling at her breast. Then she could pack up and leave for home. The girl knew because she had accompanied her mother the last few times, earlier in the summer. She had watched, fascinated, listening to her mother's explanation. She had seen the little person emerge, red-faced and damp, just as lambs came from a sheep and calves from cows. Her mother would give the baby a quick smack, and it would start to cry, and all the women in the room would break out into relieved smiles. The birth mother was exhausted. It had not been easy, but now the little child was lying on her breast, its head against her heart. Another life had come into the world, and with that the women's smiles rose into happy chatter, and their thoughts returned to their own babies, even when these were now grown men and had children of their own. These thoughts and more came into the mind of the girl as she lay in the bottom of the boat.

After a while, she saw the light was growing a little dimmer, and the sun was beginning to sink towards the horizon. She heard the voices of the men but could not make out what they were saying among themselves. The words they used were strange to her ears. The boat dipped and tossed, and she saw branches overhead. The boat stopped moving. She felt it sway as one of the men jumped out onto the riverbank. Another loosened the bindings around her wrists. Her arms felt numb and stiff, and she could hardly move them round in front of her. The man squatted down in front of her and made a gesture. For a moment, she was puzzled, thinking he was being offensive, and then alarmed, fearing he was intending to force himself on her. Then she realised he was only asking if she needed to piss or shit. She nodded, and he seemed to understand and started to untie her ankles but stopped. He called to his friends, who laughed and threw him a length of rope. He tied it around her neck and fastened one end to his belt. Only then did he loosen her ankles and lift her over the side of the boat. Ahead of her were some low bushes. Her captor motioned in their direction and, keeping hold of the rope attached to her neck, stood with his back towards her until she had finished.

Now she could see the four of them – rough young men, perhaps traders or pirates, if there was any real difference between the two. Long untidy hair, weather-beaten faces, poor clothes which had seen hard wear. They had daggers at their waists, and she had stepped over spears lying in the bottom of the boat, but no swords that she could see. Having taken them in, she looked around at the river, at the features of the riverbank. She did not recognise where she was. It was part of the river she had never seen before. She had travelled to the autumn market a couple of times with her father and brothers, but she did not think they had travelled this far.

The men lit a fire and began to heat their evening meal. One of them brought her a bowl of stew and untied her hands.

"Eat," he said, and sat by her while she ate. Then he tied her up again.

"Sleep," he said.

With the food in her stomach, and the light fading, the girl drifted into sleep.

She woke with a start, looking around for the familiar sights of home. Then she remembered, her heart fell, and a sense of dread and fear took over again. She had been woken by one of the men shaking her. He had a cup of ale which he placed to her lips. Her mouth was parched, so she drank. He handed her some bread and cheese.

"Eat," he said.

She did not really feel like eating; anxiety and loss made her stomach feel like a knot, but she did not know when she would be given food again and she hated feeling hungry, so she forced herself to swallow.

They continued drifting until, by and by, a village appeared in the distance, spread out alongside the river. The men pushed the girl into the bottom of the boat and covered her with a rough cloth, an old sail perhaps. She felt the boat come to a stop and heard bargaining going on. She could not make out everything that was said but understood enough to realise that the men were dealing for farm produce to take down the river.

After that halt, they slid along all day, staying well in the middle of the stream. It would have taken a sharp-eyed person to see that there was a girl in the boat, let alone that she was not there of her free will. The vessel was now full of goods, and the men had to bail now and then as the higher waves slopped over the side.

Towards evening, the girl could see dark shapes on the horizon far away across the plain, and as they grew nearer, she realised they were the outlines of houses, so many houses all packed into one place, and in the midst a tower, breaking the skyline. This must be a town. She had never been to a town, only heard about them in stories from her father or from neighbours when they had been away from home for days at a time. She also detected an unfamiliar smell and noticed large white birds swooping and calling overhead. The river grew wider and wider, until the far bank disappeared into the distance. The men leaned on the steering oar, and the boat turned to the side, towards the town. The girl was worried that they would cover her up again, but this time they did not bother. They steered in straight towards the riverside and, dropping oars into the water, slowed the boat down and swung alongside a rough wooden quay.

☙ Chapter 2 ❧

The boat was resting against a walkway that led up the river bank towards a row of buildings. There were heaps of goods inside and out, and men and women hurrying to and fro. The man she took to be leader of the crew, the one who could speak a little of her own language, tied up her hands and lifted her out of the boat. Once again, he held the other end of the rope and, after exchanging some words with his fellows, he set off among the houses.

"They go to chief, pay dues, make sure no trouble. You come with me," he said, leading the girl behind him.

The whole place stank, like the far end of her home at the end of winter, or the outhouse after a long spell of hot weather. She felt the walls pressing in on either side as they walked down one alleyway after another. Strange people pushed past, touching up against her in a way that she was not used to, their elbows banging into her shoulders, shoving her, almost as if she was not there. Odd shadows played as the sun sank over the houses. But no one seemed to find it surprising to see a man leading a girl like anyone else would lead a cow or a horse. Nobody gave her a glance as they pushed past, except one or two men who looked at her a little too closely for her liking. Perhaps it was normal for people to treat one another like this, like animals, in the town.

The man led her away from the quay, past several buildings that were evidently traders' houses, with goods still on display outside. One had clothes hanging in the wind, another meat, another had pots displayed on a table. Then they passed along a street of small cottages, wattle and daub, poor and shabby compared to her own home. Finally, they reached the far edge of the town, an area of small fenced-off plots where people were growing vegetables and fruits. The man skirted the plots until he came to a larger building, which evidently fronted onto a road, although they approached from the rear. He pushed open a gate and pulled the girl in behind him. They were standing in a small yard, surrounded by timber buildings. The walls towered over the girl, as if someone had taken several copies of the storehouse at home, stacked them up and arranged them in a square. At the far end was a long hall, rush thatched, with smoke seeping from a hole in the centre. As the man crossed the yard, another came out of a door opening at the other side. They exchanged greetings, and the boatman asked if the mistress was available, as he had something to show her. The girl understood all this, although they did not speak so clearly.

The boatman stood waiting in the yard, holding the girl by the rope, until a woman appeared from the doorway. She was a fat old woman, wearing a brown dress, with a tired-looking face, strangely thin above her bulging lower body. She spoke to the boatman, and he pointed to the girl. The woman looked the girl up and down, squinting a little since the light was poor. Then she stepped up close and stared into her face.

"Open your mouth," she said. The girl did as she was told. The woman looked inside. The girl closed her mouth when she looked away. Suddenly, the woman clutched at the girl's breast through the fabric of her tunic. The girl gave a start, but the woman did not react. She simply let go of the breast and squeezed the other one. She spoke to the man.

"Turn around," he said to the girl and walked around himself as she did so, so that the rope did not become tangled. When the girl had turned a full circle and was facing the woman once more, the crone spoke again.

"Have you started bleeding?"

The girl was taken aback. What sort of question was that to ask a stranger? The woman repeated the question, now in an angry tone. The girl decided it was best to answer.

"Yes," she said.

"Have you lain with a man?"

The girl hesitated – another strange question. What business was it of this woman?

"No," she said finally. "Never. There are only my father and my brothers in my house."

"It happens," said the woman in a flat voice.

It's true, thought the girl. She had heard it did happen.

"Not in my family," she said fiercely. The man chuckled.

"And the men on the boat?" continued the woman. "They didn't mess with you?"

The girl remembered the thought, the surge of fear she had experienced when the man had gestured to her the first day on the boat. She hesitated a moment too long for the old woman's temper.

"Don't play simple with me, girl. You know what I mean. Did they fuck with you?"

"No," the girl said, noticing a flash of anger on the face of the boatman.

He growled at the old woman, incomprehensible words. She gave him a curt answer and fumbled in a small drawstring bag at her belt. She took out several coins and handed them to the man. He merely grunted in reply, and she was forced to hand over another small piece of silver before he passed her the rope. He left the way he had come.

"Follow me," said the woman, and led the girl across the yard to one of the wooden sheds. She pushed open the door and, taking hold of the girl's arm, shoved her inside. The room was almost entirely dark, with just enough light coming in through the door for the girl to see there was a heap of straw in one corner, roughly bound together as a mattress.

"Have you eaten?" asked the woman.

"Not since we broke fast this morning," said the girl.

The woman untied the rope from around the girl's wrists and let her arms swing free.

"You'll remain here in this room. There's a wooden bucket in the corner for your needs. I'll send someone with food shortly."

With that, she left, closing the door and dropping a latch outside. The girl was trapped, a prisoner. She was alone, in the dark; she could not remember the last time she had felt alone like this. There was always someone with her at home, and if not someone, then the animals. She sat on the mattress with her back against the wall and pondered on her fate. She had been gone from home for two days now. They would be looking for her. But she was far away in this strange town with strange people. Had she ever felt so lost before now?

Suddenly, there was a rattle against the door, and the sound of the latch being lifted. The last rays of the dying day outlined a round figure, a young woman.

"Hey, new girl, here's your dinner." The shadow stepped into the room, carrying a bowl with some food and a wooden cup.

The girl looked up. The shadow had a rough and strange accent, like some of the people she had seen at the autumn market.

"Don't look so glum," said the shadow. "At least they're feeding you real food."

She squatted down heavily and placed the bowl and cup on the floor. At that level, she looked at the girl face to face, but with the light behind her, she remained just a shadow.

"Come on, love, eat up, and then you'll soon be as fat as I am," the shadow continued. Having said that, the young woman tried to stand up, but despite a tremendous effort, remained stuck in the squat.

"Here, pet, will you give me a hand up?" The girl stood up and the shadow reached out a hand. The girl took hold of it, and the plump figure slowly rose.

"Oh, by all the gods," she said. "I thought I was going to have to stay like that all night." She chuckled, but when the girl did not respond, she looked at her closely.

"What's your name?" asked the shadow.

"Signy," said the girl.

"Well, Miss Signy, so you can speak. I'm Gunhilde, and thanks for helping me. Come to think of it, it's probably not a good idea to get as fat as me, after all."

Gunhilde turned to go, saying, "I'll fetch that bowl and cup in the morning. You just eat up. The food's not that bad."

The girl, Signy, picked up the bowl. There was stew in it and a wooden spoon to eat it with. The stew was still warm, mostly vegetables, but with a little meat. Not as good as at home, but it would not help to add hunger to fear and anxiety. She drank from the cup – mead, and strong mead, at that. She lay down on the straw and let the events of the last two days pass through her mind.

For years, ever since she could remember, she had trodden the same paths: to the woods, to the fields, to the next farm, once in a while to the village. Sometimes, in a dark corner of her mind, she had wondered whether that was all there was to life. Sometimes, she had looked out at the river and wondered where it went. Where did the boats come from? Where did they go? Would she always just be a person standing on the riverbank, watching them pass by, until the question lost meaning, until she was caught up in the routine of childrearing, of running a home, if she was lucky going out now and then like her mother, to the home of a sick person, a person in need of a herbalist's skills, until one day she died and was no more? Was that what her life would add up to? Oh, how you shouldn't tempt the three sisters who twisted your fate! How glad she would be to be back in that routine, on her own mattress, in her own home, with the familiar people and things around her. Instead, she had dreamed. She had tempted the sisters, and they had woven a knot in her thread. They had sent four evil men, their servants no doubt, to take her away and cast her adrift, floating, floating down the broad river of life. And what would become of her? What happened to all the naughty, adventurous girls, the girls who vanished down the river? She knew the rumours. She knew what the older women repeated to the younger ones to keep them in line.

"Wake up, pet," sounded a friendly voice. "You seem to have made yourself comfortable."

Gunhilde's round shadow stood in the doorway, light flooding in behind her. The young woman came into the room. "You'd better hand me up that bowl and cup. We don't want any accidents like yesterday."

Signy rubbed her eyes and stretched her limbs, and then clambered up from the straw mattress. She picked up the bowl and cup and handed them to Gunhilde.

"Mistress says you've to come with me. She wants to take a look at you in daylight."

"What is this place?" asked Signy. "Who is the mistress?"

Gunhilde stood puzzled for a moment, and then laughed.

"I suppose I had the same question myself when I first came here. This is a brothel, darling, a whorehouse, a home away from home for all the sailors on the East Sea. And the mistress, well, she runs the house, though the chief is the chief, if you know what I mean."

Whores she knew, or at least women who were labelled as whores. There were women of bad reputation in the village, women whose men had gone off to fight, for example, and never came back; women who struggled to keep their families fed, and who were not beyond earning a bit of extra food or drink. They were frequent clients of her mother. Her mother was never critical. All women needing help were equal in her eyes, whatever the attitude of her neighbours. Come to think of it, Gunhilde could easily have been one of them had she lived in the village. Slavery and prostitution were the fates usually assigned to the women who had disappeared, Signy reflected, as she followed the plump girl outside.

The light in the courtyard blazed after the darkness of the room.

"Bring her here."

Signy heard the rasping voice of the old woman from the day before. She stepped into the yard. She felt dirty and bedraggled, more so under the gaze of the old woman who stood waiting for her.

"So your name is Signy?" said the woman. Signy nodded. "And the man who brought you yesterday, Dolk, he said you're the daughter of a farmer named Sigurt, from far up the river, and your father kept you on the straight and narrow."

"My father was a good man. My mother taught us well."

"We'll see about that, Miss Signy. Take your clothes off."

Signy stiffened.

The woman repeated her order. "Take your clothes off. I want to have a look at you."

Signy was not shy and had often swum naked in the river with the other girls when she was younger, with boys, too, for that matter, but to strip here in the courtyard of a strange building, under the gaze of this old woman…She hesitated.

"Do I have to rip your clothes off you?" the old woman squawked.

No, that would be even worse, and more humiliating. Signy glanced around. There was no one else except the old woman. She lifted her dress, pulled it over her head and stood naked. There was no wind in the yard, and she felt the warmth of the sun on her skin. For a moment, it actually felt quite good. The old woman walked around her in a circle, inspecting her carefully.

As she completed a second round, Gunhilde appeared out of the doorway.

"My, you're skinny," the fat girl commented, "and such tiny little tits." The old woman looked up and gave her servant a cold stare. "But…but you look real pretty," Gunhilde quickly added.

"Go and fetch a high stool," said the old woman.

Gunhilde disappeared into the hall, and the other two stood waiting for a moment, until the servant appeared with a stool.

"Sit on that and spread your legs apart," said the woman.

Signy did as she was told. She knew what the woman was going to do. This was something her mother had had to do on occasions, before girls got married. The woman wanted to check whether she had told the truth about not lying with a man. Well, let her check, Signy thought. Mother always said it was just a way to set men at ease, and anyway, I know I'm a virgin, whatever the old woman thinks. I've nothing to hide or be ashamed of.

The old woman finished her check and stood up straight. "It looks like you're telling the truth," she said.

"I usually do," said Signy.

"That's enough lip, young woman," said the older one.

"That won't last long here," said Gunhilde, "not seeing how cute she looks."

"Silence," growled the older woman, and she appeared to lapse into thought. After a moment, a cunning expression filled her grim features. She quickened into life and ordered Signy to put her clothes back on. She took her by the hand and led her across the yard back to her shed, ordered her inside and bolted the door again.

Later in the day, Gunhilde appeared with food and to empty the slop bucket.

"You're not to be disturbed, she says."

"Why not?"

"Don't ask me. Usually the girls are put to work right away, but not you. You've got to stay in here and eat your food for free. Probably keeping you for someone special, the chief, maybe."

Gunhilde left, and Signy was alone once again. All this obsession about whether she was a virgin or not had left her puzzled, so puzzled that she had almost forgotten to worry about her parents and her family. Now she was caught up in a strange situation. She was not so naive – obviously sex was at the bottom of the whole thing, having sex with men, but what did it mean for her? And why was it so important that she had not had a boy of her own? There were plenty of girls who had several boys before they were married. Didn't it just make sense to try things out before settling down? But those inspections her mother carried out kept nagging at her, and she remembered the men who came furtively to their door, old men, men with good farms, men who were taking younger wives, the clan chief, himself, on one occasion.

On the third day after she had been locked up again, Gunhilde told Signy it was time to leave the room and follow her into the courtyard.

"Stay here while I fetch some hot water," the fat girl ordered.

Signy stood in the yard feeling rather foolish, until Gunhilde returned with a bowl of water and some soapwort.

"Mistress says you have to clean yourself, all over."

"All over?"

"That's what she said. She told me to 'get that girl cleaned up, and into a fresh shift'." Gunhilde mimicked the rude tone of the older woman. "If you're shy, you can go over there in the corner, but if you ask me, you had better get used to being looked at in the nude. Might be just as well to start practising."

Very well, thought Signy, if that's going to be the way it is, I will, and with a sharp tug she pulled her dirty dress over her head. She stood stark naked in the yard and washed herself all over with the warm water and soapwort. How nice to be fresh and clean, she said to herself, and to feel the warm sun on my body! And she stretched her arms up into the air and shook her head so that water flew from her hair.

Just then, when she wasn't paying attention, the house door opened, and the old woman stepped out. She was not alone, but was followed by a tall man, of a similar age, her father's age, dressed in black, with his long hair drawn into a greying ponytail.

"This is the girl I was telling you about," said the old woman.

Signy froze at the sound of her voice. Her eyes met those of the tall man. He nodded, almost as if in greeting. She stood still, not quite knowing what to do. Trying to cover her private parts was her first instinct, but what's the point, she thought. He's already seen all there is to see. Let him take a good look, if he wants to. Instead, she put her hands on her hips and slowly turned round in a circle, and when she completed it, she stood looking him in the eye. His gaze did not waver from her face, but he spoke quietly to the old woman, who shouted in turn.

"Gunhilde, get here with some clothes right now! Master Laurentius wants her covered up."

The fat girl appeared with a fresh tunic. Signy dropped the shift over her head. She knew the tall man was watching her the whole time. The three sisters had spun her fate already, she reflected. If this man is involved, there's nothing I can do about that. Once clothed, she did a small bow to him and stood, trying to look as if she was a little modest farm girl, although that girl had passed away during the days she had been closed up in the room.

The tall man stepped towards her. She watched him, scrutinised him, as he moved. He might look old, but he had none of the decrepitude of the old woman, she noticed, none of the stiffness of the old men from the home village. He was dressed in a similar way to the men on the boat, but as he came closer, she saw that his clothes were of incomparably better quality, better even than her parents' best clothes. The fabric was tightly and evenly woven, and the shape of the trousers and jacket fit exactly to his body. His cloak was held in place by a brooch, and from the brooch a jewel twinkled, just like the brooch that her mother used on festival days. But the metal was somehow more yellow, the moulding finer, and the jewel was larger than any she had ever seen, even thinking of the clan chief at home. Was this the chief of the town that Gunhilde had spoken of, she wondered.

Now the man was standing right up close to her, but he turned to the old woman when he spoke.

"You're asking me to exchange this single girl for the two I brought you?"

He turned quickly back towards Signy as the old woman muttered in reply.

"Madame tells me you can milk cows," he said.

What another strange question. These people didn't seem to think straight. "Yes, sir," she replied.

"Is there anything else you can do?" He looked right into her eyes, as if he could see her thoughts and did not really need to ask the question.

"I can bake bread," she said, looking back at him, feigning innocence. The man sighed.

"I know herbs and medicines," she confessed. "My mother was a wise woman and a herbalist."

"Really," said the man, now smiling. He smiled in such a way that she knew he was smiling for her, and her alone. She could not smile back in that way. The old woman and Gunhilde could see her face, so she arched her eyebrows, just ever so much that he could see, but the women standing apart could not.

The man turned around to the old woman.

"Can I borrow her for an hour?"

The old woman looked shocked.

The man instantly registered her misunderstanding.

"That's not what I meant. I want to take her out into the market to test her," he said. "Can you find her a pair of sandals?" The old woman hesitated. "Oh, and here's my purse," he added, handing over a small leather bag, "as surety that I come back. And don't be tempted. I know exactly how much is in there."

Gunhilde appeared with a long cloak, to cover up the tunic, and a pair of leather sandals. Signy had never worn such footwear. In her village, the women and men all went barefoot or slipped on wooden clogs when the weather was bad. She could not tie the straps, and Gunhilde had to help her. She felt foolish in front of the man, as if she had revealed herself as the country girl she really was, but he did not seem bothered. He offered her his arm, and she took it, as if they were about to dance, and side by side they left the yard by the back gate.

"I expected you to be fearful," the man said.

Signy did not answer.

"But when I looked into your eyes, I found mainly curiosity."

"The Fates have shaped my future," she said, quietly.

The man laughed lightly. "My name is Laurentius. I'm a trader. I buy where goods are cheap, and then I transport them to people who want or need them and sell them for more than I paid for them. It's hard work, but I enjoy it, and I'm good at it."

He looked at Signy, who kept quiet and waited for him to continue.

"It pains me a little to tell you this, but you have become goods. A few days ago, perhaps, you were an innocent country girl milking your cow, until four opportunistic bandits happened to pass by. Since then, you have been property for sale. First they sold you to Madame, and now she proposes to sell you to me, and says that you are worth as much as two nice girls from the shores of the Middle Sea I carried all the way here. Perhaps you are worth the price, I'm beginning to suspect so, but let me tell you why the exchange would be a good deal for you. If you stay here with Madame, you'll be put to work in the brothel. Do you know what that is?"

"Not exactly, sir, but I'm beginning to suspect."

"A brothel is a place where men can pay a price for sex. Men like those who row my boat. When you're young and fresh as you are, the price will be high, especially if you're a virgin, which Madame assures me you are. Probably that would mean the chief gets the first few turns with you, before you become available for the general public. After that, with time, the price goes down, until you end up as an ordinary whore like Gunhilde. Then, if you're lucky, you get older and worn out, until you look and act like Madame. But very few are so lucky, and the less lucky ones will be long dead."

Her heart was heavy at the words he said, and she felt a new surge of fear. He stopped and turned to her. She must have been showing her feelings on her face.

"I don't think you should be wasted in a place like that," he said. "I'm not sure that I can guarantee your life will turn out better, but if I do purchase you, I can promise you that you will not end up as an ordinary whore, in an ordinary whorehouse, in a nowhere settlement like this one. I like to make a profit on my investments, and if I invest in buying you from Madame, I think I know how I can do it, even at twice the usual price."

He was standing close to her, so close he must be able to see every muscle move, hear every breath. Perhaps he wanted her for himself, she wondered.

"A little frightened," he muttered to himself. "Self-preservation," he said aloud, "requires a certain anxiety. I feel it myself sometimes, in the heart of a storm, or if I see a strange ship on the horizon where I don't expect to see one."

They had been walking along the path by the cultivated plots, back the way she had arrived with the boatman, when they had stopped to talk. Now, he turned and looked out over the plots. She followed his eyes. In front of her was a neatly tended garden, divided into small squares. In each square, a different type of plant was growing. She recognised them. Some of them were the plants her mother used in her medicines. They had clumps of many of the same plants growing behind the cottage.

She did not need to know what he would ask, so she pointed.

"That one's for fever. That one'll stop a cough. That one's used for pain when women are giving birth. That one'll settle your stomach. And that one," she added, pointing further away, "you can give to a woman who wants to stop a child in her womb."

He laughed.

"Then you might have a place in the whorehouse after all. What about that one?" he asked, pointing.

"That one's for old men who have young wives," said Signy, and could not help laughing, too, "but my mother always told me it was the women who came for it, not the men."

"Perhaps I should take some?" he suggested, but when he saw the look in her eyes, he had to stifle his chuckle at his own joke.

My face must have shown I was annoyed by his comment, she thought. Perhaps he's no better, imagining he's having me for himself, but it won't do to annoy him.

"I don't need it, certainly not today," Laurentius added hastily. "I'm a married man, and in any case, like I said, Signy, I'm a trader, and I don't spoil my own investments."

That did not make matters a whole lot better, but there was no point in quarrelling with the man who was her fate and her path out of the brothel. She had let go of his arm while they were talking, and now she took hold of it again.

"Were we going to the market, Master?" she asked, smiling up at him.

He looked down at her and patted her hand.

"You need good boots, a thick dress and a sea cloak, where we're going. You'll also need some prettier clothes eventually, but we won't find those in this dump of a town."

And so the two of them walked the paths among the houses and past the traders' booths.

Just a few days ago, I was dragged through these same alleys on the end of a rope like an animal, she mused, and now I'm on the arm of this handsome, well, he really is handsome for a man of his age, trader, just as if I'm his wife or lover.

☙ Chapter 3 ❧

By evening, the wind had started to pick up, and Laurentius did not want to miss the opportunity to leave as soon as his business was complete. His ship was beached on a slope of sand, with the wide sea stretching out beyond it. He left Signy under the care of his crew while he returned to seal the deal with Madame and retrieve his purse.

"Go to the far end, the stern, and sit down, out of the way. The men won't harm you. Make yourself comfortable while they prepare for the voyage."

It was not long before the reason for his warning became evident, and she received an unpleasant reminder of the reality of her situation. While the trader was away, half a dozen young men tied together in a chain, men with dishevelled hair, dressed in torn clothes and with bound hands, were herded – there was no other way to describe it – on board. They were beaten with rope ends until they sat huddled together in the forward part of the ship. The young men could easily have been her brothers, thought Signy, pulling her cloak around her shoulders, almost as if she was trying to hide from their gaze.

The remainder of Laurentius' cargo consisted of two large chests, which were delivered on a cart to the quayside and swung on board, where they joined several bundles of furs which had been lashed down before Signy arrived. Once the crates had been stowed, the crew began to look at one another in a concerned manner, before Laurentius appeared, hurrying along the quayside.

"The chief tried to make me pay another tariff for the goods I brought with me," said the trader to the steersman. "He gets greedier every time."

The men were already heaving at the boat, freeing the bow from the sand, as he vaulted over the side of the vessel. The boatsman took the steering oar, the crew ran out sweeps, and manoeuvred the ship away from the beach. The vessel edged forward, and the town fell away. The open sea stretched endlessly before them.

The wind picked up and spray began to fly. Even though it had been a warm day, Signy found herself shivering in the breeze. She was glad that Laurentius had bought warm clothes for her. She now understood that the strange odour she had remarked on when she was approaching the town was the smell of the sea, and the white birds were sea birds whirling, squawking and screeching, high above the mast.

As the land slipped away behind them, and the wind caught the sail, she felt really frightened. Not the anxiety for the unknown or fear of separation from her family, or even the dread of a future in a brothel, but the immediate, physical fear of being in an alien environment. She could swim, swim very well for that matter, but that was in a placid creek where you could see the banks, where there were friends around to call if you needed help. Now, she was being tossed on the open ocean, with land out of sight, and waves, real waves, rising and falling beneath the boat. The sky seemed boundless, boundless in a way she had never experienced growing up in a clearing in the forest. She felt very small, and the huge emptiness above was not space but became a weight pressing down on her. She began to feel sick, and wrapped her arms around her body, trying to hold herself together. Her stomach churned and her teeth chattered uncontrollably. What's going on? Why can't I control myself, she thought.

With the sail hoisted and land disappearing beneath the horizon, Laurentius left the boat in the hands of his steersman, and stepped forward to where she was sitting. He crouched down beside her, seeing her colourless face and trembling body.

"I've never seen so much water before," she said. "Even our river, when it was in flood, was nothing like this."

"Everyone feels sick the first time they go to sea. Some people never get over it."

"But there's nothing," said Signy, "nothing but this little boat in all this space."

"I just want to keep a good distance from the land," said Laurentius, "in case the wind changes during the night, but tomorrow we'll be among the islands. Now I want to make good use of the breeze. There'll be enough rowing to be done when the time comes."

When the sun set, the stars and the moon appeared high above, not glimpsed among the branches, but like a silver and black dome over Signy's head. There was a glittering sheen on the water, which grew and shrank as the waves passed by. It's not hard to see why people believe the sky's the home of a god, she thought.

The crew prepared their evening meal and offered her food, but for once the feeling of sickness conquered her hunger, and all she could do was shake her head in refusal. She lay against a folded sail, and the sway of the ship carried her away into sleep.

When she awoke, the sea was calmer, land was again in sight and she felt a little better. She could see they were close by a flat island, and once more birds were wheeling and diving around them. The crew noticed she had woken and came with food, and her hunger conquered her fears. She sat, huddled in the cloak with the hood pulled over her head, chewing on a piece of bread and some dried meat as the world passed by.

As the day wore on, the breeze dropped still further, until the sail hung limp, and there was no alternative but to run out the oars and begin to row. The crew pulled together in a steady rhythm, and as they did so, the islands closed in until they were passing down a long sound with land on either side, an arm of the sea almost like a river. Far ahead, Signy saw the bay narrowed, and ended in a cluster of buildings. After a while, she could make out individual houses and then the dockside.

Signy sat still while the captives in the front of the boat were rousted and driven over the side onto the land. Then rough shouts and a few blows set them marching up the slope and out of sight among the buildings. Laurentius supervised closely as the chests and furs were loaded onto hand carts and carried inside the same yard. Finally, he asked Signy to get up and follow him. Is this where I'll pass from Laurentius' hands to another's, she reflected.

She felt as if the land was rolling under her feet, and when she tried to walk, she found herself bracing for a sway which never came. Laurentius was gracious and held out his hand to steady her. As they walked together up the slope, she saw that the settlement ahead was made up of a series of long, low houses and several palisaded yards. They did not go in through the same opening where the slaves had been taken, but round to the front of the buildings where there was an ornamented gateway, leading into a smaller courtyard.

A man greeted Laurentius warmly, while casting an admiring look at Signy. Laurentius spoke to the man, but Signy could not understand the conversation, and she did not try. The man gestured for her to follow him. Laurentius disappeared between two buildings at the far end of the courtyard, presumably to check on his cargo. Signy was shown into one of the long, low houses.

"Wait here," said the man, now speaking in her own tongue. "This is the women's house."

She was still standing in the entrance when a slave girl appeared and bowed to her. The girl spoke in the same intonation as Laurentius had used to the man.

"I don't understand," Signy said.

"I'm sorry," said the girl, at once speaking in a manner that Signy could comprehend. "Your place is here," she continued, indicating a bed halfway along the far wall of the house.

Signy had only time to take off her cloak and throw it down on the bed before Laurentius appeared in the doorway.

"This looks a bit more comfortable than your previous quarters," he commented. "You'll be safe for the night here in the women's house."

"Why am I in here in comfort, when the men were taken in bonds into the other yard?"

Laurentius looked grim for a moment. "You saw the chests which were lashed amidships in the boat?"

"Yes."

"Those chests contain amber. Do you know what that is?"

She shook her head.

"It's like a jewel, and it's found along the shores of the sea we've just crossed. People in the south will pay an enormous amount for it."

"Now I know what you're talking about," she interrupted. "Mother has a charm of amber she uses against the evil eye."

"Precisely," said Laurentius, "and two chests of amber and the bundles of fur safely delivered to my partners in Frisia will bring me enough money to live on all year. But I'm not worried about the chests running off, unless some enemy or rival merchant helps himself to them. In the yard at the back of this inn, there are twenty-three male slaves I've collected on my voyages this summer, and who I plan to sell in Puttby. They're not worth as much as the amber and furs, but twenty-three strong young men could cause a lot of trouble, so they are tied up and held under guard. You're one young woman, far from home. Even though you're valuable to me, I'm not especially worried that you'll run away. Where would you run to, alone in a strange land? And so long as you stay in the women's house, no one will come and steal you. I'm not worried that you'll cause trouble. In fact, I came here to invite you to join the evening meal. We'll have a hard day tomorrow, and it's best we eat well and get a good night's sleep."

She sat at the low end of the table, among the other women. She barely understood what they were saying and did not care to speak herself. She was a captive, she knew, and she had become a slave not as valuable as the boxes of charms, but perhaps more valuable than twenty-three men who could be her brothers and cousins. What a strange world where one foolish young girl seemed to be worth more than so many strong young men!

In the morning, Laurentius was all business. Signy was taken into the big yard at the back of the trading post where the male captives had been roped together under the supervision of the yardmen. There were packhorses standing in the yard, too, big strong animals bearing the chests the merchant had said were full of amber.

"Do you want to ride a horse or walk?" he asked.

"My only experience of riding a horse is guiding our old mare to the far end of the village," Signy replied. "She knew the way as well as I did."

"In that case, you'll have to walk. Let me see your footwear." He looked thoughtful for a moment. "I think I'll find you a different pair."

A short while later, he returned carrying some felt boots and snug-fitting woollen stockings.

"For a day of walking, these will chafe less than those leather ones, especially for someone who's not used to wearing them."

When everything was in order, the signal was given. The men who had been assisting with the horses took up spears and fastened on swords and were instantly transformed from labourers into guards. Out between the houses, they walked inland, through the flat fields, past a few cottages and huts, along mile after mile of well-beaten trail. Around midday, they stopped. Water was fetched from a nearby spring, and bread was handed out. The guards and the captives ate alike. When the meal was over, the captives were driven to their feet and the march continued. Before nightfall, they reached a way-station surrounded by a palisade.

"Here there are no women's quarters, so you'll sleep with me," said Laurentius.

The trader joined several fellow merchants and talked business. The chests with the amber were not mentioned in the conversation but were carried to the area assigned as the trader's sleeping place.

Signy lay down, fully clothed, with Laurentius beside her. Was this to be the night, she wondered, when Laurentius would take advantage of her?

"I have to keep an eye on you in this place, the same as my amber," he said, patting her and turning his back to her. "This is the land of the Jutes. They're a warlike and troublesome people, and their speech is almost unintelligible, but they generally leave merchants in peace since their leaders take a share of everything."

For a while, she tried to keep a little distance, but as the night became chilly, she was forced to snuggle against the trader's warm back. Is he dreaming of me, she wondered, feeling my body against his?

In the morning, Laurentius said nothing of what had and had not passed in the night. The procedure was reversed. The boxes loaded onto the horses, the men driven out onto the road, and the march started again.

The following night passed in the same manner. Laurentius was clearly serious, Signy concluded, when he had said he didn't intend to damage his goods.

On the third day, after they had been marching for a while, the trader dropped back to walk alongside her.

"We should be at our destination by nightfall, a town called Puttby, on the shore of the salt sea."

Signy did not really grasp what he meant, but she felt she had to say something. "I couldn't understand what the people at the post were saying," she admitted. "Sometimes I thought I could hear familiar words, but other times it was like bird chatter."

Laurentius laughed as they walked along. "Your ear'll soon get adjusted, just like your legs did on the boat."

Then he lengthened his stride and made his way up to the front of the column.

Before the sun set, they reached the town, and made their way through the narrow and twisting paths down to the waterfront and the merchants' quarter. There was a set of buildings which looked very similar to the trading post on the far shore they had left behind them, but when Signy walked in through the gateway, she was struck with surprise. Instead of a range of huts and halls as she expected, the yard was surrounded by a wooden colonnade and, under the low roof, were a series of doors.

"Home from home for Factor Titus," said Laurentius, without explaining what he meant. A woman hurried towards them, giving Signy a sharp look as she did so, glancing up and down at her clothes, as if trying to ascertain her status and relationship to Laurentius.

"Jortha," he said, "Signy will be with us for a few days. Please find a room for her where she'll not be disturbed." He turned to Signy. "No need for you to sleep by me here. This is my yard, and these are my people. They understand my business. They do as I tell them, and you'll be safe."

The factor, discovered in a storeroom, supervising the storage of the furs, turned out to be a fat, red-faced man with short bristling hair and a white beard. When he spoke directly to her, he tried to use her tongue, but with a peculiar accent and many mistakes. As soon as he spoke to Laurentius, he became entirely incomprehensible. He listened to the trader, with one eye on Signy the whole time, as if he half disbelieved what Laurentius was saying. At one point, he stopped him and, turning to Signy, asked her to turn around, as she had done in the yard at the brothel. She waited for the factor to order her to take her clothes off to complete the inspection, but apparently Laurentius' word was sufficient. After a while, Laurentius patted her on the shoulder and told her she could leave them.

Was she now supposed to go to her room and wait? She decided to push her luck and, instead, stepped outside, first into the courtyard, and then out of the building altogether. In front of her was a wide pathway, and from there a long stretch of mud expanded to the horizon. She found a large boulder and sat down on it. To her left and right an inlet stretched out, edged by buildings large and small, several trading posts similar to the one behind her, but mainly small huts and cottages. Also dotted along the shore were numerous boats, resting far up on dry land. Beyond, where the water met the sky, lay the sea, she surmised; the salt sea, Laurentius had called it.

A man came past with a wicker basket filled with fish. He started talking to her, showing the fish as if he wanted her to buy some. She did not understand what he was saying, so she spoke to him in her own tongue, and he immediately stopped babbling.

"Sorry, Miss, I didn't realise you were a Saxon. Would you like to buy fish, fresh fish, just caught today?"

"I'm sorry, too," she said. "I'm a stranger here. I would have loved to buy your fish, but I don't have any money."

The fisherman touched his woollen hat and moved on.

"The fisherman called me a Saxon," she told Laurentius a little later. "What did he mean?"

"He meant you're not from here, not from Juteland, like him. There are people from many lands who meet in Puttby. Factor Titus, for example, is a Briton. He works for my business partner, the merchant Fabiansson. That's why he pronounces your language with such a strange accent and makes mistakes all the time. And why he constructed the trading yard to resemble a villa." This was obviously amusing to the trader, but Signy did not understand what he meant.

"And you," she hesitated before using his name, "Laurentius, what people do you belong to? You seem to be able to talk to everyone in their own way."

"I hardly know anymore, Signy. My home is in Frisia, to the south, but I wasn't born there. I'm named after a Roman, because my father was a citizen of the Empire, but I'm not a Roman, and there is no Empire anymore, at least not in these parts. I suppose I'm just a wandering trader, a sailor of the seven seas."

Again, she did not understand exactly what he meant, who these Romans were, what the Empire was, but she could recognise Laurentius' meaning. He didn't belong anywhere, and yet at the same time he belonged a little everywhere.

"The meal should be ready," he said. "You can sit by me."

While they ate, he told her about his life, crossing the seas from one port to the other, sometimes to the east, sometimes to the west. As new dishes arrived, he filled her glass.

"What is this drink?" It tasted strange in her mouth.

"It's wine," he said. "You should add some water to soften the effect."

Even with the wine diluted, her head started to feel a little muzzy, and the drink obviously had a similar effect on the trader, because halfway through the meal he had told her about his wife, the homestead he had up a creek in Frisia, and his two sons who had followed in his business and were trading in a far-off country called Britannia.

She looked at him a little sceptically, but then noticed a dampness in his eyes, and perhaps just the trace of a tear high up on his cheek. Was it the drink or did he really miss his family?

"I could have left you in the Danborg, in the whorehouse," he said a little later, "but when I looked into your eyes, I saw a light, a sparkle, that told me it would be wrong to do that. In the next few days, we'll part company, Signy." She glanced at him, and thought he looked a little sad. "I should stick to trading male slaves," he continued, "and not be tempted by young girls. Tomorrow, the next day or the next, some man will come by the trading post and offer a price I can't refuse. But it'll be a high price, my dear, so that the man knows he's getting something, someone, valuable, who he should take care of. I hope he'll see that same sparkle. And I'll tell him if he doesn't, I'll come back one day and cut off his balls."

It must be the wine talking, she thought. It was certainly stronger than the ale she was used to.

"I'll do my best," she said, "to sparkle."

Could I ever be a trader and buy and sell people, she wondered. Supposing I came to care about someone, would I just be able to sell them to someone else? Is that what trading does to a soul, makes it so hard that the deal, that silver, always comes first? Perhaps only a hard person could even become a trader. After all, a farmer could think highly of his animals, pamper them and feed them from his hand, and then kill them at the end of the summer and eat them. Perhaps being a trader was only one step away?

❧ Chapter 4 ☙

Signy felt sick, sick in the heart, in the morning, when Factor Titus took her to his booth in the marketplace. It was full of quality goods, she could see that, but that did not make her feel better. There were fur cloaks and hats, jewelled brooches and arm bands, beautifully embroidered shirts and cloaks. Amber, carved into jewels or threaded as necklaces and bracelets, was laid out for people from the surrounding countryside to come and see. She felt sick because she grasped that she was one of the items for sale, just like the fur cloaks and the amber carvings. She was on display, like a prize cow at a market.

"Should I show them my tits, like I did in Danborg," she asked the factor, "or let them feel my behind to see if there's sufficient meat on it?"

"Sit down and keep quiet. That's enough," said Titus, in an irritated tone. "It's not your tits that men are looking at, nor your tongue they want to hear. If Master Laurentius wanted them to see your tits, he would've told me."

At one point, the factor's wife came in and combed Signy's hair, took a woven patterned headcloth from the shop and placed it over her head. She stood back, examined her and nodded, with evident satisfaction at her own effort to enhance the presentation. Signy sat on a stool and watched the men and women come into the shop. Occasionally, a man she had noticed earlier accompanied by his wife would later come back alone, look over at her and exchange a few words with Titus or his wife. When he heard their reply, he would inevitably shake his head and walk away, sometimes casting a long glance back over his shoulder.

So the first day passed by. While Signy was curious to observe the visitors to the shop, there were long periods when nothing happened, or when the factor's wife and a customer were chatting so quickly that she could make little of their conversation. As the day wore on, she became bored, until Laurentius came into the booth. He gave her a smile and was about to speak, when the door opened behind him, and another man stepped in. As Laurentius turned to the newcomer, his smile broke into a grin.

"Why, Amalric, you old pirate, what are you doing here, so far from home?"

Signy's ears pricked up in an instant, motivated by the sound of the exchange, which she could comprehend at last. She observed the stranger carefully. His blue eyes seemed sad, a strange contrast to his weather-beaten face and close-cropped hair.

"Laurentius, you rascal! I was coming to see if you had some new labourers for me. Your lady wife sends her greetings, by the way."

Signy saw Laurentius give the newcomer a sharp look. Was he a little suspicious that Amalric, whom he had called a pirate, had news from his wife?

"I've a dozen men in the compound," the trader answered. "You can have your pick, and you can convey the asking price directly to Aggi."

"Gladly," said Amalric, catching sight of Signy. "What have you here, Laurentius?"

The pirate took a few long strides across the shop until he stood in front of her.

"You leave her alone," said Laurentius. "She'd kill you."

Amalric laughed. "I've half a dozen of these at home. I don't need another one…though you seem sharp enough, I can see," he added, addressing Signy directly.

Signy caught a tone in his voice that belied the jocularity and vulgarity of his words.

"You're still looking for a new wife?" asked Laurentius.

Amalric turned back to his friend, since it was quite evident to Signy that Amalric and Laurentius were friends.

"Still searching for a nice civilised Roman woman as a partner?" continued the trader.

"I had one, Laurentius, I had one, for a little while, and then…" He shrugged. "It's not worth worrying about." He glanced back to Signy and chuckled, waving his hand towards her. "This little pussycat, you can keep her!"

Laurentius threw an arm around Amalric's shoulders, and the two men left the booth in the direction of the warehouse. To examine the slaves, no doubt, thought Signy.

"What sort of a man is he?" she asked the factor's wife.

"Bad man!" said the wife, not as fluent in Saxon as her husband.

"He seemed so sad," said Signy.

"Bad man!" repeated the wife, clearly not willing to discuss Amalric further.

Despite the factor's wife's judgement, Signy had been perked up by the appearance of Laurentius and his weather-beaten friend. They seemed to belong to another class of person than the farmers and local landowners who made up most of the customers, to a class of person with a far-away look in their eyes, as if they were continually trying to see over the horizon.

A little later, a middle-aged man, with a paunch and dark hair around a bald patch, came in and looked quickly around. He spoke to the factor's wife. Whatever words he had used, and Signy could not make them out, he must have been asking for Laurentius, since the factor's wife waved in the direction that the trader had departed. The stranger hesitated, as if he was reluctant to take that path. In fact, now Signy considered the matter carefully, playing back the sounds she had heard in her mind, she could make out the merchant's name. It's like a game, she thought, parts of which I can really understand, and parts which I need to guess. An amusing thought came to her mind. Suppose I spoke to the man in my own tongue as if I understood what he had said.

"He left with Amalric to inspect the slaves," she said.

The dark-haired man spun towards her, with the look of a striking snake. "Amalric was here?" he said, or so she thought. The name she could make out, the rest she would guess.

"Just a moment ago," she replied, forcing herself to smile.

The man hesitated and then spoke again. "How do you know him?" he said, taking a step towards her, a threatening look on his face. Now she understood both his words and his tone. He had changed the way he was speaking, to an approximation of her own language. How should she reply?

She was saved by Laurentius' voice from the doorway behind him.

"Look but don't touch, Drusus!" the trader said in the clear Saxon with which he had spoken to her earlier. He must have heard them talking. He must have intended her to understand.

The dark-haired man stopped and turned around, saying something to Laurentius which she could no longer follow.

"I said it as much for her as I did for you," he laughed. "I don't want her to think I'm going to let anyone come in here and put his paws on her." He continued speaking in Saxon.

The dark-haired man spoke again, with an annoyed expression.

"You had that look on your face," laughed the trader again.

The dark-haired man said something else.

"She only speaks Saxon, so far as I know. You could try speaking Frankish," replied the trader.

"I did," said the man.

"You're still not going to get her. The price is too high."

"I'm a rich man," said the stranger, in words which were barely recognisable to Signy, but were evidently what Laurentius meant by Frankish. They were at least easier to understand than the gibberish he had been speaking earlier to the factor's wife.

"Whatever you can afford, then the price is double," said the trader.

"You're keeping her for yourself?" asked the dark-haired man, sourly.

"Not at all, otherwise why would she be in the booth? It's just I have a plan."

"Am I part of that plan?" said a newcomer, a younger man, who had entered unobserved.

What muddle of words, Signy thought. Some I can almost grasp, like slippery fish, and others are completely incomprehensible. I could never have imagined such a place.

The young man caught sight of Signy, and she saw him gasp.

"Whoa! Nice-looking girl," he said. "Is she on offer?" He spoke in the same garbled manner as the older man.

"Same applies to you," said Laurentius, emphatically continuing in Saxon.

The young newcomer walked over and lifted his hand to her face. His grey eyes scrutinised her.

"Hands off, Constantinus," said the older man, "you heard what he said."

"No, I didn't, Uncle," said the younger one. "Anyway, I thought you were allowed to check the goods in here."

"Not this one," said Laurentius.

"I can see why," said Constantinus, his eyes fixed on Signy. "Once you touched her, you might find it hard to let go."

"You understand my point exactly," said Laurentius.

"But what reasonable man would want to let go?" said Constantinus, turning back to his uncle.

"That's not the kind of talk I expect from a man in holy orders," observed the trader.

"I didn't take holy orders. You know that! They can't force you, and when they said it was time, I refused. I mean, I never asked to be shut up in a monastery, just because Father offended someone. I have a life to live. I deserve to live it like anyone else."

"That may be so," said Laurentius, "but you won't be living it with her."

A strange look appeared on Constantinus' face, part suffering and part hate.

"You can say that now, trader," he snarled, "but when I get my rights, when I become Governor of Britannia, then you'll have to learn a different attitude."

Signy noticed Laurentius attempting to suppress a laugh.

"You treat me with contempt," continued the young man, "all of you. Uncle, you merchant" – and, catching a stifled giggle behind him, turned to Signy, jabbing at her with his finger – "and even you, a mere girl for sale…"

"Come now, Con," said the uncle, "we've other business to see to."

Constantinus gave Signy one last look, his eyes trailing down her body, resting here and there for an extra stare.

"I won't forget you easily," he said suddenly, in perfect Saxon.

Signy felt her amusement drain away, felt herself turning cold and clammy. There was something about the young man's gaze that was both lascivious and threatening. Laurentius must have detected it, too, as he hastily led the two men towards the back of the shop to the storage area.

After a while, he returned.

"I'll escort you home this evening myself," he said. "I didn't like the tone in the boy's voice. I'm sorry they bothered you, but they were here looking for weapons, and I need to clear my stock."

"I thought you were trying to sell me, Laurentius," said Signy, "but all you do is dissuade possible purchasers."

"Did you want any of the men who have come so far in bed with you?"

"No, they were awful!"

"But Amalric was the least awful?" laughed Laurentius.

She looked up at him, and when he glanced down, he caught her eye.

"Amalric, that old rogue! I noticed it!" He stopped and examined her more carefully. "But yes, he was a handsome man in his youth, when I first knew him. An officer in the Roman army, could you guess it, before the uprising? He can still be a charmer when he's in the mood, but he's done a lot of bad things over the years."

"She said he was a bad man, Master Titus' wife."

"She would and she's right," said Laurentius, sighing. "I'm not asking you to trust me, that would be too much, though I wasn't the man who took you from your family. I wasn't the one who sold you the first time. I've given you my word that I'll find someone who'll treat you well, and who you can benefit from. It's the best I can do."

She saw the young man with the grey eyes pass by the shop the following day. He looked in through the open shutters, gave her a hungry glance and walked on, but he did not come in. Later, she saw him returning with his uncle. They were followed by a man leading a horse pulling a cart, and in the cart was a jumble of weapons. This time the two passed by without a glance.

Who were they? she wondered. People who Laurentius did not entirely trust when he was clearly on good terms with Amalric, who even he admitted was a bad man. And what had the young man meant by getting his rights? It's not really my business, of course, she reflected, but although I'm just a girl, waiting to be sold to a stranger, that doesn't mean I should stop thinking. On the contrary, I've got to make a greater effort to think than I ever did, every moment of every day. I never expected life to take this path, but it's time I started accepting the fact. Now I must own my fate, make the best of it, or I'll be destroyed by it.

On the third day, Signy had to do something to stave off the tedium, so she asked Titus' wife for some embroidery. She sat in the shop and stitched some of the patterns she had practised with her mother. That attracted a couple of ladies, but even they were shocked and horrified when they heard her price. No, I'm not a lady's maid either, she thought, and not a cheap plaything for an old man. I'm an exclusive article, for a man to be my first, and for that, whoever he is, he's going to have to pay. What a sad thing, she thought, for men to be such fools, although more than one marriage had been broken off in the home village because Mother refused to confirm that the bride was a virgin. She shrugged to herself. Few of the girls were, of course, by the time marriage came around, but there were always fathers willing to pay for Mother's affirmation. She grimaced to herself as another disappointed buyer left the shop. If I had been left at home for another year, then probably I would have given my virginity for free to one of the young men from the village, and then what would have happened to me? Would I have become a mother, married with a squalling baby in a hovel somewhere in the forest? Or if I had even then been stolen by the boatmen, would I have been lying on my back in the brothel, fucked by all and sundry, like fat Gunhilde? But, by the Fates, what am I doing in a trader's booth, far from home, in Puttby, in Juteland, a place I never suspected even existed?

She was deep in these thoughts, sewing automatically, when she heard a new voice in the store. It was a young man, tall, with long blond hair, moustaches and a beard. His clothes marked him out as wealthy, she knew that by now. The jewelled sword at his waist showed that he was a warrior. He looked a little like the clan chief's sons from her village. He was talking to Factor Titus in a heated manner. Signy could not grasp every word, but a few sank in, combined with their expressions and gesturing, sufficient to imagine what the conversation might be.

"These jewelled brooches," she thought he was saying, while pointing to one of the baskets. "I want one, no, two, as a present for my wife." His fingers gave him away.

She saw Titus' wife nod encouragingly.

"She's pregnant again" – the same word, thought Signy, with a smile to herself – "and I must bring something back for her from my journey to Puttby. I had a lot of booty from the summer raiding, and I sold it all. I've plenty of coins. Which of these are best? Do you have anything better?" He was showing the purse attached to his belt. It was fat, and jingled as he did so.

He looked around the booth for something better, even better than the regular jewels for his wife, but as he did so his eye fell on Signy. His voice fell silent. His whole body turned on its axis until he was facing her. He took a step towards her, his eyes glistening. She looked up at him from where she was sitting sewing.

"*God dag!*" she said, copying the ladies who had come into the store. These were the only Jutish words she dared to utter.

The young man looked transfixed. She turned back to her sewing and tried to concentrate on the stitches, suppressing a desire to laugh. The factor spoke. The man turned back to him. The factor spoke again and nodded. The young man looked back at her. She sensed his agitation from the other side of the store. She looked up at him again and smiled. She could imagine he was handsome, a younger version of the grizzled old Amalric. Perhaps he was a bad man, too, but if someone was going to have her, she would rather it was him than one of the fat old men who had been sniffing around the day before. The young man looked from her to the factor and back again. At that moment, Laurentius walked past the booth and, glancing in, saw the young man talking to Titus. He stopped in his tracks, turned back and came into the store.

"Hello, Thorgill, my friend. Looking to dispose of the silver you just extracted from me?" He greeted the young man warmly, placing his arm on his shoulder. The young man indicated Signy, sitting quietly on her stool. Laurentius nodded sagely, and then looked over to her.

"Signy, I'd like to introduce you to Chief Thorgill."

Signy stood up and carefully placed her sewing on the stool. Then she crossed the booth to the three men. She bowed her head to the young chief, then took his hands in hers and kissed them.

Laurentius gently laid his hand on her arm.

"I was telling the chief that you know all about medicinal herbs, but you never said you could embroider so beautifully, too."

I bet you were, thought Signy, but a moment later, she instinctively felt she was doing Laurentius a disfavour. Probably that was exactly what he had been explaining. If the chief was to purchase her for a great deal more than an ordinary slave girl, he would have to understand that he was not just getting a partner for his bed, but someone who brought other skills with her. She could be a woman who might enhance his prestige as well as satisfy his bodily lusts.

Laurentius left the factor and Thorgill to haggle over the price and, taking Signy by the arm, led her out of the shop into the street. There he stopped and looked down at her.

"Thorgill's a good man," he said. "Just this morning, I bought a whole stack of plunder from him that he had gathered together in Britannia, and as I did so, I thought he might be the man for you, so I gave him a little more than I normally would, and suggested he look in at Titus' booth for something special before he leaves for home."

"But he already has a wife! I heard him say so."

"He won't mistreat you, Signy, not after what he'll have paid, and that's why I was explaining to him about your other qualities."

"But won't his wife hate me?"

Laurentius laughed. "His wife is pregnant all the time. She's the most pregnant woman in all of Juteland. She'll probably be glad to avoid him for a bit. And besides, he'll be away half the year, raiding in Britannia."

Signy gave him a hard look.

"If he is raiding Britannia, and you and Titus are here doing business with him…do you mean that you two just bought his plunder, that he took from this place, Britannia? Titus is a Briton, from Britannia, you told me, and the merchant who owns the warehouse and this shop, they're from Britannia, too." She was confused.

Laurentius said nothing, but Signy knew him well enough by now to read the answer in his eyes. How could he explain such things to a pretty young girl? She would just have to find them out for herself, as his own wife had done years ago.

Titus came out of the store, shortly followed by the handsome warrior. They both looked very pleased with themselves. Titus spoke to Laurentius.

"It looks like I have to hand you over to Chief Thorgill," said the trader and only now, when she belonged to another man, he gave her a hug. "Congratulations, Thorgill, you've made a good bargain. Will you send your man round to the trading post to collect her belongings before you go?"

What poor belongings did she have at the trading post, Signy thought. I was snatched from my home in only my shift. But Thorgill spoke to Laurentius, the two men laughed, and the trader walked off without looking back.

Thorgill took Signy's arm and led her away with him, through the streets of Puttby, until they reached the house where he was staying. All the while, he kept looking down at her like she was going to disappear if he stopped. When they arrived, two men jumped up – his comrades or followers. He pointed at Signy, and the two men laughed heartily and patted their young chief on the back. Signy expected her new owner to take her to his room that same night, but she quickly learned that Thorgill had not become a chief by being foolish. He was a patient man, and he found her a room of her own.

To her surprise, in the evening a man appeared at her door, bearing a small chest.

"From Master Laurentius," he said.

When the man had gone, Signy opened the chest, slightly trembling, and there were the boots, the sandals, the dresses she had worn on the journey, the sea cloak, even the head band, her embroidery and, nestled in among the clothes, was a small piece of carved amber, the strange shape of a man lying on a gridiron. It was only years later, when a woman with education saw it, that she learned the carving was of a Christian martyr. He was a rich man, who had given all his wealth to the poor, and his name was St Laurentius.

⟡ Chapter 5 ⟡

Lying with a man, Signy discovered, had a lot in common with sailing on boats or learning Jutish. Truthfully, the first time was not particularly satisfactory. She had done her best, but she had been nervous and tense, and Thorgill had been unsure how to treat his new toy, his new treasure. But after a while, Signy's body and her mind adapted. Once she began to enjoy the experience, bed became more fun for both of them. She began to understand why girls got into trouble. There was a daily reminder that sexual relations should be taken seriously, in the shape of Thorgill's wife Helga's ever-swelling belly.

She had anticipated problems with Thorgill's wife, and she was right. Helga did not deign to speak to Signy directly. That would give the slave girl far too much importance. But Signy could make her own deductions from the mistress's tone when she spoke to Thorgill. She understood the word "oxen". She could guess the implication of "someone who could do proper work".

"She said you should clean out the pigs," said Thorgill, the third or fourth night they were together. He spoke, just spoke without thinking whether she would understand. "She said you should be put to grinding corn."

There's no shame in cleaning out pigs or grinding corn, Signy thought. I did both at home. Those are jobs that need to be done, and someone has to do them.

"I told her I didn't pay so much for the girl to be worn out cleaning pigs or grinding corn. We've got plenty of ugly, stupid girls who can do that."

And that only made her more angry, I can guess, thought Signy.

"I don't understand what her problem is," said Thorgill. "She's my lawful wife, the mother of my daughters. It's not even as if I've married you, and plenty of chiefs have more than one wife."

Signy was not especially grateful for his comment, but she knew better than to complain. Let Helga do that, she thought, wriggling closer to him, and letting her hands do the talking.

She was well aware that every woman should share the burden of work around a farm, whatever her status, and was a little disconcerted by the stand-off between Thorgill and Helga. She could not do nothing. That would only earn the contempt of the entire household.

"I told Helga you could sew," said Thorgill, finally. "She agreed that you would be permitted to repair clothes – the clothes of the servants and slaves, not her own," he added.

Signy was thankful for the compromise.

"I can do that," she said to Thorgill with a smile, and another, deeper smile at the look of relief that appeared on his face. "I can spin, too," she suggested. "Every girl is taught to spin."

"Very well," said Thorgill, frowning, "sewing and spinning, but no dirty jobs."

Helga had undoubtedly decided that repairing clothes was a sufficiently demeaning task to humiliate her rival for Thorgill's affections, but growing up with two older brothers, Signy was quite used to repairing clothes. And besides, she quickly realised her sewing tasks gave her a chance to meet the other people who lived on Thorgill's farmstead, people quite like her. She could listen to their speech and observe their habits, and gradually come to understand them and make herself understood.

She found a corner of the weaving shed with sufficient light to see her work and out of the wind and rain. The two slaves who did most of the weaving exchanged words with her now and then, but they mostly spoke between themselves or sang in a tongue she could not understand. With them there was no hostility. They had perhaps no husbands but lived with men from their own people, and even a couple of small and dirty children, who were allowed the run of the farmyard. The other women treated her coldly. Unfriendly treatment from Helga's own maid was to be expected. Gudrun was obliged to follow her mistress's whims and moods. Perhaps the maid had occasionally shared her master's bed before Signy appeared and was now jealous. What can I do about that, thought Signy? I would have been jealous if I was in Gudrun's situation, if an offcomer suddenly appeared and took my place in Thorgill's bed. I would have been irritated if the same thing had happened in the village at home, if I was ousted from a lover's favour, not that I would have stood a chance of becoming the clan chief's bed partner. Surly treatment from the cook maids and the brewhouse maid, the milkmaids and even the slave who actually had the task of cleaning out the pigs was harder to bear. They recognise one of their own, Signy concluded, and don't understand why I should receive special favour.

The men, on the other hand, were a great deal friendlier. She was no competitor to them, of course. On the contrary, better the chief slept with a stranger than cast his eye on their own wives or girlfriends. And she could see the calculation on their faces: you never know, if Thorgill gets bored with the pretty little Saxon girl, then maybe he'll pass her off to one of us, so why irritate her unnecessarily? Instead, they greeted her cheerily, kept their jokes on the right side of indecency, brought her pieces of clothing to fix far more often than wear and tear would justify. In short, they did everything to create the impression that they were a decent set of men and wouldn't mind if she told their master as much.

Chief Thorgill lived in a longhouse made of wood, with a high thatched roof, like a bigger version of the one Signy had grown up in, except the animals did not live with the master. They had barns of their own arranged around a farmyard, with storage for winter food. There was a blacksmith, a carpenter and the open shed where the women gathered to spin and weave, where Signy had her own corner. Thorgill and his wife lived in the upper part of the longhouse, above the storerooms, just as her mother and father had done at home. Thorgill's house was big enough so that there was space on the upper floor for more than one bedchamber. The pregnant Helga and her maid currently occupied one of these. Thorgill, and now Signy, occupied the other. Thorgill's closest men, including the two who had been with him in Puttby, slept on benches around the lower part of the house.

Signy was not invited to Helga's room and could only watch the comings and goings from afar. Sometimes she could hear Helga moaning and crying. Thorgill's wife would lie on her bed, complaining she felt unwell, with one of the serving girls bathing her forehead with a damp cloth. Then the wise woman, Irmengaard, would arrive and give her some potion. In a while, the young mother-to-be would fall asleep, and afterwards she would seem to be better for a few days.

Signy had grown up in a loving family, but in Thorgill's home she was an outsider and, as Helga set the tone, an unwelcome one. On the rare occasions when there were no clothes to repair or wool to spin, or Thorgill to entertain, she kept to herself, wandering down to the seashore, which was just visible from the house. She watched the waves and the birds, kicked over pieces of driftwood, and picked up shells, turning them over in her hand to feel and weigh them. Other times, she walked up the river which ran alongside the farmstead, or up the slope towards a low hill, topped by a clump of the few trees in the neighbourhood. When she stood in the middle, she could almost imagine she was in the forest, although a few paces in any direction, and she was back in open landscape again.

As she explored, she started to recognise some of the medicinal plants she knew from home, and she built up a map in her mind of where they grew. This new knowledge was desperately needed. She had begun to be worried. Thorgill was obviously well able to father children. There were no signs yet, but suppose she were to become pregnant? She knew it was risky for a girl as young as her to be carrying a child. Her body was not ready. Besides, she did not want to become a mother. She did not want to be pregnant, and she did not want the responsibility of looking after a child. She knew she would have to take precautions. Saying no to Thorgill was not an option. She began to collect the herbs she needed to make the medicine which would end any pregnancy if the worst were to happen. She hid her collection in the bottom of her clothes chest.

One damp afternoon, in the half-daylight, she was searching along the river for a particular root which she suspected grew there. She had seen the green parts of the plant earlier, although recently a cold night frost had killed them off. She was intent on her work, digging into the earth with a stick, when she heard a sound above her. She froze and then looked up.

"What are you doing?" came a hostile voice.

Her knowledge of Jutish was now sufficient to comprehend and respond.

"I'm looking for roots."

"Come up here, girl, at once!" A hooded figure, a woman, was standing higher up the riverbank, watching her. The woman beckoned, and Signy was obliged to clamber up, slipping and sliding in the mud.

The woman observed in silence as she struggled up the muddy bank. When she reached level ground, Signy realised that the hooded figure was Irmengaard, the wise woman who she had seen attending Helga.

"I know who you are," the woman said at last. "That little slave girl that Thorgill brought back from Puttby. What are you doing digging in the riverbank?"

"I told the truth, Mistress," said Signy, intimidated by the reputation of the wise woman. "I was looking for roots."

"And what do you know of roots? This is not a field! What sort of roots do you expect to find here?"

Signy was silenced. The woman's sharp look suggested she already knew exactly which roots Signy was looking for. But telling the truth would be to admit she intended to abort Thorgill's child. She said nothing, trying to avoid the woman's gaze.

"Do you know who I am?" asked the wise woman.

"Yes, Mistress," Signy answered.

"Was it these you were looking for?" asked the woman, and lifted several pale fragments from the basket she was holding. Signy felt trapped, and just nodded.

"So you know how to make medicines?" asked the woman.

Signy bowed her head. "Some…a little…my mother, at home, showed me."

"Did she indeed? Yes, I heard the gossip," said the woman. Her expression was hidden by her hood, but her voice felt like a blast from the midwinter north wind. "Thorgill might be interested to know that his new toy has been searching for the means to stop his child. Do you think he would be so pleased with you then?"

Signy's eyes at last met those of the wise woman. He might, she thought, since he bought me to share his bed while Helga is producing children like his best sow.

"I'm too young to have a child, too small, not ready," she said, "at least that's what my mother would say."

The wise woman's eyes held steady for a moment.

"Your mother was correct," she said finally. "It could be the death of you and the child. I don't want to have that on my conscience. Take these and make what you need, before you have an accident." She gave Signy the roots she had in her hand and reached down again into her basket. "And if you ever need a rest from Thorgill's attention, put a little of the juice from this plant in his drink. Just ever so little. Too much and it's deadly."

Signy came close and held out her hand to take the wise woman's offering.

"But remember, I know what you are doing and," she added, raising her finger, "I have one warning, Miss Signy. Don't ever try to give medicines or any other treatment to the village women. If I find you've crossed my path with your mother's cottage cures, I won't kill you, though I so easily could. I'll keep your body alive and destroy your *hugr*, your soul."

Irmengaard looked down once again into the basket, and Signy's eyes followed her gaze. She had been picking mushrooms.

Signy felt one weight at least had been lifted, with the herbs now stashed in her chest. She had better control over her situation and, at the time of the month when the risk for conception was highest, she took the smallest amount of the juice the wise woman had recommended and dropped it into Thorgill's ale. On those nights, her master simply lay beside her and talked. At first, he talked about the farm, about the harvest that had been brought in, about his fears for Helga and his hopes for the coming child. He already had two daughters, and he so desperately wanted a son. A real man had to have a son, he said, and Signy felt a little uneasy. Was he expecting her to provide him a son? Now she really wondered what would happen if someone let him know she was deliberately preventing that. She feared his anger. Irmengaard had a hold over her that could be life or death, and she was not entirely sure she could trust the wise woman.

When Thorgill had said all he had to say about local matters, he told her about his adventures as a warrior. She had already heard some of the stories from the women in the weaving room, how the big man in the area, Chief Sigg, had developed a taste for luxuries supplied by the traders, wine from the south, glass drinking vessels instead of wooden or pottery cups. His wives had been worse than he was, and eventually their expensive desires had outgrown his ability to pay for them. So, several years ago, he had put together a raiding party and sailed over the sea to a land on the far side – Britland.

"We came ashore and robbed a rich man's house," said Thorgill, who had just been a youth at the time. "You couldn't believe the amount of treasure – more than in all the booths of Puttby. We came back with enough booty to satisfy Chief Sigg's wives and keep up his lifestyle a little longer, and plenty for us, too. It didn't last for ever, of course. When the treasure ran out, we made another voyage, and another, and now we do it every summer."

Signy had already heard the result from Laurentius.

"Didn't the people of Britland become wiser? Didn't they defend themselves at all?"

Thorgill, relaxed by Signy's potion, seemed unworried.

"We had to recruit more men each time and travel further, and some of the men didn't come back, but there was always plenty of treasure to go round for the fatherless families."

"Sigg is dead now?"

"Yes, my dear," said Thorgill, "and when Oswulf, his son, took over as leader, he decided to do things differently. We had once seen a broad river that seemed to stretch inland, but old Sigg had always been reluctant to enter the river, for fear of being trapped. So as long as he was in charge we continued to voyage along the coast, the same as we did every year. Two years ago, with his father out of the way, Oswulf felt bolder and gathered together a few of his friends…" Thorgill chuckled to himself. He had evidently been one of the friends. "…and instead we sailed up the river. When the river narrowed, we pulled the boats up onto the bank, and set off into the countryside. The locals were completely unprepared. They put up no resistance. None of us were even injured, let alone killed. We simply had to show up at a farm or a house and demand the goods, and the owners were so frightened, they had handed them over straightaway."

Thorgill turned, or rather his eyes turned, towards Signy, who was leaning over him, listening with all her attention not to misunderstand a word.

"When we got back, loaded down with gold and silver, rumours spread that Oswulf had found a new source of wealth. This last summer, we put together a bigger band, men from all across Juteland, even those who had not believed Oswulf at first. We had to travel further, and the natives fought back this time. But even so, the gold and silver, glass and metalwork, the wine we drank and the women we had, they passed all our expectations."

"And it was this booty…that was the price you paid for me in Puttby?"

"Some of it, my little darling."

Signy stroked his chest.

Next summer, Thorgill told her, the raiding crews planned to make the same voyage, and when he came back laden with plunder again, he would recruit more fighters to his band, and become a big man like Oswulf.

❧ Chapter 6 ❧

Thorgill had been called away, up country, for a gathering with Chief Oswulf. Signy might have been grateful for a few nights without her lord, if it had not left her open to the mercies of all the others. She expected some new humiliation when Helga's personal maid, Gudrun, appeared at the weaving shed, accompanied by her friend and ally, the cook.

Signy slowly put down her sewing, one of the stable boys' trousers, which she was fixing for at least the third time, and prepared for the worst.

"What is it?" she said, expecting an insult or crude comment. "What do you want?"

It took a moment before she realised the look in the women's eyes was not hostility, but anxiety.

It took a longer while before Gudrun answered. "We want your help," she said finally.

And why now, thought Signy.

"With what, may I ask?"

There was another long silence, filled by glances between Gudrun and her friend.

"Mistress Helga is ill," the maid said at last.

"Mistress Helga is expecting a child. She's not ill," Signy replied.

"No, no, you don't understand," burst out the cook. "She's really ill. She's frightened she's going to lose the child. She's wailing and crying, shaking and shivering."

"And what has that to do with me?" asked Signy.

"They say," said Gudrun, casting a glance at the two weavers, who had long since stopped their work to watch the exchange, "they say that you know medicine, that you have experience in treating expectant mothers."

"The wise woman Irmengaard is the one who has experience with treating expectant mothers."

"But" – Gudrun and the cook exchanged frightened looks – "Irmengaard is away, travelling…"

"To her sister," added the cook.

"I know very little," said Signy, "and I've been expressly forbidden to treat anyone in this house or the village."

"Please, please, help us," cried Gudrun, evidently close to tears. "Please just advise us what we should do."

"You know Mistress Helga doesn't want me in her room." You know she hates me, Signy thought.

"There's no one else for us to turn to," cried the cook, holding out her hands in a plea. "We need your help…Mistress Signy."

So they were serious then, thought Signy, if they were going to demean themselves by elevating her to the title of "Mistress".

"Very well," she said, standing up and carefully placing the boy's trousers on her stool. "I'll come with you. I'll remain at the threshold and advise, but that's all."

She did not need to say more for Gudrun and the cook to turn on their heels and hurry away to the hall. She was forced to scurry after them.

She had heard crying earlier, she reflected, but she had given it no thought. With Helga's ill-temper and complaining, Signy had quickly learned to block out the sounds from the room her master's wife occupied. She was still hesitant to follow the women to Helga's sanctuary, though they beckoned and whispered as loudly as they dared to encourage her.

She stood in the doorway to Helga's room, and the cook pulled aside the curtain. Thorgill's wife lay on a low bed in the centre of the space, propped up by pillows. Her eyes stared in Signy's direction, but they did not seem to see her.

"He's going to die," she suddenly wailed, clutching at her belly. "My son is going to die."

"No, Mistress," stuttered Gudrun, taking a damp cloth from a basin by the bed and wiping Helga's forehead.

"I'm going to die," cried the stricken woman again. "My son is going to die, and I'm going to die with him."

Signy observed the woman carefully. It wouldn't be beyond Helga to simulate such behaviour, she thought. Knowing that Thorgill was away, she might easily have conceived a plan to trick me into doing something that would set me in such poor light that I'd be punished, whipped, even, or sent away.

Suddenly, Helga began to wail again, and then weep and shake, beads of sweat forming on her brow. Gudrun desperately applied the damp cloth once more and turned to Signy with a beseeching look.

"What shall we do?"

Of course, thought Signy, if I do nothing, and something happens to Helga, in the worst case that she and the child did die, then it would be easy to blame me for the disaster. Better to suppose this sickness is genuine.

She took a step forward into the room, half expecting that Helga would begin to shriek at her for intruding, but the pregnant woman simply continued crying and shaking.

In the end, thought Signy, it doesn't make a difference whether this is real or simply acting; there's a risk that the child will be harmed either way.

She took another cautious step forward. There was still no reaction from Helga. She came alongside the bed, reached out and took Helga's hand. The woman seemed entirely unaware that her rival was by her side. Signy started to worry, no longer about her own safety, but about the state of her master's wife and the baby inside her.

"How long has this been going on?" she asked.

"Since yesterday," said Gudrun, gratitude seeping into her voice.

"Her heart is beating wildly," said Signy. That was a sign that was impossible to fake.

"She's been possessed…by an evil spirit," said Gudrun, a questioning tone in her voice.

"I don't think so," said Signy. "Does she know that the wise woman is travelling?"

Gudrun hesitated. "I…I think so. Irmengaard was here the day before she left."

A new fear spread through Signy's mind. She doubted that Helga had deliberately set her up for a confrontation with Irmengaard, but in effect that was what she had done. More likely, Helga's usual worries had been heightened by the absence of both her husband and the medicine woman, heightened until they had become uncontrollable, and then she had been trapped in a vicious circle of her own making. Signy felt herself frowning. She would have to act. When it came to a choice, between a dead child or a dead mother with an angry, resentful master, and the unknown threat from Irmengaard, she knew which she would rather face.

"Keep bathing her forehead. Bathe her breast, too. Try to keep her cool. I'll come back in a little while, I promise you."

The look Gudrun gave her would have melted her heart if it had not been long frozen by the woman's earlier disdain.

She crossed the upper region of the hall until she came to her own space, the space she usually shared with Thorgill and where she kept her chest. The wise woman had only forbidden her to treat people. She had said nothing about picking plants and collecting mushrooms, and Signy had continued to add to her collection. She had wort and willow bark, and other herbs she could use to make a calming potion. That much she had learned from her mother years ago, and there had been many times they had sat together warming various remedies, sometimes in water, sometimes in honeyed mead. Honeyed mead would be best today, she thought, carefully descending the ladder to the lower hall, ducking through the doorway and crossing the yard to the cook hut.

"Warm me some mead," she said. The kitchen maids eyed her suspiciously, clearly noticing her unexpectedly commanding tone. "Your mistress is ill, and if you do nothing, then I'll ensure that the master beats you when he returns." The threat of Thorgill's anger stirred them into action.

Signy sang a song to herself, a long song about a maid and a warrior, and the troubles they had to become a couple. It was a useful song to sing while waiting for juices from the herbs to join those of the mead. Sung at a constant slow pace, it helped ensure some consistency in the broth, and the words of love and hope would seep into the brew and give it additional power.

She nodded to the maids when she was done and ordered them to empty the mixture into a beaker. She carried it back to the longhouse, climbing the ladder carefully, still hearing the sobbing from Helga's room, joined, she now detected, by that of Gudrun.

"Oh, thank the gods you're back. She's getting weaker."

There was no doubt that Helga looked exhausted. Given time, her exhaustion might even tip her into sleep and break the cycle quite naturally, but there was still the risk that her body might succumb, her heart fail or her breathing cease.

"Give her this, one sip at a time."

Gudrun looked at her questioningly.

"Give it to her," Signy insisted. "It will send her to sleep and calm her down." Still Gudrun hesitated.

"Listen," said Signy. "You asked me here. You begged for my help. Now you'll share the treatment with me, so that if something ill happens, we also share responsibility."

Gudrun took the beaker doubtfully, peered into it and sniffed.

"Gudrun," said Signy, "I've no need to prepare a poison to ensure that Helga dies. I merely need to do nothing and wait for Freya to call her naturally. Pour a little into a smaller cup and give it to your mistress. It won't take long, and you'll see the difference, see her calm down, feel her heart beat more slowly, feel the fever pass."

The maid did as she was instructed. Signy crouched by her, placing her hand reassuringly on Gudrun's shoulder, on the shoulder of the woman who had been one of her foes ever since she had first arrived. The maid lifted the cup away to fill it again, turned her head towards Signy, and their eyes met.

"Believe me, Gudrun," said Signy, softly.

As they watched, Helga's features relaxed, her breathing became steadier. Instead of staring, the mistress's eyes closed.

Gudrun looked doubtful still, no doubt fearing that the process might continue until the breathing stopped entirely, but it did not, only becoming the calm of sleep.

"Now," said Signy, recalling her mother's practice, "you go and get something to eat and drink, while I sit and keep watch. When you return, you should sleep at the foot of the bed, and if anything happens in the night, then come and call me right away. You know where I'll be, and I'll be alone."

There was no call in the night. Signy glanced in the door of Helga's room in the morning and received a timid smile from Gudrun in return. It was enough. The sewing and the spinning still needed to be done. Young Grunwald would still need his trousers repaired, so he did not have to keep wearing his uncle's.

☙ Chapter 7 ❧

Signy did not expect gratitude from Helga, especially as Gudrun reported that Thorgill's wife could not remember anything of her illness. Others did, however, and the looks Signy now received might not be quite called respect, but perhaps rather suspicion, alarm, even. It was one thing to be rumoured to be a herbalist, quite another to have proved that she was, however much of an exaggeration, she thought. The concoction I put together isn't the only cure I know, but there's not a lot more I can do with any certainty, she had to admit to herself. There's a big difference between sitting beside calm and experienced Mother and doing it all myself.

There was no avoiding another nagging fear, either. She had defied Irmengaard's order. Not only had she treated a patient without the wise woman's permission, but she had treated her most important patient. Perhaps she had saved Helga's life, but that would be small thanks to balance against the wise woman's threat. Irmengaard knew where to find her once she returned. There could be only one reason the black-hooded figure was crossing the yard in her direction.

The wise woman stopped in front of the weaving shed, her eyes on Signy. She raised her hand to point.

"You," she said, "broke the word you gave me."

To save a life, thought Signy, but the words caught in her throat.

"You," said Irmengaard, "will come to my house tomorrow, when the sun is one hand from the horizon."

Signy could find no words to reply.

"You won't defy me again?"

Signy nodded. The wise woman turned and strode away.

The weavers observed her departure with fearful awe, and then they turned their sorrowful gazes towards Signy. She saw they had reached their conclusion. Signy was a dead woman walking.

Signy found Irmengaard picking herbs in her garden. The air was cold, but the wise woman clearly knew how to protect her plants from the killing frost for as long as possible. Irmengaard said nothing when she caught sight of her visitor, merely beckoned for her to follow.

The doorway to the woman's cottage was low, and Signy noticed Irmengaard had to stoop to enter, as she had to herself. Inside, it was warm, despite the chill. A fire crackled in the middle of the room, the smoke lazily climbing to where it could seep out through the thatch. Signy stood on the threshold, not daring to take more than one step inside the wise woman's domain. Irmengaard herself crossed the room to a low table and set down the material she had brought with her from the garden. Then she turned to Signy and threw back the hood of her cloak. Signy was shocked to see the wise woman was not the old witch she had expected, but was perhaps around her mother's age, if not younger. Irmengaard undid the clasp and removed the cloak, folding it carefully and placing it on the top of a chest which stood next to the wall.

In the dim light that filtered in through a skin-covered window, and the orange glow of the fire, Signy could see she was slim, dark-haired, and when she looked closely, dark-eyed, too, very different from the majority of the people who shared Thorgill's homestead, not unattractive to look at, in fact.

Irmengaard noticed Signy's appraisal.

"You were expecting an old crone?" she asked, though obviously anticipating no answer from Signy. "Most of them do, when they come here for the first time. I would be a crone, too, if I was forced to labour in the fields or grind flour or spin and weave." She paused as if contemplating Signy. "Let this be my first lesson to you. If you want to preserve your looks, let your mind do the work."

Signy stood rooted to the spot, anxiety forming a pit in her stomach.

Irmengaard reached for the pin that fastened her dress at the shoulder, and with a deft flick unhooked it and let the garment fall to the ground.

Signy could not stifle a gasp. The wise woman's body was covered in tattoos, rows of dots and spirals around her breasts, down her stomach and down her legs, and out along her arms.

"Do you know who you're dealing with?" she asked in a flat, faintly hostile tone. "Do you know what these signify?"

She waved her hand up down her body to ensure that Signy understood she was referring to her ornamentation. It wasn't easy to make out the patterns in the firelight, and as Irmengaard moved and the flames danced, her shape seemed to shift, until all that remained was a disembodied voice. The wise woman did a pirouette to show the patterns covered her back as well, including two schematic staring eyes, but when she completed the turn, there was a smile on her face.

"You have a lot to learn, child, because you're still a child, despite your position in Thorgill's household." She laughed. "One day you'll realise what a risk you were taking to cross my path. You'll realise how lucky you are that it was kind Irmengaard, daughter of Brenn, you disobeyed and not certain others of our sisterhood with shorter tempers and fewer scruples."

She stopped speaking and let her eyes rest on Signy's face. Signy's instinct was to look away, but a voice inside told her to hold the wise woman's gaze, despite her fear.

"I owe you an apology," Irmengaard said at last, "perhaps two. I've treated you very unfairly. I should have been more sympathetic to a young woman in a strange land, far from home. Instead, I'll admit, I was annoyed when the slave women's gossip reached me, whispering that Thorgill's new purchase from Puttby, the pretty little Saxon girl, claimed she was a medicine woman. I was angry when I found you by the river looking for roots, because that confirmed the rumours were true. No one would clamber about in a muddy ditch looking for obscure roots unless they knew what they were looking for. So I threatened you in the most childish and immature manner. When I returned from my journey, I heard a new story, a story that you had saved Mistress Helga's life while I was away, and not now from some foolish slaves, but from Gudrun herself. I was furious, I confess. I sat and ruminated on how to punish you, to betray you to Thorgill, for example, but you'd just saved his wife and child, so that would be futile. No, I would have to concoct some means myself to show you who is the only wise woman in these parts."

She laughed again, a little bitterly.

"A most foolish woman, in fact, I was soon taught. I was sitting in this room, brooding malevolently on your fate, when the goddess, Freya herself, came to me and beat me to the floor. Literally," Irmengaard emphasised, pointing to a spot by the fire. "I was lying there when I came to my senses. The goddess was angry, she said, at my arrogance, at my refusal to accept her gift."

The wise woman took a step towards Signy, who stood silent, frozen.

"Do you understand what that means?"

If she expected a reply, she did not hear one.

"It means you were sent here, to me, by the goddess. I should have seen that at once, of course, from the look you gave me when we met by the river. Of course, you were frightened. Who would not be, caught red-handed by someone with my status, but there was defiance, too, deep down."

She paused and took a breath.

"Was your mother a priestess…of Freya?"

"No," said Signy. "My mother…"

"…was a humble farmer's wife?" Irmengaard completed the sentence.

"No," said Signy, "she was proud to be the wife of a good man, a farmer, and proud to be able to help the people of the village. We had priests, like everywhere, priests of Tyr, but they lived in the house of the clan chief."

"You sound like you're no great lover of priests." The wise woman looked thoughtful for a moment. "That was to be my second apology, but I'm afraid I messed it up. I apologise for demeaning your mother, twice now. I, too, first learned my arts from my mother, not my birth mother, though, but my foster mother."

Signy had no conception of how to respond. Her nervousness exacerbated her still inadequate grasp of Jutish, and besides, it was disconcerting to have to speak to a naked woman whose body appeared to shimmer and almost vanish at times during the conversation.

"Let's say this, then," said Irmengaard after a pause that seemed to last for ever. She took two quick steps, wrapped her arms around Signy's neck and placed her lips against Signy's.

Then she stepped back.

"Friends or enemies?"

"Friends, if the gods wish it," said Signy, still unconvinced.

The wise woman turned away, stooping to where her dress still lay in a heap on the floor. As she did so, the eyes imprinted on her back held Signy's gaze as tightly as the living eyes in her face. Irmengaard pulled up the dress and fastened the brooch, and once her body was covered, Signy's courage returned.

"Tell me," she whispered, "could you destroy my soul but keep my body alive?"

Irmengaard turned slowly and gazed at her. "Could I? I've heard it said that it's possible, but…"

Signy detected a note of vulnerability in Irmengaard's voice, and with that her fear started to fade. The wise woman was certainly strange, but Signy remembered her own mother, how she sat inconsolable, staring into the fire after a day when a child or a mother had lost their lives despite all her efforts. Sometimes the wish to perform exceeded the capability.

"Now sit down on this log by the fire," said Irmengaard, quickly recovering her self-assurance, "and I'll sit beside you, and we'll share some food and drink. You can tell me who you are and how you came to be here, or should we say, how Freya found you and guided you to my door."

It was hard to see her journey that way, Signy reflected, but as she recounted her kidnapping, her rescue by Laurentius and the kindness he had shown her, she felt she might just discern the hand of some higher power that steered her fate.

"I had a dream a short while before you arrived," said Irmengaard, as Signy's tale reached an end. "A yellow cat came to me and asked to become my apprentice, my follower. A cat! Now I realise that cat was you, in the form of an animal. Have you ever felt that you've taken on another shape and visited other people or places?"

Signy found it hard to suppress a laugh. The whole suggestion was absurd. Those were stories people told about sorcerers or some mythic warrior heroes, not farm girls.

"I simply want to learn," said Signy. "I want to learn the skills my mother didn't have the opportunity to teach me, to make medicines, to help women in childbirth, not just the easy cases, but difficult ones, too. To help men, too, if the occasion should arise."

"I'll teach you, don't worry," said Irmengaard. "I'll teach you more secrets than your mother could, if you let me."

The wise woman stood up.

"What must I do?" asked Signy.

"You must come to me at the next full moon," said Irmengaard, turning towards her.

"How will I explain my absence to Thorgill?"

"Thorgill won't argue, I promise."

When the midwinter feast had been celebrated, and the days grew longer, a summons came from Chief Oswulf ordering Thorgill to join him at his hall to discuss the next summer's expedition. Helga had just given birth, to yet another daughter, healthy and with a loud voice, and although Thorgill would have conventionally taken his wife to the council of war, neither she nor the child were up to a trip across country in the uncertain winter weather.

"I'll have to make do with the next best woman," he said, an ironic smile on his face. Signy had already begun to suspect that she might not merely be the "next best woman". Thorgill had not complained at all about the nights when she had left him alone to sit with Irmengaard. Perhaps he had been content to share his bed with Gudrun again, as the maid had now admitted he had done before Signy had come. Perhaps he was secretly proud that his find in the market had been taken up by the wise woman. Having a priestess in the household would undoubtedly add to his prestige, and maybe now was an opportunity to throw a warning or two in the direction of Oswulf. So Signy read matters from the somewhat confused ramblings of her bed partner.

She was dressed up in borrowed finery to accompany Thorgill on the visit. She was not yet a practised horse rider, although the men of the household had been quick to offer her training when they heard she had been forced to walk across the width of Juteland.

The journey to Oswulf's hall left her tired and sore, and the reception given by the other womenfolk was reserved. Signy understood they were unsure if she was just a slave, a favoured bed mate, or even a second wife. Since Chief Thorgill had chosen to bring this woman to such a prestigious meeting, they evidently decided to avoid causing offence, though in view of her dubious status, Signy was placed well down the table when it came to feasting. She was quite satisfied with that. It provided her with an opportunity to watch and learn on her first visit to the big chief's hall, without being forced to participate actively in customs she did not know or understand.

"It's disgraceful," said Thorgill, when he realised she had been asked to sit among the wives of some of the lesser warriors.

"Don't worry, my lord," she said, and kissed him. "I don't want to embarrass you in front of the high-born ladies with my foreign accent and poor manners."

Thorgill soon forgot her position when the drinking and eating began, and she was grateful to keep out of sight when Oswulf's wife carried round the drinking horn, and cheers and toasts to the success of the coming summer rose to the rafters. The men and women she sat with were not so proud. Surprisingly, she found that several of the women were Saxons and had stories similar to hers.

"They came in the night!"

"I screamed and shouted!"

"He threw me across the back of a horse and carried me off."

"I was so sick on the boat. I puked from beginning to end."

"And now look, here in Juteland and in the bed of the heroic warrior, and I was destined for old Cumbolanus." That girl was from Britland, or Britannia, as she called her home.

The women laughed among themselves, casting glances at the men clustered around Chief Oswulf. And they described the strange land over the seas.

"The houses are built of stone, at least the rich people's houses," said the heroic warrior's girl. Laurentius had told her, Signy recalled, of the city of Rome, which he had visited years ago, a whole town built of stone.

"The rich men wear skirts instead of trousers and cut their hair and beards short," commented another.

"A lot of them don't have beards at all!"

"And the women wear gowns you can see through! Can you believe it!"

One woman even spoke a few words that sounded like nonsense, and the others collapsed into laughter.

"What was the joke?" asked Signy, wondering.

The woman sitting beside her laughed again.

"She said, 'Can you tell me the way to the toilet?' in Latin."

"Latin, what's that?"

One of Signy's new friends leaned towards her.

"It's the language fine people speak over there." Her neighbour looked shrewd. "They think they're Romans, but they're no better than us."

When they arrived back from the council, the blacksmith and the carpenter were put hard to work, and soon smoke and steam, and the sound of beaten iron, filled the winter air. To Signy's relief, Helga made a good recovery from the birth, and soon handed the baby over to a wet nurse. Thorgill's duties as a husband took precedence, and he spent more time with his wife, which improved Helga's temper, but did little to improve her feelings towards Signy, difficult as they were to judge, since the two women barely exchanged a word when they met. Evidently, Signy's journey to the chieftain's feast had only added another source of resentment.

Signy judged it better to keep out of the way of her master's wife, and once the last of the snow melted and the days grew lighter, she started borrowing a horse from the stables to improve her riding skills. At first, the men who cared for the horses had been surprised that she took the initiative, as few of the women cared to ride. She suspected they had gone behind her back to Thorgill to make sure of his permission to let her use the horses. Evidently, he had not stood in her way.

Eventually, she developed enough confidence to ride over to a neighbouring farmstead, where the house mother was one of the Saxon women she had met at the feast. Their stable folk had been mightily surprised at first, when Thorgill's woman cantered across the fields and pulled up into the yard, but Thorgill was a law unto himself, and they supposed his woman was likewise. As spring went on, these visits became more numerous, and Signy began to get on good terms with the several of the neighbouring warriors and their wives. The men would all be part of Thorgill's band in the summer, and the chief was pleased that his girl was contributing to a sense of solidarity.

She did not need a horse or Thorgill's permission to visit Irmengaard. She merely had to tramp across the fields to the outskirts of the village once the evening light started to fade. The other women might have watched her go, might have felt she should have stayed with them, spinning the thread that would be needed when the bright daylight returned and the weaving looms would be busy, but they said nothing. Everyone knew the wise woman. Everyone had needed her help, and they did not question her judgement. If the Saxon slave girl was worthy of her attention, they were not going to argue or complain.

◌ Chapter 8 ◌

Signy had dismounted and was leading her horse towards the stables when she was surprised to see Helga crossing the farmyard. She was more than surprised when Helga headed straight in her direction. Her timing could barely be worse, Signy thought. She was tired and sweaty after riding to a farm some distance south from the settlement to deliver medication and an amulet to the mother of a sick child. Irmengaard had requested her help, since she had another patient to care for in the opposite direction. Signy immediately understood why Irmengaard had chosen to send her. There was nothing much wrong with the little boy and, in all honesty, the mother had been in more need of the calming draught.

Signy was wearing men's breeches under her riding cloak. Her hair was half bound up by a piece of plaited leather, and the hood of her cloak had fallen away during the ride, a sign perhaps of her dubious status – still a slave, but now half-respected assistant to the wise woman, half-married to the chief. Helga, as befitted the mistress of the household, was dressed in a fine robe, with glittering brooches at the shoulders and bangles hanging from the cuffs. An exquisite belt hung from her waist with a jewelled purse, and the household keys well visible. Her hair was plaited and covered by a spotlessly clean scarf. Her smile was as carefully constructed as the styling of her hair, and for the same purpose.

"Signy, my dear," she said, in a tone dripping with honey, "Thorgill tells me that he'll be taking you with him on his voyage. That will be such a fitting opportunity for someone with your" – her eyes passed down Signy's dirty figure and returned once more to her face – "characteristics."

With that, she turned and made her way back across the yard.

Those are the most words she has addressed to me all year, thought Signy, watching her retreating back, and she certainly came out of her way to ensure I heard them. She looked down at her body, at her feet. Her tunic was stained. Her trousers were of rough wool and tied with a length of twisted cord. She was wearing a pair of muddy boots. Suddenly, she laughed to herself. All that is missing is a sword, and I might pass for a slight and soft-faced warrior.

She collected her normal clothes from a peg just inside the stable and made her way down to the stream that ran behind the farmyard. She was naturally suspicious of Helga's announcement. She knew nothing of raiding, other than one short experience as a victim. She was just beginning to feel at home on Thorgill's farm, to have Irmengaard as a friend and mentor, beginning to know some of the neighbouring women. Perhaps it's simply that Helga hopes that I might not return, she concluded. I might be killed in some battle, captured and raped and put to death by hostile natives, or maybe just lost overboard on the voyage.

She stripped off the dirty riding clothes, took up a wooden bucket, dipped it into the stream and emptied it over her head and body. The water was cold, and she was still standing slightly dazed when she heard a voice behind her.

"So you'll be joining us on the voyage, Mistress Signy?"

She recognised the sound of young Grunwald, the boy who had brought his trousers to be repaired so many times during the winter. Unfortunately, her robe was hanging from a tree branch out of reach.

"Everyone seems to know what I'll be doing except me," she said. "If you could be kind enough to pass me my dress."

The boy turned, now red-faced, took the clothing from its place and handed it to her. Surely she was not the first woman he had seen without clothes, though it was not really fitting that a farmhand should be ogling his master's girl. His reddening ears betrayed that he knew that, too.

"If I am, then I suppose I'll still have the job of fixing your trousers wherever we go." Now he had lost the blustering attitude that he had when he had first spoken to her. "And be careful I don't have to patch you up as well."

A few days before, one of the slaves had cut himself while attaching a new blade to a scythe handle. She had heard his cry and ran, needle in hand. A couple of quick stiches and the wound was closed, though it would be days before they could be sure no corruption would set in. Vinegar from the kitchen and sphagnum moss would help but were never certain.

She slipped the brooch pin through her dress to hold it in place.

"I'll fetch your clogs," offered the boy.

"There's no need," she said quickly. "They're in the stable, and I have to pass back that way."

"Am I to sail with you?" she asked Thorgill, stretched out beside her.

"I thought so," he said. "There have always been a few women who've accompanied us on the voyages. Some of them have even taken part in the raiding. Big strong girls can wield a spear as well as a man, and they have eyes and noses for perfumes and spices that are valuable spoils."

"But I'm not a big strong girl," she pointed out quite reasonably, "and I can't fight!"

The Jute chief rolled over to face her with a chuckle. "There's plenty else you can do."

"Such as stir trouble among the men, when you have your girl and they don't."

"Don't get your hopes up," he replied. "I'll be away from the camp most of the time."

"Camp?"

"Yes, we'll do as we did last year. Set up a camp beside the river, and you can stay there. Skalgrim's cook'll be coming, and Oswulf has agreed to bring a couple of goats and some boys to take care of them. You can do what you do here, make repairs, treat any warriors who are injured…I heard how you helped old

Foggi…Okay, you'll have to grind corn and maybe scavenge while we're away…"

"And if I don't want to go…"

Thorgill's eyebrows curved upwards.

"If I want you to come, you have to come, Signy. You have to do as I say. My men have to do as I say, even though they're not bound to me as you are. We go, together. I'm the leader. They're followers. You're a follower. That's all there is to it."

Irmengaard laughed when Signy told her what Thorgill had suggested.

"I dripped it in Helga's ear, when I had the chance," she said, looking very pleased with herself. "It'll be good for you and Helga to have a break from one another. And besides, it'll be a test for you. You'll discover how much you've grown, as a healer, and as a woman."

And then she kissed Signy on the cheek.

"Helga's pregnant again," said Signy. "Gudrun told me."

"Another girl," said Irmengaard. "The sticks said so."

"You cast sticks?"

"Gudrun and I did."

"Gudrun, why?"

Irmengaard lifted her finger and placed it against Signy's lips.

"You're not the only one weighing whether to carry Thorgill's child in the hope it would be a boy."

That gave Signy a great deal to think on as she crossed the fields back to the farm. If Helga became the mother of Thorgill's son, that would only strengthen her place. Helga was Chief Skalgrim's cousin, after all, and Skalgrim himself was foster brother to Chief Oswulf. It was Helga's duty to deliver a son to Thorgill.

I've done all I can to prevent myself carrying Thorgill's child, she said to herself, short of avoiding his bed altogether, which I can't do, and I don't want to do. I have my reasons, and Irmengaard agrees. On the other hand, if Gudrun were to have a son before Helga, and he's Thorgill's son – well, that's by no means certain, the way Gudrun sleeps around – all else would be forgotten. Gudrun would fly high above me, might even threaten

Helga if the sticks are correct and her baby is yet another girl. That would be an awkward situation, she reflected, and not at all to my benefit.

But Gudrun wasn't pregnant, that Signy was quite sure of, because Helga's maid had been carrying a child. The father lived on a neighbouring farm. Signy and Irmengaard had sat with her for three days while the poison worked, and the life within her had been extinguished.

With the planting season complete, the boats were sealed and put in the water, and the preparation for the journey over the sea reached a climax. Warriors gathered from far and wide, and not just warriors, but farmhands and young boys like Grunwald, hoping for their first chance to join the raid. The moon was full and high in the sky when the boats left. Providing the weather stayed fine, they could see their way at night almost as well as during the day for the time the journey would take.

Signy sat in the stern, out of the way of the rowing men. At her feet was a small chest containing the little she could bring with her: clean clothes, and some medicines, some herbs she had picked, and some she had received from Irmengaard with strict instructions on how they were to be used. Oswulf's boat was in the lead, his privilege as leader of the expedition.

On the third day, the lookout, a particularly sharp-eyed youth, reported that he had spotted land on the horizon, and soon enough, standing in the stern beside Thorgill, Signy could make out a low coastline far in the distance.

"Is this Britland?" asked Signy, peering out at the smudge of brown on the horizon.

"This is the part of the coast that Oswulf's father raided in the past," said the steersman.

"And many others," added Thorgill. "It's useless to go there now. The few Britons who remain are thoroughly prepared, and besides, many Angles and Saxons have moved in. They won't put up with any interference from Jutes."

"They're poorer than we are," laughed the steersman.

Oswulf swung his boat around to the north, and the oarsmen set to work again. One whole day and into the next and then the land receded. Signy wondered if they were drifting out to sea, but Thorgill assured her that this was the entrance to a great bay, surrounded by marshy swamps. Oswulf followed the coast, and Thorgill and the others followed after.

"Oswulf will call a halt," said the steersman. "We'll wait here for the tide to turn."

"Is the water too shallow?" asked Signy, now familiar with the rising and falling of the tide along the coast of Juteland.

The steersman shook his head. "No, my dear, but we'll never be able to row up the river against the flow and the tide, but wait until the tide changes…" He gave her a shrewd smile.

Thorgill and his band were at ease, the oars drawn in, waiting for the signal from Oswulf's boat, waiting for the judgement of their own steersman.

Slowly, the vessel shifted, turning gently in the water, until the steersman adjusted his oar.

"Oswulf's pulling away," shouted the lookout. The steersman grimaced, but even Signy could see that the rope to the anchor was now taut as the boat was pulled towards the river.

"The hand of the gods," laughed the steersman, seeing her watching the anchor line. "Use it if you dare!"

The boat edged forward as soon as the anchor was lifted, and by the time the stone had been hauled on board, the vessel was already slipping into the river mouth.

"It'll move all the faster as the tide builds and the river narrows," said the steersman. "If the gods are willing, we won't hit a sandbank. Keep a sharp eye out there, young Ferland!" he yelled to the lookout in the bows.

The tree-lined waterway reminded her of her home. Was it really less than one year since she had been sitting on a similar river watching the boats pass by, wondering where they were coming from and where they were going? Would there be girls like her watching from the bank of this river with fear in their hearts as they recognised the pirates? Last year, she had been a victim, and now, not even a year later, she was one of the plunderers.

The water tore on, eddying and swirling around hidden shoals and all-too-obvious obstructions, half-submerged tree limbs, small islands, and even an abandoned watercraft, twirling dangerously in the flow. After an age of rushing water, Signy had the feeling that the surge was dying down.

"Now's about the time to find our mooring place," said the steersman, "before the tide turns and we're drawn back down the river again."

A cry went up from the lead boat, and Thorgill pointed. They had reached the stretch of the river where they had made their camp in previous years. Above this point, the stream narrowed, and there were too many rocks, small waterfalls and rapids for easy passage, especially if they had to make a hasty retreat. One by one, the boats swung into the bank. The men leaped out and pulled them up out of the river with strong, practised arms.

The landscape was flat and empty, not a house to be seen, but there were sufficient trees along the bank that before long the sound of axes rang out, and the first lengths of wood were being dragged together to form some simple shelters. Other men had grabbed digging tools, and Oswulf was marching around indicating where he wanted the ditch cleared out and the palisade from last year patched up. Foraging parties were sent out, even ready to bargain for food with the local farmers, at least for now. Warriors were despatched to hunt for deer or wild pig, and they returned saying they had seen the Britons in the distance, but the area around the campsite appeared to have been abandoned.

Thorgill scowled. "This area was full of farms when we landed the first year."

There were no signs of farms now. No crops had been planted. Even the fruit from the trees where the farms had previously stood had just fallen to the ground and rotted.

In a couple of days, the warriors left, taking the road to the south, while Signy, the other women and a few boys and older men remained behind. The men and boys continued cutting down trees and dragging them to the campsite. Piece by piece, the brushwood filling the gaps in the palisade was replaced by solid wood.

After a couple of days, some of the warriors returned, driving a small herd of cows and some pigs, and leading several people they had seized. The cows and pigs were corralled, and the captives put to work assisting in the camp, with blows and curses to dig, blows and curses to haul timber, blows and curses to stand up, and blows and curses to lie down.

Signy took charge of dealing out the food to the captives, just enough so that they could work. It was a trying task, but brought her into contact with the Britons, accustoming her ears to the talk, to their garbled attempts to speak Saxon. Not that it helped. It was obvious they hated and feared her just as much as the men.

The road from south to north passed about half a mile inland, where the ground was a little higher. It took a while before Signy dared to walk that far, but once it became evident there were no enemy waiting in ambush, she began to explore along the track that led through the fields to the road. To her the road itself was remarkable. It was no mud path, beaten down over the years by the feet of people and animals, but a strip of stones and pebbles, fitted carefully, and stretching off as far as the eye could see, straight across the flat countryside. She crouched down and swept her hand across the surface. Someone has made this, she thought, foot by foot, yard by yard. She could see, too, where someone else had had to patch it, where holes had appeared in the surface, and a less skilful craftsman had filled them in with gravel and earth. She set off to the north, peering down into the ditch by the side of the road to look for herbs, any that could make the porridge tastier, and any that might be useful for medicines.

Presently, she caught sight of a low stone wall and then another. She stopped, and her eyes travelled along the wall as it ran beside the road and then turned in among the overgrown plants and out of sight. Hidden among the long grass were the ruins of a building, perhaps the foundation of a wooden house like Laurentius' warehouse, or one of the houses of stone she had heard about. There was a small path leading inside, probably made by animals. She stepped off the road and took the path into the ruins. Between the walls, the ground was strewn with rotten wood, broken tiles and fallen stones, half-buried, as if they had lain there for years. She kept tripping over stones, until she realised they had been laid out in a series of paths, and then she noticed that some of the plants growing between the paths were familiar. They were the very herbs she had been looking for. Someone with a knowledge of medicinal plants must have lived here long ago. She bent down and picked those she needed and tucked them into her dress. In other places, quite novel plants were growing, and some of them had brightly coloured flowers. She picked one and sniffed it. A soft fragrance filled her nose. She made her way out of the broken building back to the road. It would be dusk soon, and it was better to go back to the camp while there was still light, but tomorrow she would return and see what else she could find.

In the following days, she realised there were several buildings scattered by the road. Among the ruins she found vegetables growing, the remains of the gardens planted by the people who used to live here. Onions and a tangle of beans had sprung up. If they stayed long enough, perhaps there would be beans to harvest. At the northern end of the village, she noticed that the road divided. The main track continued straight across the flat land, while a second road turned west, inland, to where she could see wooded hills rising in the distance. She sat on a fallen stone and wondered about the people who lived here. Who were they? What did they do? Where had they gone? She brushed her foot against one of the stones and saw that it had been carved. There was the figure of a woman in a long dress, with her hair bound up on her head, and letters above and below. She had seen such images carved into the glass beakers at Oswulf's feast. She reached down and ran her finger along the slots cut into the stone. It was a message from the people who used to live here, but she did not know what it meant.

Mainly, the people left in the camp waited: waited for the foragers to return with food, waited for the warriors to come back, until one day they did. Oswulf, Thorgill and several other senior warriors were riding horses, and there were more cattle and pigs, and a few scrawny sheep and goats, but no gold and silver.

"We scoured the countryside, from farm to farm and cottage to cottage. The people must have seen us coming, as there was never anyone there when we arrived. No valuables, no weapons, only the farm animals that had been left behind, and few of those," said Thorgill, lying beside her that night. "The men are tired and dispirited. In previous years, it was so easy. We'll rest a few days, and then we'll head north to see if we have better luck."

They departed, leaving behind a couple of casualties who had sores and blisters from ill-fitting clothes and boots. Signy was soon busy preparing salves for their painful skin.

When Thorgill and the warriors returned, the results were just as meagre: a few more cows and pigs, some sacks of food and cheap-looking cooking pots. What was worse, in one place the natives had put up some resistance. It had not taken long before they ran away, but they had fought enough that several of the Jutes had nasty injuries. Signy got to work, applying medications and binding their wounds. They were grateful for her care, but her efforts did little to lift their mood.

"Are we going to have to go home with nothing?" Signy asked.

Thorgill had no real answer.

"It'll be a humiliation," he said, at last. "It'll make it very difficult to recruit next year. Men'll hesitate to join us if the results are so pitiful. There are always other leaders to follow, making magnificent promises."

Thorgill's spirits were so low that he simply lay next to Signy thinking, staring at the ceiling of their little hut. Signy imagined their return to Juteland, almost empty-handed. Thorgill will look weak, she thought. He'll look at me and be reminded of the failed raid, by Helga, if no one else. He might even begin to think that I've brought the bad luck. I can imagine Helga whispering into his ear that everything had been going well until he had squandered his gains on the little Saxon bitch. Me, who is seemingly barren, while Helga and Gudrun are plump with healthy sons. The gods are punishing him for vanity and waste, Helga would say. What will my fate be then? Even if I submit and take the risk of bearing a child, I'll be at the bottom of the heap. I might be sent away. I might even be returned to the gods with an apology, bound and screaming as the water closes over me. I doubt even Irmengaard could help me.

Thorgill's light breathing betrayed he had fallen asleep, but Signy lay awake, her thoughts running around in her head, until she was forced to get up and duck out of the hut for some fresh air. She stood for a moment and stared out over the palisade, into the moonlit countryside, towards the village and the road the raiders had so fruitlessly followed, to the woods and the hills beyond.

People like her had lived here once, people who planted herbs, people who enjoyed flowers for their colour and scents, people who built houses and farms, she imagined. People who worked hard to lay the stones for walls and roads. She could almost see women working in the gardens, men hammering away at the stones. She saw soldiers, like the old men in her home village who had come back from the wars, striding along the roads. She saw a trader like Laurentius, leading a line of mules, or maybe a column of slaves, up from the south, through the village. They came to the place where the roads met. She saw their shapes and heard their voices. Which way would they take? Would they continue north, or…no, the man like Laurentius waved his hand, and one by one the mules turned onto the road to the hills, and two by two the slaves followed, to a life of backbreaking toil and hardship, but where…where?

"Thorgill! Thorgill!" she called, rushing back into the hut.

Her master stirred, blinking.

"You rode north and south. Why haven't tried the road to the west?" she asked.

He looked at her, sleep still in his eyes, his forehead wrinkled in question.

"I rode there last year. It just leads into the forest. There's nothing there."

"But Thorgill, no one makes such an effort to build a road like that, so many stones, so carefully cut and laid out, if it doesn't lead anywhere. It must lead somewhere!"

Thorgill looked at her doubtfully. "It leads into the forest, and up into the hills."

"It's a road…for soldiers and traders. I was shown them by the gods."

"Shown them?"

She shook her head. "I saw them, well, perhaps I imagined them, but you have to imagine, Thorgill, imagine what might be beyond the forest, beyond the hills. The road must lead somewhere."

Why doesn't he understand? she thought. Why doesn't he see there's no choice but to try? We can't go back with nothing. *I* can't go back with nothing.

She was right, she knew it; beyond the hills must lie another land, just as the river which flowed past her old home had led to new lands. With the comfort of being right, she laid down her head and fell asleep.

In the morning, in the daylight, she repeated what she had said in the night, but Thorgill only shook his head and repeated what he had said.

"There's just forest and the hills. Nothing."

By the gods, she thought, if he doesn't act, then I'll have to go myself. I'll make a run for it, run for the hills, and either he'll have to let me leave, or he'll have to follow, and then, then…

And she looked at her master, and he must have seen the expression in her eyes, because for just a moment he seemed anxious.

"You're frightened," she whispered, "frightened of the forests and the hills."

"We don't know what's living there," said Thorgill. "There could be wood folk or elves. I had a cousin who travelled north, across the sea to where there are mountains and forests, and we never saw him again. They said the trolls had taken him."

"But I used to live in the forest. There's nothing harmful. A few wild pigs, perhaps, and wolves, maybe even a bear, but those couldn't harm a band of armed warriors. I walked the paths alone, and so did my mother. I never saw any trolls or wood folk. A brave and strong man like you should be willing to try that road. You haven't been that way before, and who knows what lies at the end?"

"Well, I'm not sure, and who will follow me? You can't come!"

I'll damn well go on my own if you daren't, she thought again.

"I can make you a charm," she said. "I'll make you a charm against the wood folk and trolls, and I'll make one for any other man who dares to take the road with you."

Thorgill grunted. She guessed the meaning of his grunt. His woman had implied he was a coward and did not dare take the west road. Would he have to spend the entire winter looking into her eyes while they ate poor porridge because he had been a coward?

"Those charms you mentioned, would they really work?"

Signy had to make an effort not to laugh.

"Remind your followers I'm a girl from the forest, and I know the ways of the wood folk, and I'll make charms that'll certainly keep them away."

She left the camp for the entire morning, taking with her some small pieces of fabric, torn from the tunic of one of the raiders who had died. Thorgill watched her sceptically as she disappeared out of sight. In fact, she had no real plan except to gather some objects and sew them up in the pieces of cloth. Then she had an idea: the perfumed flowers in the ruined garden. They would do the trick. She sat for a long while on a low wall in the sun, stitching the cloth, and into each piece, she stuffed flowers and added a few herbs for good measure. When she got back to the camp, she gave them to Thorgill and asked him to sniff.

"I picked these flowers in the cottage garden. They smell of men's homes. Tie those pouches around your neck, and the necks of your men, and the scent will keep the wood folk away," she said, looking very serious. It was not only Thorgill who knew she was a friend of Irmengaard, so they did as she said.

Thorgill and Oswulf called a council of war. Oswulf was doubtful about Thorgill's plan.

"No one in their right mind would set off far from the shore, away from the boats, up into the woods and the hills," said Oswulf. "Everyone knows those wild places are full of evil spirits. There can't be any riches to find up there."

Thorgill made no mention that it was Signy who had suggested the plan, but he did have a cunning idea of his own.

"What about all those stories of dragons guarding gold in caverns, don't they live in wild places? Might there be a dragon with a hoard living up in the hills?"

Oswulf snorted into his beaker of ale.

"If you want to go and get killed by a dragon, that's your own business. I'm not taking the chance."

"Will you let me try?" asked Thorgill.

"I'll give you five days, and if you're not back by then, the boats will sail."

❧ Chapter 9 ☙
Thorgill's Saga

On the fifth day that Thorgill and his band had been away, Oswulf finally gave the order for the boats to be loaded, ready for launch to catch the morning tide. Everything of value in the camp was packed up, the animals slaughtered and butchered, bread baked, and barrels and leather bags filled with fresh water from the river.

Signy was almost overwhelmed by worry. What should she do if Thorgill didn't return in time? Should she turn tail and leave with the others? Had she enough faith and concern for her master that she should remain? Or should she run for the hills? If she returned to Juteland without Thorgill, her life wouldn't be worth living. Helga would blame her for her husband's disappearance, even if she was unaware of Signy's part in persuading Thorgill to leave on the expedition. If a new master came to the farmstead, Signy would not be the valuable bed partner that she had been to Thorgill, but just another slave girl, to be used, maybe, and then put to work under Helga's orders. And supposing someone did know her part, one of the men who had chosen not to accompany Thorgill. She would have no life, no life at all. That was the bitter truth. If Helga didn't have her killed at once, then Skalgrim or Oswulf would take the matter into their own hands.

It would be better to run away and take her chance.

Without her thinking, Signy's legs took her along the path leading from the camp and through the deserted village. It was late in the day. She sat on a stone by the road junction, staring towards the distant hills. She was hot and thirsty, and the sun was dipping towards the horizon, when she heard a faint noise across the still fields, a noise that could be the sound of the evening breeze, approaching rain or even that of marching feet. She imagined in the far-off distance the road seemed to change colour, as if there was a grey tint to its surface. Could that be Thorgill? She set off running along the road. What if it was an enemy? Then that would mean Thorgill was dead, and whatever happened to her would not make a difference. She ran and ran until she was short of breath, and she stood panting in the middle of the road. She heard a shout from up ahead, and then there was a figure running towards her. In a moment, she could see it was Thorgill. His blond hair was streaming behind him, and as he came up to her, he seized her in his arms and whirled her around, and then he put her down and held her and kissed her like he had never done before.

He did not say a word, just gripped her tightly against him, but as the rest of the group came striding towards them, tired but proud, she saw the packs they were carrying. She saw the horses ladened with goods. She saw the captives, bent under the burdens they were carrying. And when the Jutes saw her clutched in Thorgill's grasp, they cheered and whistled.

Oswulf was standing at the gate of the camp when they entered. Whether he liked what he saw was difficult to discern, but as the human porters dropped their packs into a heap in the middle of the camp, and he heard the clang of metal on metal, Signy saw relief flood over him. It would be difficult to prevent Thorgill gaining credit, but at least the expedition he had led was ending in success, and as clan chief he would have his share of the booty. He greeted his young ally with as much warmth as he could muster and congratulated him on his success. Signy could see his conflicted emotions in his expression, but she did not care. That night, Thorgill was the toast of the camp. The butchered meat was unpacked and set to roast, the ale unloaded, and the drinking horns passed round. And later, when Thorgill lay beside Signy, he thanked the gods that they had brought her to him.

She heard the saga in halls up and down the coast of Juteland that winter, the story of Thorgill's raid over the hills. Sometimes Thorgill told it himself if he was fishing for new recruits to his band. Sometimes the tale was sung, usually more poetically, by a man who fancied himself a bard, or another hoping by flattery to be among those selected as Thorgill's companions for the following year. Neither the version that Thorgill told in public, nor that of the poets or would-be crew members quite matched the version Signy first heard from Thorgill in the days after he returned.

> *My housemen followed with willing hearts that dawn, together with the best of Skalgrim's and Oswulf's bands.*

This she knew was a lie from the very start, only included to flatter Oswulf. No one from the chief's band had joined and only a couple from Skalgrim's, and only then those who had friends or relatives among Thorgill's own followers.

> *We set off as the sun rose and strode away into the haze of morning. We walked through fields and by abandoned farms, hedges and small woods, a spirit of adventure in our hearts.*

Another convenient fiction. Not one of the men would have taken a pace, even Thorgill, if she had not handed out the amulets to each and every one of them, muttering a self-invented incantation as she did so.

> *We rose and broke our fast with jokes and sang brave words as we entered the forest and the trees closed around us. We followed the wonderous path which, as if slashed into the earth by the hand of a giant, led straight through the woods and up the mountainside.*

In fact, they had fallen silent, she knew, fingering the amulets nervously. Some had hoped the road would end and they could turn back with their honour intact, without having to face any forest-dwellers or treasure-guarding dragons. They were still ignorant of the fact that Thorgill was merely following a suggestion from his bed partner.

Soon we could see nothing but trees ahead and trees behind, but our brave songs and cheerful laughter kept away the beasts of the forest and the threats of the wood spirits.

Thorgill had told her, Signy recalled, that he had fingered her charm more than once and held it to his nose to check the scent still diffusing from the sachet. The merchant had warned him he was buying a special woman, he told himself. Irmengaard had assured him that Signy was one of Freya's chosen, a sorceress. Just now he needed all the sorcery he could muster to pass through the forest and over the hills.

At the very summit of the mountains stood a fearsome landscape of ruined buildings. Some had tumbled down, mere heaps of stones, while others rose up into the sky, high above our heads, with a thin mist curling around them and, between the ruins, glimpses of caverns and tunnels leading deep into the mountains. This must be the abode of dwarves, we thought, mining ill-gotten riches from inside the earth, or a place once inhabited by man but now the scorched and poisoned home of evil beasts, and we drew our swords, ready to take on the cursed denizens of this desolation.

Strange, Signy thought, that in just the kind of place where there might have been a dragon guarding a treasure, they had hurried on as fast as they could. Of course, Thorgill had made up the dragon story, but his followers didn't know that.

Soon we caught glimpses of blue sky ahead through the thinning trees, and all at once we stood on the edge of the forest, as if we had journeyed through hell to a wonderland. Ahead of us stretched a landscape with a small river curving its path through fields and orchards. We gathered in the shadows of the trees, seeing the road stretching on down the valley. Here and there small houses and people working in the fields. But above all, not far from the road, stepping down the hillside, was a palace from travellers' tales or the house of the gods. The walls were shining white, and the roofs blazing red, exceeding all the houses we had seen before in its magnificence.

She wished she had been there to see the magnificent house, while it still stood perfect, unharmed. Thorgill was incapable of giving any sort of proper description. It obviously had not been a hall, like his own, like Oswulf's, like her old clan chief's. The nearest she could imagine was Laurentius' trading post in Puttby, but somehow built of stone.

> *We could see no guards, no soldiers, only two women carrying baskets coming from the gateway and setting off towards the place where the labourers were working, when we burst from the trees shouting our cries of victory.*

In his public narration, Thorgill never mentioned the quarrelling that preceded his decision to rely on bluff. There was a certain bravery in bluffing, of course, but an entirely different type than that of dashing from the forest, swords drawn, with shouts of triumph in the air. In reality, Thorgill organised his band into a column, and they marched down the road as if they belonged there. Thorgill admitted to Signy he was so tense as they approached the house that he was holding his breath. He could scarcely believe that a fool would leave such a house unguarded. What if his bluff had failed, thought Signy. What if the stone house had not been a dwelling, but a fort? Then the story would have had a different ending. Then there would have been no story.

> *We ran through the gate, into the yard, taking the enemy by surprise, the shock of our attack preventing any resistance.*

Why tell such a series of untruths, she thought. Why appear brave and foolhardy, rather than admit that their approach had been carefully calculated and clever? Because that's how men like Thorgill had to appear, she concluded, if they wanted to draw cheers and envy from their audience.

What had actually happened? They had marched up to the gate, fearful that someone would slam it in their faces. When they ran into the yard, there had been no one there but flies buzzing around a dunghill and horses shifting in the stables. Somewhere in one of the buildings they could hear the sounds of a millstone grinding corn and women's voices. No one to be taken by surprise; no one to offer any resistance. It wouldn't have been much different, she reflected, if a host of armed strangers had suddenly invaded Thorgill's own yard.

With a great cry, we ran through the house, putting the defenders to the sword.

Who were these stout defenders? Signy knew the answer. An old man who fell with a cry, his blood spreading across the pavement; an old woman who came out of a room nearby, hearing his cry of despair; and a little boy, who ran from the room where the woman had been, stood for a moment looking down at her, before a blow from Thorgill's sword sent him, too, sprawling lifeless. Those had been the three brave defenders. Three or four men and half a dozen women had been drawn by the grinding of the gates, and now stood in shocked silence.

My eyes could hardly take in what I saw as I passed from room to room. Gold and silver, jewels and ivory, embroidered cloth and rich garments, too much for us to carry away. Beyond the kitchens stood the wine cellar, a drink for the banquets of chiefs in Juteland, but in that house available in a flood.

Before long, his followers were roaring and drunk, Thorgill told Signy, and their attention turned to the women. Dairymaids or cooks were shoved down, their clothes ripped away, forced, petrified, into silence. Before long, most of the raiders were incapable of doing anything, rob or rape, and lapsed into a drunken stupor.

"You should have mixed the wine with water," Signy told him, recalling Laurentius' advice.

"It's a bit late to come with that wisdom now," said Thorgill, "and in any case, how come you know so much about wine?"

More than most of you do, evidently, she thought.

Just then, in the midst of our plunder, came a noise from outside the gate, and I mounted the lofty wall to look out.

A great host of natives stood clustered in the road, waving their weapons and cursing us in defiance. Few as we were, we had no choice but to teach these people they must leave their conquerors alone.

Thorgill had to hide a cringe at this point, Signy noticed, whenever he told the story, or disguised his face behind a goblet when someone else was singing. Of his group, there were now only three or four sober men with him. The rest were drunk or occupied with the women. It was just as well that the men outside the gate were obviously farmworkers, not fighters, and carrying tools, not weapons. If they had been more courageous, better organised or better armed, the raid might have come to a quick end. There was no honour in mentioning that Thorgill and the three or four sober Jutes had been quite sufficient to deal with a few drudges.

I ordered the gate to be swung open and rushed out, taking the enemy by surprise. They had no time to flee before three or four of them lay dead on the ground, and others soon would be. The remainder ran.

A couple of drunken raiders had rushed off in pursuit, Thorgill recalled, while he stood and caught his breath. The whole situation had begun to get out of hand, thanks to the wine. He watched the remaining peasants flee down the road, and cuffed those of his band who had followed them once they shamefacedly returned.

"They went to raise the alarm," said Signy, the first time she heard the story, "to run and fetch the local chief and his band of warriors."

"The old man was the clan chief, I suppose," said Thorgill.

"And the old man had no hearth warriors, only peasants?"

"More fool him," said Thorgill. "Now he's dead and we took his treasures."

"But were there no soldiers at all over the hills?"

"Listen to the story, woman, and you'll hear what happened."

You're still feeling very pleased with yourself, I can see that, thought Signy.

The dusk began to draw in.
"I'll take the first watch," I said to Radwulf, Skalgrim's man. "Get some sleep. I'll wake you later, and you can take the second."

"And what about the rest of the men?" asked Signy.

Thorgill shrugged. "Fuck them, I thought, while I surveyed the carnage in the yard, the heap of valuables, the broken wine jars, the drunk men, the semi-naked and weeping women."

He had gone into the house, found an unbroken glass cup and helped himself to wine from one of the jars. Slowly, the excitement and tension drained from him. The raiders had built a fire in the yard, brought bread, cheese, meat and beer from the kitchens.

I threw the beaker into the corner of the yard where it shattered into a thousand pieces. There are times when a leader must show he is above the crowd. I stood over the gate and kept watch in the dark night. After Radwulf took my place, I lay down and fell into a deep and undisturbed sleep.

You always have to be the hero, thought Signy. But then it had really been a brave deed to lead his band over the hills into the unknown, and the men had been brave to follow after him. Maybe it was being too hard on them to insult them out for getting drunk when their victory had seemed so easy? So easy, in fact, that Thorgill felt compelled to make it sound heroic.

"Gather up the treasures," I ordered, as the glowing sun peeped over the treetops, "and pack the valuables into bundles."

In the morning, the majority of the band did not look or feel at all well, and Thorgill had cursed out those who were in the worst state. He had difficulties, too, in getting the women to prepare food for his band. Hardly surprising, thought Signy, after what they had been through.

No sooner had we eaten, than the lookout called again.

"Soldiers on the way!"

Far off in the distance I could see cavalrymen trotting along the road, then pulling up their horses up, pointing and gesticulating.

"Let them sit and chatter," I said. "There's nothing to be gained by waiting around until some better-organised defence shows up and, besides, we have the deadline to meet with Oswulf."

There was always laughter round the table when he said that, some of it at Oswulf's expense. How close the big man had been to missing out on his share of the loot! But at the time, it had been a serious worry. What if Oswulf left them to their fate, a small band of raiders in a hostile country, burdened down by loot and captives? He took his share in the end, thought Signy, though he had done nothing.

"We leave at dawn tomorrow," I announced, "and when I say we leave at dawn, I mean it. Anyone not in a fit state to join us will be left behind, to the natives."

Goblets and bowls were beaten flat, precious metal and jewels were stripped from furniture and ornaments, everything to reduce the load. I scoured the women's quarters. I could not imagine our fine women wearing any of the clothes I found, more suited to a whore in Puttby, but there were bottles of perfume and cosmetics, and by following my delicate nose in the pantry, I found a great heap of spices.

When the neighbours and volunteers dined in Thorgill's hall, they were treated to a sample of what he had found. The tastes were strange but stimulated not just the palate but also the imagination. Signy thought of the herb garden she had found in the ruined village. Maybe there had been plants there that she had not appreciated, ones that could have seasoned food, or even provided new medicines. She had a lot still to learn from Irmengaard, that she knew, but perhaps there was knowledge that lay beyond even the wise woman's understanding.

It would have been gratifying if I could relate that we won a great battle against the foreigners, but even though we kept watch all day and could see people coming and going on the road, no one approached the hall. The cowards would trot up, then seeing our fearsome faces, they would leave, and later another crowd would gather, uselessly cursing their fate.

The night was chill, and we remained inside the house. We built a fire in the middle of the tiled floor of one of the rooms, wrapped ourselves in blankets and slept around it. I paced the house from the fire to the kitchens, where a guard sat watch over the women, to the stables, where the male captives still sat, tied up, to the gatehouse, to the upper storey, and back to the fire, until I could keep awake no longer.

Sometimes Signy wondered whether Thorgill was lying to her, that the capture of the rich man's house had not been so easy, and that he and his band had had more trouble than he was willing to admit, that they had had to fight, even. But then all of them had come back, more or less unwounded, and there was no denying the riches they brought with them.

The first rays of dawn were just beginning to filter through the trees on the hillside above the house when we woke. The men stretched their stiff limbs and threw some last wood, the remains of a table and some gilded chairs, onto the fire, throwing sparks which drifted upwards in the warm air. The horses and captives were led from the stables and loaded with their burdens, the women driven from the kitchen and roped to the end of the line.

What better did they deserve, thought Signy, since they had put up so little resistance? Thorgill told her he stepped out into the garden and cast a final glance at the corpses of the old man, the old woman and the child who still lay where they had fallen, now surrounded by a cloud of buzzing flies.

"Too bad, old man," I said to his corpse. "You should have spent more on your defence and less on luxuries. I hope there are many more old fools in this land who have the same priorities!"

It did not make sense to Signy that no one had tried to stop Thorgill and his band. Didn't they have any warriors in that country? Were they so wealthy that they could leave precious jewels and silver and gold lying around unguarded? Why did the chief have no armed followers to give him honour and show his worth?

> *The yard doors were swung open, and the first of the horses passed through the gateway, down the entrance road, and up the hill towards the forest. I stood in the gate as each passed by. The horses, the captives, sullen and glaring, the women, perhaps a little grateful that I had spared them a second night like the first, and finally the last of our heroes. I saw smoke seeping from the windows and between the roof tiles of the house where the ceiling had caught fire in the room where we had been sleeping. As I cast a last look back, I could just make out a tongue of flame licking up the side of the building, a fitting funeral pyre for that foolish old chieftain.*

"What had happened to the horsemen who had been watching?" asked Signy.

Thorgill shrugged. "I don't suppose they dared ride up to the burning house until they were sure we'd gone."

"Were they all such cowards?"

"How am I supposed to know? I never spoke to them."

He turned to look at her.

"Not everyone who's cautious is a coward, Signy. The old chief Sigg, Oswulf's father, was cautious, but he was no coward. He fought many battles, always in the centre of the line, but he didn't like to risk the lives of his men. You have to have the measure of a man before you can say whether he's a coward. And if you want to know the truth, I was a little worried they would follow us, so perhaps I was the coward.

"One man among the captives was having problems walking, or at least pretending to. I wasn't sure if he was genuinely frail and finding it difficult to keep up or if the old bastard was pretending, trying to slow us down in the hope that some pursuers would catch us. Then I had an inspiration."

> *At the middle of the day, we reached the desolate mountain top with the ruined buildings. We had come through unharmed once,*

so perhaps there were no dwarves and trolls after all. However, there was no need to tempt fate. An offering should be made.

"Only fitting," echoed around the halls at this point.

I walked the road until I found what I needed: a doorway, with a lintel across it, a little over the height of a man.

When our band and the captives had assembled, I dragged out the limping captive.

"Pull him up," I ordered. A rope was tied around his ankles, and soon the limper was dangling helplessly.

"Gods," I called, "accept this sacrifice, and protect us when we come this way again!" Then I stepped forward and cut the old man's throat.

It was the right thing to do, thought Signy. The gods had sent her the vision. They must have been keeping watch over Thorgill and his band, must have frightened the peasants who ran away, sent terror into the hearts of the horsemen who did not dare come near. They would expect a tribute. She was no expert on sacrifices. In her home village, Tyr's priests had taken care of matters: a horse, an ox, always one of the best. A man would surely be an adequate offering.

Everyone in every hall knew the rest of the story.

⍰ Chapter 10 ⍰

News of Thorgill's success spread throughout Juteland. Signy's role in persuading Thorgill to cross the hills did not feature in the version of the story that the bards told from hall to hall. Would it be so shameful for a chief to admit he had taken advice from a girl? Was it better to invent a whole cascade of nonsense, a false reason, false actions, only justified, only unquestioned because of the outcome, she thought. But in the end, it hardly mattered. Thorgill himself knew he would never have crossed the hills had Signy not persuaded him. Even before they had set sail from Britland, he had told her that she was no longer a slave. She would be considered part of the family, his wife from now on, wife number two, of course, but, he assured her, still his wife.

On their return, Signy was wise enough not to challenge Helga in the household. On the contrary, she tried to keep as much distance from her as possible, but at least she no longer had to mend torn clothes in the weaving shed. She now supervised two slave girls, Leema and Martha, who had that task.

Thorgill and his followers had so much treasure they hardly knew what to do with it. Of course, the riches had to be shared out, a portion to Oswulf and a portion to Skalgrim, which they would then share with their retinues. That still left plenty for Thorgill and the warriors who had followed him. When Thorgill had returned from the *thing*, he had with him a couple of items for Signy as a special reward: a jewelled bracelet and a necklace of coloured beads and glinting red stones. She would never be able to wear them in Helga's presence, let alone in the company of Oswulf's wives. But she knew she had them. She placed Thorgill's gifts at the bottom of her chest, next to the amulet

Laurentius had given her, and covered them with a length of rough linen.

The merchants of Puttby were flooded with treasure, so much so that Thorgill felt they were making unreasonably low offers and decided to dig a hole behind his house and bury part of the gold and silver there. He dragged a large stone over the place and swore Helga and Signy, and the two men who helped him, to secrecy.

"So a god sent you a vision? Did you go into a trance?" Curiosity was mixed with worry in Irmengaard's voice. "Did you use herbs or mushrooms?"

"No," said Signy, slightly confused, "I was tired and worried, and couldn't sleep, and there was a little moonshine, but I could see them clearly – mules and slaves, almost as if it was daylight."

"Signy, don't you understand? Did you see any cats in the ruined village? Freya must have seen your plight. She must have sent you guidance in your desperate situation."

Signy could not help frowning.

"Why would Freya be interested in me? Why should the goddess care whether Thorgill gets rich or not?"

"She doesn't care about Thorgill, my dear. She cares about you. You're one of her sisters. You must be destined for great things. I told you so."

Perhaps, thought Signy, otherwise why would I have been stolen from my home and brought here? Why would Thorgill have decided to spend – waste, according to Helga – his spoils on me, and then insist I accompany him on his expedition?

"If the gods can steer our fate," she said, at last, "then I'm worried that I acted mockingly when I made the amulets for the men."

She had told of her discovery of the village and the herb garden laid out by some wise person long ago and lying untouched, a treasure waiting for her. Signy told Irmengaard about the fears of Thorgill's followers before they ventured into the forest, and how she had picked flowers and herbs and tied them into the bundles, and she told of Thorgill hanging the old man and cutting his throat.

"You're right that you should be careful not to mock the spirits, sister," said Irmengaard, raising a warning finger. "Most likely they were not offended this time by your little posies, judging by Thorgill's triumph, but you must always humbly make the right sacrifice for good fortune. An old man, I don't know. Maybe he should have hung up Leema or Martha and left the old man for the beasts."

"I won't forget," said Signy.

"Perhaps he should have sacrificed you," laughed Irmengaard, "since you brought him success." There was too much sincerity in her voice for Signy to ignore it. The older woman reached out, placing a comforting hand on Signy's arm.

"Do you wish to see your future? I asked the gods to show me, while you were away in Britland. I was fearful you would not return, but…"

"Did you see something awful?" asked Signy, horrified by her friend's faltering words.

"No, that's what was strange. I couldn't see anything of your future at all. I saw many people trying to talk to me, but all I heard was the barking of dogs and the bleating of sheep. It was as if the Fates were deliberately hiding your future from me. Perhaps they would be more willing to show your own future to you?"

"If the gods were unwilling to show you, Irmengaard, I don't wish to ask. Let them plan for me what they will."

But Signy soon found out that Irmengaard herself had a plan for her.

"I spoke to Thorgill," the wise woman reported, "and he had to agree, of course. The more the gods favour him, the better, that was his simple conclusion."

She smiled.

"You're to accompany me to the festival, to the sacrifices we make to ensure the sun comes back promptly next year," Irmengaard told Signy. "We'll travel two days, into the centre of

Juteland, and there we'll meet many other wise women, and the priestesses of Freya."

"Are you sure? I'm merely an ex-slave and an ignorant Saxon," asked Signy.

Irmengaard sighed. "You'd better get used to the idea that you're no longer a slave, that you're Thorgill's wife and have slaves who answer to you."

"I know, but…" Signy had heard stories about the meetings of priests and priestesses in the forest. Her mother had never been part of those circles. She had always preferred to be a practical helper to the village women, knowing her herbs and roots, simple amulets made from objects gathered in the woods, and a few homely incantations. Worship and sacrifices, those were bigger matters for people who felt themselves called.

"But you've been called," Irmengaard insisted. "Being called is not a choice. It's in the hands of the gods."

How could Signy argue with Irmengaard? She was well aware that the wise woman had some authority among the priestesses. The tattoos on her body were practical evidence, but the strangers who paid visits, and Irmengaard's absences, now more frequent when Signy could take care of routine matters, supported her conclusion. What harm was there in going to the ceremony, when her friend would be there to explain and protect her?

They could have completed the distance in half the time if they had been able to ride, but Irmengaard refused Signy's offer to find a horse for her, and pointed out that the journey was part of the ritual, preparing the mind for the festival. And as they walked, one after the other, along endless paths through the fields and marshes, that is what Signy attempted to do.

Their tired feet led them to a clearing on the borders of a wide lake. A cluster of booths, open shelters, really, lay just beyond the edge of the trees and, between them and the water, Signy could see a group of women stacking timber to make a large bonfire.

From the site of the stack, two rows of poles led down towards the lake, where a short pier led over the water.

"Irmengaard," came a voice in cheerful greeting, as they threaded their way towards the wise woman's customary lodging, "do you have the sacred drink with you?"

Signy glanced around and saw the bulky figure of Ornfrid, who lived on Oswulf's domains, bustling towards them.

"I have, don't worry," replied Irmengaard cheerfully. The ceremony could not take place without the brew Irmengaard had been preparing, the brew which would place the women in the right frame of mind to feel the significance of the sacrifice and open them to visions of their totem animals and the sacred beings.

Ornfrid's gaze fell on Signy, and her brow furrowed.

"Haven't I seen you somewhere before?"

Ornfrid was one of the most important priestesses in this area of Juteland, and Signy had already felt nervous about meeting her.

"Ah, now I remember, you were at Oswulf's feast, weren't you? I remember your face. A pretty stranger, Thorgill's Saxon girl, so they told me." She reached out and touched Signy's cheek.

"My apprentice," said Irmengaard.

"I heard you had a new girl with you," said Ornfrid, "but I didn't expect such a…well, so young, and a newcomer to our land."

"Signy's mother was the village midwife," said Irmengaard, slightly sharply. "She already knew more than many of our women do before she came to me."

"So you have gifts, then, my dear," said Ornfrid. "Make sure you use them wisely."

The older woman turned back to Irmengaard.

"You *did* bring your staff of office this year, didn't you?" she asked, giving her colleague a hard look.

"I…I…might have…"

"You haven't forgotten it again, have you?" grumped Ornfrid. "How can you take part in the ceremony without your staff? People won't know who you are or show you the respect your position among us deserves."

Irmengaard opened her mouth to argue, but before she could utter a word, Signy found her own voice.

"I have your staff here in my pack," she said firmly. "I'm sorry, Irmengaard. I saw you had left it when we were on the way out, so I popped it in my own bundle."

She slid her bundle from her shoulder.

"You brought the staff of authority in your own bundle," said Ornfrid slowly, her face turning pale, "the symbol of the gods' favour. What sort of omen is this?" she muttered, turning and vanishing among the huts.

"Don't let her bother you," said Irmengaard. "She gets so wound up about nothing. And give me that bloody staff, though everyone knows who I am without any symbol of authority. They all drink my potion without complaining."

For most of the following day, the senior priestesses were taken up with business and rituals, to which Signy was not invited, in a hut at the east end of the clearing. With Irmengaard occupied, she was left on her own. She spoke to several of the other young women, farm girls like herself and eager to learn the secrets of the medicine women, and just as eager to take on the aura of mystery associated with being a priestess. Together with a girl called Neema, she carried firewood to the bonfire, and afterwards they shared some of the food they had brought. Neema had never been a slave girl, and Signy was careful to be vague about her own background. Neema was the younger daughter of a poor chief and her father had apprenticed her to the local midwife so he would not have to find a dowry for her. I might have been a slave, thought Signy, but at least I have a husband and a place in the world again, in a strange land, perhaps, but maybe I'm better off than I would've been, married to a farm boy at home.

Her thoughts were disturbed by the pounding of a drum. The sun had begun to set, and the dignitaries processed from their hut towards the fire. Signy spotted Irmengaard and Ornfrid in the procession, as well as a horse, a couple of goats, and a naked, painted man being led on a rope.

Neema pulled at Signy's sleeve.

"It's time for us to distribute the meal, and your Irmengaard will share out the blessed mead, and then the sacrifices will begin as the sun sets."

The purpose, Signy knew, was to ensure that the sun would return warm and strong in the spring.

The blessed mead had an oddly bitter taste, but Signy felt she was obliged to support her mentor by drinking heartily.

It did not take long before she realised that she might have made a mistake. The beating of the drums began to sound as if they were pounding in her head, and the dancing flames from the bonfire took on evermore fantastical shapes. She saw snakes and dragons and flying birds, until she had to look away to avoid being lured into the fire.

Chanting started, and one by one all the women and girls took up the chorus. The words were strange, and it was difficult for Signy to follow their song. She was far away from the main action, sitting with the junior women, but at least she could see the priestesses at work. The goats were slaughtered, their blood spattered over the nearest participants in blessing. Their heads were cut off, and Signy could just make out the shape of Ornfrid leading a group between the rows of poles and out onto the pier to throw the heads into the lake. The goats' bodies were quickly skinned and set to roast. The same happened to the horse, though it was necessary to stun the struggling beast with a blow to the head before its throat was cut. The body was hung up on an arrangement of timbers, while the blood drained into a cup, which was passed around the fire. When it came to Signy, she flicked a few drops from the cup on her face and passed it on. By then the horse had also been beheaded, and the severed head carried down to the lake in procession and thrown into the waters coloured orange by the setting sun. Finally, it was the turn of the man. His arms were tied behind his back, but his feet were free, and he seemed to accept his fate, walking between Irmengaard and the high priestess down the path and along the pier, where he stood for a moment, before the women placed their hands on his back and pushed him in.

Signy was already on her feet, swaying to the sound of the drums. The ring of women joined hands and began to circle around the fire, then they let go, and each woman turned in place, and then she had her hands back on Neema's waist and the chain began to circle again.

Signy woke up to a burning sensation in her eyes, and when she opened them, she realised that it was daylight. The last she could remember was the great shout which went up as the man hit the water and the high priestess raised her arms to the setting sun. After that, the effects of the drumming, the dancing and the blessed mead must have taken over completely.

She was lying on the turf, and someone had placed a cloak over her. She still felt dizzy and disorientated after the events of the night. Slowly, she drew up her knees and pushed herself into a half-sitting position. At that moment, she had the first of two surprises. She was naked under the cloak, and she could not remember taking off her clothes. She felt round about her, but her hand did not locate any garments. She glanced around and then sat up. The cloak slipped down her body and she had the second surprise. Her breasts and upper torso seemed to be covered with ash. She looked at her left arm, twisting it around to see it was daubed with swirls of ash. On her other arm, too, when she checked that. Alarmed, she pulled the cloak aside and found that her belly, her legs, all over, in fact, were covered by swirls and dots. She only dimly recalled the events of the evening: the man being guided towards the lake and the painted women sending him to his final destination. Had Irmengaard and the high priestess been naked then or was her memory playing tricks on her? The ash on her body reminded her of the tattoos that covered her friend, but how had she come to be decorated like this, and why? She jumped up, the cloak in a heap at her feet, staring down at herself, her body and her legs, oblivious to a voice calling her name.

Then she looked around and saw Irmengaard a little distance away, seated on a fallen tree trunk, beckoning to her. She became aware of the chill of the morning, picked up the cloak and wrapped it around herself once again, and headed over to her friend.

"You're smudging all my symbols," said Ornfrid, who was sitting beside Irmengaard, close to a small fire.

"Symbols?"

Ornfrid laughed.

"Yes. I painted you up so beautifully. Let's have a look at what's left," she added and, catching Signy by surprise, pulled playfully at the cloak. Signy's covering came away in her hand.

"Sit down, dear," said Irmengaard protectively, patting the log, "and have a cup of mead…Nothing in it this morning." She gave Signy a sympathetic examination. "You look shattered."

"Painted me?" muttered Signy.

Irmengaard and Ornfrid laughed together.

"You were with the spirits," said Irmengaard.

Signy sipped at the mead. This time it tasted fresh and needed.

"I'm covered with ash," she muttered, still confused, and placed the beaker on the ground. "I need to get cleaned up."

She saw Ornfrid frown.

"You'll wash away my careful designs," she said, and turned to Irmengaard. "Which bits do you think we should make permanent?"

"Here," said Irmengaard, touching Signy's left shoulder, just above her breast. "The head of the lynx is a mark of the sisterhood that everyone recognises, and she's certainly earned the sign like the other novices."

"I…I…need to find my clothes."

"They should be over there," said her friend, pointing towards a small clump of trees where a couple of other women were sorting through a heap of garments. "It's where we pile them every year, so no one has to remember where they've dropped them. There's a stream a little further over, beyond the trees, if you really need to wash."

Signy struggled to her feet again and turned to leave.

"And here," said Ornfrid, patting her on the rear. "I drew a nice lynx right here on her tail bone. You'll remember it, won't you, Irmengaard? You've one there yourself."

"Because *you* put it there, when *you* decided I was destined for the priesthood."

Signy left the older women and crossed the clearing to the pile of clothes. The girls were as naked as she was, lifting up dresses and cloaks one by one to see which was theirs. As Signy approached, she saw one of them was Neema, who raised her eyebrows.

"Someone's been having fun with you!"

"What do you mean?" asked Signy, slightly irritated.

"You're daubed all over. It's a bit smeared, but I can make out two ravens and, turn around…"

Signy stood stock still, but Neema only skipped around her.

"…and a boar…nice, and a lynx head. Wow…you're as fancied up as the high priestess. They're not going to turn all of these into tattoos, are they?"

"I hope not," said Signy, spotting her dress among the ones the girls had discarded. "I don't remember a thing. I feel like I've crawled through a hearthplace. I need to get washed."

"We'll come, too," said the second girl, finally finding her own clothes, and together the three set off for the stream.

"You were dancing behind me, holding on to me," said Neema, as they stepped carefully along the path. "Once we passed the high priestess, we all turned round to circle back, and there was another girl there, not you. What happened?"

Signy did not answer. Her eyes fastened on the place just above Neema's left breast.

"You've got one there – a tattoo," she said.

"Of course. I got it last year, after I was sworn in," said Neema.

"And me, too," said the other girl, half twisting towards Signy.

"Wait. Stop," said Signy. "Turn around the other way." But the girl was confused. "Turn around, Neema," Signy said frantically.

But Neema froze, frowning. "What is it?"

Signy grabbed at her hips and twisted her round, but there was nothing to see, no tattoo on her back.

"I'm sorry," she said, "I'm not feeling right, and there was something Irmengaard said."

The other two exchanged puzzled looks and they resumed their walk to the stream. Signy's thoughts were on an altogether different track, trying to dredge up a memory of the events of the night before, trying to link the priestesses' words and the comments Neema and her friend had just made. Why *had* Ornfrid picked her out of the dance? What *was* the significance of the fire-ash decoration? There were times when she felt like she was being pulled into the sisterhood against her will. Irmengaard and now Ornfrid treated her with an importance she did not think she had. Anyone could see visions. Anyone could pick up something a friend had forgotten and bring it with them. That did not make her special, just a girl who had been taught by her mother to be thoughtful and observant.

But as they reached the stream, and Neema and the other girl plunged in screaming, Signy's thoughts went back to another stream, to that fateful day, her last day beside the river which ran past her childhood home. She had not been thoughtful or observant then. She had been dreaming, and by some dreadful twist of fate, her dreams had led her here.

The tattoos stung where Irmengaard pricked them in with dye. One she could see on her left shoulder, and the other, out of sight, was just above her rear. That one hurt most. Pain and discomfort were a necessary part of growth, she understood. She could only imagine what Irmengaard must have gone through with all the decoration on her body. That was the sign of a senior member of the sisterhood, and she was only a novice. She understood that, too, but that did not stop her asking.

"Why did Ornfrid insist on the second tattoo? Neema only had one."

Irmengaard laughed. "Well, apart from the fact that Ornfrid thinks you have a pretty bottom, and that it would look even better with a little cat head above it…" Her laugh died away. "All the marks have their own significance, and a second tattoo marks out a novice as a special recruit, someone the priestesses all agree has been favoured by our goddess. For that reason, the other girls, Neema and the rest, who might only hear rumours, can see that you've been chosen by the marks on your body. And anyone else who chances to attend our celebrations, from the Goth lands, from the Svear or even the Northland, who does not know you personally, they'll know too. And if you continue on this path—"

"I'll be covered, like you?"

"Ornfrid's daubings weren't just for fun, Signy."

Even if the gods were not willing to reveal her future, the priestesses seemed to have already mapped out a path for her as patterns on her body.

☙ Chapter 11 ❧

Signy had other, practical cares that winter. From being a slave, she had become a mistress to Martha and Leema, two of the battered and frightened women captured from the villa, the women who Irmengaard had suggested would have made better sacrifices than the old man. She had watched the women on the journey over. They had never set foot on a boat, never seen the sea, and they had been sick and huddled together every moment of the journey from Britland to Juteland. She remembered only too well being torn from her home and carried across the sea and forced into the life of a slave.

At first, the women grovelled and quivered whenever they saw her, obviously imagining her to be some species of horrible heathen ogress – pretty to look at but with a soul of darkness. Signy did not have the heart to be severe with them. Martha was manageable. She had taken care of the old lady who lived in the villa and was used to housework. But even with Martha, Signy found being a mistress difficult at first. Martha spoke no Saxon or Jutish, and Signy had picked up only a few words of British from the slaves captured previously. The two women mainly communicated with signs and gestures, smiles and nods or shakes of the head. However, day by day, Signy learned a few words of Martha's language, and Martha learned a few of hers. Neither knew enough to converse, but sufficient to give and take orders.

Signy was surprised and pleased one day when, by means of a few words and many gestures, Martha offered to arrange her hair in the style she had seen on one of the drinking vessels Thorgill had brought home. For the rest of the day, she walked around imagining herself as the goddess on the cup until reality struck home again. *I can never be friends with Martha. I might* not be a goddess, but I'm the mistress, the wife of the man who tore Martha from her home and loved ones.

Sometimes Signy found Martha weeping silently, and as the months passed and Signy understood her better, she discovered that Martha had been promised in marriage to one of the young men from the estate. By chance, he had gone into the town that day, and she had never seen him again. At times like that, Signy felt a terrible guilt. What right do I have, a mere farmer's daughter, to lord it over Martha, to have absolute authority over another person? Because the Fates have decided it should be that way?

Leema was a more challenging problem, since she was pregnant. Perhaps Helga would be lucky to have Leema as a wet nurse for the next daughter Irmengaard so confidently predicted, Signy concluded. When the time came for Helga to give birth, Irmengaard took care of her. Signy had to step in as midwife to the slave girl. She was relieved to pass the lactating Leema on to her new duties under Helga's sharp tongue.

Signy, herself, had her obligations as Thorgill's favourite, especially now she had the status of wife. As had become his custom, shortly after the midwinter festival, Oswulf called the chiefs together to plan the forthcoming campaign. If the earth had been frozen or snow had fallen, Helga could have made the trip in a sleigh, but as it was, it had been raining constantly, and the tracks were reduced to mud. It would only be possible to reach Oswulf's hall on horseback. Helga would have to remain at home, and Signy accompanied Thorgill once again. This time, however, Thorgill was the toast of the feast, and Signy could not hide among the lesser men's wives. As an honour, reluctantly due to Thorgill, Signy was given the duty of carrying the drinking horn to the high table. I wonder, she thought, when she heard the news, if Oswulf has been told how I talked Thorgill into his expedition?

The big man's ambitions for the following year knew almost no limits. This was Oswulf's chance for fame. If he was successful this year, there was a good possibility that he could be elected High King of all the Jutes. For that reason, he was ill-disposed to listen to other men's advice.

"He's determined to take a town," said Thorgill, "and he claims to have an ally who can help him."

"Who?" asked Signy.

"The envoys were supposed to attend the war meeting, but they've been delayed by the poor state of the roads. It seems they'll be at the feast."

"And you, what did you say?"

"I held my peace, my darling. Oswulf's already sufficiently jealous of me. I don't want to provoke a quarrel. I suspect Oswulf wants the town for himself. I'm just happy he'll allow me to go my own way."

Signy was dressed as finely as possible for the feast, not by Martha, but by Oswulf's wives' maids, and in Oswulf's second wife's gown, hastily taken in at the waist. When the servants let her see her reflection in the polished metal mirror, she thought the gods must be playing a joke on her.

The feast was no joke, however. Oswulf's hall was filled to overflowing, and when Signy paraded in with the ceremonial horn, the noise was deafening. She made her way up towards the high table, the long gown trailing behind her, carefully mounted the step to the dais, and then, bowing her head, passed the horn to Chief Oswulf. While he called out his toast and drank, she took a quick look along the row of dignitaries seated beside him. Thorgill, of course, and Skalgrim, who would be second in command of the coming year's raid; old Radwulf, who had ridden with Thorgill last year; then a row of other self-important-looking men, who had not been with them the previous year but were obviously hoping to hitch themselves to Oswulf's tail. She took the horn from Oswulf and handed it to Skalgrim, and from Skalgrim to Thorgill, and so on, until she reached the end, and two faces she did not recognise: young men, dressed for riding, not for feasting.

"Your health, my lords," she said in Saxon, realising they could be foreigners, perhaps even the envoys that Thorgill had mentioned.

The darker of the two took the horn.

"Your honour, Mistress," he replied, with a heavy accent, taking a drink and passing the horn to his companion. It gave Signy a chance to look him in the eye, while the other man drank.

"You're no Jute," said the man returning her look. "Chief Oswulf's wife?"

"I'm Mistress Signy, Chief Thorgill's wife," she replied carefully with a smile and a bow, and in doing so her eye caught a glint of gold on the man's shoulder, a medallion dangling from the brooch which held his cloak in place.

"Your master?" she asked, her eyes indicating the portrait in the centre of the disc, a man with short-cut hair and a trimmed beard.

The stranger laughed quietly and shook his head.

"The emperor," he said, "of Rome."

"Our master's the emperor's man," said his companion, reaching out with the drinking horn.

"This is a sign," continued the first man, raising the medallion with his finger, "of our embassy."

Signy noticed a perturbed expression cross his face, before a scowl from the warrior sitting beside the envoys signalled that there had been more than enough pleasantries for Jutish custom and, taking the horn, Signy bowed her head again and continued with her duties.

"The two envoys," she asked Thorgill in the morning. He had returned from the feast too late for sensible conversation. "What sort of men were they?"

"Young men," he replied. "Their chief couldn't make the journey himself in the winter, so he sent them in lieu."

"Was Oswulf annoyed? He had placed them very low on the table."

"He was satisfied with the offer they read out for him, and with the sight of his ally's seal on the document. It seems it's the custom among these Romans to write important matters down, instead of speaking them out like real men."

"So the important man is a Roman, though his servants…" But she held her tongue. "So Oswulf will take the town?"

"Yes, and Skalgrim and I will lead our own raids. Once the town has been plundered, we'll unite in the lands over the hills. That's what was written down. Oswulf's wishes first, and everyone else's afterwards."

"Isn't it always so, my love," said Signy, soothingly, "that high chiefs must come first?"

Thorgill looked at her fiercely. "After next year, I'll follow no man, but make my own way."

It was only later when Signy was reflecting once more on the feast that she realised the envoy's disturbance had been caused not by the sight of her breasts as she had first suspected, but because he had caught a glimpse of the tattoo on her shoulder. So, the influence of Freya's sisters reached even to these foreigners, these servants of a Roman, she thought, because sure as eggs are eggs, as her friend had once said, the two envoys were no more Romans than she was.

Men flocked far and wide to Oswulf's host, by land and sea. Boats lined up along the shore from north to south, awaiting men and animals for the journey. Quantities of food and drink were loaded aboard with servants to prepare it. The blacksmith brought his assistant; even a priest was added to the party. Some of the younger men wondered if there was a chance to plant crops, and perhaps remain behind through the winter. Some Angles had done that, they had heard; built small villages along the coast, welcomed their friends when they returned in following years and were gradually spreading out across the land. Surely the Jutes could do likewise. Oswulf might have great ambitions but, ultimately, he was a simple pirate, an opportunist, though he was glad to hear every suggestion that made him feel more important. Who could resist his leadership if he was the first Jute lord to found a settlement on the shores of Britland, and in a town, at that? Fortunately, others around him, wiser, more thoughtful men, were aware that there was a big difference between leading a raiding party and conquering a land.

It was natural that Signy would be included in the expedition, and if Signy went, now Martha would have to come as well. As the time for departure approached, the women packed a chest with the things they needed: clothes, spare boots, Signy's jewels, her medicines and tools — especially her medicines and tools, those for everyday problems and those which would be needed to treat injured warriors. She and Martha packed everything in, and then Martha sat on the lid, while Signy closed the hasp.

Only Irmengaard was worried, still troubled by her attempt to read Signy's future.

"Won't you try," she said, "to see what will come? I care about you. You've become important to me. I'll miss you. I want to know you'll come back safe to me."

"I don't want to tempt the gods," said Signy. "Let them tell Oswulf his fortune, but don't bother them with a nobody like me."

Irmengaard snorted. "You don't know who's important in the eyes of the gods. Who persuaded Thorgill to take the west road last year? You or Oswulf? And where do you think that inspiration came from?"

"I don't know," Signy admitted. "Sometimes I think it was a sign from the gods, but at others, I feel that I was tired and half-asleep, and dreamed the whole thing."

"But who sends us our dreams?"

That was a question without an answer, thought Signy, given some of her dreams. During the winter, she had tried to puzzle out how her thoughts had led her to suggest to Thorgill to take the road over the hills. If she could only understand how that had happened, it might provide a clue how to proceed in the future: to rely on the guidance of the gods or be guided by her own imagination. The gods seemed fickle and unpredictable. One moment they had punished her for presumption by arranging for her to be kidnapped, and the next they pushed her into the path of Laurentius, a man who seemed to have some honour and decency, trader and slaver though he was. And then, what had they been intending when they had paired her with Thorgill, a pleasant enough man, but otherwise a very ordinary Jute chief?

"No, Irmengaard," she said firmly. "I'm not going to try to outwit the Fates. Let them spin what they want for me. I'll accept the life that comes and live it to the best of my abilities."

☙ Chapter 12 ❧

There was nothing either Signy or Irmengaard could do to prevent the future arriving, however obscured from human view it was. The weather was fine, with a good breeze, and Oswulf's priest pronounced that the omens were auspicious for departure. Hundreds of people assembled from their lodgings in farms and cottages all around the district and gathered on the shore by the boats. They dragged their vessels down to the water's edge and, as the tide came in, the boats lifted and floated, and the crews, Signy and Martha among them, scrambled on board. Trumpets sounded, and all along the coastline the raiders took to the waves.

By the second day, Signy, considering herself an experienced traveller, was standing in the bow beside the sharp-eyed lookout, young Ferland, the salt spray in her face, gazing out as the boat cut through the waves. On either side, she could see other vessels speeding across the water.

On the third day, the beauty and excitement of the voyage came to an abrupt end. Not through a storm, thank the gods, but because the cloud sank, and a blanket of mist crept around them. Thorgill ordered the sail to be lowered and let the boat drift, just steadied by the oarsmen. He knew they were near the shore, and he did not want to run aground in enemy territory. As the day wore on, the mist lifted, and they could clearly see the coast. They saw people standing on the beach with boats ready to launch. Had they been spotted? Thorgill hastily ordered his crew to pull with all their might. Slowly, the coastline faded away to a thin stripe, and then sank below the horizon. The steersman adjusted the course, and they headed cautiously offshore, until it was time to glide into the long bay and ride the tide up the river to the landing place. They saw boats before them and astern, and when they reached the bend in the river with the shallow beach for landing, there were already several pulled up on the shore.

The camp had suffered during the winter, but at least the native inhabitants had not destroyed it. The people who had arrived with the first boats were already clearing out the ditch and straightening the poles that made up the palisade. Signy found the hut that she and Thorgill had used the previous year. Half the thatch had come off and water had leaked in, but they could soon patch it up and begin to dry it out. Signy and Martha set off along the river to find reeds and dry grass and, with the help of a couple of Thorgill's band, they had the roof repaired by the following day. A little annexe was built where Martha could sleep, along with a cow and a pig they had brought with them from Juteland. It was not luxurious, far less so than home, but this was camp life. Luxury would come later, over the hills, or perhaps in the captured town, if Oswulf and his ally permitted it.

The chief was not among the first arrivals, but eventually Oswulf's boat pulled ashore. Skalgrim, the tough old veteran who acted as Oswulf's advisor, arrived a day later. Once he was ashore, the big man called everyone to gather and hear their leaders.

Skalgrim spoke first. "Soon all the boats'll have arrived, and the camp'll be packed with warriors and their followers. The food we brought with us won't last long. Hunting and scavenging won't be sufficient. We have to make a move, even if just to find new supplies."

"We must wait for the stragglers," said Oswulf, taking his turn. "Ravnberg and Ulvholm have not yet arrived. I must also receive word from the Duke that he's in place to assist us."

"The Duke" was the title Oswulf had given to his mysterious ally.

"We'll use the time to get organised, make sure our equipment's in order. Sharpen your swords and spears, make sure boots are repaired, and then we'll send out our expeditions. I'll be taking the biggest party south to attack the town," announced Oswulf.

There were nods of assent, led by Skalgrim. Oswulf's word was law, even for him.

That was natural, thought Signy, huddled quietly at the back of the assembly among the women. There was no need to cause quarrels at this stage by questioning Oswulf's leadership. Signy knew Thorgill had his own opinions, though he was careful not to show them. Once honour and riches had been won in the field, then it would be another matter.

"Skalgrim will take his followers north," Oswulf continued. "You'll be sending scouts ahead to find the villas and the town which lies up the road," he added, smiling at the old warrior.

The natives put up a good deal of opposition to Skalgrim the previous year, thought Signy. Those people must live somewhere, and Skalgrim probably knows how to teach them a lesson. She saw Oswulf glance around the assembled group.

"Finally, Thorgill will lead the remaining raiders back over the hills to lands beyond the forest."

During the cold and dreary days of the winter, Signy had imagined herself riding over the hills alongside Thorgill, part of his triumphal army, but the reality turned out a great deal duller.

"Signy, my dear," he said, placing his hand on her shoulder and using his softest tone. "You'll have to stay here in the camp with the other women. You'll be needed here, in case of accidents. There are bound to be casualties when Skalgrim and Oswulf return, even if they have tripped over their own spears or fallen drunk from their horses. You can patch them up and give them some salve. I'm sure it'll do them more good than an incantation from the priest."

"I'm not going into competition with Oswulf's priest," she said.

"That's just as well," said Thorgill. "Just keep your head down and don't offend anyone, especially Ulvholm. He's furious at being left in charge of the camp. He's taken the task as an insult, but he'd be useless in a fight. I can't believe that there are many warriors or soldiers where I'm heading," he continued, "and if there are, there are many more of us than last year, so they'd better stay away. On the other hand," he added, grinning, "where there are horses, there are wealthy people, and where there are wealthy people, there's property worth stealing."

"And a town, not far from the villa," said Signy, reminding him of what Martha had told her.

"Perhaps I'll capture a better town than either Oswulf or Skalgrim," Thorgill laughed.

"Will you need my charms?" Signy asked. "Martha and I can make enough for everyone with the help of the other women."

"With the warriors I have this year, I'll be unstoppable. All the riches over the hills will be at our mercy," said Thorgill, not wishing to give a straight answer. "We'll mop up the area before Oswulf even arrives. Just make sure you follow after as soon as you can. I'll reserve one of those villas for you."

"I'll make you a charm, anyway," she replied.

Oswulf moved out first, a messenger from the Duke by his side, leading his contingent down the south road, and later the same day, Skalgrim left for the north. Thorgill and Signy had one last night together, before she tied the good-luck charm around his neck and waved him off, standing in the shadow of the camp gate until he and his followers had vanished out of sight along the road to the west.

When we get back to Juteland, I will have his child, she said to herself. She felt she could be a mother now.

With the raiding parties gone, there was still plenty to be done around the camp. Signy and Martha tidied out the hut and moved the pig to a separate pen that the young men had constructed. Tonight, Martha would sleep with just the cow, unless Signy let her take Thorgill's place inside the hut. Elsewhere, the blacksmith had set up a new shelter and constructed an earthen hearth. His assistant was busy blowing with a bellows bag to heat the coals. They would need a lot of charcoal to keep him satisfied, and several of the older men, no longer fit enough to march with the bands, were beginning to set up a kiln to burn a new batch.

Signy decided to walk out to the old ruins to gather some of the herbs that had been growing in the abandoned garden the previous year. They were back in Martha's homeland, and it wouldn't be wise to trust her maid too much, Signy reckoned. How much did the slave woman know about this part of the country? Even if Martha had lived on the other side of the hills, she could probably find her way back, so Signy had forbidden her to leave the camp. Though she would have liked company, she made her way alone down the track and along the road to the deserted village. She took the little path towards the ruined garden, smiling to herself when she saw the same herbs growing, and noticed a few of the scented flowers she recalled peering up among the weeds. She filled her pouch with herbs, and then made her way round to the patch of flowers. A few low stones remained of a wall and, feeling the soft sun on her face, Signy sat down.

I wonder, she thought, if I allow my spirit free, if I can discover the spirits of the people who used to live here, who used to walk among these small stone houses and in this garden. She closed her eyes and allowed her body to relax, hearing the buzz of the bees, the rustling of a small animal among the vegetation, and tasting the scent of the flowers, but no voices spoke to her, no faces came. No wonder, she thought. I don't know their names or their words. How could I reach out to them and they to me?

She opened her eyes and noticed a mark that made her heart stop. A little to her left was the print of a foot in the earth. She had not spotted it when she sat down. It can't be mine, she thought. I didn't come that way and, besides, it was the print of a boot. Can someone else in the camp have found this place? We've been here several days, and there are hundreds of people. Probably some curious person had made their way over to the ruined village for a little peace and quiet like I did.

She plucked several of the flowers and looked again at the print. There was more than one, and they seemed to come from the direction of the road, but where did they lead to among the fallen stones? She followed the tracks into the undergrowth until she came to the stump of the rear wall of the building. From there, she could see the camp in the distance. She saw the people carrying wood inside, the smoke rising from several of the small buildings. She peered down at the ground. The grass and plants were flattened. Someone had been lying there. Who could it have been? A couple of the men lazing away from work, or perhaps someone had taken one of the maids out here to be in peace, get a little privacy away from the prying eyes and comments in the camp. She crouched low, her hand against the crushed vegetation, and as she stood again, she happened to glance up towards the camp, spread out in full view before her. An uncomfortable thought struck her. Supposing someone had been watching the camp. They could lie behind the wall and see everything that was going on, and if anyone came out of the camp, they could quickly slip away through the ruins and across the road. She turned on her heels and did the same, this time looking carefully for footprints. Yes, there they were, the same prints, right up to the edge of the road.

She crossed the neatly cut stones and found the same prints on the other side, disappearing into some vegetation which had been pushed down and crushed. She hesitated for a moment, and then continued forward through the undergrowth, past another wall, to where the ruins stood a little higher among some taller bushes. The prints continued across a small clearing, and then her heart sank. She could see not just footprints, but hoofprints in the dirt, and a pile of horse droppings. The horse had obviously gone and with it, its rider. She contemplated the pile of droppings. How long had they been there? She wasn't an expert tracker, but they certainly looked pretty fresh.

She returned to the hut and showed Martha the flowers she had picked. Martha sniffed at them and smiled. She murmured a word, their name in her own language, Signy supposed, but her mind was elsewhere. She went inside the hut to sort out the herbs and place them in her chest. When she came out again, Martha had thrown some wood on the fire and was beginning to heat the evening meal. Porridge again, Signy supposed, but Martha had also been busy while she was out and bargained with one of the boys for a rabbit he had managed to catch with a snare.

"I must go and see Ulvholm," Signy said. "I'll be back before long."

She crossed the camp to the hut which Oswulf had recently vacated and where Ulvholm had now taken up residence. The camp chief was sitting on a log outside the hut, and in front of him was a fire with a cauldron steaming over it. As she approached, the man reached inside the cauldron and withdrew a piece of meat. He was contemplating his catch, glistening on the end of a spike, when she stopped in front of him. He slowly raised his eyes from his dinner and contemplated her instead, examining her from head to toes, but not meeting her gaze.

"What do you want, woman?" he asked.

"I've seen something," she said, "in the ruined village." Then it struck her. Chief Ulvholm had probably never set foot outside the camp. He would have no idea what ruined village she was talking about. "By the road junction," she added hastily.

"I gave an order that no one was to leave the camp," said the chief, eyeing his meat once again, "especially women."

"Nevertheless…" Signy began.

"Nevertheless, nevertheless, what in hell do you mean by addressing me like that? Have you been defying my orders?"

"I didn't know of your order, my lord."

"Because you were already wandering around up to no good," said the chief, now taking a bite from the chunk of meat.

"I saw boot prints and horse droppings, probably fresh ones. I think—"

"Unlike some others, I don't give a damn what you think, little girl. Don't imagine you know more than I do. Don't think you are better than you are. Just because you're supposed to be Thorgill's wife, that's no reason to act so proud." He munched, then swallowed. "I remember seeing you at the winter meet, flouncing about in borrowed feathers, as if you were so important. A little Saxon whore like you wouldn't know the difference between horse shit and…" His eyes lighted on the rest of his dinner. "…oatcakes," he grunted, picking one up and stuffing it into his mouth.

For a moment, Signy felt sick. The impression that he was eating a piece of horse dung was almost overwhelming. She was about to repeat the word "nevertheless" when her senses told her that would not be a good idea.

"Now clear off," said the chief. "Go back to your cooking, and don't try to teach me my business. And don't go wandering out of the camp again, unless you want a lesson in obedience." His eyes again wandered over her body, and she did not have to guess what form the lesson might take.

Is the man mad, she thought, to risk picking a fight with my husband, and Thorgill himself already looking for a reason to quarrel with Oswulf and his followers?

"Very well, my lord," she said, in her most humble tone, well-practised from her first months with Helga, and backed slowly away.

The sun was beginning to go down when she returned. Signy and Martha sat by the fire, each lost in their own thoughts. The boy came over to ask how the rabbit tasted. He had been standing by the gate, watching them eat. He was clearly rather proud that someone as important as Chief Thorgill's wife might be tasting his rabbit.

Signy glanced up at him. His eyes gave him away. I know what you're imagining, she said to herself. You're thinking I might be Thorgill's wife, but I'm probably no older than you. And I'm quite good-looking. How long would it be, while the raiders were away, before there started to be problems in the camp, men and women mixed together, with not enough to do?

Suddenly, there was a shout from above. The lookout had spotted horsemen approaching through the dusk.

"From the direction they're coming, it must be Thorgill returning."

The boy jumped up, gave Signy one last glance, and ran back to his post by the gate. Soon it would be sundown, and then he would swing the wooden door shut until morning, as he had been ordered. She knew he did not want to be caught out of place.

A thought flashed through Signy's head. Thorgill had left on foot. Why would he be returning now on horseback? Would it have been so easy to find horses in the woods, and if so, why would he have come back so soon, instead of riding on? Her mind jumped to the footprints and the hoofmarks. Where there was one horseman, there could be others out among the abandoned fields. If someone was watching, they could have waited until the warriors left so they could attack the camp. To hell with Ulvholm, she thought, and jumped up.

"Shut the gate!" she called, but the boy and his friends hesitated to obey a woman's order.

The lookout shouted, "They're coming in fast."

The horsemen had broken into a gallop. The first rider was in through the gate before the boy realised he really should swing it shut. The horseman was not one of Thorgill's men. He was a stranger, who lashed out with an axe, and the boy fell to the ground. Two old men picked up spears from a stack beside the gate and ran towards the intruder. Several more horsemen had pushed their way inside and, throwing well-aimed spears, felled the men. The first rider had already dismounted and was pushing the gate wide open. More and more horsemen surged in, filling the space at the entrance, taking in the camp with their cold gaze, while others pushed in behind – ten, twenty, even more.

Signy crouched down beside Martha, watching the invaders. "We can be seen in the light of the fire," she whispered, laying a hand on Martha's shoulder and drawing her back into the shadows.

Martha leaned over to Signy and whispered in her ear, "Britons."

Martha's own people, thought Signy, although that did not mean they were necessarily her friends. She knew, from Martha's stories, that there were many groups of Britons, and their quarrels had left them vulnerable to chancers like Oswulf.

In a moment, there was a bustling among the horsemen as they separated to make way for two newcomers. From the way they carried themselves, Signy concluded they were chiefs. The one nearest to her was heavily built and had long blond hair, a moustache and a beard.

"Saxon," Signy whispered to Martha, hearing words in Saxon, but West Saxon, not the dialect of her people. That will keep her in her place, she thought, if she thinks my people have come.

At first, she could not see the other man, but when his horse took a step forward, he stood out clearly. His hair was short, she could see that, and his beard was trimmed, too. He had a cloak fastened over his shoulder, and wore a short tunic and leather boots. Her heart took a jump, as if she had seen a ghost. She had seen figures like that before. He was just like one of the men on Thorgill's best drinking vessel, the ones who stood talking to the goddess. Or the heads on the coins she had seen. People that Laurentius had called Romans. She had assumed those were images from long ago, idealised from the gods, but the leader of the invaders could have stepped down from one of the vessels or the medallion that the envoy had been wearing. Had Oswulf been betrayed by the man he had called "the Duke"?

She felt Martha's hand clutch her arm and turned to her. "What is it, Martha?" she whispered, but the slave woman was petrified with fear, her eyes nearly bulging from her head.

The short-haired man was giving orders. His voice was quiet but carried through the gathering gloom. His followers obeyed instantly. Once in a while, he turned and exchanged words with the big man beside him. She could swear even the short-haired man, the Roman, spoke in Saxon when he did so, but she was too far away to make out what they were saying.

There was a yell, and she turned to see the blacksmith rushing out of the smithy with his heavy hammer raised to swing at the intruders. Another figure, his assistant, jumped out behind him, a glowing iron in his hand. There was a red burst in the gathering dusk. The blacksmith screamed as his assistant lunged at him and turned, distracted. In an instant, one of the intruders struck him down with his sword. A cold shiver took hold of Signy. The blacksmith's assistant was a slave, a Briton, she knew. Had the man taken the opportunity for revenge? Supposing Martha did something similar? Where was the knife she had used to cut the rabbit? But Martha still clung to her, clearly terrified by the horsemen.

Again there was a disturbance. Now the old priest was advancing, calling in a loud voice, cursing against the intruders in the name of the gods. She saw some of the dismounted warriors hesitate, and the big Saxon drew his horse back a step, too. She heard what the priest was shouting. They were strong words, of threat and doom. Saxons and Jutes shared the same gods. The Saxons among the attackers probably understood what he was saying. Even she reflexively looked up, half expecting to see circling ravens. Then the Roman waved a hand to two short-haired warriors, and they stepped towards the cursing priest and cut him down. The curses faded away along with the life-spirit of the curser.

Now, at last, the camp chief put in an appearance.

"What in the name of Woden…" Ulvholm began, and then came to a halt. "…is going on here?" he added in a fainter voice, seeing the group of armed men in the middle of his camp. He did not have a chance to say more before he was bundled to the ground.

By now, almost all the riders had dismounted and were beginning to search through the huts, rounding people up as they found them. Two of the intruders came over to the fire where Signy and Martha had been sitting and spotted the women crouching in the shadows. Martha was trembling and holding tight. Signy remembered how she had been raped by the Jutes last year. She must be terrified the same would happen again. *What about me? Will I share her fate?*

They shouted one word. "Up!"

Signy hesitated, fearful of becoming a victim.

"Up!" they shouted again.

Signy stood and drew Martha with her.

The men spoke, some quick words in British that Signy could not follow. She saw Martha nod her head. The men spoke again, softly, directly to Martha. She nodded again. Then they turned to Signy and spoke to her. It was too quick, too quiet, all the sound rolled into one. She did not know what to reply. She just heard

Martha whisper next to her, "She's a good woman. She cared for me. Don't hurt her," and then the men reached forward and grasped her. There was nothing Signy could do. It was useless calling out. Who would she call out to? It was useless screaming. They would only beat her or worse.

One of the men led Martha away. Signy watched her go, back to her people. The other soldier took a hard grip on Signy's arm, and, half dragging, half lifting her, marched her over to the pen where the pigs had been housed. He shoved her inside, and she tumbled down. When she picked herself up, she found herself sitting alongside the two women from the bakehouse and the blacksmith's wife. Shortly after, two other women were pushed into the pen, strangers who had arrived with Skalgrim's boat. The women crept to the back of the pen, to the darkest part they could find, and huddled together, peering out into the darkness. Signy could no longer see what was going on outside, only the shadow of a man standing guard over the pen. She could still hear shouting and talking, but after a while, even that died down. The women crept as close together as they could. The blacksmith's wife began to cry, and one of the bakers tried to comfort her.

Presently, there was an exchange of words outside the pen, and a second soldier appeared. He was carrying some wooden bowls and had a metal pail in his hand. He looked over towards the women with a smile on his face.

Signy thought she understood. "Dinner," he seemed to say. For once she was not hungry. Whether she was too scared to feel hungry or she had already eaten enough of the rabbit stew earlier, she was not sure. None of the other women wanted food, either. The soldier looked around hopefully and seemed disappointed that no one took him up on his offer. Then he shrugged, turned and left, making a comment on the way out that both he and the guard obviously found funny.

One by one, the other women fell asleep, but Signy sat awake for what seemed like for ever, until there was a banging noise, and she woke with a start. She looked around in a daze to find it was daylight, and she was sitting squeezed into one corner of the pigpen with a soldier leaning over her. He carried the same wooden bowls and pail.

"Break…your…fast," he said, speaking very slowly and unnecessarily loudly in British, and with a smile plastered across his stupid face. "You're…going…to…need…it." Was he the same fool as the night before, thought Signy, as her mind ran quickly backward over the events of the previous evening. There was a pit in her stomach now, no longer just fear, but the beginnings of hunger. When would she be given another meal, if she ever got another meal, she wondered. The soldier looked at the sullen women hopefully.

Signy spoke up.

"Me," she said tentatively, as when she attempted to speak British to Martha. The soldier gave her a big smile and dumped a clump of oatmeal into one of the wooden bowls. He pulled a wooden spoon from his belt and handed it to her.

"Anyone else?" he asked hopefully. The other women kept silent, so he said something cheerfully to Signy, "All the more for you," perhaps, and getting no response, left the pigsty.

Signy ate the porridge, while the other women watched her as if she was eating a baby. It was just plain boiled meal and water, but she had eaten worse when she was a child. When she was finished, she held on to the bowl and spoon, and in a little while the simple, cheerful soldier returned.

"More?" he enquired.

She shook her head, and he reached out and took the bowl from her. With her stomach full, she started to wonder what was coming next. Amazingly, she and the other women had not been raped or mistreated. They'd been left to sleep in peace. But this had happened to her before, she recalled. They were property again, she and the other women, property that was too valuable to destroy wantonly.

Before long, the cheery soldier came back, this time with a bucket of water and a drinking cup. Just what I needed, thought Signy, and swallowed a whole cupful of water. Her initiative sparked a little life in the other women, who passed the cup among themselves, taking a few gulps. If I can only keep my mind working, she thought, then the worst might be averted.

The camp round about had begun to bustle as the sun came up. Signy examined her companions. Their clothes were caked in mud and worse from sitting all night where the pigs had been lying. Their hair was plastered with dirt. What a mess they were! What a mess I must be, she thought, but perhaps that was just as well if they had become unattractive objects to rapists. On the other hand, these soldiers didn't appear to be rapists. She and her companions had been left alone. The man who had brought the food didn't smell of stale wine or beer. He didn't seem to be hung-over or angry. There was no lust in his eyes. She'd heard no screaming or shouting in the night, not even any drunken singing or loud laughter. Only the little jokes exchanged between the man who had fed them and whoever was on watch.

Soon after, the guard stood up a little straighter, and the face of a young man appeared over the fence of the pigsty.

He first spoke in British, and then repeated it for good measure with exaggerated politeness in halting, sing-song Saxon. "Good morning, ladies. Now we are going on a little walk."

What did he mean? His first intention was clear as he waved to them to stand up. The guard came into the pen and held out his hand. Signy reached out, and he pulled her upright. The other women stood looking stunned and blinking, stiff after an uncomfortable night, tottering a little as their legs took their weight. The young man opened the gate, and the guard ushered them out.

Once she was standing upright, Signy could see more of the camp. The young boys and old men among the Jutes were roped into a line, their hands tied together. Ulvholm was not among them. Signy and the other women were pushed out of the pen, and with nudges and prods, moved to the end of the line. No one tied them up, however, so they just stood, waiting. Signy looked round to see if she could see Martha, but there was no sign of her. She did see two soldiers dragging at the reeds she and her maid had so carefully arranged on the roof of Thorgill's hut just a couple of days before. Two others came out from the hut, and she saw they were carrying her chest. Away from the hut, they stopped and placed it on the ground, pulled at the hasp, opened the lid and looked inside. She expected them to take out her clothes and find her jewels, to claim them as plunder, but they made no move to disturb the contents. A third man came over and peered inside, too. He shook his head, made a dismissive gesture, and they closed the lid once again. At that moment, there was a shout, and Signy realised that the column of captives was being urged to move forward.

Signy thought ruefully of the footprints and traces of the horse she had seen the day before as they were marched away from the camp. Someone, one of these men, must have been watching. As she glanced back, she saw there were large gaps in the palisade already, and smoke rising from burning huts. They headed off across the flat fields, the fields that Thorgill had passed by just two days before. Where was he and what had happened to him?

The captives and their escort marched on and on through the morning. Signy was glad she had eaten the oatmeal and drunk plenty of water, and she wondered how the women who had taken no breakfast were feeling. Her answer came a short while later when the blacksmith's wife keeled over and fell down in front of her. A soldier ran up. The rest of the women cringed, expecting blows or a knife, but instead the man pulled out a leather bottle and handed it to the blacksmith's wife. This time she drank greedily, and the march resumed.

At midday, the sun was high in the sky and there was no shelter. Someone must have had mercy on the prisoners, since the column stopped moving, and the chief with the sing-song voice came walking by.

"Sit down, sit down."

They collapsed gratefully and gracelessly onto the road, but with a gesture he urged them onto the grass beyond the ditch. After a short while, there was the sound of horses approaching, and half a dozen riders appeared at a trot, including the short-haired leader and the big Saxon from the night before. When they pulled level with the sing-song man, Signy saw the short-haired leader lean down and speak to him. The two of them laughed, the sing-song man patted the horse, and the riders moved off. These strangers seemed so calm and confident in every action, as if they were in complete control.

Where was Thorgill? Where was Skalgrim? Where was Oswulf?

After a little while, soldiers came by with water, and then a short time later, the line of people was urged to its feet and ordered to march again. Thorgill took this road, thought Signy. Where is he?

They walked all day until the sun set behind the hills. Signy's feet were tired and sore, and she was beginning to feel hungry again. Suddenly, they were told to stop, and the whole line collapsed onto the road, not waiting for any clearer instructions. Signy felt like she would never be able to get up again. The cheery soldier reappeared, and Signy's hopes for food rose. Sure enough, as he came nearer, she heard him calling out, "Dinner?" in a hopeful manner. Someone must have told him to use the Saxon word. This time none of them refused, and each one received a ladle of the same oatmeal. When he reached Signy, he looked a little apologetic at the monotony of the food.

"It's the same as we're getting, love," he said in British, not bothering whether she understood him or not.

Signy gulped it down quickly. She held out her bowl as he came back up the line.

"Good lass," he said, scraping around in his bucket and giving her another ladleful. She didn't care what the others thought. She felt sick and tired and frightened, but she didn't need to feel hungry on top of everything else.

They had been sitting by the side of the road for a long time, when the remaining men and boys in the line were commanded to their feet. The women started to stand, too, but were told to sit down again. After a while, the men were marched off along a side road and disappeared out of view. Silence fell once again on the sitting women. Are they marching to their deaths, Signy wondered.

A couple of guards sat a little way up the road, chatting. The last rays of the sun gleamed over the top of the hill ahead of them.

The guards jumped to their feet: the sing-song chief was back.

"Ladies, ladies, on your feet again. We haven't finished for today, but I promise you tonight's lodging will be cleaner than yesterday's…once we get there."

One guard positioned himself in front, and the other behind, and they set off again up the road. It was nearly pitch black, but the road was smooth and straight and walking was easy so long as you kept your eyes on the person in front. Just try to keep upright, don't let exhaustion take over, and keep placing one foot in front of the other – there was little more that Signy could bring herself to do or think.

They came to the edge of the forest and passed under the dark canopy. A sickly smell hit Signy, the smell of blood, the smell of dead bodies. She saw the other women could smell the same, and they were looking around from side to side in alarm. At one moment, she thought she saw a naked body. A little further on, the stench became worse, and she imagined that she had seen a whole heap of bodies by the side of the road, stacked like fallen timber. Then an evening breeze trickled through the trees and started to clear the air. There was no more smell, and no more eerie sights. They had been dead bodies, Signy was sure. They couldn't be anything else. What had happened? Were these Thorgill's men, lying dead by the road?

She tried to calculate their progress, but it was hopeless. She was too tired, and the result was impossible to contemplate. The strangers were obviously comfortable in marching their prisoners up this road. The footprints in the ruin, the horse shit, the little jokes between the men, the casual friendliness of the soldiers and the officers…Either they didn't know there were any Jutes nearby or there were no longer any Jutes on the road.

The women kept on walking for what seemed like half the night. The pace was easy and slow, but the road led up and up. Stepping on became automatic, almost like sleepwalking. It seemed to take an age before the trees thinned out. Then Signy remembered more of Thorgill's story, how eventually at the top of the hill they had come across ruined buildings and troll caves. Just as Thorgill had described them, ruined buildings appeared in the light of the moon, but instead of being deserted, they thronged with life. Not with trolls or giants or dragons, although flames could be seen winking among the fallen walls, but men and more men, and out in the dark she could once again hear Saxon voices. As the road levelled out, the soldier at the front of the column called to someone ahead and, after receiving a reply, led them into one of the ruins. There was a fire burning in the middle of what must have once been a large square room, but which had lost its roof. Two soldiers, standing by the fire, moved away when the women were directed in and went to stand by the door. The women looked around and sat down one by one. In sheer exhaustion, without saying anything, they lay down and slept.

❦ Chapter 13 ❦

The women seemed to have been forgotten. Food and water were delivered, the guards changed regularly, and morning and evening they were escorted to the latrines, but otherwise they were left alone to contemplate their fate. There was little they could see from their prison. They could hear voices of men, Saxons and Britons, and occasionally a woman. There were no windows in the walls and the door was narrow. It was demeaning to stand by the entrance, trying to catch a view of a world which consisted mainly of guards' arses.

On the second morning, the two bakers were called for and taken away for most of the day, and in the evening they returned tired and sore from having ground flour the whole day. They could give no news. Their guards spoke no Jutish, and they had not understood what was being said to them, just that they were to turn the hand mills until they were allowed to stop. They had smelled baking bread but had not been allowed near the bakehouse. They had received the same oaten porridge as the women who had stayed behind.

Signy had plenty of time to consider the situation. They were captives, and that meant she was once again reduced to being a slave, because that was the inevitable fate of captives. Supposing the enemy found out she was not just another camp follower, but Thorgill's wife? Martha knew what Thorgill had done, knew he had killed the old man. She knew who she was, and worse, supposing they discovered the old lady's jewels in her chest, the ones Thorgill had stolen from the villa? Martha had told her she'd never seen the old lady wear them, but the maid knew where they had come from and she knew where they were hidden. The Britons would kill her for being a thief and the wife of a murderer. Her only hope would be that the end was quick.

Those fear-filled moments did pass. There were times when she felt more hopeful. She had been taken once before, she reflected, and matters had turned out reasonably well. Maybe they would again. But she was no longer a virgin, promising booty for the right man. She was used, definitely used, and although that had given her experience she lacked when Thorgill first took her, that only made her a more suitable candidate for a whorehouse. What talents did she have of use to a slave holder other than a pretty face and a young body? She was no baker. She could not weave like the blacksmith's wife. She could not make pots or garments. She could sew and spin, but any girl could do that. Her talents lay elsewhere, but they were not ones which were obviously evident. How could she be a medicine woman without her medicines and her tools? What use was it being a sister of Freya in a land where, so Martha had told her, many people worshipped entirely different gods, where being a priestess might be a liability rather than an advantage? At best, she could hope to be some man's plaything for a while, and then when he grew tired of her, to be discarded to the most menial work. Unless, of course, the Fates had something else in mind, she thought. I'm still me, my mother's daughter, my father's dear child, even looking hard, Thorgill's pretty Saxon girl, Irmengaard's apprentice. I've been the cup bearer in Chief Oswulf's hall. I imagined that riches might be found beyond the hills. All of this I've done. I can do more if only I keep my eyes open, my ears listening, and don't allow myself to be overwhelmed by the situation. I wanted to see for myself what was down the river, beyond the forest, and now the Fates have made that inevitable.

On the third day, there was a stir in the camp. Voices were louder, there were the sounds of metal on metal, arms and armour clashing together. Towards evening, the women heard orders being given, soldiers assembling, and they could see the shadows and outline of an organised column through the rectangular opening of the door. More orders were shouted in the still evening, and the women followed the footsteps as they faded away down the road into the forest.

The camp was dark that night, and the following day was eerily quiet. The few voices outside were muted. Their breakfast was brought to them by a silent old man in place of the usual guard, and afterwards the same man escorted them to the latrines. As they walked among the buildings, they could only see a few figures flitting here and there in the distance. The previous days had felt tedious and long, but with the absence of sounds and the tension in the air, this day felt endless.

Dusk came and night fell, and the women huddled together, hushed like the rest of the camp. Well into the night, they were woken by shouts from outside. Torches lit up the road, and the sound of marching feet and the clink of armour in motion could be heard once again. The women sat up, staring out into the darkness, now broken up by flames of orange. Again there were voices giving orders. Signy could hear the sound of Saxons telling people to keep moving. There were curses, and a cry as someone received a blow. More feet, more voices, the tones different. Were there Jutes out among the shadows? The women pressed forward to the entrance and peered out into the dancing flames and their reflected glow.

Suddenly, one of the women who had arrived with Skalgrim gasped and shrieked. "I can see them!"

Jutes walking, stumbling through the night outside.

"Let me through!" she cried, and tried to push past the guard on the door, but he turned and roughly shoved her inside again, where she stumbled backwards and collapsed weeping. A second woman looked around the edge of the door, shielding her eyes from the brightness of the flames.

"I'm sure they're Skalgrim's men," she said in a hoarse whisper, worry in her voice. She called out abruptly, hailing one of the marching men, and a voice called back, two words before it was cut off with an oath and an order to shut up.

"Beaten. Dead."

The woman turned back, her face in tears. Her husband had been one of Skalgrim's warriors.

Signy tried to fathom what had happened. Had there been a battle? Was that why the soldiers had marched off the day before?

But if these were Skalgrim's men, where were Thorgill's men? As the sound of the marching captives died away, a brief hope filled her that Thorgill and his followers might also have been captured and led away to another place. Gradually, a kind of quiet fell once more over the camp, a kind of quiet, broken by the sobbing of the two women, and her heart sank again. Signy lay down, closed her eyes and let sleep take away her cares.

In the morning, nothing seemed to have changed, as if the vision in the night was no more than a dream or a nightmare. The same old man came with the porridge, and when they were escorted from the hut, the camp appeared as empty as it had on the previous day. Now a great dread filled the women. What would become of them if their menfolk had been defeated and killed? There was no hope. The day lay on them like a weight. They could scarcely talk among themselves, and mainly sat in silence, staring into the embers of the fire with ever-sinking hope.

The evening meal came, and several of the women felt so sick at heart that they would not touch it. Signy felt sick, too, but she steeled herself to follow her usual strategy and forced herself to eat. Dusk fell, and the women sat, waiting for the customary order to follow the old man to the latrines. But before he put in an appearance, there was a disturbance at the entrance: a low voice gave an order, and the guard moved aside. Two figures stepped into the space, and Signy's heart gave an involuntary leap. She recognised their silhouettes, and when they spoke, she recognised their voices. They were the two leaders she had seen on the first day, the big Saxon and the short-haired Roman. They took a couple of paces forward. The women shrank back towards the wall.

The short-haired man spoke first.

"We…are…not…here…to…harm…you," he said, speaking slowly, in British, as if he expected to be understood. "Can…anyone…here…speak…British?" His voice was clear, and he was obviously trying to sound friendly. Signy thought she caught his words but said nothing.

The big Saxon spoke.

"Can anyone here speak Saxon? We know there were Saxons among the Jutes."

Why should they answer? What did these people want?

The two men conferred, looking from one woman to the other. The Saxon spoke again.

"We'll treat you well. We need your help to stop the fighting. We need someone who can help us talk to your chief."

Signy heard what he said. Were they such fools to think these women, bakers, maids, farmers' wives, could talk to Oswulf? The short-haired man was looking straight at her, as if he was singling her out. Did he recognise her from some brief glance in Oswulf's camp? Had someone told him she was Thorgill's wife? Had he realised she could speak Saxon? Was he a wizard who could see into her heart as Irmengaard seemed to? Her eyes met his, and almost without thinking she stood up, drawn up by his gaze. She stepped over the crouching bakers and stood in front of the men. For a moment, her eyes were still caught by the regard of the short-haired man, and then she broke the look and bowed her head.

"I will help you, my lords, if it's for the sake of peace," she whispered, almost to herself, as if she still had to convince one part of her that this was the right thing to do. The short-haired man reached out and placed his hand on her shoulder. She felt its warmth. She felt its weight, but the grip was light, quite gentle, not the grip of a man who was intending to use violence.

"You speak Jutish?" asked the big Saxon.

"Yes, Master."

"And what is your name?" asked the short-haired man, this time in Saxon, once more trying to sound friendly.

"Signy, Master."

The big Saxon looked irritated and not at all friendly.

"You sound like a Saxon, not a Jute," he said. "What were you doing in the camp of the Jutes?"

"I was Thorgill's woman, Master."

"The chief? His wife?" asked the big Saxon, suspiciously.

"No, Master, only his woman, his servant."

The Saxon grunted, then whispered a few words she could not understand to the short-haired man, who nodded and looked grim.

Signy peered up at him, trying to observe him without catching his eye.

Suddenly, he spoke. "Can you ride…a horse?"

"Yes, Master."

He looked thoughtful, exchanged another couple of words with his companion, glanced at the cluster of the other women and shook his head.

"Thank you, Signy. With your help we may be able to save many men's lives." He turned and called to the guard. There was another shout into the darkness, and a third man ducked in through the doorway. The Roman spoke to him in British. He spoke quickly, and she could not catch what he was saying.

"Follow him!" ordered the big Saxon.

The newcomer smiled at her and beckoned her to follow him, out of the hut and into the camp.

"My…name…is…Cull, Miss," he said in halting Saxon.

"I speak a little British," she whispered back. "Where are we going?"

The man, Cull, looked down at her in surprise.

"You need to be clean," he said, speaking slowly and softly. "The governor needs your help in the morning. Follow me, and you'll be alright. I'll take care of you." He had an accent which made it hard to understand everything he was saying, but she felt the warmth of his tone. It sounded like he really meant no harm, she believed. It sounded like he really wanted to help her. She could feel it. Perhaps she could trust the short-haired man. The big Saxon was another matter. He was a type she knew very well, and he had probably weighed her up instantly, too.

❧ Chapter 14 ❧

Signy followed the man named Cull through the camp to the far end, where he shouted through a doorway and a woman emerged. There was an exchange of words she did not understand, but she understood the order that followed.

"Come here," the woman ordered, using the tone Signy had almost forgotten. "Take all those filthy clothes off, right now."

Signy hesitated. They wanted her to strip. She looked around. The man at least had gone, but that was not her worst fear. The woman would see her marks. She would call the man back, tell him what sort of person she was. He would take her to the leaders, the short-haired man and the Saxon. The short-haired man hadn't held back when he had ordered his soldiers to kill the priest in the camp. She would beg, grovel, abase herself, promise to do whatever he wanted, just to save her life.

"Hurry up, love. We haven't got all day." The woman's voice broke into her panic, reminding her of Martha. Of course Martha knows that I'm friends with Irmengaard, the wise woman, she thought, but had never commented on the tattoos. Maybe, maybe, the Britons didn't understand? Maybe such marks meant something different here?

She slowly lifted up her tunic, tugging it over her head. If the woman noticed the mark, she said nothing, merely held out her hand for the dirty garment. Signy ran her fingers through her hair. She could feel it was filthy and matted.

"Don't you worry, love," said the woman. "We'll take care of that."

Signy thought she understand what the woman had said. Perhaps it was just her imagination, but at least she felt the woman's tone had softened a little. A second woman appeared, carrying a pail of water which, without warning, she emptied over

Signy's head. The water was freezing cold, and Signy gasped and cried out. The two women laughed and began to comb her hair. They did not try to be gentle, and even if they had, it would have hurt to get out the tangles. By the time they had finished, she was cold, as well as naked and wet. The women seemed momentarily at a loss as to what to do. They could not let her put her old dirty clothes back on, but she could not go unclothed in a camp full of men.

There was a discreet knock from behind the wall. She heard Cull's voice again. "We found some clean clothes in one of the chests. You can use these."

The woman handed Signy a tunic, and she gasped, almost with a laugh of relaxed tension. She recognised one of her own tunics. The strangers must have her chest somewhere close by. She slipped the garment on, and the two women led her over to a nearby fire.

"Sit," they ordered, and she did so, letting the warmth flow over her, drying her body and eventually her hair.

Had she done right, she thought, to say she would help the enemy leaders? They had probably killed Thorgill, she'd already concluded. They were probably responsible for the deaths of all the cheerful young men who had welcomed her to Thorgill's farm, joked with her in those early days when she had been alone, come to her with their torn clothes and later, when they learned of her skills, their torn skins and broken limbs. He had said, the Roman, that he wanted peace, but the Britons had already ended so many lives, and probably mostly wanted to save their own. But she was a woman, alone in a strange land, her husband and master was likely dead. What choice did she have but to obey, to find a new master, and hope he would be a kind and decent man as, taken altogether, Thorgill had been? The man with the short-cut hair had spoken with a soft voice, hardly sounding like a warrior, though he had not hesitated to order his men to cut down the blacksmith and the priest, and no doubt Ulvholm, too. Well, Thorgill had also killed people, and stolen and burned, and she had been proud of him for doing so. Probably her husband and his house warriors had raped and assaulted women, though

Thorgill had not boasted of that in her hearing. All in all, she calculated, perhaps it would be in her best interest to serve the short-haired man, to obey his orders to the best of her ability and hope that some good would come of it. At least the warriors who followed him were sober and had left the women alone.

She awoke early and, for a moment, thought she was back in the prison with the other Jute women, but instead she was in another small hut, which she had shared with the women who had washed her. Her hut-mates had clearly already got up, so she stretched her limbs, stood up, walked to the door and looked out. There was no guard to be seen. She looked to her left and her right. They were on the edge of the forest, and the road rose to the left through the ruined and half-repaired buildings. There was no one else around, just one of the strange women, bent over the fire. Could they stop her if she ran, but where would she run to? She walked over to the woman, who heard her coming and stood up.

"Get something to eat," she said abruptly. "They'll be coming for you soon, and I want to get your hair braided."

Signy sat on a nearby rock and took a bowl of stew and a spoon, and in a moment the woman walked round behind her and began to work on her hair. In a while, Signy saw Cull coming down the road towards them. He was carrying a bundle of cloth over his arm. He stopped when he saw her. She gave him a timid smile.

"Clothes," he said, grinning in return. "I hope they fit."

She took hold of them. Of course they would fit. They were her own riding clothes, the ones she had sewn and embroidered herself. She had imagined wearing them to ride with Thorgill through the land he had won, but instead, she was going to use them for what, she wondered. She went inside the hut and pulled on the tunic and a pair of soft trousers. She knew they made her look a little like a man, but that could not be helped. She walked out of the hut and caught Cull's gaze. She recognised the admiring look he gave her, the look of a man who could not help but smile at a pretty woman. Even the two old women smiled. They're proud of their handiwork, she thought. They've converted a dirty and smelly prisoner into a girl almost fit to be…the wife of a chief.

Cull pulled himself together and gestured to Signy to follow. Reaching the top of the hill, she saw two horses waiting with a pair of grooms. They were not big horses, but she was glad of help to mount the unfamiliar animal. Cull gave the order, and the horses began to walk down the road and into the trees. At first, he said nothing, but as they rode together, he could not hold his curiosity.

"You said you speak British, Miss?"

"Little. I had British maid in home in Juteland," she said, squeezing her mind to remember the right words.

The man shook his head and sighed. "I don't speak Saxon so good…nor Latin." He sighed again and fell silent.

"What happen now?" she asked, eventually coming up with a suitable question.

"I don't know," her companion answered. "Marcus, the governor, our chief…he has his own way."

"The man short hair, Roman?"

Cull now laughed outright.

"He'd be glad to hear you call him that," he said. "The Roman…aye, that's the fellow."

It had taken hours for the women to walk up the hill, but on horseback the journey down went much faster. Soon she knew they must reach the place where she thought she had seen dead bodies. She was sure they had been bodies. She felt the horse moving uneasily, slightly nervously, beneath her, as if the animal also detected something uncomfortable, but there was nothing to be seen. No corpses, no dead people, perhaps some marks on the road that might have been blood, though she could have been imaging what was not there. And then Cull stopped, indicating to the left, to a path they should take through the woods. The horses walked on, for a little while, up a hill, and then all at once they were out from the trees and among the huts of a small encampment. Signy saw that they were on the hillside overlooking the flat plain and the fields. Far away in the distance must be the river, the road and the remains of the Jute camp. A boy stepped forward and took her reins, and she swung herself off the horse. Whatever awaited her, she was about to find out.

Cull led her into a hut, a single room, roughly built from unfinished logs, plastered with mud. He called out a greeting as they entered, and Signy saw the leader with the close-cropped hair standing inside the hut. Marcus, the governor, Cull had called him. To Signy's surprise, he was carefully examining a square of wood as they entered and looked up when he heard Cull's voice.

"Thank you, Cull," he said briskly when he saw them. "Are you travelling back to the mines this afternoon?"

Now, in the calm of the day, after a good night's sleep, clean and well dressed, she could understand his speech a little better. Perhaps he was even making an effort to be understood.

"I was planning to stay," Cull said, as if addressing an old friend and not his chief, she noticed, "but I can ride back if you want."

His chief handed him the wooden tablet.

"I would be grateful if you could make sure this message gets to Edwulf before nightfall."

Edwulf's another Saxon name, Signy thought, as she examined the room. A simple bed was arranged across one end. A chest, a table and a pair of wooden stools were the only other furniture. On the table were several beakers and a pair of jugs.

Cull took the tablet and left. The leader turned to Signy, switching at once to his strange-sounding Saxon.

"My name is Marcus Lucullus Ursinus, and I am Magister Militum of the province of Britannia Prima…in charge of the army, that is," he said, and paused.

Signy bowed her head, unsure of what this meant.

He continued. "I suppose that there are people who have already concluded I have asked you here to take to my bed." He paused again, looking at her cautiously, as if this was the first time such a thought had come into his own mind. Perhaps it is, she reflected. Last time he saw me I was a bedraggled, dirty and smelly captive, a Jute slave woman. I can guess from the way Cull and the women eyed me I look a lot different now.

The man scrutinised her from top to bottom, as if memorising every aspect of her, and then he spoke again. "Perhaps you do yourself. It's the custom, I know."

She looked up. It was the first time she had seen him clearly, too. He was older than she had imagined, about the same age as her father, she thought. His hair was dark, but there were signs of grey here and there, and it was thinning a little. The creases around his eyes were deeper than those of a young man, and there was a scar across his face. Now she was close to him, she saw that he looked tired and strained. Perhaps he would also rather be somewhere else than in this hut?

"That is not why you are here, Mistress…er…Signy. Tomorrow, I plan to have a parley with the leader of the remaining Jutes. I have been told his name is Oswulf."

Signy dared not speak. Probably he would prefer to be at home, she thought, with his wife and children, a beaker of ale in his hand, maybe listening to the song of a bard.

"I need someone to convey my words to him in a way which he will clearly understand. I would have preferred someone…" He hesitated. "I would have preferred a man," he continued, "but we must use the tools which the gods put in our hands, and I realise you might have some influence with these people."

Signy remained silent. His look suggested he was a man who thought a great deal, who could play with words. Maybe he was a poet himself, she wondered, or invented riddles.

"My friend Gisla," he began, "tells me that you were the concubine of one of the leaders of the Jutes, one Chief Thorgill. Is that correct?"

Concubine…What on earth was that? It was not a Saxon word. So far, she had been careful to avoid telling them she was Thorgill's wife, and it might be best to continue.

"Yes, my lord," she said, hoping the word "concubine" was not an insult.

"This man, this Thorgill, was the leader of the first band who came in this direction. Is that correct?"

She nodded.

"My friend also told me that you are a Saxon, from the east, by your accent. How did you come to be with the Jutes, then?"

"I was kidnapped and sold as a slave, sir. Chief Thorgill bought me from a trader."

The man said nothing, merely sat, apparently lost in thought. Signy could no longer hold silent.

"My lord, can you tell me what happened? Where is my master…and his men?"

The man looked straight at her.

"They are dead, Mistress. Your master and every one of his men."

Signy felt a shock run throughout her body. It was all she could do to hold herself upright on the stool. The man saw it, too. A tinge of sympathy softened his features, but his voice continued calm and low.

"Chief Thorgill was undoubtedly a brave man, and a skilled warrior. He fought hard, but he made two mistakes. First, he led his band into my province last year. He killed an old man and his wife, friends of mine, and their grandson, and he stole their property. He also allowed his men to rape and carry off the servants of the house, and he sacrificed an innocent man to his gods." Now a tone of anger had crept into his voice. Signy got a grip of herself and sat straight on the stool, observing him.

"Then he made a second mistake, and a worse mistake for a leader. He underestimated his enemy. I would guess he assumed we were weak and unprepared. Because of that, he led his men into a trap. He paid the penalty for his mistakes." The anger in his voice had passed. Now he just looked sad.

Signy's mind went to Helga, to her friends in Juteland, to the mothers, wives and sisters who would never see their menfolk again. She felt tears welling in her eyes.

"I understand your sorrow," said the man, assuming she was thinking of Thorgill. "I too have lost friends in the battle. There are moments when I also feel like weeping."

Signy sniffed and gulped, and then raised her head. Her eyes met his. She felt like a fool. What was she doing breaking down in front of this man? She wiped away her tears with the sleeve of her dress.

"The past cannot be undone, Mistress…Signy. And tomorrow you will have a chance to shape the future, to help me ensure that no more men die, no more women in my country are weeping for their husbands and sons." He paused for a moment. "No more women standing on some far shore looking out for their own menfolk who never reappear, either."

"What do you want me to do?" she whispered.

"We have been watching Oswulf, and tomorrow he will return to the camp."

She plucked up the courage to ask, "Was it you who had been hiding in the ruins?"

"It was not me, personally, of course," he answered with a slight smile, distorted by the scar on his cheek, "but yes, we have been waiting and watching. Our scouts were observing the – your – camp from the ruins."

"I saw traces, the place where he lay, the marks of his horse's hooves. I didn't know what they meant," she sighed.

The man smiled again. He seemed to have relaxed a little. "Perhaps if more of your people had been as observant as you, they would not have been in the situation they are today."

"And Chief Skalgrim?" she asked. "What happened to him? I think we saw some of his men in the night."

"There was a battle, again," he replied, taking her seriously, she thought. "Many deaths on both sides, but we prevailed. Skalgrim, the leader, and his house warriors are dead. Many of his men, too, and others taken captive. Only Oswulf and his band are left. Either we fight him and he and his men die like the others, or he has the sense to go back to his own land and never return. That is the choice I want to give him. I would rather he took a message home as a warning to others, but, if he chooses to fight, then we will fight. Your role will be to repeat my words, exactly as I say them, in Oswulf's own tongue so he understands precisely what I mean. You will be my voice. I hope he will be willing to listen to me. I hope the fact you belonged to the household of one of his chiefs will mean that he is willing to listen to you. I hope we can win this battle with words alone."

"I will be your voice, my lord," she said quietly.

"Thank you," he replied, standing up suddenly, turning away towards his worktable. I belong to this man now, Signy thought. What choice do I have? He might speak softly, but his words are still commands. She had seen his men obey his soft words in Oswulf's camp.

He turned back to her. "My men have prepared a hut for you. It will not be comfortable, but better than the place where I last saw you. I'll place a guard on the door, so you are not molested."

He crossed to the entrance and exchanged a few words with someone waiting outside. Then he beckoned to her.

"Follow this man," he said, indicating a young warrior. "You will be safe. He will find you food. Take care to sleep well. I'll see you in the morning."

He turned back into his hut, and the young warrior led her away.

❧ Chapter 15 ☙

Signy was woken by the sound of horns blasting loudly not far off. She sat up in alarm, fearing that the camp was under attack. But the horn sounds died away to a sporadic bleat, and the sound of men's laughter filtered in through the cloth covering the entrance to her shelter.

"Ah, thought that would wake you up!" The young warrior stuck his head through the opening. He disappeared once more, while Signy struggled to her feet. There was little to distinguish camp life among the Jutes and among the Britons, she concluded, rubbing her back where she had been lying on the hard ground.

Just then, Cull peered into the hut, saw she was decent and came in. He was carrying a gold neckband and a jewelled brooch.

"Gisla thought you should wear these," he said.

She took the neckband. It was heavy, heavier than any neckband she had worn while with the Jutes. Had it really come from the grim Saxon chief? Why had he honoured her like this? He must know what sort of person she was. Cull fitted a cloak around her shoulders and fastened it with the jewelled brooch.

"Merely a loan, of course," Cull pointed out, "while you are serving the governor, but Chief Gisla thought you must look impressive, as if you've already earned a special place among us."

He stepped back and examined her.

"Very fine." He smiled and whistled. "You're a damned fine-looking young woman, do you know that?"

A smile from the young warrior, returning with a beaker of ale and a bowl, revealed he probably thought the same.

The area outside the hut was thronged with men. There was scarcely room to squeeze between them. Signy tailed the red-headed Briton as he pushed through the crowd until they reached several well-dressed and important-looking people standing around the governor. As Cull approached, they turned, looking past him and directly at her.

"Here she is," said the governor, "our interpreter."

The big Saxon, Chief Gisla, stepped towards her, examining her.

"Quite a princess today," he said with a slightly mocking smile, tapping her on her shoulder, "to have been found in a pigsty!"

He is so difficult to read, she thought. To him, I must be just an East Saxon farm girl who had been bedded by a pirate, and yet…am I a possible princess to him or merely a dressed-up pirate's whore?

The governor stepped forward and took her arm, and his touch made her feel more at ease. He gestured towards the other men.

"You have already met Chief Gisla," he said, "although it was dark, and the surroundings were not the best. And this is Prince Merwyn of the Welsh, my daughter's husband, and Chief Paul of Breedon, and Chief Horvath."

The three strangers greeted her with minimal changes in their facial expressions, as if they were examining livestock. It was clear they shared the same doubts as the big Saxon.

"I think we should start," said Gisla. "It'll take some time for us to line up on the road, and we need to get to the Jutes before they manage to load their boats and flee."

"I would be quite content if they fled," said the man introduced as Prince Merwyn. She now recognised him as the man with the sing-song voice who had led the escort for the prisoners.

"No," said the governor, "Gisla is right. We need to confront them and convince them they should not come back. Let's get moving."

The leaders made their way through the camp to a gate in the palisade. Cull and Signy followed. When they passed through the gap, Signy found herself looking down over a steep hill defended by pits and sharpened wooden stakes. At the foot of the hill lay a field, trampled and muddy. On the far side of the field, she saw a vast number of horses waiting. She had never seen so many horses in her life, not even at the horse fair. They continued down the hill, picking their way among the obstacles. When they reached the column of horses, the governor and Chief Gisla walked towards the head of the line. Cull, taking Signy by the arm, stayed a few steps behind. At the very front of the column, three men with lur horns were standing in the road, and beside them were three other men holding banners which fluttered in the morning breeze, one embroidered with a red dragon, the second with a rearing bear, and the third with a golden lion, stretching its claws across the field of white cloth.

Oh, by the gods, she said to herself, and Thorgill thought this land was undefended!

Gisla gave a signal, and the men with the horns and banners mounted the horses at the head of the column. Behind them were two more handsome, splendidly decorated mounts, and behind these were the two modest beasts that Signy and Cull had ridden on their journey down from the mine. Gisla gave another signal, and the men with the horns put them to their lips and blew a long blast, the wail she had heard earlier. Signy, hearing a noise behind her, turned and saw an endless number of men getting onto the horses standing patiently behind them.

Cull spoke to her. "We should mount, too. Do you need help?"

She shook her head, at once feeling the weight of the necklace around her neck.

Gisla was still standing beside his horse. He glanced back at her and frowned. Then he reached over to one of the grooms and took the length of rope the boy had been using as a lead. He walked over.

"Hold out your hands, wrists together!"

She did as he ordered.

Without saying more, he bound her hands and tied them to her bridle, and then drew the rope across and knotted it to Cull's saddle.

"Hold her tight!" he said, in a most unfriendly manner. He might have loaned her his jewellery to make the impression she was trusted, but he obviously did not trust her.

The governor raised his arm in the air, the horn players gave another blast, and two by two the horses were urged into motion.

Signy recognised the route, the long straight road across the fields to the junction where the ruined village lay. It had taken them much of the day to walk this way on foot. On horseback, they arrived in sight of the remains of the Jute camp by early afternoon. As they reached the junction, the men in the lead raised the banners, and the horn players began to blow, the wailing sound drifting across the fields. This time the Britons were not hiding sneakily or riding in disguise. They wanted the Jutes to know they were coming. When the men with the banners reached the north–south road, the entire line of riders came to a halt. The horns blew again, and the man carrying the lion flag trotted forward along the road until he reached the path leading to the camp. There he shouted at the top of his voice. To Signy, his words were indistinct, but she understood he was calling the Jutes to come out and meet them. There was no direct response to his call, but from her vantage point on horseback, Signy could see men moving around in the wrecked camp. Probably they knew their comrades were dead or captives. Probably they were looking out at the Britons and arguing about what they should do. Some would want to defend their honour and fight to the death. Others would be fearing the same fate as their comrades and wishing they were once more sitting by their own fire, sleeping in their own bed at home, and arguing they should launch the boats as quickly as possible. What would Oswulf decide? There was movement in the camp and eventually half a dozen horsemen rode out.

Gisla turned. "Bring her forward," he said to Cull, and then turned to Signy. "Now we'll see what use you are."

He untied the rope from Cull's saddle and refastened it to his own. Then he drew Signy's horse forward until it was level with his, between him and the governor. The Jutes walked their horses towards them and then stopped, shouting distance away. She recognised Oswulf at the head of the group. Most of the other mounted men were typical warriors, men she might have encountered around the camp, but there was one who stood out. He was not a Jute. She would have noticed *him* in the camp. Could he be the man who Oswulf had boasted about, his ally, the Duke? He looked like a Roman, too, like the governor. And yet, and yet, there was something uncomfortably familiar about him, as if she had seen him, but somewhere else, somewhere far, far from this field in Britland. Signy thought she saw the governor shift uneasily on his horse. She glanced across at him and he looked back, the faint trace of a question on his face. When she turned back to look towards Oswulf and his companions, the strange man had pulled his horse alongside the chief's and turned to speak to him. The change in profile gave him away.

"Drusus," she whispered to herself. The man who had leered at her in Factor Titus' booth!

Then she heard the governor's voice beside her.

"This man is Chief Oswulf?"

"Yes, Master."

"Then repeat what I say in a way that a Jute will comprehend."

"Greetings, Chief Oswulf," the governor said, slowly, in his stilted Saxon. Signy repeated the words in Jutish, as loudly as she could without straining her voice.

There was no immediate response, so the governor continued.

"I am Marcus Lucullus Ursinus, Chief of the Dumantes, from the west of Britain, and leader of the army that stands behind me."

Signy was tempted to glance back, to check that the army was still there, to estimate what impression the assembled troops might give to Oswulf, but with an effort she concentrated on repeating the words of the man on the horse alongside hers.

"Your men entered my country and slaughtered my countrymen." He seemed to be struggling to find the right words, not surprising, since he was still speaking in Saxon, a language that was too obviously not his own. He stopped, glanced across and nodded. Signy translated what he said. Out of the corner of her eye, she saw Gisla watching her, grimacing. She knew she had said nothing wrong, not added anything nor taken anything away. Did he even understand what she was saying when she spoke Jutish? Supposing he misunderstood something she said. She felt a little anxiety creep in.

The governor began again. "I am a man of peace, and my countrymen only want to live in peace. But if our peace is broken, we will take up arms in our defence, and we will seek retribution." Signy translated his words, and she saw this time that Gisla nodded towards the governor. I suppose now you are satisfied with my translation, she thought.

The governor continued. "We have defeated your companions, Chief Skalgrim and Chief Thorgill, and they and their men have gone to meet their ancestors." Signy translated once again.

The governor continued, "I have come to offer you peace, to allow you and your men to return to your boats, and to leave our country without any more bloodshed."

Signy repeated his words. The governor stopped talking as if he was waiting for a reply. Oswulf sat on his horse, looking grim and impassive. Signy watched him. She tried to put herself in his place. She had seen and heard him speak often enough. She felt a growing worry. The way the man beside her was speaking was not the way to address a man like Oswulf. She knew Oswulf's kind of man. She knew what language Oswulf would respect, and it was not reasonable words. The governor sounded like a merchant bargaining with a fellow trader. Men like Oswulf only respected boasting, aggression, threats of violence.

Then the Jute began to speak. "My friend here says that you are a liar and not to be trusted. He says you killed his brother for no good reasons, and for that he has a blood feud with you, and you deserve to die."

For a moment, Signy was confused by Oswulf's reply, but she repeated it in Saxon.

"That has nothing to do with you and I, Chief Oswulf. I am here to discuss your attack on my land and on my people."

"A blood feud with my friend is a blood feud with me," replied the chief.

"What your friend says has nothing to do with the offer I have made to you, to leave in peace and never return."

"We could settle everything now, man against man, you against my friend."

That was a reasonable offer, thought Signy. They could mark out a square with sticks, and the two could fight to the death. From what she had seen of the two men, she did not doubt for a moment that the governor would make short work of Oswulf's balding ally.

However, Oswulf then spoke again. "My friend says he is a noble man, and it would be beneath his dignity to fight a mere farmer and thief."

You friend's a damned coward, with no honour at all, no more than you have yourself, thought Signy, and her blood began to boil. She felt an urge to speak, to tell the Jute what had happened and what fate waited for him in words that he couldn't avoid understanding. She looked at Marcus, but he seemed still to be waiting patiently for a reply to his offer.

She felt she had to do something. She felt she had to act. She could not help herself. She could not remain silent.

"If your friend is too cowardly to fight like a warrior, then you should listen to the words of the king and tremble," she shouted. "You know me, Oswulf…Signy, Thorgill's wife. I served you the mead horn in Thorgill's hall at harvest time, and in your own hall at the feast where you planned this raid. Look at these men behind us, and know there are hundreds more, all skilled warriors and mounted on sturdy horses. Each one is ready to drink from your skull and the skulls of your men, to nail your heads above their door. And even now their sons are marching home with your women as their slaves. They have slaughtered Skalgrim's band, and they have cut down Thorgill's band. Every man is dead. The crows have eaten their eyes, and the wolves have eaten their hearts. The dogs and pigs are feeding on their carcasses. Witches and ogres are pissing on their graves. Thorgill's helmet and sword are nailed to the wall of the king's house, and I, who was proud to be Thorgill's woman, have been warming the bed of this mighty man. If you don't leave at once, his men will slaughter you like a pig at the start of winter, and every one of your men likewise. You will die like dogs, food for vermin. You will be dishonoured in the halls of Juteland for evermore as fools and knaves who rashly took on foe incomparably more powerful and cunning than you are. Your mothers will tear their hair. Your wives will have to take skraelings to their beds in shame of your memory. Your children will have to marry trolls."

She stopped to gather her breath.

Oswulf shouted angrily. "I'm not going to listen to your gabble, you treacherous Saxon bitch! How dare you speak to me!"

Signy heard Gisla shout out beside her, in stumbling Jutish.

"She speaks the words of the king!" He glanced quickly towards Signy. "At least what he should have been saying," she heard him mutter to himself, and then he turned to the governor. "Advance the men, Marcus, slowly."

Signy glanced at Gisla fearfully. Her stomach clenched. She could have sunk right through the horse into the ground. She was supposed to have repeated the governor's words, and instead she had only blurted out her own foolish thoughts. Had she made a mistake? Had she pushed these men into a battle?

The governor raised his arm and waved to the horsemen behind him.

"I don't know what you said," he hissed, "but you are to repeat my words, nothing more."

She was about to try to explain, when he spoke again in a calm and reasonable tone. "Keep your tongue straight in your mouth if you want to keep your head on your shoulders. Now repeat after me. You cannot defend the camp, Chief Oswulf. My men have burned the gates, pulled down the palisade and filled the ditch."

Signy watched Oswulf as he spoke. Listen to him, she thought, desperately, please, Oswulf, listen to him, otherwise everything I said will come true. She took a deep breath, collected herself and repeated the governor's words exactly, straining to sound calm and reasonable herself. Gisla looked over to her. She glanced across at him nervously. The big Saxon gave her a smile. Did she see him wink his eye, too? Had she won him over?

Oswulf began to speak. "My men are brave and valiant warriors and you, so-called king, will lose many men if you dare attack us."

Signy repeated his words in the Saxon language, taking care to leave out the "so-called".

The Jute chief spoke again, and Signy translated.

"I have many captives from among the Britons," he said, "and every one of them will die if you dare to attack."

As she finished speaking, Oswulf turned and shouted something back to the camp. Some more of his men appeared from among the shattered remnants of the palisade, including his ally, Ravnberg, and they were dragging three captives with them, two short-haired men and a woman. The Jutes pushed them roughly forward until they arrived at the place where Oswulf was sitting on his horse.

One of the captive men started to speak. There was no need for her to translate, no possibility. It was all she could do to follow him as he spoke in British.

"Oh, King! I am Alban, son of Chief Gerontius of Durolanium. This is my brother, and this my sister."

Signy looked at the three young people. Oswulf must have been successful on his raid and captured their town, she thought. How many captives did he have in his camp and how much booty?

Oswulf leaned down from his horse and spoke to Ravnberg, who lifted his sword and, without any warning, hacked at the young man who had just spoken. The Briton fell to the ground, blood pouring from a wound. The woman beside him screamed, and the other man cried out. Ravnberg stabbed a couple more times and kicked his victim as he lay on the ground.

Oswulf spoke again, and Signy translated his words, her voice trembling. "Now you can see I am not bluffing. These are my conditions. My men will be allowed to board their boats unmolested and take their booty with them. While they do this, your men will not approach nearer, or else all the captives will suffer the fate of this man."

"He wants to save his face," said Gisla.

"Tell him I accept his conditions," said Marcus, "but on two terms of my own. First, he has to leave the captives behind him, unharmed, and second, he is to swear a holy oath in front of his men that he will depart and leave Britannia in peace."

Signy translated the words. When she was finished, Oswulf shouted angrily that he wasn't going to accept any conditions put forward by a woman, especially a Saxon bitch and a mere whore of a slave.

"He refuses to bargain through a woman's voice, Master," said Signy.

The governor turned to her. She saw anger flashing in his eyes. "This man is tempting Fortuna," he said. "Say this. We are given the tools that we need by the gods, and we should therefore respect them. This woman was brought to me by the gods as a trophy in battle to speak my words, and I am proud to use the gift of the gods. Signy, use their name for the god of war so they know I think you are a gift from the war god."

"Tyr," she said. "Tyr, the god of war."

As she spoke, a grim smile spread over the face of the Jute leader.

"You are a cunning man with words, so-called king," he called out, "and I hope you are as skilled in bed with Thorgill's witch."

Signy felt herself redden as she translated the words. Before the governor had a chance to react, Oswulf continued, and she was forced to listen to him again.

"Thorgill was a fool to ride over the hills when there was booty for all in the east. He was a fool to listen to a woman, that same strumpet and harlot who is sitting beside you, who bewitched him and spun spells on him, and led him into reckless ways. His rashness brought trouble on him, and on his men, while his whore has already wriggled her way into his enemy's bed."

Signy translated, although omitting the insulting references to herself. She could hear Gisla chuckling. He obviously understood well enough. So you think this is amusing? she reflected.

Oswulf continued. "There will be no need for me to convey any message to the Jutes to stay away. The empty boats and the brotherless men will serve well enough. But, since I'm a man of honour myself, I'll let it be known that there's a chief who calls himself king in the west of Britain, leader of many skilled warriors who only wish to be left in peace to enjoy their women. That should get their attention."

Signy translated approximately, and as she did so, Oswulf drew out his sword. He was about to raise it, when the man beside him, the so-called Duke, took his arm. They exchanged a few words, and Signy saw Oswulf laugh.

The man Drusus urged his horse one step towards them. She could not make out a word of what he was saying, but evidently the governor did so. She saw him turn red and angrily reply, before turning to her.

"Do you know this man, this Briton?"

"No, my lord, but I've seen him once before in Juteland."

"Do you wish to return to the Jutes?"

Signy was horrified. Was she now going to be turned over to Oswulf and Uncle Drusus? "No, Master," she gasped, "they would kill me."

She saw the governor glance at Gisla, and the big Saxon shook his head.

"Then you stay."

The governor spoke again, and Signy heard Oswulf laugh.

"May you enjoy that barren witch. May she cast the same spells on you as she cast on Thorgill, and in case she is not enough to satisfy you, mighty king, you can have this one as well." He waved towards the woman hostage, before raising his sword above his head. Signy listened as he swore he would depart in peace and never return.

The governor watched him, and when Oswulf had returned his sword to his scabbard, he too swore, and asked Signy to repeat his oath to Gisla, so that the Saxon, a man, could call out the words.

"I consider myself a friend and a brother to the Jutes. May we live in peace together. I swear that my men and I will remain on the west side of the road until you and your followers have boarded their ships and left. In the name of God and his son, Jesus Christ. Amen."

Signy did not need to translate, as Gisla repeated the oath in half-jumbled Jutish, and swore by quite a different god, and in reply Oswulf spoke again.

"He is letting the woman go," said Signy, "as a token of his sincerity." The Jute warriors released their grip and Ravnberg pushed the woman towards the Britons. At the same time, they dragged the second man back towards their camp. He cried out and he struggled but was silenced by a blow. The young woman half stumbled forward, and then looked around helplessly, clearly not knowing whether to continue or follow her brother back to the Jutes' camp.

"Call her," whispered Signy. "She doesn't dare to come."

She heard the man beside her call out, "You may come to us. Run, before he changes his mind."

The woman began to walk hesitantly, until Cull suddenly dashed out between the horses, across the space towards her. He caught hold of her, lifting her from her feet, and carried her back towards the waiting Britons.

As the Jutes retreated, the governor drew his horse up beside Signy's. Then he took out a knife and leaned across. She thought he might be about to stab her, but instead he cut the bonds around her wrists. Gisla saw him do it, untied the rope from his horse, and handed it to her.

"You are a free woman, Mistress Signy," the governor said.

"Thank you for not swapping me for the princess," she said. "I may be a mere slave girl, but I will repay you one day."

A thoughtful expression came over the governor's face. "I don't understand why Drusus was with Oswulf. Why did he want you?"

"I saw him only once," said Signy, "at a trading place in Juteland, years ago, him and his son – no, no, his nephew."

"My enemies conspire together," the governor sighed. "It's to be expected."

Should I tell him what I heard about "the Duke"? Better not, she thought. A mere slave should not know about such matters.

"If he is your enemy, he is my enemy, too," she replied instead.

❧ Chapter 16 ❧

Signy turned her horse towards the road through the ruined village, drained by the tension of the negotiations, by the insults she had received, and by the sight of the young man hacked to death before her eyes. She had done her task as best she could, she thought, and now they had said she was free. Free to do what? Free to go where? She had no one, nothing. She did not notice the curious, even respectful, glances. She only vaguely heard when the governor leaned over to her and thanked her, saying to his listening companions that he would be in her debt for ever. She only reacted when Gisla pulled his horse alongside hers and reached over and patted her on the leg. For a moment, she felt offended and threatened, but then she realised he meant well.

"You got it right, my dear. A brute like that wouldn't understand Marcus' fine words. He needed the message plain and simple, however angry he got," he chuckled. "I was just trying to imagine his own wife. Would she be worth fighting for?"

Signy looked at him, a little perplexed. She shook her head, and Gisla laughed again.

"My baubles…keep them. You earned them, and in a decent enough manner, but," he added, tapping her arm where the bracelet dangled, "don't forget, you're one of us now," and with that he rode off. Who is us, she thought, warily watching the big Saxon leave.

As the leaders reached the main group of troops, many of the waiting riders had already dismounted and hobbled their horses. Some were scavenging brushwood and branches to make fires. The governor, Gisla and the men who had been with them disappeared among their followers, giving orders, issuing instructions. Signy was left by herself, not quite knowing what to do. She dismounted and, using the rope that had formerly been her bonds, she tied her horse to a projecting stump, a fruit tree that must have been cut down for firewood – by who, the Jutes or the Britons? Either way, there would be no more fruit from that tree for years. She took off the heavy necklace, undid the brooch and folded the cloak, and put them into a bag that was slung over the horse.

She heard Cull's voice coming down the road and looked up. He was talking to the younger Saxon she had seen earlier in the day. They had both stripped to their tunics and were striding briskly towards her. They greeted her, seeming now to accept her as one of their fellows.

"Horvath and I are going to collect the body of the young man who they killed," said Cull.

"What has happened to the lady?" asked Signy, realising she was not the only woman in the camp. There was another, in a worse situation than she was, who had been taken captive and then seen her brother cut down by her side.

"Fulvia?" said Horvath, and pointed back along the road.

"I'll go and find her," Signy said.

She found the sorrowing woman alone by a campfire. She put her arms around her and whispered into her ear, not quite knowing what she was saying or if Fulvia could understand a word.

Signy awoke with a start, a hand shaking her shoulder.

"You were calling out," said a stranger's voice from a face she only dimly recognised. She had been dreaming that she had fallen off Thorgill's boat, and no matter how hard she swam, she could not reach the shore.

The chill of dawn was still in the air, but the camp was waking, men talking quietly, the sound of the horses grazing. There was no food to cook, little enough to share in this deserted and plundered place, and Signy and Fulvia sat by the remains of the fire, waiting to be told what to do next. After a while, a messenger ambled up, saying, "You're to come to the chief's council."

They tidied themselves the best they could and followed.

The governor, Gisla, the prince and the other chiefs were sitting around a fire in the middle of the camp. The governor rose as they approached and greeted them. His council looked more like a group of bandits than patrician warriors. They must have spent the night in the open beside a fire just as we did, thought Signy.

"Mistress Fulvia, Mistress Signy," said the governor in greeting, and beckoned the women to sit. He turned back to the men right away, continuing to speak quickly, though his eyes betrayed he was talking about Fulvia.

"You don't understand a word, do you, my dear?" said Gisla. The governor stopped, clearly irritated by the interruption. Gisla held up one finger and turned to Signy. "We can't stay here," he said, "but we have to make sure the Jutes clear off. Then Marcus has promised to escort Mistress Fulvia and her people home. It'll take a couple of days. We can't all go…just a few of us."

"You will ride with Merwyn," said the governor hastily, as the group of men got to their feet, "over the hills to Competum Novum, and wait until we get back."

What choice did she have but to do as she was told, in a foreign land, among strangers?

When Prince Merwyn gave the signal for the main army to turn towards the hills and start the journey home, Signy rode up the line of men until she was just behind him. How odd, she thought, that I've travelled this road with the prince before. Does he even recognise me as one of those exhausted, wretched, stumbling captives?

The day was well advanced by the time the column reached the mining area at the summit, where they had to stay for the night. Signy tied her horse at the edge of the trees and went on a search, hoping to find the other women who had been taken prisoner with her. Perhaps she could use her change in fortune to help them. She walked among the ruins and fallen stones until she found the roofless hut which had been their prison, but it was empty.

"My lord," she asked the prince at the evening meal, "where has everyone gone who was here before? The prisoners, the old men, the women?"

"We sent them away," he replied, "in case we had to fight. The women and the old men back to their homes, the prisoners…I can't say where they might be."

In the morning, they rose early, and for the first time, Signy saw the valley stretching below, the fields green with newly sprouted and bountiful crops, the river with lush meadows on either side where cattle were grazing. She thought back to her parents' poor farm – a few small fields cleared from the forest, a cow and a pig. The view seemed like paradise. No wonder Thorgill had wanted to return, perhaps dreaming of making this land his own. To the side of the road, she saw the house that Thorgill had raided. Even now, when some parts were still a skeleton of burned timbers and others only roughly repaired, she could hardly believe her eyes. Is Martha in there, she wondered, reunited with her man, resuming the life which had been so horribly interrupted? She strained her eyes for her former maid, but, of course, there was no sign of her. There were, however, plenty of people at the side of the road who waved and cheered as they passed by. The news of the victories over the Jutes had already spread across the countryside. Has anyone heard my contribution, Signy wondered, hopefully not the whole story, but only the ending.

The troop continued on, down the hill past the villa and between the fields. Signy knew they were heading towards a town. Martha had used a British name, Four Corners. Competum Novum, the governor had called it, such a complicated and strange name. She expected to see a cluster of wooden houses, huddled together at a road junction, smoky, black and stained, like at Danborg or Puttby. At first, she did not recognise the town as they approached, only seeing a long wall stretched across the road before them, curving around to the left and right, like the palisade of an enormous camp. As they came nearer, she saw the wall was constructed of stone, and the road ran straight up to it and in under an archway.

Signy could never have imagined the sight which met her eyes. Stone-paved streets which led in every direction, lined by neat stone houses, some thatched and some tiled. Small shops with their goods spread in front of them, a bakehouse, a shop selling meat, another with shoes and leather goods. Just as they reached an open area where four roads met, the prince beckoned her to follow as he passed through a gateway and into a courtyard. This must be some sort of inn or hostel, Signy concluded, similar to the ones I stayed in while I was travelling with Laurentius. The walls of the courtyard were painted white, with the windows and doorways picked out in red. She heard the sound of running water, and saw, in the middle of the yard, not a well head, but a stone urn with water flowing over the sides and draining away through a round basin. Without thinking, she jumped down and led her thirsty horse to the fountain.

A voice brought her back to reality. It was Prince Merwyn calling her. A servant took her horse before she followed him through a low archway into the building. Inside, the walls were also painted red and white, and she was amazed to see the floor was decorated in a dazzling black-and-white pattern made up of small stones. The prince stopped by a doorway and knocked. There was a voice from inside, and he entered. Signy followed. Seated at a table was a young man, blond and muscular, a younger version of Chief Gisla. The prince greeted him cheerfully.

"Edwulf, my friend, may I present the young lady who Marcus dug out to help us negotiate with the Jutes, a fellow Saxon, am I right?"

Signy recalled the name from her first meeting with the governor as the young Saxon looked her up and down.

"Edwulf Gislasson," he said, saluting somewhat dubiously. "Marcus did send a couple of messages about an interpreter, but I must admit I didn't fully grasp who he meant."

The prince laughed. "I'm already planning a poem, and we'll sing it at the next feast." He turned to Signy. "What do you say, Mistress Signy, would you like the bards to sing your praises?"

I've heard the bards sing men's praises, she thought, and it was all lies.

"I'm sure you can do a great job with a poem," said Edwulf, with a grin, "but let's leave planning the feasting until a future occasion." He turned to Signy. "I wasn't expecting a woman guest. That bit my wife's father forgot to include in the message. Now we need to find you a suitable room. The whole hostel has been taken over as our headquarters, and of course, we are all men. I suppose we could lodge you in the town."

"I wouldn't do that," said Merwyn, serious for a moment, "in the circumstances."

"No, I suppose not," said Edwulf, and scratched his short beard. "Well, if you can just wait here a moment, I'll go and find a servant to speak to the hostel keeper, and we'll find a spot for you."

He went out, his arm around Prince Merwyn's shoulders, and Signy was left alone in the room. At first, she just gazed at the painted walls, the decorated ceiling, and the floor which was laid out with pictures. In the middle was the image of a man, almost naked, carrying a winged staff rather like Irmengaard's. She bent down and touched her fingers to it for good luck. Then she stood up, and taking a pace or two backwards, found herself by the table where Chief Edwulf had been sitting. Lying on the table was a wooden tablet like the one she had seen the governor holding when she had first come into his hut, those few days before, the same one, perhaps. The tablet was made of two halves, each one filled with wax, and scratched into the wax were all sorts of marks. She recognised them as being writing, words, like she had seen inscribed on some of the pottery and jewels in Thorgill's house, on the stone in the ruined village, or the magic signs Oswulf's priest had drawn when he wanted to call on the gods. Beside the tablet was another rectangular object of a type she had never seen before. When she tried to pick it up, it fell apart in her hand, and she gasped. The object was made up of a lot of sheets, thin and almost transparent, and on the sheets were more words, one after another and, here and there, small pictures of many colours. She took one sheet and turned it carefully, and there were more words, and another, with more words. If words were magic signs, this must be a sacred object of some sort, she thought, and carefully put it down. She took up the tablet to examine it more closely. Just then, Edwulf returned with a broad smile on his face.

"We've found you a bed," he said. "The servant's just moving your things there."

"I don't have any things," she stuttered, "just the bag on my horse, my cloak and—"

"There was a message from Marcus about a chest to be delivered to you. Aren't those your things?"

"My chest, my chest, my little chest…yes, those are my things," she cried, and then she sighed. "I'm sorry, my lord, it's been so difficult. I hardly know where I am."

"I hope you feel you're among friends here," said Edwulf. "Marcus seems to think highly of you. In the message, he asked that we take special care of you."

The Saxon smiled again. He noticed she had the tablet in her hands and reached out to take it from her.

"Is this the message?" she asked, handing him the tablet. "I've never learned to read or write. What's written here?"

Edwulf chuckled.

"No, Mistress, that isn't the message. I was just making a list of supplies." He ran his finger down the tablet. "Oats, 10 sacks; Barley, 15 sacks; Rye, 8 sacks. We've enough to make bread for a couple of days, but if we don't send the army home soon, we'll all have to survive on beer."

"And this," she said, laying her hand on the book and opening the pages.

"That?" He glanced up at her. "I think Marcus left it. Sometimes we young men laugh at him behind his back because he likes to read so much. But this time he taught us a lesson. He found the idea for the ambush in the forest in one of these old books he's been reading."

"Is it some kind of magic in this…book, then, my lord?" asked Signy.

"Well, let me see," said the Saxon, frowning. He picked up the book and opened it at the first sheet. "It's written in Latin, and my Latin's not much good, despite my wife's efforts to teach me. Here: 'The whole of Gaul is divided into three parts.' Oh, I know this one. Amanda made me read it once, part of it, anyway. It's all put down by a man named Julius Caesar, telling about his wars in Gaul. Sometimes, I think my wife's father imagines him-self to be Julius Caesar, although old Julius came to a sad end."

"Oh?"

"His friends stabbed him to death," said Edwulf, sighing, "so they say, but it was many years ago and in a far-away country…long before I was born. That's what I've heard, anyway."

Signy looked from the young man to the book.

"And these are his own words, telling his own story?"

"Something like that, I suppose."

"Do you think a girl like me could learn to read, and maybe write as well, like you can?" she said in a small voice.

"I don't see why not," laughed Edwulf. "I was about your age when I learned, and it was a girl who taught me, and she taught me so well, I married her."

Signy was silent, looking at the book and the tablet.

"You're married to the governor's daughter, right?"

"I am, my dear Amanda, and very lucky for that," he answered.

If I find the right person to teach me to read and write, and if I'm good enough at it, they might want to marry me, she thought. She felt her eyes beginning to tear up and was angry at her self-pity. She straightened herself and took a deep breath.

"Perhaps it's best you show me my room," she said, suddenly embarrassed, "and then you can continue with your grain supplies."

She followed Edwulf up some stairs to the upper level, and he showed her into a room, a cleaner and tidier version of the ones she remembered from Juteland. A large window with shutters looked out onto the town. There was a bed, a small table, some stools and her chest.

"Oh, there's my chest." She sighed with relief.

"I'm glad," said Edwulf, "and I can add one thing. I've spoken to the maid, and she'll take you to the bathhouse, but you might need to wait. Most of the men are away, but it would cause a bit of a stir if you turned up while they were bathing."

He laughed, not unpleasantly, though; she must have looked puzzled.

"A bathhouse, what's that?"

The Saxon laughed again. He was obviously a man who found it easy to laugh.

"I was confused myself, years ago when I first came over to Britannia with my father. Why would anyone want to go and sit in a pool of warm water, when they could bathe in a fresh river? My father still refuses to go to the baths." He shrugged. "My wife follows Roman ways, of course, so I've had to get used to the Roman habits."

His eyes twinkled, seeing Signy still perplexed.

"It's like a swimming hole," he said, "except warm and inside, and the bath attendant will clean off all the dirt and sweat from travelling. You should try. I'll tell her to send a servant for you."

With that he left, and she was alone again.

She opened her chest. The clothes were in disarray. Someone had been searching inside. Of course, that's how they had found her riding clothes. She took the garments out, one by one. The bottom tunics, her best ones, were still smooth and neat. Had the things beneath remained untouched? She lifted the length of rough cloth and took out the leather bags she and Martha had placed under it. In one were the herbs and plants that she needed for the medications, and beside it a little wrapper with needles and thread of fine, twisted gut. She put the herbs back and took out the second bag. It had not been touched, either, and inside lay her jewels, the ones Thorgill had taken from the half-burned house she had passed on the road. Sadly, she thought, I can never show them off to anyone, but so long as I have them, I will have something I can barter if I ever need to. She replaced the second bag in the chest and laid the cloth on top. Just in time, as there was a knock on the door, and the voice of a woman behind her.

"Mistress, the master told me to take you to bathe. Will you follow?" With Edwulf she had been able to speak in Saxon. What a relief that had been! The maid sounded like Martha, but she spoke so quickly that Signy barely understood.

She walked after the maid, along the corridor and down the stairs. At the end of a long passageway, they came to the door to the bathhouse. Waiting for her was a robust-looking middle-aged woman. Signy stood still, not knowing what to do.

"Are you the foreign lady they was talking about?" asked the attendant, eyeing her sceptically.

"Yes," said Signy, replying in nervous, broken British. "I not know do."

"Take your clothes off," said the attendant.

Signy lifted her hands and then froze – this woman would see her marks. But the others, in the camp, had made no comments.

Once she was naked, she could only stand and wonder what would happen next. She was willing to try to learn Roman habits, but how to start? Another bucket of cold water? Was that what was meant by a bath?

"Just do as I say, Miss, 'cause more gents'll be along soon, and I don't want them ogling you in this state, which they would. Go through that door and get in the pool. I'll make sure no men come in until you're done. They used to have mixed bathing here, until the bishop put a stop to it. Just as well, if you ask me. All sorts of hanky-panky going on."

It was too much, too many words. Signy did not try to comprehend the woman's prattle anymore, and merely followed her gesture through an arched doorway, where she saw a pool of water.

"Just get in the bath," called the woman from the entrance. "I'll send your clothes to be washed."

Signy gently lowered herself into the pool, until the water reached up to her chin. What a strange feeling, like being in the swimming hole, but warm, warmer than any river. She sat still, feeling her body relax.

The attendant reappeared. "Very well, Miss, time to move on. I've got the gents needing to be in."

Signy climbed up the steps on the far side of the pool and followed the attendant to the next room. The air was baking hot. She could feel the floor burning the soles of her feet. She was sweating, drips running down her face and trickling over her body.

"That's good! It'll clean your pores," shouted the attendant from the doorway, though it did not feel good at all. "You just stay in there for a while and sweat. Get all the dirt out of your system."

Signy felt like bread baking in an oven. All at once she could take it no longer. She hurried through the next doorway, and could immediately feel cool air. Ahead was another inviting pool and she jumped in. The moment she hit the water, she screamed aloud. It was cold, as cold as the river at home in the early spring.

"You seem to have got the idea quickly, Mistress," the attendant commented in an approving manner, when she finally came up. "Now climb out and I'll clean you off."

Signy followed the attendant to the next room.

"Lie on that bench," the woman ordered, picking up a flask and dripping the contents on Signy's back. "It's just oil, Mistress." A scent of flowers filled the air. "There we are, all done."

Signy looked around for her clothes.

"They took them to be washed," the woman said, handing Signy a long robe. "You just pop back to your room and put on some fresh clothes, and you'll feel as good as new."

She did as she was told, and it was true, she did feel good. If this was a Roman habit, she could easily get used to it. Perhaps she was new, a new person, no longer a Jute slave who had been forced to sit in a pigsty, but one of the elegant ladies she had seen on the vases. Not just for a day, as she had been when Martha arranged her hair, but for the rest of her life.

And then she thought of Irmengaard, and a tear came to her eye. She would never see her friend again, never be able to tell her where she was and what she was doing.

Accept the fate the gods send you, her friend had said. *Be prepared!*

No wonder even such a wise woman couldn't see my future, she thought, and if she had, neither of us would have understood what we saw.

☙ Chapter 17 ❧

There was no guard on Signy's door and none at the gate from the hostel to the street, but she was surprised to see an armed man standing in the passage which led to the yard at the rear of the hostel. This piqued her curiosity. Perhaps she would find the missing women there, she thought, and went to investigate. The guard spoke up as she neared him.

"It's better you don't go in there, my lady." She stopped. The guard's words were difficult to follow.

"What? Why not?" she asked.

"Prisoners, dangerous enemies, and sick people," said the guard.

Signy glanced through the gate and saw several women standing by a well in the centre of the yard, talking together.

"Women," she said, pointing. "Not dangerous."

She was unsure what the guard said in reply, perhaps something like "Women from town, treat injured soldiers," but a stubborn feeling grew within her. How dangerous was the yard compared to what she had been through during the last few days?

"You stop me?" she asked.

"No, my lady. Just not a good idea," said the man.

She understood that well enough, but went through, anyway. The women glanced at her as she emerged from the opening into the yard. They were plainly dressed and carrying baskets. Then she realised she was dressed as a lady in the eyes of the guard, in the women's eyes, as a higher class of person, a person you did not stop, you did not question too closely, but whose place was not the rear yard of a hostel.

There was a portico running around the yard, and instead of walking out into the sunshine, which would have inevitably brought her close to the whispering, watching women, Signy walked around under the eaves, in the shade. She saw that the buildings would normally have been used as stables or storerooms, but now she heard the mumble of voices inside. She picked out snatches of British and Saxon. When she heard the Saxon, her curiosity got the better of her, and she looked in at one of the doorways. There were several men inside, some sitting on stools, and a couple lying on low beds.

"Good morning, Miss," said one of the men.

She greeted him politely in return. The men, she reasoned, must be the wounded survivors of the recent battles. She heard steps behind her – one of the women approaching. She stepped back from the doorway to allow her into the room. The wounded soldiers greeted the woman warmly as she busied around.

Signy continued on her way around the yard, until she reached the far side. Here it felt distinctly colder, permanently in the shade, and the buildings were not as clean and bright as those nearer the entrance. She saw a man, standing in the shadow of the corner.

"Wait, Miss," said the man, stepping forward and showing himself to be another guard.

Signy stopped, but then her ear caught the sound of voices once again.

"Who there?" she asked.

"Prisoners, Miss," replied the guard. "Dangerous enemy prisoners."

"Jutes?" she asked.

"Don't know, Miss. They just told me to come here and make sure none of them get out…" The guard said more, something derisive, judging by the expression on his face, but there were too many words, too quickly. She was lost after the first few.

"I look them?" she asked. The guard continued to frown, obviously puzzled why anyone would want to be bothered with a lot of wounded enemies, especially a finely dressed young woman. "I help them," she added.

The guard looked even more confused. "Why would you want to help them? The sooner they die, the better," he muttered, but his comments were wasted.

"Can't stop you, Miss," he finally acknowledged.

Signy looked into the first room. The low whispering stopped as her shadow filled the doorway. The smell of untreated wounds, of urine and excrement filled her nose. Someone lying in the shadows moaned, and another voice called out, "Who's there?"

The voice brought back memories, memories of a farmstead, memories of young men laughing among themselves at the thought of the adventure that awaited them. Instead, they were lying in a stinking cowshed, probably expecting to die just as the guard was hoping.

"I'm Signy," she said in Jutish, "Chief Thorgill's wife, taken prisoner by the Britons." That at least was no lie, even if it was not the entire truth.

As her eyes adjusted to the gloom, she could make out the figures inside the room. She felt the tension and heard the slight adjustments of posture as she spoke.

"We're from Skalgrim's crew," said one of the men. "They've left us here."

"Can you get us some help, Mistress?" said another. "Bjornfot here is in pain. He's dying, Mistress, but does he have to become a rotting corpse before he dies?"

She took another step into the room. Some of the men wore rough bandages over sword cuts, and another still had on the jerkin he had been wearing when he had been stabbed by a spear. Blood stained the site of the wound. At the back of the room, a man lay on the floor. She could not see him well, but she did not need to. His wound had become infected; she could smell it. She remembered a case her mother had treated, a man who had been out hunting and tripped over a fallen branch. The javelin he had been carrying had pierced his belly. He had lingered for weeks. She could hardly bear the thought of it, even now.

"How many of you are there?"

"There are six of us in here, counting Bjornfot, and some more in the next room, and perhaps the next after that. They won't let us out. We have to piss and shit in the corner. My lady, we're all going to die if we're left here."

These young men would have gladly died on the battlefield, facing the enemy with honour, but they were frightened boys now, abandoned in this dark and stinking room, ashamed to have been taken prisoner. What can I do to help them, she thought, brushing a buzzing fly away from her face. The medicines in my chest…I didn't have a chance to use them in the camp, but now they could help. And I can fetch water from the well I saw in the courtyard. I doubt the guard'll stop me.

"Very well," she said. "Promise me you'll not cause trouble, and I'll try to help you. My mother was a wise woman and I learned some of her skills."

Another one of the men spoke up. "Mistress, I remember now. We heard in the camp that we should go to Thorgill's wife if we needed medicines. One of his men told us, but we never greeted you, Mistress. We didn't need you then…"

Most of all they needed hope. They needed hope so that they would take care of themselves. She looked around the room and noticed there was a shuttered window high in the far wall.

"Does that window open?" she asked.

"No, lady. It's barred on the outside."

"I'll come back," she said. "And when I do, those of you who can stand or move must get to work."

She left the room and continued on her way. She did not need to ask the situation in the neighbouring rooms, if they could be called that. A glance in the doorway told her that the situation was similar.

The guard watched her leave through the gateway at the far end of the yard. She stepped out into the alleyway that ran behind the hostel. From there she could see the wooden shutters which blocked the light and air from getting into the storerooms where the men were housed. If she stood on tiptoes, she could just reach the wooden bar that held them closed. She reached up and pushed. The bar would not move. She stretched her arms. Her strength was at its limit, but she still could not move the bar. Despairing, she stepped back, and looking around, noticed a piece of timber lying further up the alley. She picked it up. It seemed solid enough. She reached up again and, using both arms, struck the bar with the length of timber. It shifted slightly. She struck again, and there was clear movement. A third blow, and with a sudden jerk it came loose, tumbled to the ground, and the shutters swung open.

She could hear the men inside.

She moved along to the next set of shutters and repeated the process, and then to the third. She returned to the yard through the gate. The guard observed her suspiciously.

She crossed to the well. The women from the town had gone now. She drew up a bucket of water and carried it across to the first room.

"Clean out that shit and piss into the yard," she ordered the men. "In future, when you piss, piss out of the door, and cast your shit through the window into the alley. There must be no shit and piss in this room."

The men looked rather shocked at her plain-spoken orders, but started to swill the floor. She went to the second room. The men there were in no better condition, and were confused by the sudden opening of the shutters and the stream of light that had flooded their prison. She gave the same instructions and was about to repeat them for the third roomful of men when there was a shout from inside.

"Mistress, it can't be you!"

"Grunwald?"

"Oh, by the gods, it's Signy! We're saved! Have you come with Oswulf?"

What could she tell them, that she had also been a prisoner, but she now was one of their enemies?

"Grunwald? Ferland? What are you doing here? I thought you were all dead."

"We should have been, Mistress, but they had mercy on us who could walk."

"Some chief reckoned he could get a good price for us if we got patched up."

"He reckoned wrong, though, because nobody's come to do it."

Signy stood for a moment, taking in the familiar faces from Thorgill's farm. After all, she was not quite alone in Britland. No, she had not betrayed them. She had been placed here to help them, to save them. Her hands found her hips, and a little of the authority she had acquired as Thorgill's wife returned.

"You should be ashamed of yourselves," she said. "This room stinks, and so do you. Once I've fixed up the worst wounded from Skalgrim's crew, I'll be back, and then we're going to get this place cleaned up!"

She made her way through the hostel to the bathhouse. When she looked in, there was no one there. She had remembered correctly: by the entrance was a pile of linen sheets, and a couple of robes like the one she had worn yesterday. She could tear them up for clean bandages. She tucked them under her arm and snuck back to her room. There she took the leather bag of herbs from her chest and made her way to the yard.

The guard at the gate said nothing. She greeted him in a friendly manner as she went past. Who was he to question her in her fancy clothes and braided hair? The second guard merely watched her. Probably he was suspicious of what she was doing, she reckoned, but would it be in his best interest to interfere with whatever she was up to? If she was staying in the hostel, then she must be associated with the leaders, with an important officer, at least, maybe his wife or girlfriend. Or maybe she had come from the slave merchant, and it wasn't his job to tell her what to do and what not to do, so long as the prisoners stayed where they were.

She bathed and cleaned the wounds as best she could and bound them up again with a mixture of spider's web and herbs. She saw that simply having their wounds treated had already made the men feel better. Their postures had changed, their backs straightened. Those who could stand were doing their best to help her.

When she had finished the walking wounded, she turned her attention to the young man, Bjornfot. There was nothing she could do for his wound. She could only reduce his misery. She mixed some herbs she knew would dull his pain in a beaker of water and lifted it to his lips. He was too weak to drink, but she held the beaker to his mouth until he had swallowed the contents, and let his head back gently to lie on the pile of straw which served as a pillow.

She turned to the least injured of the men in the cell, the one who had remembered she was a wise woman.

"Your name?"

"Asser, my lady."

"Asser," she said, "I'll leave a beaker of this mixture with you. Give it to Bjornfot in the evening. Make sure he drinks it all."

She went from room to room, assuring them she would be back the following day.

When she returned in the morning, there was a clear difference. The fresh air wafting through the rooms had cleared the stink. She could see the men felt better, their eyes brighter, a couple of them actually smiling when they saw her, and when she took off the bandages, where there had been infection, there were signs of healing. Only Bjornfot showed no signs of improvement. She crouched down beside him, feeling his brow and holding his hand.

"The sickness is raging inside him," she said to the watching Asser. "There's nothing more I can do."

She left the room and stepped out into the yard. She rarely felt the need to pray, but at this moment she stood and reached her arms up to the sky and asked for guidance. She stood for a short while, considering the situation. Did the gods speak to her, she wondered afterwards, or was it only her own thoughts that clarified? She remembered the advice she had received from Irmengaard. Her skills could be used to bring life into the world, but they could also be used to bring death. For Bjornfot, death would be a mercy. Inside her bag, she had a small pouch, and inside that, an even smaller one, and inside that were the materials she needed. With great care, she dropped a little powder into a beaker of water and went back inside the room. The young man lay delirious. He was calling for his mother. Signy squatted down and placed the beaker to his lips. He was too weak and too sick to drink it himself, so she poured the contents into his mouth. He swallowed and coughed. Signy stood and tossed the beaker through the open window into the street outside, where she heard it shatter. She could not risk anyone else drinking from it. Then she crouched again and placed her hand on the young man's chest. She could feel his heart pounding, his lungs heaving for breath. As she waited, she sensed the pounding grow quieter and the breathing shallower. Soon his heart would stop, and his breathing would come to an end. His cellmates gathered round, watching over their dying friend.

Suddenly, she jumped up. Like a strike of lightning, a thought had come to her mind, as if the gods had really spoken to her. She rushed from the room and out into the portico. The guard was standing in his customary position, half-asleep. She took two steps towards him and laid hold of his spear.

"Oy, what yer doing?"

"Just let me borrow this," she said, and pulled it from his surprised grasp. He gave out a shout as she disappeared back inside the room. She pushed her way through the men and crouched down again. Bjornfot's breathing was weak, but he was still alive. She took the spear and placed it beside him, wrapping his hand around the shaft. Now when his spirit finally left him, it would meet those of his ancestors with a weapon in his hand, as a warrior.

The room grew a little darker, as the figure of the guard blocked the doorway, but he stayed on the threshold, where he didn't disturb the cluster of people at the rear of the room. Bjornfot gasped, took another breath, then gasped again, and that was his last. Signy felt for his heartbeat. She placed her ear against his mouth to check for his breath. She could feel no movement in his chest, no breath, no life. The men surrounding her gave out a great cry, which was taken up by the Jutes in the adjacent rooms; a shout to commend Bjornfot's spirit to the gods. Signy eased the spear from his grasp and handed it to the still-waiting guard with a word of thanks.

"The boy dead," she said. "Someone take his body."

The guard's face was filled with astonishment.

"Are you some sort of sorceress?" he spluttered, but she had neither the words nor the strength to provide an answer.

When Signy came to visit the Jutes on the third day, Bjornfot's body had been taken away but, in departing, his spirit had lifted the spirits of the remaining men from Skalgrim's crew. She noticed a difference, both in the men themselves, and in their attitude to her – respect, perhaps even admiration. She could see from their expressions that they knew that her medicine had hastened their young friend's death. She knew that they had been brought up to fear and respect wise women for just that reason. She hoped that they understood that she, Signy, Thorgill's woman, had gone beyond bringing only the deliverance of death. That she had respected the dying Bjornfot and helped him die as a warrior. She hoped that they would feel that she respected them, too. Wounded and weakened as they were, they were still warriors. They had fought and been defeated in battle. That was the will of the gods for reasons they might not understand, but that did not mean they were no longer men, and what the gods had taken away, one day they could give back. The men's voices were louder, their greetings more cheerful, even a few jokes and jesting comments had begun to creep into their chatter, especially from the boys who had known her from Juteland, who weren't quite so impressed by her fancy clothes and the way her hair was arranged, because they remembered her darning their tunics. But Signy understood their jokes and comments were a sign that a miracle had happened. They had thought they were doomed to die, but their lives had been saved. Now Signy herself could afford to smile as she moved from room to room.

When she went to collect water from the well, Signy also realised there had been a change in the attitude of the women taking care of the wounded Britons and Saxons. At first she reckoned they could not grasp why anyone, let alone a high-ranked woman, would care for the Jutes. Then they must have realised she was one of them, a foreigner, an enemy, taking care of her own. Perhaps they had heard that she had been brewing potions in the hostel kitchen and imagined she was practising magic. Well, she thought, they only had to look in the direction of the Jutes' cells to see what sort of magic it was, nothing more than cleanliness and hope. Now they could hear loud voices and laughter from the quarters where the Jutes were once dying in misery.

She saw them gathered in the courtyard and watching her from a distance, as she moved from room to room.

"How dare you?" one called out, and her friends nodded and grimaced.

Signy couldn't afford to let them disturb her as she left the portico and crossed the yard to the well.

"Took the guard's spear," mumbled one.

"What other weapons has she smuggled into the cells?" grumbled a second.

In the days in the hostel, she had begun to make out the words used by the Britons a little better, and thought she understood what they were saying. As she approached the women, one of them spat at her. There was no mistaking that message. She stopped and looked up at them. She saw their faces, hard and angry, and took a step back. What was this? Another woman spat. Another cursed.

"Jute witch! Whore!"

A third picked up a stone lying in the yard and flung it towards her. There were more curses. Other women picked up stones and came towards her, ready to throw them. She backed up again, wondering how she could protect herself. She looked around for the guard, but he was nowhere to be seen. Another stone flew, close by her head. A third hit her in the belly, and she struggled to keep her balance as her foot slipped on the damp cobbles. The women came nearer, menacing. One, drawing a knife from inside her gown, took a step towards her.

"Stop at once!" came a loud voice from behind Signy's back.

The women's faces swivelled towards the man who had just entered the yard. The woman who had pulled out the knife simply turned and ran for the gate. The others fell to their knees and pressed their heads to the ground. Signy looked around to see who it was, and found that the governor himself was striding towards her. Now she realised why the women were crouching in fear. This was not the governor in dirty field clothes she had seen in the camp, or even the tidied-up governor who had bargained with Oswulf, but one obviously fresh from the baths and in full uniform. His beard and hair were neatly trimmed. He was wearing a white tunic, leather jerkin, and a broad belt decorated with plates, shining like gold. His purple cloak was draped over his shoulders, fastened by a gold clasp. His boots were polished and glinting. The shock of the women's attack and the surprise of her master's appearance were too much for Signy. Her knees began to shake, and she slowly sank down, much as the women had done.

The governor reached down to her and lifted her to her feet.

"Merwyn told me that you were here, caring for your countrymen," he said, wrapping his arms protectively around her. The crouching townswomen started to wail, as they realised what a horrible mistake they had made, what a foolish step they had just been about to take.

"They are frightened for their men," said Signy, casting a glance towards the women.

Marcus held her for a moment longer, and then, releasing his embrace, turned to the women in the yard.

"Go," he said, and the townswomen scrambled to their feet and fled.

With his arm still around Signy's waist, he crossed the yard to the rooms where the Jute prisoners were held and looked into the first one.

"Did you heal these men? I heard they were at death's door. It's a pity those stupid women didn't ask for your help, instead of throwing stones. If our men had received the same treatment you've given yours, they'd have been much better off."

"What will happen to my friends?" she asked, indicating the three rooms.

He looked serious.

"The healthy captives have already been taken to be sold as slaves, to Hibernia, probably. I suppose these will go the same way, eventually. You've seen the hostility. It would not be worth their own lives to keep them here in Britannia."

"But…" But it was pointless. What could she do for them, even Grunwald, Ferland and the others from Thorgill's crew?

It was saddening that she had helped to heal them only for them to be dragged away to a life of servitude. Was that a better end than the honourable death she had tried to give Bjornfot? How was she to know? She had been sold as a slave once, and now she stood with the arm of the governor around her waist. He had held her, and she had felt so secure in his embrace, so safe nestled against him, after the fright of the women's attack.

"Tomorrow we must leave here," he said, with a final glance at the Jutes. "The raiders have gone, with the exception of these few here, and the army must be sent home. There are animals and crops to be taken care of, and the other business of the province doesn't cease just because a group of Jutes decides to attack us."

"Shall I come with you?" she asked.

"I hope so," he said. "I'll arrange for these men to be cared for. I suspect those women will be more careful in future who they insult, but I think your patients have mended sufficiently that ordinary treatment will complete the process. If nothing else, healthy slaves are valuable property, and I'll find someone whose interest it is to see that they regain their strength and health, if for no other reason than it's good business."

Signy knew that only too well. As dying men, the Jutes had been hated and worthless. As healthy ones, they might be equally as hated and perhaps even more feared, but they would be worth something to somebody, and with the world the way it was, that would have to be sufficient.

☙ Chapter 18 ❧

Few of the governor's companions remained in the hostel. Chief Gisla had left for the south, after giving Signy a hug like a bear, his hand behind her back, on the exact spot where the lynx tattoo was hidden. Prince Merwyn's laughter was no longer heard in the house, nor the voice of the harp-playing poet who Signy had caught one day, singing to himself, in a corner of the courtyard. The governor's retainers and Edwulf were the among the last lodging with local families or sleeping in barns and outhouses around the town, and the day came when even they were ordered to congregate outside the gate to start the journey home.

"Edwulf is travelling directly to Verdaris," the governor told her. She knew the name, the name of his home. "I have to take a longer route, a few more days to take care of business in the city of Walcastrum. Will you travel with Edwulf or with me?"

There was only one answer, of course.

"With you, my lord."

"Hm," he said, "it'll be boring, and it's probably going to rain, but if you insist, I'll tell Cull's boy, Malcolm, to keep an eye on you."

Let it rain, she said to herself, but I'm not straying from you, Master. You've become my pillar, my beacon in this strange land.

Some of the men had horses, but not all, so the journey was taken at walking pace. The party trudged west along an old road constructed hundreds of years before by the Romans.

At the end of first day, they reached a hostel, a smaller version of the building they had stayed in at Competum. They ate in the refectory. Marcus, Edwulf and Cull sat at the high table. Signy was assigned a place lower down, among the few women in the party. They had been among the servants taking care of the men – their food, their clothes and shelter. She did not recognise them. They regarded her with indifference, even hostility. Perhaps my reputation as a friend of the Jutes has spread, she wondered. Perhaps they also think I'm a witch.

In Walcastrum, while the governor paid a visit to his sister, who was married to a local landowner, Signy was housed with a tailor. The tailor and his family were irritated to have a guest forced on them. Food and drink were short enough at this time of year, especially after the levies to feed the army, and now they had another mouth to feed. By gesture, she offered to assist with some sewing. The man reluctantly agreed, observed her first efforts with scepticism, and then with a grunt handed her a cloak that required taking in, to be used by someone else in the family now that the owner had died. It was a good cloak, she reflected, and the new owner should be pleased to receive it. Not like the thin material she had inherited from her older cousins, or leggings that had already seen duty for her brothers.

By the time the governor returned to the town, and the word went out for his followers to assemble in the marketplace on the following morning, the tailor was sorry to see her leave. His only child had married a farm hand and moved out of town. There was no one to carry on the business. Would the Saxon girl be interested in staying as his assistant?

His wife bid Signy a hearty farewell.

On the first evening of the journey south, they came to a place where the hostel was in ruins. The walls still stood, but the roof was missing in places. People passed by on the road, to judge by the charred wood, ash and rubbish scattered around, but the buildings were uninhabitable. The men made up fires in what had been the courtyard. The women cooked a stew of meat and barley. When they had eaten and drunk, they wrapped themselves in their cloaks and slept where they had been sitting. Not everywhere in Britland is splendid and orderly, Signy reflected, her head resting against her saddle bag. Soon the site of this hostel will look like the ruined village by the Jutes' camp, just an outline of stone and the remnants of a few gardens.

As the journey continued, she felt the mood lifting in the party. Despite the discomfort, they would soon be home, to their own hearths, their own families. What will my fate be, she wondered. I have no hearth to return to, no family waiting for me. I might be free, but what does it mean to be free? Free to go thirsty and hungry? Free to get wet and cold? Free to beg for a roof over my head? Free to desire friends in a land where I know no one, and can hardly speak the language, and where people seem so quick to turn against me? Free to be a victim of a crime, a rape or murder, perhaps; and no one cares whether I live or die.

And what am I going to do with myself? How am I going to feed myself? I was a child when I was taken from my home, dependent on my family, learning from my mother. And then what have I been? Not perhaps a whore like Gunhilde, the fat girl in Danby, but the next best thing – a man's plaything. I've no skills I can use and retain my honour. A healer, you say? Yes, I can heal, but a healer has to be trusted. It took me the whole long time in Thorgill's house to gain trust, and I would never have done so without Irmengaard. No one will help me here.

And then she became irritated with herself again. She was focussed on the past, once more feeling sorry for what had been lost. She was thinking like a farmgirl, as if the whole world simply consisted of the fields around her house, the life that villagers led, had always led, would always lead. Hadn't the gods picked her out to voyage over the seas, to show her the world beyond the forest and the river, to learn new skills, to become a new person, to change others' lives even?

Just when she had started to become comfortable with her life in Thorgill's farm, to slip into the role of a chief's wife, to consider becoming the mother of his children, a caring matriarch of the estate, her life had been upended again. The governor and his men had grabbed her as roughly and cruelly as the river thieves, and forced her into a new path, to live a new life, to learn new skills. So what could she learn in this place, among these people, that she would never have experienced on her home farm or in Thorgill's house? She already had an inkling of the answer, but she could not conceive how to bring the result about. The book, the scratchings made by Edwulf Gislasson, that was what lifted one person above another in this land. A duel between Edwulf and Thorgill would have been a close-run match. But Edwulf could read the book, and Thorgill would have used it to light a fire. Edwulf could reckon exactly how much corn and beer he had in his barns without even going to see, and Thorgill had to walk over and count, and even then, she had noticed, he often counted wrong. If I have the chance, she told herself, I will learn to read and write, to count with more scratches than I, II, III, and speak Latin like a Roman. The tailor had meant well, she thought, and no doubt there would always be cloaks that needed sewing, leggings and shirts to be made. No doubt I could have put up with his wife the way I put up with Helga, but I'm not a village girl anymore. I'm not going back to being a village girl. I'd rather be a whore, rather die, than be such a failure.

Even on horseback, at the pace of marching men, the journey had begun to become tiresome until, as the sun dipped below the western horizon, the party passed a cottage where a woman with two small children stood in the entrance, keenly examining the band of men. There was a burst of laughter from behind her, among those marching on foot, and a cheer. She turned and saw one of the warriors break from the group. The children ran towards him, hugging his legs, and as he struggled free, he embraced the woman. Father was home from the war, and he was whole and healthy.

The scene was repeated with small variations as they continued. At one cottage, she saw a woman scan the troop in vain, not seeing her husband. One of his friends stepped out to speak to her. As he did so, the governor signalled a halt and jumped from his horse. Signy watched as he walked back along the road to the woman, now clutching her head in her hands and weeping. She watched him talking and finally embracing her. Signy guessed he was reassuring the woman she would be looked after. Then he returned to the head of the column, his gaze on the ground, shaking his head, hiding his face. She wondered how many times this scene was being repeated in Juteland. She imagined Helga as one of the weeping women. Who would reassure her? Who would take in the harvest and prepare for winter? Who would become a father to Thorgill's children? Would Oswulf had mustered such compassion for the widows and orphans of the men he had left in Britland, or did he see their loss as an opportunity to extend his own power?

Signy's thoughts were interrupted by a sight which made her heart jump. A little way from the road stretched an enormous building, its white walls tinged pink by the setting sun, stepping down the hillside, and above it, a high tower, with two or three figures, outlines against the sky, waving in welcome. How many days have they stood there, how many evenings, looking out for their returning menfolk, she thought.

The governor swung his horse into the tree-lined lane leading up to the house, and the marching men turned after him. Ahead was a gateway, and the massive wooden door swung open as they approached. Inside was a yard, lit by blazing torches and filled with the shadows of waiting people. Signy passed under the gate, and her horse came to a halt, shaking its head and snorting as it recognised home. The governor jumped down and hurried towards a waiting woman with a small boy, perhaps five or six years old, standing by her side: his wife and son, no doubt. Signy pulled her eyes away from the scene to look around the yard. Everywhere men and women were embracing. Young children were jumping up and down to see their fathers, while the older ones tried to look mature, and came forward to take hold of the horses. Signy sat still, not quite knowing what to do, gazing up at the buildings around her, the tower, the blazing torches. This was not a mere chieftain's hall. This was a palace, a building from the sagas. What was she to do in a place like this? She felt someone tapping her leg and glanced down. It was a young woman, about her own age.

"Excuse me, Miss," she said. "The mistress is asking for you."

Signy dismounted and followed the girl across the yard. As she did so, the governor's wife, the mistress of the house, came towards her. In the half-light, Signy could see she was simply but elegantly dressed. Her brown hair was bound up, held in place by a comb, and her eyes were dark, soft, like her skin and her round cheeks and swelling bosom. Her look was friendly, but reserved, as if she was unsure about this strange woman accompanying her husband.

She held out her hands in a hesitant embrace.

"My name is Bryna," said the governor's wife. "Welcome to our home."

"I Signy," replied Signy, bowing her head, nervous once again of her British speech.

The woman, Bryna, took a step back, looking carefully, assessing her.

"You must be tired after your journey," she said. Signy was taken off guard by her perfect Saxon, but before she could say anything in return, Bryna turned to the maid, who was standing a little behind her. "Julia will show you a room, and I will ask Master Barnulf and Mistress Maud to make a place for you at the evening meal. Now, I must take care of my husband."

The maid led Signy through a doorway into the house. She had been impressed with the interior of the hostel in Competum Novum, but even in the half-dark she saw that this house was a great deal finer. The corridor was tiled in a weaving pattern, and the walls were painted with scenes of trees and plants, almost as if she was still standing outside and walking through a garden. They passed through another arch and into a portico running around the house and facing out into an open area. She could not see clearly, but she could smell the perfume of flowers in the evening air and hear the sounds of birds fluttering in the darkness. It must be a real garden, she thought, and not just herbs and vegetables. The maid led her through an archway until they reached a flight of stairs, and then along a corridor on the upper level. She was shown into a small room.

"You may stay here, Miss," said the maid, lighting an oil lamp so the space was filled with a soft light. Signy was evidently not the only occupant of the room, since there were two low cots, one neatly made up and the other obviously barely tidied. Presumably the occupant was now down in the yard greeting the men.

Signy sat down on the undisturbed cot.

"I'll go to find your baggage," replied the maid, leaving the room.

Signy lay back on the bed and closed her eyes. It was all too much at once. She needed to block out the world to process what she had just been through, but her attempt was interrupted by a discreet knock. She hardly had the strength to answer. A rotund, friendly-looking woman came into the room and over to her, gazing down with concern.

"Welcome, Miss," she said. "I'm Maud, the housekeeper, wife of Barnulf, the steward." Two men stood behind her carrying Signy's chest and her saddle bags.

"You're to join us for the evening meal. Julia will come and fetch you before we start," said the housekeeper, sticking to the safety of her native language.

When they had gone, Signy stripped off her travelling clothes and folded them carefully. She opened her chest and took out a long tunic. Lady Bryna has been very careful to put me in my place, she reflected.

She had been housed in a servant's room. She was dining with the steward, not the master, but the steward of this type of estate, what sort of a man could he be? Almost as fine as the master, Signy concluded. She shook out her hair, and, gathering it in one hand, pushed a carved bone comb into it. That was all the jewellery she thought to wear, the look of a modest servant at her best.

Again, a discreet knock at the door, and this time Signy jumped to her feet. Julia saw she was ready and led her out along a dark corridor into the depths of the building. They arrived at a small hall, lit up by several oil lamps and candles on a long table, flanked by benches. She saw Maud standing beside a burly-looking man about the governor's age, just a little grey in his short-cut brown hair. The steward, she concluded, relieved that she had made the right choice in her clothes. Barnulf caught her eye in acknowledgement of her presence but showed no sign of moving to greet her. Instead, his wife came over, a hand outstretched, and indicated the place where she should sit, not at the top of the table but not, at least, she considered, at the bottom. The other house staff arranged themselves along the benches. The meal was served, but before they started, Signy was surprised when the man bowed his head and said a few words she could not follow. The other staff bowed their heads in silence as he spoke. These people must follow the Christ, Signy thought, that Martha had described to her. Yet another matter to learn and remember.

When Signy returned to her room, the other cot was occupied by a sleeping form, a rather rotund young woman, who did not stir as Signy prepared for the night. In the morning, when she awoke, the woman had already risen and left. Signy sat wondering what the habits of the house were, what she was supposed to do when all the others must have their allotted tasks for the day, then the curtain over the door was pulled aside and her room companion appeared, accompanied by a distinct odour of the cow barn.

"Oh, hello," said the young woman cheerfully. "You've woken up, now. Sorry they put you in with me. I must go to bed early and get up early, too…to milk the cows. I'm sorry," she repeated, "but I'm just a milkmaid, not a fine lady like you."

Signy sat perplexed. There was something she could not quite get straight, and then it dawned on her. Her roommate had been speaking to her in the Saxon tongue. Judging by her accent, she was evidently a Briton, but she managed at least as well as the governor and many of his entourage.

"Thank you," Signy replied. "I'm not such a fine lady as you might think. I've milked plenty of cows in my time." Well, not quite true. Her family had only ever had two cows at most. "You speak the Saxon tongue very well."

"Thank you, Miss," replied the girl with a smile. "I grew up in Master Edwulf's household. Mistress Amanda is a kind mistress, and I was always very careful to listen to his men." She paused for a moment. "You have to know when those boys are teasing you."

"I'm sure," said Signy. "That's also something I've had to put up with."

The girl sat down, put her hands on her knees and observed Signy very closely.

"Miss, can I ask you something? I don't mean to be rude, but they said you are a sorceress. Is that true?"

There was no doubt about the meaning of the girl's words, thought Signy, uneasily surprised, though the newcomer's expression seemed to be one of curiosity rather than hostility.

"They?" was all Signy managed to say,

"Some of the women in the farmyard. They said you are a witch who raised a man from the dead, one of our enemies, in Competum, and that the master is in your power."

Signy felt her guts tighten into a knot. How had such a rumour spread around the house before she had even managed to get out of bed?

"Is that what they are saying of me?"

The girl nodded. "Yes, Miss. Miss, it's nothing I'm bothered by myself. I'm quite happy they put you here with me," she added defensively.

"It's not true, what they are saying…what's your name?"

"Meri, Miss."

"I'm just a healer, Meri. Yes, I came with the raiders from Juteland and I helped my friends. I know some of the women were angry that I helped the men who had fought their men, but they were my friends, and shouldn't we help our friends if we can?"

"It wasn't me, Miss, that said it."

"No," said Signy, nervously pulling her robe tightly around. Sooner or later, she thought, the girl will catch a glimpse of my tattoos. Would she know what they meant if she had lived with Saxons? Would that confirm I'm a witch?

The immediate risk was averted by a sharp voice from the corridor outside, and the curtain being abruptly pulled open.

"The mistress wishes to speak to you. There's small beer and bread in the servants' parlour, if you need to break your fast." It was the maid, Julia, and the friendly demeanour from the day before had evaporated.

The parlour was empty, the staff already at work. Signy forced down some beer and a couple of oatcakes. Julia stood watching her, saying nothing. Once it was evident Signy had finished, the maid led her down the corridor towards the master's rooms.

They passed through an archway which was an opening to the summer morning. Spread out in front was a beautiful garden, the one Signy had caught the scent of the evening before, with paths of gravel crossing hither and thither, meeting in the centre at a fountain, which even now was spraying water high into the air. Between the paths were beds containing here flowers, there herbs, and in the middle of some of them trees had been planted. She would have appreciated it more had her breakfast not felt like a stone in her stomach.

Julia stopped at a door and knocked. Bryna was sitting on a low stool beside a table. Close by was another stool, and she gestured to Signy to sit. Her face was friendly, but Signy could see a certain seriousness behind her smile.

"Have you slept well, Miss Signy?" she asked. "Did you eat well?"

No reply was expected, since she continued immediately. She's as nervous as I am, thought Signy.

"My husband has told me about you, how you helped him. Perhaps he spared some of the details, but I wasn't born yesterday, so I can guess much of what he left out."

What had he said, wondered Signy, and what had his wife imagined?

"My husband told me you had done him a great service in his dealings with the Jutes. He said that you had been worth a hundred warriors and that, thanks to you, there are many men returning to their homes today who would otherwise be dead."

Signy kept her gaze on the floor. She could almost feel Bryna's brown eyes probing her, as intrusive and analytical as the men's hands in Titus' booth.

"He also told me that they had taken you from the Jute camp. You were together with one of their leaders?"

"Chief Thorgill, my lady. He was my master. I suppose I was a sort of second wife to him, and besides, I know how to use herbs and plants to treat sickness and wounds, and he thought I would be useful in the camp."

"Undoubtedly," said Bryna, falling into silence. Signy wondered if she had said too much, something wrong.

Bryna stood up, walked across the room, turned abruptly and returned to her stool.

"I want to be clear. There is a rumour going around the household that you are a sorceress. Some women who were at the camp in Competum returned home while you were accompanying my husband to Walcastrum, and when they saw you arrive yesterday, they spread a tale about a Jutish woman who had used spells and magic to raise several wounded enemies from the dead. Not only that, they say, this woman placed a curse on the master, meaning my husband, so that he does everything that she wishes. Fanciful, I appreciate, but not without a touch of truth, if I've grasped Marcus' mumblings."

Signy offered up a thought of gratitude to her roommate, for having forewarned her by her indiscretion, but even then she could not immediately find any reply.

Bryna said nothing, either, for what seemed like an endless while. Then she spoke again. "You were merely being useful, I suppose."

"I was doing my best to help my friends."

"Exactly, but your friends are not the friends of the women of this house."

She stood up again but did not look directly at Signy. "I understand," she said, "that you are under my husband's protection because of the service you did him. I also understand we do owe you a debt of gratitude, probably including those women who are spreading gossip. I assure you nothing untoward will happen to you while you remain here. I will do my best to ensure you are seen as an honoured guest. But I cannot suppress all malicious talk and cruel looks. I've had you placed with Meri.

She's merely a milkmaid, I realise, but she speaks your tongue quite well for a servant. She has a good heart and means well, if you can put up with her talking."

Bryna took a deep breath as if she was relieved to have said what she had to say.

"I have talked things over with my husband," she continued. "Besides being young and pretty, you are obviously an intelligent and resourceful woman. My husband feels an obligation to help you, but I am afraid the opportunities are limited here at Verdaris for someone who has been the…second wife, shall we say, of a chieftain, even if he was a Jute." Bryna paused.

Signy watched her struggling to choose the right words. She could see that Bryna did not want to be rude, but it was obvious that her hostess had no desire for her to remain in the house.

"I don't want to stay where I'm not welcome," Signy said. "I had to endure that for a long time in my former master's home."

"I didn't say you're not welcome, Mistress. Rather, we have no opportunity here for you to employ your talents. We have no need for…"

A second wife, thought Signy.

"…another healer. You might find a better opportunity to practise your art elsewhere."

Especially if I already have a reputation of being a witch, Signy thought.

Bryna seemed to collect herself and turned to face Signy. "Supposing my husband and I had the means to help you. What would you choose to accept from us?"

Signy let the first thoughts race through her mind, without saying them out loud. What could she say that would not offend Bryna, that would not make her an enemy? Not a roof over her head. That was obviously not on offer. Not gold or silver, of course, that would be too simple, foolish and greedy, and besides, she had no need of them.

"My lady," she said at last, "I'm grateful that the gods gave me the chance to help your husband and to bring the fighting to an end. I was just a tool in their hands. They didn't wish to see more men die. I'm just an ignorant farm girl who has wandered from place to place, on a path set out by the Fates, and this has brought me to your land and your home."

Bryna smiled, though there was scepticism in her smile.

"Miss Signy, if we simply wait for God to choose our fate, we may wait a long time, believe me. Sometimes we have to see what God is offering and take it for ourselves, otherwise He may not be so forgiving to offer it again."

She sounded like she spoke from experience, thought Signy.

"Mistress Bryna, do you think it would be possible for an ignorant girl like me to learn to read and write?" She hesitated. "Master Edwulf thought so."

Bryna laughed, but now kindly, perhaps as much from relief as anything else.

"Master Edwulf should know," she said. Her eyes sparkled briefly, and for the first time, Signy felt she had seen the real Bryna for a moment, not the one who was disconcerted by this younger woman with a doubtful reputation. "I'll see what I can do, but this is nothing I can arrange in the waving of a hand. Until I can, I'll do my best to make this house comfortable for you. I'll speak to the women who are spreading falsehoods and remind them you are my husband's, their master's, guest." She reached for a small bell. At its sound, the maid Julia reappeared, and she and Bryna began to speak quickly in what Signy now knew was named Latin, after the Roman Emperor, the language the leaders used. This discussion was evidently not meant for her ears. The maid nodded vigorously several times, flushing red, glancing at Signy with ill-suppressed hostility, through a long diatribe from Bryna.

When it ended, she simply said, "Follow me," and Signy had no option but to accompany her.

"It's the mistress who the does the healing in this house," said Signy's roommate, stretching out her arm. "See here where one of the cows caught me. It was a nasty gash, but it healed up just fine."

The scar had healed nicely, thought Signy, but it was strange that the mistress of a house like this should perform such a task. Chief Oswulf's wives would never have sunk to treating the sick, and Helga…impossible to imagine. Healing and herbalism were not honoured occupations but were treated with suspicion and a little fear. They were matters to be left to women who were a little strange, like Irmengaard and Ornfrid, like herself.

Meri was sitting on her cot, leaning against the wall, her feet stretched out in front of her. With the extra practice, her Saxon was flowing better, and Signy thought she seemed more at ease with the stranger who had been dumped on her.

"Barnulf said we were to stop spreading nasty gossip and you should be treated like one of the family," she went on. "Some of the girls'll listen, I suppose, but I know it's true. You are a *seithr*, isn't that what they call a sorceress where you come from?"

"How so?"

The girl swung around and stood up.

"I saw your witch mark, while you were sleeping." She pointed towards Signy's shoulder.

"You mean this?" asked Signy, pulling back the corner of her robe.

The girl nodded. "It doesn't bother me, though. I don't mind if you're a witch. I wish I was."

"I'm not a witch, Meri," Signy insisted, "and that's not my witch mark. And I have another one. Do you want to see it?"

The milkmaid nodded dumbly, so Signy turned around and lifted her dress.

"Oh, by Jesus," Meri shrieked, and then burst out laughing. Signy dropped her robe and sank once more to her cot.

"Now you've seen all there is to see. I couldn't hide it, if we're going to share this room. But listen, I'm not a *seithr*. If I was, I promise you, I wouldn't be here. My old master would be living comfortably in the land of the Jutes, and me with him, maybe the mother to his child. But because I can't see the future, not my own nor anyone else's, he's dead, and I'm here with you. Yes, I can heal people. Yes, I can fix up wounds, just as your mistress fixed yours, but I don't place curses on people, and I can't raise people from the dead or steal their souls."

"But…"

"But, yes, I was friends with a wise woman in the land of the Jutes, and she was – is – a priestess of the old religion, and she took me as her apprentice, and those are the marks she gave me. I know that doesn't look good in a Christian household, but there's nothing I can do about it. I promise you I shan't make any sacrifices or invoke Thunor or Freya…well, only at the full moon, and never on the Christ's day."

"You know what," said Meri, with a serious look on her face. "I'm glad you got put in my room. I kind of like you, whatever Julia says. Will you come with me to the dairy? I'm supposed to churn some butter, and I could use some company."

❧ Chapter 19 ❧

With Meri's cheerful assistance, the attitudes of some of the other girls in the kitchen and yard began to improve. None of them could speak Saxon as well as the milkmaid, but they started to teach Signy more words of British and encourage her to use them.

One afternoon, with the morning milking completed, and some free time before the evening duties started, Meri beckoned to Signy.

"Come with me. Some of us are going down to the river to wash our clothes and clean up. The boys have been told to stay away."

A bathe in the river sounded inviting, and the look on Meri's face was enough encouragement to join her.

Several of the younger girls were waiting by the door which led out to the farmyard and from there, via a short track through the fields, to the river. The girls were still reserved around Signy, though they chatted merrily among themselves. Never mind, Signy thought, it's good to get out of the house.

While the other girls stripped and hesitated cautiously at the edge of the water, Signy lifted her robe over her head, placing it on the grassy bank, weighted down by a stone. Then she walked out into the water, and once it had reached her thighs, plunged in. The river by Verdaris was hardly impressive, nothing like the vast flow which had passed her childhood home, but deep enough away from the ford. What a joy it was to feel the cool stream, and for a little while, she just moved enough to stay afloat and let the current carry her downstream. Then she rolled onto her stomach and swam slowly back to the washing place. In the centre, the flow was quite strong, and it took a little effort to make headway, but soon she reached a calmer stretch, and with a couple of vigorous strokes, came into the shallows where she could put her feet down and wade to the bank.

She was greeted by stunned silence.

She stood petrified herself. Had the girls seen her tattoos and were now convinced, as Meri had been, that she was indeed a witch?

Then the silence was broken.

"We thought we'd lost you."

"We thought you'd been swept away, like Quallius' sheep last winter."

Signy felt a huge surge of relief. The girls had been worried on her behalf.

"Have you never swum?" she asked.

"No," came the united answer.

"Only the boys do that!"

"Some of them dare!"

"Would anybody like to try?" Signy offered. "I'll hold you."

For a moment, there was silence again, and then a voice piped up, one of the kitchen girls, Coela.

"I dare!"

Signy led the hesitant girl out into the deeper water, and then took her by the shoulders.

"Lie back," she said. "Trust me, I'll hold you."

The girl leaned back.

"Now lift your feet!"

Coela did as she was bidden, and suddenly she was floating.

"Aaargh," she screamed, laughing and kicking her feet, so that water flew everywhere, and soon the other girls were splashing back, and Coela did not even notice that Signy had drawn her out into the river, so that they were both floating free.

When they returned to the shore, they were met with the congratulations of the others. "It's not so dangerous," Coela laughed.

Then Signy felt a damp hand against her back, just where the tattoo lay.

"Signy," asked Coela, "why do you have these marks?"

She was just about to try to explain, when Meri spoke up, quickly and loudly in British, spinning a tale that they were her clan marks, and that all the girls in Juteland had tattoos.

"Just so the men know who they're going with!"

"Especially when they can't see your face," added Signy, patting herself on the rear.

The ice was broken, the barriers down, and now the girls crowded round and began to pepper her with questions about her old life, and how she came to Juteland, and about the battles in the forest, and how she had assisted the master in his meeting with the Jute chieftain. It was long after dark and they had begun to get cold before they clambered up the bank, and along the path to the house, to be met by the irritated cook, who had had no help all evening, and who they now expected to serve them a meal, did they?

Julia remained frosty. Signy suspected she was jealous, as Gudrun had been jealous when she first arrived at Thorgill's house. She doubted the governor paid much attention to Julia, and perhaps the maid really wished *she* was a sorceress who could throw a spell on the governor to increase his interest. The atmosphere did not improve after the mistress of the house handed Signy a grey wool dress decorated with a coloured band around the edge, similar to those worn by the other women.

"Now you will look like one of us," Bryna said, "and not a complete stranger."

Not still an enemy, at least, thought Signy, who could not help wondering if Julia's attitude was a reflection of Bryna's own true opinion, well hidden behind kind-sounding words and smiles.

"I hope to have a reply in a few days," Bryna went on, "to a letter I sent to Corinium." Signy had learned that Corinium was the chief town of the province. "My husband has a friend in town, and I'm sure he can help you."

Signy had barely seen the governor since she arrived at his house. Such an important man was busy, no doubt, she thought, visiting the halls of nearby chiefs, probably having to sit through the same sort of feasts and songs about his victory that Thorgill and I had last winter. Once she had crossed paths with him in the stable yard, not long after the mistress had given her the new dress, and she was overcome by emotion, twirling around to show the sign that she was now one of his household. Otherwise, she resolved to keep her thoughts to herself if ever they crossed paths.

At least now, when she had a growing group of friends, she no longer felt the need to be defensive the whole time. She had begun to feel a little happier in the villa, though she often thought of the people she had left behind – Irmengaard, Gudrun, the flock of children around the farm and Thorgill would come into her mind – and it was hard to suppress tears. At such moments, she felt like everything was her fault: Thorgill's death, Skalgrim's death, all the men's deaths, and the boys from Thorgill's farm who would be sold as slaves, even the sorrow and anger of the widows and orphans around Verdaris. She was responsible, because her imagination had led the whole world astray. But then Meri or one of the others would find her, throw an arm around her and tell her of some plan they had to go to the woods to look for mushrooms, or invite Cobb from the village, who could play the pipes, to organise a dance, and didn't she think that Huw was sweet, and would make a good husband? The latter Signy doubted, as she had quickly learned that Huw had been with almost every girl on the estate and seemed to have no plans to settle down with any of them. The governor's home might be built of stone, not wood, with a beautiful garden, and rich fields and orchards round about, with fat cows and strong oxen, but people were the same people, everywhere.

Signy's acceptance by the servants only seemed to exaggerate Julia's resentment.

"They're going to send you away," she began, finding Signy alone in the garden, weeding the plants. "She said they don't need a malevolent witch like you here, a friend of our enemies, upsetting the household and the labourers."

Signy said nothing. She knew very well she would have to leave sooner or later. Julia's opinion did not matter, but her silence did not stop the maid.

"They were going to send you to Chief Gisla's house, since you're only a Saxon, but they didn't want you worshipping pagan gods and stirring up trouble. Then they were going to send you to Mistress Milesia, but our mistress didn't think you were good enough for her friend."

"I'm sorry, Julia," Signy said, in the hope of stopping the flow, "but I don't know who you are talking about."

"Of course, you don't know Mistress Milesia, who our mistress lived with before she married our master. She's our mistress's best friend, and we'll be going to visit her later in the summer. Without you, of course, since you're being sent to the merchant Fabiansson…"

Somewhere in Signy's mind, the name stirred a memory.

"…and he knows what to do with girls like you," Julia added with a mean laugh.

Signy was left grasping at a memory. Laurentius' business partner, the merchant who owned the warehouse in Puttby, the shop where she had been put on sale, his name had been Fabiansson, an unusual name. Too unusual to be a coincidence. She felt the blood drain from her face, and she felt faint.

Julia must have noticed the change in her expression and realised that her shot had hit home.

"Fabiansson sells slaves to Hibernia," the maid continued relentlessly. "He already sent a bunch of Jutes there. I heard it in the marketplace when we visited the townhouse. And he's expecting a whole lot more from Competum. Maybe he'll sell you to Hibernia. Then you'll live in rags and get to milk cows all day long just like your fat friend, Meri."

With that, Julia turned on her heels and marched off.

What a bitch, thought Signy, but is there any truth in what she said? Did Bryna dislike her so much she was going to be made a slave again? After all the kind words? After what the governor had promised? She felt like crying. She could not go on weeding anymore, but sat down on a small stone bench beside the steps which led up to the portico.

A moment later, so it seemed, there was the crunch of footsteps on the gravel near the bench, and a soft voice asked, "Are you well, Signy?"

She recognised the voice, that of Bryna. She had to gather herself, hold herself together, not let the panic take over.

"Yes, Mistress," she gasped. "I'm just nervous about what's ahead for me."

"There's no need to worry. Cull rode by this morning with a message from Merchant Fabiansson. I had written to him to ask if he could provide a roof for you."

So that much was true. Bryna had been in contact with the slave dealer.

"He's an old friend of ours, and dear Deacon Baxter, a good man, has offered to teach you to read and write. They've helped my husband on many occasions over the years, and I'm sure they'll see taking care of you as a pleasure."

Signy's heartbeat began to normalise, and she felt her body coming back under her control. She let go of the edge of the bench, which she had gripped for support without realising it.

"I've never lived in a town. It would be a big step for me," she said, as a way to buy time and distract attention.

Bryna smiled again.

"Not for you, Signy! You've been through so much. I don't think that Fabiansson and Deacon Baxter will hold any surprises for you."

Signy felt another surge of nausea. It was not the surprises she was worried about, but what she already knew.

Bryna continued with a smile. "My husband will be home tomorrow with the final arrangements." She paused for a moment. "And Fabiansson has a daughter, too. Her name is Megana. I'm sure she'll be a good friend for you, better than I could ever be."

She can't be such a good liar, thought Signy.

"I'm sorry you'll be leaving," said Meri. The news had spread throughout Verdaris before Signy had managed to regain her room.

"I am too, a little," said Signy, "but you know I want to learn to read and write, and Mistress Bryna said she has found someone who can teach me. Do you know Merchant Fabiansson and his daughter?"

The milkmaid shook her head.

"I saw the merchant once in the yard, but I've never seen his daughter."

No doubt a merchant's daughter avoided anywhere as lowly as a yard, thought Signy, a picture of Oswulf's wives in her imagination.

"What about a…Deacon Baxter?"

"Oh, he's a hoot," Meri laughed. "He comes here every festival and makes up the absolutely worst riddles."

Then she turned serious.

"I'm so jealous," she said. "And I can already write a little, just numbers. Mistress Amanda showed me. Look: one." She drew her finger across her palm: I. "Two." She repeated the gesture: II. "Three" – III – "and five is like this." She held up her hand, spreading her fingers out. "So you draw it like this" – V – "and then four, you have to hide your thumb behind your hand, like so," she said, drawing IV on her palm.

"That's wonderful," said Signy, who only knew how to use marks to count. Meri really did know the signs that the masters used to track their work, as Edwulf had done, and as Barnulf, the steward, did. "What about letters, then?"

The milkmaid shook her head.

"They all run into one another. I can't keep track of them."

"It can't be too hard," said Signy, "if Edwulf and Barnulf can do it."

Meri looked at her closely.

"You think so? You mean anyone could learn to read and write?"

"I must, Meri, and you could, too," she said, suddenly insistent. "I don't want to spend all my life milking cows and making cheese, bossed about by someone like Julia. Once I was the wife of a chief. Once I served the cup at my prince's table. If I'm going to do that here, I need to be able to read and write and speak Latin and count and…"

Her breath ran out, and she sat down on her cot. She felt Meri's arm around her, and noticed her friend was crying.

❧ Chapter 20 ☙

The gods supplied a sunny day for the journey to Corinium. Bryna's relieved to see me leave, no doubt, thought Signy, and some of the servants, one at least, a little jealous. The chief stable hand, a man named Jarmi, took charge of the packhorse carrying her chest. As they approached the town, they passed a series of strange, small buildings.

"The tombs of the old Romans," called Jarmi, pulling up his horse and dismounting. "They didn't like dead people living in the town. This is the tomb of the Ursinus family, where the master's first wife, Hypatia, is buried."

Neither of them could read the inscription carved into the limestone.

"I remember her; a good woman," the groom added. "The master always stops at this tomb on his way into town to pay his respects. I thought we should do the same."

"Quite right," said Signy, and they stood in silence for a moment.

They continued along the road, leading their horses past the last few tombs until they reached the town gate. As they walked down the main street, Signy saw taverns and shops, more and larger than in Competum Novum, though some were empty, it appeared, the shutters closed even though it was the middle of the day.

"Here's the market, what they call the forum," explained her companion. The square was surrounded by more shops and more taverns, with people sitting outside, eating and drinking. At the far side was a large stone building, like a massive longhouse, roofed with tiles and with carved decorations along the frontage facing the square.

"That's the basilica, where our governor rules the province," Jarmi said, "and beside it is the Christian church."

"Is that where the master lives when he is in town?"

Jarmi laughed. "No, no one lives in the basilica. It's just full of rooms for scribes and lawyers. The master has a townhouse in Oak Street. We'll not go there today because I've to take you to Merchant Fabiansson, but I'm sure you'll see it before long." He took on an important air. "After I've dropped you off, I'll pay them a visit to see if there were any horses or packages to take home."

"Don't you think this is a very fine town?" asked Signy.

Jarmi looked very wise. "In its way, yes, but you should see the towns on the mainland. Once I was there with the master, years ago…"

They had passed the forum and turned down a smaller street. Before Jarmi could continue his anecdote, they arrived at a large gate, closed off by two wooden doors. Set into the wall at one side was a smaller gate. The stable hand dismounted and stuck his head into the entrance. One of the two wooden doors swung open. When Jarmi led his horse inside, Signy's followed, tugging her through the gate. As the yard came into view, she felt her heart begin to pound and sweat trickling down her back. She gripped at her horse, stumbling alongside, almost falling. All around the yard were wooden buildings, stables, storehouses and a row of undefinable rooms on an upper storey, almost identical to the yard of the warehouse in Puttby, where she had waited to be sold in Factor Titus' shop. Fear flooded over her. All her thoughts became questions. Was this a trap? Had she been tricked? Had she been given to Fabiansson to be sold again?

Jarmi, paying her no attention, had disappeared into one of the buildings. Signy felt her breathing become shallower and shallower and faster and faster. She felt sick. She closed her eyes and leaned against her horse. With the sight of the yard blocked off, she slowly began to feel better. How long she was standing like that she did not know, but shortly she heard voices, two men talking.

"This is the girl that the mistress sent to you, Master Fabiansson," came Jarmi's familiar voice.

Signy opened her eyes, trying hard to block out her surroundings. Across the yard she saw a middle-height, rotund man, with short white hair and a trim white beard. She focussed on his face.

The older gentleman walked towards her. She kept her eyes on him as he approached. Behind him, half out of sight, was a young woman. The man held out his arms to greet her.

"Fabian Fabianus," he said, "known to my friends and enemies as Fabiansson." He reached towards her. She was trembling and could hardly hold herself upright. She almost expected him to clamp a pair of hand irons on her wrists.

"Miss Signy, you're welcome," the merchant continued. "My friend Marcus has been full of praise for you, and Lady Bryna especially asked me to take care of you."

"I…I'm so sorry," Signy stuttered. "I…I don't think I'm feeling well. Your yard…"

Fabiansson looked worried, looked around at the yard.

"Father," came a sharp voice. "This yard is no place for Miss Signy. Have you forgotten what Uncle Marcus told you? Bring her into the house at once." The voice broke through Signy's thoughts, drove away her fear. She shifted her gaze to the young woman. She had the same rotund build as the man she called her father, but that was not what made her remarkable. While the father was pale and white, the young woman was dark, her skin brown, as if she had been working in the fields all summer, but her clothes revealed she had never worked in a field in her life. And her hair was black, black as a raven's feathers, and cascaded in unrestrained curls down to her shoulders. Her eyes were brown, so brown they, too, were almost black.

The woman stepped past her father and, taking a firm hold of Signy, without an apology drew her across the yard, through a door and into the house. She pushed Signy onto a bench just inside the door. Signy's knees gave way, and she collapsed down without arguing. She closed her eyes again and tried to control her breath. The young woman did not say a word, but went into a nearby room and came back carrying a large beaker.

"Drink this," she said.

It was ale, good-quality ale, and with a strong, honey taste. Signy felt her limbs were trembling less. Her heart began to beat more calmly. The young woman stood watching her. The merchant himself stood a little distance off, clearly puzzled by what had happened. The young woman turned to him and began to talk at a rapid pace. Signy could not make out a word of what she was saying, but the old man was evidently getting a tongue-lashing.

The young woman turned back and crouched down beside her. Her dark eyes met Signy's.

"Mistress, you're among friends here. I can guess how it must look to you, but please believe me."

By now the room, the pantry in which they were sitting, had filled up. A stable hand came in with the bags and Signy's chest, two maids and a manservant appeared from somewhere inside the house. Jarmi, Fabiansson, everyone was looking at her, wondering what was going on.

The young woman sat down on the bench next to Signy and took her face in her hands, turning it towards her. She placed her own face close to Signy's so her luxuriant hair blocked the view of the rest of the room. She looked straight into Signy's eyes.

"You'll be safe here, Signy. You're in the room next to mine. I'll take care of you."

It was a moment before Signy realised she was speaking in perfect Jutish.

That was the first time Signy met Megana. They could laugh about it later, but it was no joke at that time. Megana had even forgotten to tell Signy her name or explain who she was. Once the servants, the merchant and Jarmi had been sent about their business, Megana had led her through the rambling building until they reached the living quarters. Signy was still so confused, she hardly noticed her surroundings or where they were going. She just walked beside the dark-haired woman, all her effort going to placing one foot in front of the other without falling.

They reached a room with walls of white plaster and a floor laid in light stone, with blue, yellow and green tiles set into it, here and there, in no particular pattern. The low bed had a light-coloured cover on it, soft and smooth. Even the ceiling was painted white, with contrasting dark wooden beams. Not a room for a slave, not a room, even, for a servant. Megana helped Signy down to sit on the bed, then let her lie back. She held Signy's hand in hers as if Signy was a patient, an invalid.

"Thank you," Signy whispered. "I don't know what came over me. I just…"

"You don't have to apologise," said Megana. "I've been there."

She must have seen Signy's puzzled expression.

"I've been in Puttby. I lived in the warehouse. I was there for half a year. Learning the business."

The young woman stopped and looked at Signy. "Uncle Marcus, my godfather, told us your story."

"But I can't remember telling him."

"He finds things out if he cares to," said Megana. "Anyway, I've stood in the yard at Puttby, and looked around, and thanked God I was the daughter of the owner, and not one of the slaves."

She let go of Signy's hand, stood up and began pacing about the room.

"And…my mother was a slave," she said. "She was sold, just like you were, from one merchant to another until my father bought her. She hates the yard, too. She never goes there. She says it reminds her of her past."

"Your mother?" asked Signy, weakly.

"Yes. My father has a wife, Mistress Priscilla. Their marriage was arranged between two merchant families here in Corinium, when they were just children. She's still alive, but after my brother was born, she devoted herself to Christ. Now she lives in the priest's house by the church. My father was still a young man, so he did what he's best at and bought a new woman, my mother."

Megana had wandered over to the other side of the room while she was talking, and now she came back and sat on the bed. She took hold of Signy's hand again.

"Much, I suppose, as you were sold to your man."

"I was stolen from my home," said Signy.

"And taken to Danborg," said Megana. "I've been there, too."

"A trader, a man named Laurentius, bought me."

She felt Megana's hand tighten around hers.

"Do you know Laurentius?" Signy asked.

"I know Laurentius," said Megana with a grimace, and stood up, pacing relentlessly. "Just business," she said from the far side of the room. "You were something to be bought and then sold on to someone else."

"Megana," asked Signy, using her name for the first time, and rolling onto her side to watch her. "Have you ever bought and sold people? Even though your own mother was a slave?"

"You've been through Puttby. That's the business we do there. Furs, slaves and amber, from Puttby to the mouth of the Rhine, and then other traders transport them up the river, towards Italia and Rome, or else down into Francia."

By now Signy was sitting on the edge of the bed, observing Megana.

"I'm sorry, Megana. I didn't mean to be moralising. My man in Juteland was a robber and a murderer, and I loved him in a way… and I encouraged him. I'm not perfect."

Megana came over and sat down beside her, so close Signy could feel her pressing against her.

"You don't have to be sorry. If my mother hadn't been sold to my father, I wouldn't be here, here to be who I am, an intelligent, educated and determined individual. And if you hadn't been sold, you wouldn't be here, either. You're intelligent and determined. I can I see it in your eyes."

Megana jumped up from the bed and turned towards Signy.

"Stand up! Stand up!" she shouted excitedly. "I want to hold you!"

Signy stood up, a little wonderingly, and Megana wrapped her arms around her and kissed her. Signy stood shocked and stiff, but then her body melted as she felt Megana tight against her. After a moment, she gently pushed Megana away and smiled at her. Perhaps Mistress Bryna was right, and this Megana could be her friend.

❧ Chapter 21 ❧

The two young women were sitting on a stone bench in the caldarium, the hot room of the bathhouse at the rear of Fabiansson's compound. They had used the baths several times since Signy's arrival, but she was still not comfortable with the heat. Megana, on the other hand, seemed to need the warmth despite the summer weather outside.

"My father's relieved that you're feeling better," said Megana. "He was worried that you'd fallen sick or been possessed by some malignant spirit." They were both naked, the sweat running down their contrasting skins in streams.

"I *was* possessed, for a moment, by awful memories, but I'm so grateful you've taken care of me, your father and mother, too. Your father's been so kind, and your mother's so beautiful," said Signy.

Megana's mother, Soraya, was tall and slim, and her skin was brown, like a piece of well-polished wood. Megana had clearly inherited her colours though not her build or spirit. Soraya was almost silent, whereas Megana talked all the time. Where had she come from, wondered Signy, and what had brought her to Corinium? When she spoke British to include Signy in the discussion, her voice had a curious and exotic tone, but she clearly preferred to speak in another language to Megana and Fabiansson, one that Signy could not comprehend at all.

"Greek," Megana had explained, "the language of the east. There's no one round here who can speak it – except Baxter, and Uncle Marcus, of course, though he sounds like a book of philosophy."

"Your mother never goes out of the house?"

"She used to go out when she first came," said Megana, "but people would come up and touch her to see if the colour would come off her skin or feel her hair – quite openly in the forum."

"But Deacon Baxter's an Ethiopian…" Signy began. Megana had introduced Signy to her old tutor a couple of days before, and she could not imagine anyone touching the deacon uninvited or tugging at his hair.

"Father was involved in several troublesome quarrels," Megana continued. "Some men were angry that he was betraying his wife in a disgusting manner. Others stopped him in the street and asked him how much his girl had cost, and whether he could find one for them. In my mother's land, women stay in the house, and their husbands take care of the business. She decided she preferred it that way."

"Is that what makes *you* so angry," said Signy, "the way your mother's been treated? Has the same thing happened to you?"

Megana turned towards her. "Me, angry?"

"I've been watching you, in the office, when the farmers come in, and the tradesmen."

Megana laughed. "I've a bit of reputation in this town, Signy, as you'll soon find out. They think I hate men. I don't hate men, but I hate being patronised. I hate being pushed around by people who think they know better than I do."

"Has your father been looking for a husband for you? Do you have suitors?"

Megana laughed again. "All too many suitors, but do you think they're really interested in me? They want this…" She waved her arm around to encompass the bathhouse and the buildings beyond. "If I was married, all this would be taken by another, and I would be as much a slave as my mother has been."

She glanced towards Signy. "I'm as interested in men as any woman, but a husband…Listen, you've met Laurentius."

Signy nodded.

"When I went out to Puttby – I had begged my father to go to the mainland, so he sent me to Puttby to drive out any ideas of the glamour of being a merchant, I suppose – I met Laurentius the first time. He was just passing through, on his way from somewhere to some other place, as he always is. We talked. I told him my hopes and ambitions. He told me about his life."

"He told me, too," said Signy.

Megana continued as if she had never heard the interruption.

"The next day he'd gone – Upåkra, I think, at least we travelled there later in the summer – but he stayed in my mind, talk about the glamour of being a merchant. Just because he's rootless, I thought, he can't tie *me* down, either. No obligations on either side. I had never had a man before I went. I just wanted the experience, and he saw that I did. That summer he passed through Puttby half a dozen times, and I joined his boat – Upåkra, like I said, and the Danborg, did I ever tell you I had been there?" She sighed and looked into the distance. Almost without thinking, her hand slid down her body as if she was imagining his hands on her.

"Then the first storm of autumn passed through, and he said I had to return home. He can't have told Father, and we've never mentioned what happened afterwards. So…despite what the inhabitants of Corinium might think, I've absolutely nothing against men…in their place."

"He never touched me," said Signy. "Laurentius. I stood in front of him, stark naked, and he never touched me. We even shared a bed."

"But he found you a man in the end," said Megana, with a serious look.

"A husband, eventually."

"And *I'm* not going to put you off looking for another."

"I've got used to having a man," replied Signy. "I'll find another. I don't know how and when, but first I must educate myself, to be like Lady Bryna, like you. In this land, I must read and write, speak Latin properly, and count and reckon, and make plans, see everything from all points of view, by thinking, by reasoning, you call it."

"Let's cool down a little," suggested Megana, and they crossed over to the tepidarium.

"Baxter's a decent enough tutor," Megana continued, "though he's a deacon of the church."

"You don't think he'll be concerned about this, about what it means?" Signy tapped the tattoo on her shoulder.

"The mark of Freya," said Megana.

Signy stared at her. "Is there nothing you don't know?"

"A great deal, but I told you, half a year in Puttby, and I kept my eyes and ears open. And this one's for Freya, too, isn't it?" She stroked her hand over Signy's lower back.

"I think that one was a bit more of a personal touch," said Signy doubtfully.

"I don't think they'll bother Baxter, if he catches a glimpse." Megana smiled. "He has a few tattoos of his own from twenty years of service in the legions, though it's a bit hard to make them out. But he knows Vergil, Homer and other classics of Latin and Greek literature." Megana glanced across at Signy. "Don't worry, you'll soon know what I mean. Herodotus, Aristotle, Pythagoras and Euclid, calculation and geometry, what a muddle of knowledge…all the things he taught me. Eventually, he simply had to borrow books from Uncle Marcus' library and give them to me to study myself."

Signy looked at her with wonder, impressed by her new friend's enthusiasm.

"They don't agree…the philosophers," said Megana. "That's what annoyed me. I was left with more questions at the end than I had at the beginning, and there's no one here to talk to about it."

It was Signy's turn to laugh. "Do you think you can turn me into that person, your person to talk to about things?"

Megana did not smile, looking only serious. "Someone," she said, "someone to talk to. Someone who's interested in more than just men, like the silly kitchen girls."

"Even kitchen girls might want to read and write, Megana, have you ever thought of that?"

Megana was silent for a moment, gazing at Signy.

"I've had that thought, but I…well, I just assumed I was judging everyone else by myself. People do that, you know. Am I judging you the same way?"

"No," said Signy, as Megana stood up and beckoned her into the frigidarium. "You're an example to me."

There was a flask of scented oil on the floor. By now Signy knew the routine, and poured a little on her hands and began to rub it all over herself.

Megana turned her back to her. "Will you?"

"Of course," she replied, spreading the oil over her companion's back.

"Sometimes I feel so alone," said Megana. "The men here, with a few exceptions, Uncle Marcus, for example, are crude and only interested in money and property."

"And sex?" asked Signy.

"Of course, but don't get too hopeful. Turn around and I'll do you now. Where's the strigil, so we can scrape this off when we're done?"

Signy saw the small, sickle-shaped scraper perched on the edge of the water trough where they could stand while the oil was cleared, and where they could splash themselves with cold water. She ran her thumb along the edge. It gave her an idea.

"Megana," she said, suddenly serious. "You've opened your home to me. You've welcomed me when others have been suspicious or even hostile. I know you hope I'll be your companion, and I really wish that I can live up to that, although please be patient. It'll be a long road I have to travel. In my country, when two men leave on a journey, to fight in the war, they make an oath to each other, to be like brothers, to help one another, to support one another, to die for one another or take vengeance if it comes to that."

"I know that practice," said Megana, turning towards her. "The Greeks did it, too. They swore by their blood."

"My tattoos," Signy said, "are a mark of that sort of sisterhood, a promise I made in Juteland to my friend, Irmengaard, and which I'll never be able to fulfil now. I...I could swear to be *your* sister here and now on our journey together, if you would be mine."

"You've taken a long time to ask."

And with that, Signy pressed the strigil against her thumb until it began to bleed.

Signy took Megana's hand in hers. The scraper was barely sharp enough to make a cut, and Megana winced as it bit into her flesh. Then she and Signy clasped hands while their blood dripped onto the floor, and the water ran pink around their feet.

"Sisters," said Signy.

"A promise," said Megana, "until death."

❧ Chapter 22 ☙

"I've been speaking to Uncle Marcus," said Megana. "He's agreed to give me the buildings around the old temple of Minerva."

"The house you told me about, in Bakers' Street," said Signy. She felt Megana's hand on her shoulder, as her friend sat down beside her on the stone bench overlooking the still pool of water in the centre of the inner courtyard of the Fabiansson house. A pool that was reputed among the servants to be bottomless.

"That's right. It's been abandoned for years. The temple was dissolved ages ago, when the first Christians came. It was never a very successful one. The caretaker would have lodged in the house next door. I think other people must have lived there after the temple closed, but no one has recently."

"It's strange that the Romans imagined that wisdom would be represented by a goddess, a female. What a contrast to the Christians!"

"We would have space for several girls or young women to come together and learn."

"I'm a little jealous," said Signy. "I like being special, Deacon Baxter's only student."

"You'll still be special," said Megana. She patted her friend.

"I know! And now you've got me thinking of the dairy maid who shared the room with me in the governor's house. Meri's her name. There must be other girls like me and like her who would love to learn but have never had an opportunity."

"There, you see, we've already found our second pupil. Once the girls of Corinium hear about the Minerva House, they'll be lining up, I promise."

"Dear Megana, of course I'll help you with the school, and I'll work hard to be an example for the others."

"I'm sure you can do more than that," replied Megana, standing up and holding out her hand to draw Signy with her. "Come on, let's go and take a look at our new project."

The two young women walked through the town along West Street until they reached Bakers' Street. Once that part of the city had really been thronged with bakers, and there were still several shops displaying loaves and offering a place for people to bake their own. At the far end, towards the forum, were the remains of a small temple, plundered for stone when the Christian church had been constructed. Beside it was an abandoned house. The door was aslant, and a family of cats had taken up residence. There was dust and dirt everywhere, and in one place, the roof had fallen in, but the house was sturdily built of real stone, and underneath the debris on the floor they could discern a tiled pattern.

"It must be hundreds of years old, from the time when the Romans first came to Britannia," said Megana. In the centre of the house was an overgrown atrium. This would be a great place for a herb garden, thought Signy. Maybe Megana's right, and there's more I could do than simply be an exemplary pupil.

In the rear were kitchens and a storeroom.

"What a wonderful place!" said Signy. After growing up in a cottage built of logs and mud, she could not believe it might be possible to live in such a beautiful house.

"What a mess!" said Megana. "How much is it going to cost to put this right, and where am I going to find the workers to do it? Now I'm going to have to go begging to Uncle Marcus again for a subsidy! I should have been more tactful."

"Can you persuade your father to ask his friends?"

Megana sat down on the edge of the dried-up water cistern.

"Father's been acting strangely recently," she said. "I don't know what's the problem. He seems preoccupied. He's been away from the house a great deal. And when he's here, he's started having difficulties in reading documents written with a small hand. Sometimes I have the impression he's forgotten things he has told me already."

"You do most of the work as it is, Megana."

"But you've seen it's not easy. Men don't respect me the way they respect Father."

Signy placed her arm around Megana's shoulders. "I wish I could help you in some way, but I don't know anything about trading and town business."

After the shock of her first experience, Signy had largely avoided the big yard at the back of the Fabiansson house. However, since she was living there, she had occasionally forced herself to walk through the open space to confront her fears, to drive away the demon. Now, before the harvest was brought in, the warehouses and barns were largely empty. The only occupants were strings of packhorses carrying bales of wool and baskets of salt. Signy was returning from an arithmetic lesson with Deacon Baxter, when she slipped in through the side gate. She thought she heard voices from the rooms above the yard, and she felt uneasy. Was her imagination playing tricks? Had old memories returned, despite all her effort to banish them?

Fabiansson had returned from the north the previous day, she recalled, seeing the merchant descending the stairs from the upper gallery.

"Who are the people up there?" she asked.

"Those men?" replied Fabiansson. He looked uneasy, recalling Signy's reaction when she had first entered the yard. "I…I…was in the north, my dear," he said, placatingly. "There were some slaves to be brought south, from Competum Novum."

"Jutes?" asked Signy.

"Well, yes. Magister Ursinus and Counsellor Aurelius employed them to repair the villa at Stationum, the house that the raiders burned last year, but they've completed their work and are no longer needed."

"The villa that my…that Chief Thorgill raided."

"That's correct. It's only right these scoundrels were forced to repair it. Now, they'll have to be sold on, to Hibernia or Gaul."

Could these be the men whose wounds she had treated in the hostel yard at Competum Novum? She had almost forgotten them, assumed they had been sold as slaves long ago.

"May I go up and speak to them, Master?" she asked.

"I've told you not to refer to me as Master," said Fabiansson, "and, yes, of course you may."

Signy bounded up the stairs, listening for the voices. A man's face appeared in a doorway. She could see him look once and then again, and then turn back into the room.

"Who's there?" she called. "Tell me, who are you?"

There was Grunwald, the stable boy from Thorgill's farm; Ferland, the lookout on Thorgill's ship; Hrasmus, who loved to whittle; and Asser, Skalgrim's man. Others stuck their heads from the other doors. She ran from one to one, offering her hand, calling their names. How fit they looked, tanned and strong!

"He can't," said Signy, under her breath, "he can't send you to Hibernia."

She heard feet on the steps behind her.

"Signy, what are you doing? Father said you had run up here to see the slaves."

"Megana, these men…they're my friends from Thorgill's farm, the ones I helped in Competum, the injured men I treated. I didn't mend them so they could be sold to Hibernia. I couldn't bear it."

Megana looked from the watching faces to her friend and back again, and then she burst out laughing. "I've just told Father we'll need workers to repair the Minerva House. He said to use these slaves."

"You mean they'll be staying here?"

"For the time being." Megana turned to the man in the doorway and switched to Jutish. "Your name?"

"Grunwald, Mistress," he replied, having no idea who this newcomer was, not knowing Signy's place in the house, confused because a stranger addressed him in his own tongue, snatching an uneasy glance at the wife of his former master. Megana noticed his look and, furrowing her brows, turned and walked back along the gallery to the stairs. Signy followed her.

"These boys," she said, when they had reached the yard. "You saved their lives. They respect you. I can see that."

She stopped and turned to Signy. "I can't make any promises. It's expensive to keep slaves fed and clothed if they have nothing to do. Troublesome, too. But while the Minerva House needs to be repaired, we have work for them." She smiled. "You asked how you can help me. Make sure they do their work and stay out of trouble. I can see they'll give more loyalty to you, true loyalty, than they ever will to me or my father, merely their owners."

So the Jutes stayed, lodging in the row of rooms above the stables, and every day threading their way through the town to the Minerva House, where they cleaned away the rubbish, removed the fallen rubble, reconstructed the roof and polished the floor tiles. As their work came to an end, Signy sent a message to Bryna, painstakingly scratched out on a wax tablet under Megana's supervision, begging on behalf of the dairy maid, Meri. Soon a small cart arrived from Verdaris, carrying the milkmaid and her meagre belongings: the first pupil for the Minerva House, with, to Signy's great surprise, a heap of furniture and cooking pots, as a gift from Bryna to Megana's new venture.

Soon other girls followed.

One of the clerks in the governor's office thought his daughter would benefit from a little schooling.

"I can't afford a tutor," he explained, "not that there are any in Corinium nowadays."

The owner of the Fox Tavern sent his girl. "I've always had difficulty keeping track of the money. Now my wife Leesa's ill and can't help me anymore. My daughter'll be far more use round the tavern if she can take care of the money."

A little while later, a worried farmer's wife appeared. "My only child, my daughter, was in the hay barn with one of the farmhands. I don't want her getting into trouble."

Not if she is to inherit the farm, thought Signy.

"Perhaps being with the other girls will keep her straight," the good lady continued.

"We'll do our best," Signy replied, though neither Megana nor I are the best examples in that regard, she added to herself.

During dinner at the Fabiansson house, Megana, her father and Soraya usually spoke in Greek. The habit was hard to break. They were not intending to be rude to Signy. They had always done so. It was a convenient way to talk about private matters without the servants being able to understand. Signy began to pick up some of the words, assisted by Deacon Baxter. Nonetheless, she found their conversation hard to follow, and often her mind drifted away to her own problems. She was surprised, therefore, one day, when Fabiansson deliberately switched to speaking in Saxon.

"I have some news that'll interest you, Signy," he said, with a glint in his eye. "You know I've been away at Verdaris."

"Half the town has been there," said Megana.

"If you mean Counsellor Aurelius and Flavius the Treasurer?"

"And Theo and Pacius, and several of the other clerks with them. It's been impossible to get any legal business completed."

"We've had our own business to complete," said the merchant, "important business. The leaders of Britannia Prima have decided that Marcus should no longer be *magister militum* only. They've proposed he should be acclaimed as king."

Signy must have looked puzzled, because Fabiansson turned to her with an explanation.

"The Empire of the Romans has gone, for ever. Really, it's been gone a long time, a good twenty years, and it won't be coming back. Times have changed. The provinces are getting new leaders. Many of the lands round about have always had princes, and some have had high kings all along – Hibernia, Dalraida, for example, even Gwynedd. Britannia Prima's no longer a Roman province, and we need a man, a leader who can compare with their leaders, to unite our chiefs, to administer fair and unbiased justice, and, of course, to be the uncontested leader of the army. A king, in other words, and Marcus is just the man."

"And you men have decided among yourselves that this is the best solution?" said Megana.

Fabiansson ignored her interruption.

"Not only that, but the leaders of West Britain have decided to put up a new hall, a King's Hall, where justice can be seen to be done, where we can meet and celebrate the passing seasons and high days of the year. It must be bigger and finer than any of the halls which have been appearing here and there recently, fit for a king, in fact."

"What's wrong with the basilica?" asked Signy. "Isn't that a fine enough building?"

"And where will this hall be located?" asked Megana, a hint of irony in her voice.

"The basilica is a very fine reminder of the old days," said Fabiansson in a kindly tone, before turning to his daughter. "We thought the hall should be built by Corinium, and I've been given the task."

"Father," said Megana "don't we have enough to do?"

Fabiansson sighed. "I know, my dear, but Marcus asked me specifically, and I couldn't say no. I know I'm not as sharp as I once was but you, my dear daughter, are worth two men."

"Always, always, a woman has to be worth two men," said Megana, later.

Nonetheless, once the Jutes had finished at the Minerva House, they moved to the old Roman army camp outside the town walls and started clearing the area to prepare for construction. All winter they toiled, levelling buildings, filling in ditches, and once the ground had frozen, they were despatched into the forest to fell the trees that Wulfthere, the master builder that Fabiansson had called over from Frisia, had selected as the posts for the new hall.

Signy had no active role in the building work, though she followed the progress through her conversations with Megana and the reports she received from the labouring Jutes. She still had much to learn at the school, though her skills and knowledge rapidly outpaced the other students since she benefited from the individual attention of the deacon and coaching from Megana. On days when the weather was poor, she sat in Megana's workroom, watching and listening as her friend haggled with stewards and tradesmen, dealt with correspondence from other merchants and, above all, slowly assembled the materials and craftsmen needed for the construction of the King's Hall. Time was short. The notables and chiefs wanted their king to be acclaimed by midsummer, and at least the shell of the hall had to be ready by then. Signy saw how Megana and her clerk kept careful track of the prices of the items, sometimes pulling out old and dusty manuscripts to check details from previous years, how Megana used her arithmetic to calculate the costs and the payments to request from the treasury. She marvelled at Megana's ability to write a letter in Latin to Aquitania, to Bononia, or a few words in British to Aquae Sulis or in Saxon to Puttby and Laurentius. She was determined to be able to do the same one day, and that kept her at her studies when others were relaxing.

In the spring, when the warm weather came, she supervised the girls at the Minerva House in laying out a herb garden in the centre of the atrium. She wished she had room for the scented flowers and the carefully trimmed trees she had seen at Verdaris, but they were in town, space was limited and she needed to focus on the essentials.

She accompanied Fabiansson's wife, Mistress Priscilla, and her friend, Mathilda, on their rounds to the poor of Corinium and the surrounding villages. The Christian ladies were willing to overlook a tattoo or two because they recognised her healing skills. Word had begun to circulate among the womenfolk that Signy could prepare medicines and charms that really worked, and as time went on, people began to make their way discreetly to see her for treatment. Before long, she could find her own way throughout the city and knew almost all the servants' entries and back gates of the town, from the poorest widow to the Ursinus house itself.

☙ Chapter 23 ❧

By summer, the walls and the roof of the hall were completed, and a podium constructed at one end of what had been the parade ground of the Roman encampment. A great feast was arranged to celebrate Marcus' acclamation as king: meat and drink in plenty, pretty girls to serve it, bards, polite and bawdy, to sing. A poet was engaged to compose an epic about the battle with the Jutes, and the marvellous way that King Marcus had slaughtered them and sent them on their way, humbled and defeated, never to be seen again. There were flashy gold presents to be given out, swords or belts, carefully decorated depending on the rank and closeness to the new king, and luxury items to be taken home and displayed to wives and girlfriends. The whole process was barely controlled chaos, of course. The treasury had been drained almost empty to buy food and drink and pay people to cook and serve it.

Signy had done her part, at first simply as a desire to take some burden from Megana. Just because a king decided he wanted a hall to be built and a feast arranged did not mean that the daily tasks of trading came to a halt. On the contrary, all the fine stuff to give out, to eat and drink and to look at and admire, had to be gathered together, and a good part came from outside Britannia, from Gaul and beyond. Signy had helped arrange feasts in Thorgill's hall and found that the townspeople and country dwellers round Corinium were looking forward to the same type of entertainment enjoyed by the people of her home village and those who lived around Thorgill's farm.

As the day of the ceremony approached, another motivation crept up on her, seeped into the cracks of her mind unawares. She wanted to impress the governor, the king as he soon would be. She wanted him to see that the dirty little girl he had rescued from a roofless ruin was a person with determination and talents who had made a contribution to his celebration. Why she felt she needed to do this was difficult to put into words. The motivation was driven by memories, the memory of the moment she first saw him ride into Oswulf's camp, the moment when his eye met hers in that ruin, and above all the memory of how safe, how protected she felt, when he held her in his arms, those few moments in the courtyard in Competum Novum.

All the dignitaries of the land had been invited: the leaders that Signy had met in the war camp, Chief Gisla, Prince Merwyn and the others, the administrators from the city, Aurelius and Flavius, landowners and their wives from far and wide, everyone, in fact, whose good will was necessary for the success of the new ruling order. There were far too many people for the accommodation that was available. Even Fabiansson's yard was full of servants and warriors, horses and wagons, the stables packed with horses, and the surrounding rooms filled to overflowing with grooms and maids. The ceremony and acclamation would take place on the parade ground, in the sight of all the people, but the list of those who would pass through the door of the feasting hall and into the presence of the newly chosen king was correspondingly limited. Fabiansson was invited, but since neither Mistress Priscilla nor Soraya were interested in accompanying him to the noisy celebration of drinking and eating, Megana was tasked with keeping her father out of trouble.

Signy felt a pang of jealousy. Of course, Megana had more responsibility for the construction of the hall, and even procuring all the trappings for the feast, but even if she had been at the bottom of the table, Signy would have liked to see Marcus and hope to catch his eye. If she was merely standing outside in the crowd, the king would never know about her contribution. Probably, in fact, he had forgotten about her entirely. They had not spoken or even passed in the street since the day she left Verdaris. Obviously, he had been busy with his duties and responsibilities, with his son and daughter and his lovely wife.

She stood on the edge of the throng, looking out over what had once been the legionaries' parade ground, at the mob surrounding the fountain cascading with wine and ale. That had been Fabiansson's idea. He had seen something similar in the south lands, at some festival, and thought it would go down well in Corinium. Signy, herself, was on her third bark beaker of wine, though the effect it was having was far from agreeable. She was feeling exceedingly sorry for herself, having watched all the guests parade into the hall, and thinking she should have been there, too, instead of out here, among…what was the word that Megana used for the general public? The res publica. No…the common people. Yes, here she was, one of the common people, and her own reflections on her situation merely made her feel worse, because it was above all stupidity for her to think she was any better than the people gathered around the fountain, singing and cheering and dancing to the pipes. Why couldn't she feel the spirit? Why couldn't she just walk down and join the dance? Because she had watched him walk into the hall on the arm of his wife, and realised *she* wanted to be the woman on his arm, and *she* wanted to be the woman in his bed, this night, tomorrow night, every night.

That was a truth that had been hidden from her and she was now forced to recognise. She wanted Marcus for herself. It was ridiculous, of course. She couldn't have him and just now, she pitifully reflected, taking another swig from her beaker, any other man would do. How long had it been since she had lain with a man? Since that last night with Thorgill before he marched off to his death?

"You seem very pensive?" came a voice by her shoulder.

"What's that to you?" she said, turning to the stranger, barely visible in the glow of the blazing torches arranged around the parade ground.

"I'm feeling a little pensive, too."

"Well, why don't you go down and fetch a beaker of wine, and relax a little?" Signy muttered.

"It doesn't seem to be doing you any good, and in any case, I'm not here to enjoy myself, but to observe and report."

“And for that you need to stay sober?”

Their eyes met.

“Here, take this,” she said. “You’re right. It’s not making me feel any good. I’m just observing, too, observing my master.”

“And your master is?”

“My master is sitting in there,” she waved at the hall, “with a crown on his head.”

“I see,” said the man, “you’re one of our beloved King Marcus’ servants.”

She looked at him again, noting his sarcasm, and pursed her lips. “And just who is your master?”

“A man who’s interested in King Marcus and his sayings and doings.”

“Well, you won’t find out much from me. As you can see, he doesn’t have anything to do with me, nor me with him, the more’s the pity.”

The man frowned and sipped at the wine cup, evidently feeling there was some meaning behind her words that he could not catch.

“What do you say if we drink another toast to the king’s health?” she said, taking the stranger by the arm.

“I…er…” But it was too late; he was drawn down into the milling mass, where the host of the Fox Tavern and his girls were filling beakers from the fountain and passing them out.

“I hardly feel it’s right to take part,” the stranger said, as they pushed their way back, fresh wine in hand.

“You’re not an invited guest?” she asked.

“Well, no, quite the contrary.”

“An uninvited guest,” she said, sliding her arm around his waist. “I feel like an uninvited guest myself. That makes two of us. Where are you staying?”

“That’s a problem. I’ve nowhere to stay. I was just thinking of hiding up in one of the barns and leaving at first light.”

“That sounds like an excellent idea,” she said, pulling him towards her and pressing her lips to his.

When she awoke, it was morning, or at least early dawn. She opened her eyes and saw the stranger sitting a short distance away, against the wall, wearing his leggings and tunic. She sat up, not immediately recalling that she was naked, and merely brushed her hair from her eyes.

"I'm sorry," he said.

"What do you mean, you're sorry?" she replied, still half-asleep.

"For bringing you here and sleeping with you."

"What's come over you?" she said. "I wanted to come. And why are you dressed? Come here and lie down." Her head hurt a little trying to sit up.

He shook his head. "It was all a mistake. I'm sorry."

"A mistake?"

He seemed to gather himself before replying. "To…to have sex with a priestess…it seems wrong."

She groaned aloud and lay back on the pile of hay they had heaped up the evening before.

"I didn't realise last night," he said, "in the dark, but this morning, I couldn't help but notice, when your back was turned to me…"

"Of course you couldn't see last night. I was lying on my back," she said.

"Only the first time," he replied, "but it was dark."

Why is he making things so difficult, Signy thought.

"And then, I got to thinking. I've seen a mark like that somewhere before. It took me a while to place it, because the last time it wasn't on the girl's rear, but on her chest." He tapped himself. "Just above her left tit when she leaned over."

Plenty of girls have this mark, Signy thought, as she lay staring at the ceiling.

"And it wasn't just that," the man continued. "Once I got a good look at you in the light, I thought I recognised you."

"What do you mean?" she said, sitting up again.

"That's just it," he said, waving to her, vaguely in the direction of her tattoo. "I've seen you before, not like that, not bare-chested, of course, but near enough."

Now she was interested. What in hell was he talking about?

"Stop hiding over there," she said, "and come here."

"You won't…curse me, or something?"

"Of course I won't fucking curse you. I only want to get a look at you, since you seem to have been examining me very carefully."

Yes, there is an air about the man that seems familiar, she thought. Maybe that was why she had felt comfortable talking to him, maybe why she felt it was reasonable to kiss him, to lead him to the hayloft, to strip off her clothes and let him have his way with her, no, to eagerly join with him. The comfort of familiarity, somewhere at the gut level – or maybe lower.

She sighed, reaching for the dress she had so eagerly discarded the night before, and wrapping it around her body.

"Where do you think you have seen me?"

"In Juteland, at a feast. Oswulf the chieftain's feast."

Oh, by the gods, now his features snapped into focus.

"The envoy, the Duke's envoy!"

He nodded, looking slightly embarrassed.

"I'm sorry, I never expected…I mean, fucking a priestess is bad enough, but a chieftain's wife…"

"Tell me your name," she ordered.

He looked hesitant before replying.

"Alwynn," he said. "Alwynn, son of Blugrimm."

"Well, Alwynn, son of Blugrimm," she said, "my husband's dead, and a priestess deserves a good fuck as well as any other woman, especially when she hasn't been getting one recently. Thank you for what you did last night, and" – she tugged at his arm – "what you're going to do before you leave."

Now he looked even more alarmed. "What do you mean?"

"You know what you said about not cursing you…Well, I have a proposition, Alwynn, servant of my master's enemy, and mine, too. I know who your master is, this so-called Duke. He's Drusus Astrebanus, and if I climbed down that ladder and called for help, especially dressed like this, you would be hanging from your heels in the marketplace before midday."

"But you're not going to do that?" There was a genuine note of anxiety in his voice.

"No, I'm not, and I promise not to curse you, but to carry kind memories of you, if you'll only go and find some food and drink, then come back here and take your clothes off again, now I'm sober and can appreciate you better. Here's my dress as a hostage. If I don't keep my word, you can give it your next conquest, and I'll have to walk naked through the town to reach my home."

She looked a mess, and Megana was not slow to notice.

"Where have you been? You look like you've been dragged through a haystack."

"I went out and got fucked."

"You what?"

"I was upset and alone, so I went and I got fucked by a stranger, and it was very nice, and we did it again this morning, but now I feel lousy and hung-over, and I need to get cleaned up."

"I think you do," said Megana, hands on her hips, "and when you've done that, we need to have a good talk."

Signy did not dare disturb Megana in her workroom, and it took a while before her friend found her sitting in the atrium, half-asleep.

"What the hell did you think you were doing?" said Megana when she found her. "You could have been murdered!"

"It turned out he wasn't a stranger," said Signy. "We'd met before, and exchanged about five words, in Juteland."

"Why, of all days, yesterday, did you go out and pick up a man? I mean, you've been living here more than a year…"

"You had your party inside with the better people. I had to find my own fun. They were giving out free wine, and—"

"You don't have to pay for the wine here. If it was only the wine, you could get drunk every evening and go out into the forum and find some fun, as you put it. There are plenty of women in this town who do just that. I'm not stopping you. No, Signy, I know you too well."

"I love him, Megana," Signy said softly. "I've loved him from the moment I set eyes on him. I want him and I can't have him."

Megana narrowed her eyes. "Who exactly are we talking about, Signy?" And then her eyes opened. "Oh, by the gods, you're not serious. Not…not—"

"Marcus…yes…I helped him. I helped him, Megana, and nobody thought to ask me to the feast. So I went and got pissed, and the more I drank, the more I wanted him, until I got carried away, and I must have vaguely recognised the man, and I went away with him, and we had sex several times…in a hayloft…and I enjoyed it, and…I'm not a whore, Megana…I don't sleep around, but if I can't have the man I want, can you blame me for taking another one? I mean, I can't replace men with work like you do."

"What the heck is that supposed to mean?" said Megana, shaking her head and eyeing her friend. "You want to bed our glorious monarch," she said finally. "Well, I admit I missed my chance."

"You…and Marcus? But he's your godfather!"

"What do you think goddaughters are for? When a man loses his wife, they're a convenient replacement, unless, of course, their father doesn't argue their case."

"Megana, now you've got *me* confused."

"I missed my chance, Signy, when Hypatia died and Marcus was looking for a new wife. It could have been me if Father had had more sense. I would have been a great wife for Marcus. He's not the slightest bit interested in trading, and look how Bryna has a free hand at Verdaris."

"But Bryna's twice your age, and Marcus even more so."

"Darling," said Megana, putting her arm around Signy, "you're the one who just said she wants to bed my godfather. How old do you think you are? You can never be his wife, Signy, unless something happens to Bryna, and even then…"

"I don't need to be his wife. I wasn't Thorgill's wife. He bought me to go to bed with, don't you remember?"

Megana looked thoughtful for as moment.

"You're serious, aren't you?"

Signy nodded, tears coming to her eyes. "I love him. I want him, Megana, and I went and spent the night with another man because I couldn't be with him."

"Oh boy, you *are* serious," said Megana, seeing Signy's tears. "Sister, this is going to take some heavy thinking."

No stranger, thought Signy later, when her mind was clearer, but Alwynn, Drusus Astrebanus' man. He had been in Oswulf's hall, and now he was nosing about in Corinium, spying on the festivities. Probably he had been one of those who had betrayed Fulvia's father and opened the gates of her town to the Jutes. If he was here, then Drusus could not be far away, nor his nephew, and that could mean trouble, trouble for her and trouble for Marcus. Perhaps she should warn the new king, but how? She had promised she would not betray Alwynn. On the other hand, the Frisian seemed to have been genuinely worried that he had taken advantage of a priestess. Even a brute like Alwynn could be superstitious and fear the gods. Men, she thought – and women, too, she reflected, were not much better.

Signy's daily routine did not take her near the forum or the basilica, otherwise she might have crossed paths with the new king. The girls in the Minerva House told how he still walked alone through the streets of Corinium, sometimes stopping to chat with townspeople. Was that really the way that a king should behave? Signy had read, in one of the old books the deacon had made her struggle through, that the Roman Emperors sometimes snuck out at night in disguise to hear the voices and opinions of the plebs, more often, though, to party and play tricks. She doubted they went out alone, more likely with several toughs to protect them if the situation got out of hand.

"I think he's a bit soft on me," laughed Meri. They were shelling beans at the time.

"Who?"

"Counsellor Pacius," replied the former milkmaid. "He's always hanging around and telling me stuff."

He probably likes girls with big breasts, thought Signy instantly, and then cursed herself for being foolish and mean.

"He's probably just trying to impress you, since he's new to the position."

If I was more honest, thought Signy, I would admit that Meri is quite pretty now she has put aside her servants' clothes and takes more care of her appearance. Why shouldn't she have a fine boyfriend? She has been brave enough to try schooling, just as I advised her, and wasn't that the whole point, to fish ourselves a better class of husband? And besides, a lot of men did fancy girls with big breasts, Signy reflected ruefully. Big breasts were a characteristic she definitely lacked. If Counsellor Pacius was interested in Meri for that reason, he might have a little competition.

"Anyhow," continued Meri, not wishing to miss the opportunity to relate what the Counsellor had told her, "Pacius said that he and Treasurer Flavius think that our king would appear more dignified if he was accompanied by bodyguards when he travels around. They're recruiting men to make up the guard."

"And what sort of men are they looking for?" Signy asked.

"Ones with big spears," whispered Meri, with a smirk.

"Grunwald would make a good bodyguard," Signy said to Megana later in the day, "much better than he is as a carpenter."

If she could wangle Grunwald into the guard, it would solve two problems. First, Drusus Astrebanus was no longer the only one interested in knowing where Marcus was and what he was doing. Second, the young Jute obviously fancied her, and while she might have enjoyed his attentions if she had still been merely a farm girl, that was long in the past. He could put his spear to better use. But, for just that reason, she knew he would stay loyal, and having a loyal man in Marcus' guard would have a definite advantage.

"Counsellor Pacius owes me a favour or two," said Megana with a smile and half-closed eyes. "It's payback time."

A few days later, Signy was pleased to see that Grunwald was one of the four men, stepping smartly, with shouldered javelins, escorting the new king on his duties. Marcus' days of chatting with the ordinary inhabitants of Corinium had ended.

❦ Chapter 24 ❦

When the great feast was over, and the king and his wife had departed for visits to the magnates and potentates around the newly named Kingdom of the West Britons, Signy returned to the school bench: Latin grammar with Father Felix and reading aloud, usually from the Christian Bible, under the watchful eye of his friend, Mistress Mathilda. While the other girls practised on the abacus – Signy had had enough of that helping Megana organise the feast – Deacon Baxter taught her the basics of geometry from a battered copy of Euclid and a tattered manual on laying out military camps.

"You look exhausted," said Signy, catching Megana one morning in her workroom.

Megana put down her stylus and tapped her tablet. "Look at this," she said. "Carvings from Gaul, wall hangings from Belgica, and gilded furniture. In Grandfather's time, I could have sent a messenger to Londinium and got my hands on everything, but now, it all has to be ordered piece by piece."

"Is there anything I can do to help?"

Megana observed her thoughtfully. "Maybe there is," she said, searching about on her desk. "Maybe you can put your geometry – the deacon said you're a far better pupil than I ever was…"

"He's teasing."

"…to some use," she continued, handing Signy a wax tablet covered with numbers, some entirely scratched out and others redrawn so they were almost indecipherable. "It's only simple clerk's work, but I can't make head or tail of these numbers Master Wulfthere has provided concerning the stables. He estimates everything in his head. He has no idea of keeping records. Each building ends up a little different."

Signy glanced down at the tablet. The symbols made no sense to her either, but then why should they, she reflected.

"You'll have to go out to the building site," Megana went on, picking up her stylus again. "But don't let Uncle Marcus disturb you. He's always up there nosing about. He tries hard not to be a nuisance, but he still distracts the workers."

Signy took the tablet round to show the deacon, who scratched his head and rubbed his beard.

"You should copy the relevant pages out of the geometry book to master the principles. It would be good practice," he said at last, "but you might find the army manual more use."

She gave him a hug. "You'll help me if I run into problems, won't you?"

"I wish I could," he said, "but I'm travelling tomorrow, down to the monastery at St Penn's, and I'll be away for several weeks."

"Will you be meeting other Christians, like when I went to the festival with Irmengaard?"

"No, my dear," he said, calling for beer, "it's one of my duties to supervise Mistress Milesia. Let me tell you the story…"

And so they sat until long after dark while Baxter told the tale, and by the end Signy had reckoned out that supervising the mysterious Milesia was far from a duty.

But that left her alone with the task of reconciling Wulfthere's estimates and Megana's obsession with precision.

She enjoyed walking through the site, talking to the craftsmen, watching the Jute boys, as she thought of them, levering posts upright, swinging beams into place. As the skeletons of the buildings took form, she recognised the shapes that the deacon had shown her in the geometry book. If she could only understand how to take the lines she saw in the book and match them to the posts and beams, or reduce the knowledge of the carpenter to a drawing, then she could list all the materials and make sure they were delivered to the site when they were needed. It was difficult, though, because the geometry book was written in Greek and not terribly practical, whereas the master carpenter knew exactly what he was supposed to do, and had little interest in explaining his thoughts to a nosey young woman.

One day, she was sitting on her stool watching some labourers constructing a roof truss. As they manoeuvred the timber into place, she sketched on the tablet and checked with the book as she made her calculations. She heard footsteps behind her, and a shadow fell over her page. She glanced around and saw it was Marcus, and for a moment, her mind froze. She had been so carefully concentrating on the geometry, she had forgotten she was thinking in Greek.

"Hello, Master, it is a long time since we met," she said in that language.

"Hello, Mistress Signy," he replied. "I did not know you could speak Greek."

She could hear the surprise in his voice. She did not dare look up at him, but sat with her head down, staring at the geometry book. "Only a little that Megana taught me," she replied.

"Am I disturbing your work?" he asked, looking down at her. He was, but not in a bad way. "Euclid?" he remarked, with a chuckle. "I think that must be my old copy."

"Yes, Master," she replied. She felt her body go tense. She had to tell him. Something she had been thinking about ever since Megana had casually mentioned that he had the habit of visiting the building site – except Megana never mentioned anything casually.

Could she put the thoughts that had circled her head into words? And now she had been trapped into speaking Greek!

"Marcus, I have something to say to you. I love you," she said in a rush. She did not look up. She knew he must have heard her, must have understood her, by a faint shift in his shadow and in the sound of his breathing. "I have loved you ever since I first saw you, the first time you rode into the camp." She wanted to say more but dared not. It's love for you that has driven me to educate myself, to learn Latin and Greek, and geometry, so I can be worthy of *your* love, she wanted to say. It's why I've been sitting here, in this building site, day after day, hoping you would show up.

He said nothing, simply standing looking down at her.

Signy glanced up at him in return and smiled. You heard me, she thought, what do you think about that now?

"We're short of wood for completing the stable," she said, now in British, breaking the spell of the moment. "Now I know the reason from my calculations. I must ask Wulfthere to order the correct amount from the stock before we start the next one."

"Are you doing this work for Megana?" he asked, still looking baffled.

"I'm trying to help since she's so busy," Signy replied. She stood, gathered up the book and the tablet, and as she did so, a man, one of Fabiansson's servants, appeared and took hold of her stool.

"Where to, Miss?" he asked.

"I'll leave you to your work," said Marcus, but she knew his eyes were following her as she stepped around the puddles and through the mud of the building site to where the master carpenter was standing. Her heart was still racing. He must have heard what I said! Did he understand me? Would he believe me?

Perhaps it did not matter, since Grunwald told her he was leaving town the following day and would be absent on a tour of the eastern border for the rest of the summer.

"I told him right to his face," she said to Megana, who simply shook her black curls.

"And what did he say?"

"Nothing," admitted Signy. "Maybe he didn't understand me. I spoke in Greek. You know how terrible my accent is."

"Signy, dearest, sometimes you do try me." Megana smiled. "Maybe he was too shocked to say anything? Maybe he understood all too well, and you scrambled *his* thoughts. Uncle Marcus isn't the quickest of thinkers, but he generally comes to the best answer in the end. So what do you plan to do next?"

Megana had hit the nail on the head.

"I've been thinking. Perhaps I could persuade Wulfthere to build me a little cottage, up by the King's Hall, and I could live there. Then your servants wouldn't be bothered by patients coming asking for me at all times of the day and night."

"You mean a cottage like your mentor in Juteland?"

Signy frowned. She hadn't thought of it that way, but Irmengaard's cottage on the edge of the village had certainly given the wise woman freedom to pursue her life her own way, without prying from the neighbours.

"I could have a garden, too, and grow herbs. If we begin right away, I could already harvest some before winter sets in."

She spoke to Wulfthere and showed him a little sketch she had drawn: a small house, with a kitchen and storeroom, and a place to sleep above. The master carpenter studied her plan, found a level piece of land, and put the Jutes to work. It was Signy's house, so they did not need much encouragement.

Megana tried, albeit half-heartedly, to dissuade her from moving.

"Isn't it dangerous to live outside the city walls? Won't you be lonely?"

"Megana, my dear," she responded. "The area around the King's Hall has become a small village in its own right. The bodyguards live in one of the buildings from the old Roman camp, and several of our labourers have put up small homes along the Londinium road, now they have women living with them."

Ferland had been so quick off the mark, he already had a little son.

"The stables and barns are full of animals, and the people who look after them. And I'll still come to the Minerva House every day, and I can still keep the room next to yours, can't I? And besides, I'll be right there, on site if anyone needs my help or advice, and I'll find a maid, a girl from town, so I won't be alone."

⋖ Chapter 25 ⋗

Marcus had returned to town and left again, travelled to Verdaris to supervise the harvest, then he had been in Corinium again for the autumn court of justice and left, and now he was back again. All this Signy knew thanks to Grunwald, who passed on news he snapped up as he went about his duties. While she occasionally visited the Ursinus house to treat an injury or sickness among the household, she always tried to avoid the place when Marcus was present, for fear of crossing paths with him again. She felt embarrassed that she had blurted out her feelings to him. He was the king, after all, and married, and older, and well…what if he thought she was just a silly girl? She *was* on the way to becoming a different person, but the progress was not sufficient, that was quite obvious.

One of the maids had burned her arm in the kitchen and Marcus' housekeeper, Silke, had asked Signy for help. Signy had dressed the wound and promised to return the following day. Now, at the appointed time, she came to the service gate at the rear of the house and was surprised to find it open. She went in, crossed the yard and found Silke and the maid waiting for her in the kitchen. She examined the burn, which was healing well, smeared on a little balm and bound it up again.

"Will you stay for a bite to eat?" asked Silke.

Signy hesitated. She would have enjoyed sitting and gossiping for a while, but she knew the master was home. He could call for Silke at any time, and if she did not respond quickly enough, he would come to find her. It would be better, Silke often said, if he knew his place, which was not in the kitchen, but the governor, as Silke still called him, was altogether too informal, and so a nuisance at times.

"Thank you, but not today, Silke," Signy said, gathering up her basket.

"The master will be travelling to Verdaris tomorrow," said the housekeeper, reading her thoughts.

"Then I'll bring a bottle of the elderberry wine we've been making. Maria has been helping me. She's learning fast. I'll see myself out."

She returned to the gate and stepped out into the alley. It was dark, but a light snow had fallen earlier in the evening, and the white covering on the paving reflected enough of the moonlight for her to see comfortably. She knew her way, and any troublemakers in town knew her, too. Many of them had required her help at some time or another. She was just about to turn into Boot Street, which led out past the shoemaker's into the main square, when she heard a cry behind her.

"Signy, Signy, come back. Come back."

There was a desperate tone to the shout that made her turn on her heels and hurry back to the Ursinus house. The maid with the burned hand was standing at the gate, tears streaming down her face. The girl grabbed Signy's arm as soon as she came within reach and started to pull her into the yard.

"The master, the master, someone has attacked the master!"

Signy felt her heart jump. She needed no more dragging but ran through the kitchen and into the residential part of the house. As she emerged into the atrium, she could see several people bent over towards the far end on the right-hand side.

One of the figures turned towards her at the sound of her steps.

"Thank the gods…Mistress Signy." It was Grunwald.

Signy crouched down. Marcus was prostrate on the pavement of the atrium, halfway out of his workroom. The light was not good, not made better by Grunwald and Silke bending over and blocking it.

"Step back, please," she said. She noticed Marcus move, open his eyes at the sound of her voice. He was alive, at least.

There was blood seeping from his thigh, through the frayed edges of the cloth of his leggings. Another thumb, she thought, and there would be nothing I could do, but this looks like a flesh wound, though nasty. The leg wound did not account for him being half-conscious. Probably he had hit his head when he fell.

"You can carry him to his room," she said, and Grunwald called to the other guard, who was hovering a little way away.

"This one won't be going far," said the man, who turned out to be Captain Beltrice, the chief of the bodyguard. Signy followed Grunwald's gaze, and saw a crumpled shape, slumped against the rim of the water cistern, like a rag doll.

"The man intending murder," muttered Grunwald to Signy, "but I dealt with him."

The two guards hoisted Marcus from the ground.

"Take care," said Signy, grasping at his thigh and squeezing it tight.

The three of them bore the wounded king into his room and laid him on his bed.

"We must remove his trousers," said Signy. "Can you do that, Silke, while I find what I need in my basket?"

The housekeeper and the guard captain drew down Marcus' leggings. Signy could hear him wincing, as the cloth pulled at his wound. She took out a flask from her basket, let a couple of drops of the contents fall onto a spoon.

She bent over the supine king.

"Take these, now, my lord. After that, you won't feel anything." She placed the spoon against his lips and let the drops slip into his mouth. She held his wrist, feeling his arm relax as the medicine took effect. Then she let it gently down and bent over his leg. The wound was deep, but fortunately had gone straight into his thigh muscle. She let a couple more drops of the medication run into the wound.

"Fetch me some old wine, Silke," she said, "some that has gone bad." The housekeeper knew her needs from previous occasions and hurried off to the pantry.

"Will he live?" asked Grunwald.

"Of course," she said, glancing up at the guard. "You, of all people, should trust me. He won't be able to walk for a while, and then he'll have a limp until it's fully healed."

She placed her hand on Marcus' chest, feeling it rise and fall gently. Through her fingertips, she could just make out the beat of his heart.

Silke returned with the stale wine and a clean cloth. Signy washed the wound and, with an expert hand, stitched together the sides with a sharp needle and a length of twisted gut. Then she wiped the whole area again with the stale wine.

"Let me bind up his leg tightly with a piece of cloth. The medication I gave him should last until morning. Then I'll come back and take another look at the wound."

There was a sudden shout from outside.

"Hey, Grunwald, what's happened to the murderer?"

The big Jute disappeared from the room. Signy patted Marcus' thigh, listened one more time to his breathing.

"Take good care of him, Silke," she said, as she left. "Make sure there's someone to sit with him all the night in case he wakes. He mustn't try to get up."

"I'll do it," said the housekeeper, "but first I must send a message to Mistress Bryna, once the stable boy is ready with a horse."

Signy went out into the atrium again, where the two guards were standing shouting at each other. There was no sign of the fallen man.

"I thought you said he was dead," said Beltrice.

"I stick him with sword. No one ever survive." Grunwald's British was not his strong point.

"It looks like someone did," said the captain sourly, "unless he had an accomplice who came into the house while we were busy."

The two guards hurried towards the front entrance. Signy followed them. Just then her eye caught a fallen object tucked in the angle of the cistern edge. She bent down and picked it up: a dagger, more than a foot long and razor-sharp. She was about to call out when she stopped herself. The assailant's dagger, she thought. She knew a little about weapons. Thorgill had fancied himself as an expert. A dagger of this quality might come in useful, she thought, and the murderer won't be needing it.

With great care, she slid the weapon into her basket, under the cloths and bottles and flasks and small bags, where no one would see it.

The guards were coming back.

"Not in house," said Grunwald.

"No point going out to find him at this time of night," said Beltrice, "at least until we have the rest of the guards here to secure the building."

"I send messenger to barracks, one house boy," said Grunwald, disappearing into the rear of the house.

"I'll be going then," said Signy to no one in particular, and stepped out of the front door of the Ursinus house into the snowy street.

That was the first time I touched him, she thought, the first time I felt his heartbeat. But, but oh, how I wish it had been under other circumstances. How close it was to all my dreams being dashed! Instead, instead, I've had a chance to help him, to care for him. You shouldn't leave him alone like that, my lady, her thoughts jumped to Bryna.

She turned to the left and was about to turn once more to take the short alley out towards the forum when she saw a pair of shadowy figures crouched down, a little further along the street. She gripped the short knife she always carried at her belt, but instead of hurrying away, something drew her towards them. Trouble was not unknown in the streets of Corinium, the sort that led injured men to her hands, but more usually the result of drinking and quarrelling than back-alley robbery. The first thought she had was that the two figures were assisting a friend, perhaps a man who had drunk too much and fallen.

"Halloo!" she said, loudly, not wishing to surprise them.

The man closest to her turned abruptly. There was no sign of cold steel in his hand, she was relieved to see. She had no desire to be another stabbing victim herself or get into a knife fight with a man.

As she came nearer, she saw, as she had thought, that there was a third figure lying on the ground.

"Let me through," she said. "What's happened here?"

The man who had faced her stepped aside but did not answer her question. She bent down to take a closer look at the fallen figure, a man, dressed in black, with an obvious bleeding wound in his side. She swore to herself. Could this be the assailant, the man who had attacked Marcus, the man whose dagger she had tucked in her basket? Why had she come this way? Why had she not taken the back alley? Why had she not rounded the corner and walked on?

She stepped back, half-ready to turn away. Instinctively, she glanced along the street towards the door of the Ursinus house. There was no one to be seen. Obviously, they must all be inside, caring for their master, sending messages hither and thither. Her eye caught a trail of blood drops in the snow, from the door to the place where she was now standing. The man must have used the last of his strength to stagger out of the house while everyone was distracted and stumble along the street only to collapse here, in the shadow of the wall.

"Do you know who he is?" she asked.

"Our master," said one of the men. "He's injured. He's going to die."

She crouched down. The man certainly looked pale. He must have lost a lot of blood, but perhaps his clothes had kept the wound from opening too far.

"You can't move him," she said, "not when he's like this. The wound will open again, and he'll bleed out, like a slaughtered pig."

"We can't leave him here," said one of the men.

"No, you can't," she said, with another glance back to the Ursinus house. "That will be certain death for him, too."

The strangers looked at her doubtfully.

"Give me your cloak," she said, taking hold of the first man's cloak.

"Hey," he replied.

"Give it to me," she said, "if you want to save his life." She stood up, looked him in the face. "Listen, I'm a wise woman. I have the power of healing. I've tended injured warriors. This man need not die, if you do as I say." Though I don't know what state he'll be in if we do save him, she thought. "Give me your cloak," she repeated.

The man handed her his cloak and stood shivering in the cold. You won't take any harm from a little cold air, she thought, as she pulled out her knife, slit the edge of the cloak and tore a long strip from it. She bound the cloth tightly around the unconscious figure, reinforcing the protective effect of his clothes.

"Now make a sling from the rest of the cloak and lay him gently on it. Try to move him as little as possible."

She watched carefully for signs of bleeding as the men eased their master onto the cloth stretcher.

"Pick up the corners and carry him to wherever you have come from. Stay away from the main streets. I'll come with you."

The two men seized the corners of the cloak and slowly started to trudge along the street. Signy once again glanced back, relieved to still see no sign of life from the Ursinus house. The three of them continued until they had almost reached the south town wall.

"We need to cross the main street," whispered one of the men.

"Wait then, and I'll check the way is clear," Signy whispered. Why am I doing this? she thought. This man almost killed Marcus, almost destroyed my dream. But I want to know who he is, who these men are, and eventually, if I have to, I can end it all. One drink from my flask to warm their spirits and they'll all be dead. She quickly peered out into the main street. It was deserted, apart from a single figure, silhouetted against the snow, far away beyond the forum. No searchers, no followers, no hue and cry. She waved to the two men, and they hurried towards her, ducked across the main street and down the alley on the far side.

"Where are we going?" she asked.

"To the deserted tavern. We've been living in the stables, behind the yard."

Who in the gods' names are these men, she wondered, and why did their leader attack Marcus in such a desperate and suicidal manner?

The men took a pair of sharp turns into ever-smaller alleyways, until they shouldered open a narrow gate into the empty stable yard of an abandoned tavern. She had passed the dank and gloomy place on numerous occasions, and never had the idea that someone could be hiding there. They carefully closed the gate and continued towards one of the empty stables. Well inside, it was almost pitch black, but somehow they managed to deposit their injured master onto a heap of straw covered by a rough blanket.

"Make a light," she said, "if you can. I need to remove his clothes and clean his wound and bind it." She swore again to herself, cursing her luck. It was the second time this night she had to carry out this operation, and now in far worse conditions and on a patient with much more severe injuries. One of the men, stumbling around in the murky room, finally found an oil lamp and struck a flint. A flickering glow diffused into the space.

"I need more light," she said. "A torch held up, at least."

There was a rustling behind her, and a sudden burst of extra light. Just don't drop it and set the whole place on fire, she thought, as she leaned once more over the recumbent figure.

There were signs of fresh bleeding through the strip of cloak. She undid it slowly, slowly.

"Come here, you, and hold tight, like this," she said, addressing the man who had nothing in his hands, and showing him where to grip his injured master's waist. She took out her knife and slit up the man's jerkin, then dragged at the cloth to tear it apart. The wound was fairly clean. The sword must have been razor-sharp. Oh, Grunwald, she thought, you have taken care of your weapon.

"Keep a tight hold," she said. "If you loosen your grip, he'll die."

She checked around the wound for pieces of cloth that had been driven in by the sword blow, using the point of her knife to prise them out. She did not dare explore too deep, for fear that the flow of blood would resume.

"That'll have to do," she said, reaching for a phial of resinous fluid. She dribbled it over the wound, took a sharp needle and a length of sinew from her basket, and with deft movements ran half a dozen stitches across the wound to hold it closed. She tore off a new length of fabric from the cloak and bound it tightly around the man's belly.

She stepped back and took a breath. She had been concentrating so hard on the wound that she had not looked at the injured man's face. Now, in the light of the burning torch, she could see what she had not had time to see in Marcus' courtyard or been able to see in the street – the man's features. Even now, drained of blood and in the flickering light, she understood the whole story of who he was and why he had carried out the reckless deed. The man she saw was Drusus Astrebanus.

She turned to look at the men beside her. The first, the man who had assisted her by holding Drusus, was unfamiliar, but the second, the man holding the torch, she recognised at once.

"Alwynn," she said faintly.

"I hoped it was you," he said. "I prayed it was you when you joined us in the street. Only you, Mistress, could save his life."

"Give him this, a pinch in water, whenever he stirs," she said sharply, handing Alwynn a small pouch of light brown powder. "He must not stir, must not move, roll, try to get up. Do you understand?"

The torch bobbed as Alwynn nodded.

"He must lie completely still. You can dribble water into his mouth, spoon in a little weak gruel if he can swallow it, but don't under any circumstance allow his body to twist. If he moves, he'll die in that instant."

She stepped back.

"Show me out into the street. I'll return tomorrow, after midday."

She looked from one man to the other.

"Your secret is safe with me," she said. "You must trust me if you want to keep him alive."

She stepped out of the deserted tavern and into the dark street. A light snow was falling. If it continued, by morning all trace of their footsteps would have vanished. No one would know that Drusus Astrebanus, the so-called Duke, the traitor, lay severely wounded inside the abandoned building. No one, that is, but his retainers and herself. She took a deep breath and started to walk along the street. In the heat of the moment, she had felt possessed, as if her physical body had taken on a life of its own, as if her hands, her feet, her eyes knew what should be done to save a life, no matter whose life. But now, in the silence of the midnight street, she had to face the question: what should she do next? Alwynn and his unnamed companion could not leave without abandoning their master, and it would be the simplest task to go to the guard – she had to pass their barracks to reach her cottage – and tell them where the man who had tried to kill the king was lying. Taking the outlaws would not be simple. No doubt all three would die, but they wouldn't be the only ones. The two Frisians would go down fighting, and she had seen enough of Alwynn to know he would not be overpowered easily.

On the other hand, so long as they were compelled to nurse their master, she knew where they were. She could control the situation. Marcus' enemy, her enemy, had been delivered into her hands.

⚏ Chapter 26 ⚏

Signy was furious as she made her way through the alleys towards the deserted tavern the following day. Bryna had arrived from Verdaris at dawn and had brusquely taken over Marcus' nursing. She had barely even acknowledged the assistance that Signy had given her husband. *Perhaps she's jealous,* Signy thought, *because I'm a better healer than her. Perhaps she wants to take her husband away from me, in case, in case...*

Signy pushed open the gate and stepped into the tavern yard. Almost immediately, the man who wasn't Alwynn appeared from the stable, a dagger glinting in his hand.

"Peace," she said, "it's only me."

The sound of her voice relaxed the man. He let the hand with the dagger drop, then stuffed the blade into his belt.

"He's sleeping."

Signy's own fury was pushed to one side by the challenge she was facing.

"Very good. I've come to clean the wound and change the dressing. That's all I can do. Otherwise it's in the hands of the gods."

The stable was almost as dark during the middle of the day as it had been during the night, but as her eyes adapted, she carefully scrutinised the face of the man lying peacefully on the straw bed. There was no doubt now. She had last seen this man on a horse by the side of Oswulf, demanding that she be handed over in exchange for Princess Fulvia. What had been his interest in her? None, she supposed, from Drusus himself, except perhaps thwarted pride that Laurentius had been so dismissive of him when he had first seen her. But perhaps otherwise with his nephew…She had seen the younger man's lascivious look in the booth, the glance at the window later in the day, the desire on his face. Perhaps Drusus had hoped to tie his nephew to him using her as a gift.

Well, my friend, she thought, now you're in my hands. One small movement with my knife or a little too much potion and you'll die, but if I choose, you'll go on living. The power of life and death, here in my hands.

You have skill; use it wisely, Ornfrid had said. Today, Signy said to herself, I choose life for you.

She stripped away the bandage, bathed the wound once more in old wine, and closed it up again. "Today's not the critical day," she said to Alwynn and his companion, "but in two or three days, we'll see if he becomes feverish, if the wound begins to stink. If so, there's little more I can do, but if the wound stays clean, then…we shall see what his fate will be."

She packed up her medicines into her basket and stepped towards the door.

"Alwynn, you I know, but you," she said, turning to the other, "what's your name?"

"Liutmann, my lady," said the second.

"Well, Masters Alwynn and Liutmann, you know who I am, the servant of our king—"

"Then," said Alwynn, interrupting, "why are you saving the life of his enemy?"

"I've been given the gift to heal. I've been taught the secrets of life and death, and I've chosen life for this man, because the gods guided me to him, and I've learned not to question their guidance."

It was the best explanation that came to her mind at the moment.

"But will you tell the king where he is?"

"There's no need," she said. "The king's enemies are my enemies, though in his case I have my own personal reasons to fear your master. Now *I* have the power over his life. There's no need to involve the king. I've already said, do as I tell you and he shall live, if the gods wish it."

She wished she could keep quiet, to stop prattling in this ridiculous manner, but the truth was she was not yet sure what she would do. The gods had placed this enemy in her hands. If they wanted him to die, they would have steered her feet away, through the rear gate, or unhesitating, undistracted up the street to the forum. Since they had led her to him, clearly they wished him to live, but why? That was the riddle that was troubling her, making her babble like a drunk.

"Take care not to attract attention to yourselves," she said, forcing herself to sound logical. "The town's agitated now the attack on the king is widely known, and the body of the vegetable seller, the man your master murdered before he sneaked into the Ursinus house, has been discovered. It's not a good time to be a stranger in Corinium. I'll return tomorrow."

I must be possessed, she thought, as she turned the corner of Bakers' Street towards Fabiansson's yard gate. If Beltrice or some other person discovers what I've done, my days on this earth would be as few as those of Drusus and his retainers. I have to keep my mouth closed, not reveal a word. No one must know, not even Megana. And I can still let him die if I choose, she added, as if to reassure herself.

When she arrived at the Fabiansson house, the whole place was abuzz.

"Have you heard the news?"

"Someone tried to kill the king!"

She was exhausted, drained. She did not want to start a conversation with the kitchen staff. She made her way through the maze of rooms to try to reach her own sanctuary undisturbed, but, turning a corner, she was almost knocked down by Megana coming towards her.

"Have you heard the news? Someone tried to kill Uncle Marcus!"

"I know," she said, "I was there."

She slumped down on a nearby bench, set her basket on the pavement.

"Do you want to tell me?" said Megana.

"No," she said, "he'll be alright. A flesh wound. Bryna'll take care of him."

"She's not as skilled as you."

"She's his wife," said Signy.

"They don't say who did it."

Signy gave her a weary gaze.

"The man escaped," Megana continued. "They thought he was dead, but somehow he staggered away."

"I know," said Signy. She was torn. Really, she did not want to say more. She wanted to escape to her room, to lie in peace and think it all out. Megana sat down beside her, and as she did so, Signy noticed the small scar on her thumb, the place she had sliced months before when they had made the promise.

She took a deep breath. "I know who the attacker was," she said. "It was Drusus Astrebanus. I was there, I told you, and I recognised him."

She hesitated again. No, despite their oath, she could not say more. Saying more would place Megana in danger, too. She had to bear this worry herself.

His eyes were open when she came on the following day. She bent over to look into them, to try to see the state of his soul. Registering her presence, he began to speak.

"Xancha," he said, looking blankly into space, his eyes drifting to left and right. "Xancha, have you come back to me?"

"Xancha?" she muttered, glancing towards Alwynn and Liutmann. They shook their heads. He must be delirious, she thought, lost in the netherworld. The gods must have confused him. She hoped that was a good sign, a sign that his body was fighting against whatever rot could be gnawing at his wound.

"Xancha," he repeated, "don't you remember the winter we spent together in Arelate? What fun we had, and how we cuddled together when we were cold. I'm cold now. Won't you comfort me?" A vacant smile spread across his face.

In his madness, he was speaking Greek, not the Greek learned in books, but the Greek that Soraya spoke, that Megana erupted into when she had had a bad day and a glass too many of wine in the evening.

"Xancha must be someone's name, a girl, perhaps," she whispered.

"He's spoken of such a woman before," said Liutmann, edging closer.

"I remember, Drusus." She crouched down and murmured in his ear, hearing Megana in her mind's eye and trying to copy her intonation.

"You still look so young," he said. "How do you do it, when I'm so old and tired?"

"It's magic," she whispered, "magic you can use, too, if you want to, to get better."

"Xancha, you were so beautiful in those days. The little mole on your breast drove me crazy. I couldn't keep my eyes off it the first time I saw you dance."

She froze, not knowing what to say. The man was deranged, living in the past. What was he seeing?

"And then I had you all to myself, for the whole winter. I know I was suspicious you slept around. I was wrong, I admit, now when you have come back to me after all these years. You must have loved me in your own way, though I didn't see it at the time."

"We all loved you, Drusus," she said, a feeling of horror creeping over her, "me and your friends." She hoped to the gods he had some friends who might have loved him.

"Those were times when we were all young and had fun, Xancha. They never came again, not in all my days."

"Better to sleep and dream, Drusus, and I'll be waiting for you."

She bent over, kissed his forehead and backed out of his view. She was trembling and sweating.

She stepped outside into the air of the yard, fresh after the foetid room and the bizarre muttering.

"What was all that about?" she asked the two Frisians.

Alwynn frowned. "I didn't understand a word," he replied, "and I never heard of any Xancha."

"Yes, once when he was drunk," said Liutmann, "and maudlin!"

"Maybe," replied his friend.

"You think his disturbed soul was reliving the past?" said Signy, feeling a little calmer. "Or communicating with the dead?"

"Babbling, more like," muttered Alwynn.

Perhaps he would have something useful to tell me, she thought, if I play along a little, something about the old times.

"Give him the medication. Keep him quiet. Make sure he gets enough to drink, and perhaps something to eat if you can, during his lucid periods. I'll come again tomorrow."

"How long before we can move him?" asked Alwynn.

"Not yet. Not until his wound is clean and has closed," she answered. And until I've had the chance to learn more, she thought.

She walked through the darkened streets of the town, taking several byways and checking behind her to make sure she was not being followed. If she could squeeze some reminiscences out of him, she would need some means to write them down, a wax tablet or some papyrus sheets, and those could be found in the Minerva House.

I can't tell anyone what I'm planning to do, not even Megana, Signy thought. Even Alwynn and Liutmann will have to be misled, in case they suddenly lose their trust in me. I'll have to tell them I need to understand his past to formulate the treatment better. That isn't completely a lie. If I can capture his delusions, I can offer prayers, put together charms that might soften his madness once his physical condition improves. I can't let his thoughts take the same path which led him to attack Marcus, not when I'm responsible for his being alive.

Her heart was in her mouth as she threaded her way through the town to the abandoned tavern the following day, again taking a circuitous route, although why anyone should be following her was unclear. She had heard rumours in the town that Drusus was the guilty man and that his body had vanished, but everyone assumed he had died, an end, the public concluded, he certainly deserved after killing the vegetable seller and attacking the king. Everyone assumed he had companions with him who had carried the corpse away, away into lawless eastern Britannia where no one would find him. There was nothing to associate Signy the healer with the murderer.

"He was quiet during the night," said Alwynn, "but now he's uneasy again."

"The medicine wears off," said Signy, "but that's important. If he's asleep all the time, we'll never know whether he's recovering."

"Come and see," said Liutmann. "He was muttering about a Bryna."

"Our Bryna…the queen?"

"How am I supposed to know?" grumbled Liutmann. "I know he thought he was once engaged to a girl called Bryna, in Treviri, but nothing came of it. There's got to be more than one Bryna in this world?"

"I suppose so," said Signy, distractedly. But there's a tangle of threads here, she thought, and I hope I can unravel some of them.

"Leave me here with him for a little while, friends," she said. "I'll take care of him if you need to go into the town for food or drink?"

Alwynn and Liutmann exchanged glances. They had to trust her, she calculated. They had already placed their master's life in her hands. They had placed their own lives in her hands. Why not take the chance to go outside? They would need to hire, or perhaps steal, some horses at some point. A little reconnaissance would never hurt.

She heard them leave, then settled down by the bed, pulling out the wax tablet, unfolding it and taking up her stylus.

"Now Drusus, my darling," she said, in the same attempt at colloquial Greek he had responded to the previous day, "tell your Xancha all about Bryna."

His eyelids flickered and opened. His eyes stared ahead.

"Her father betrayed me," he said. "Milesia betrayed me."

Signy felt a cold drip of sweat run down between her shoulders, and the room was not warm.

"How, my darling, how? Tell me." She held the stylus ready, ready to jot down anything he was going to say.

"It was before I met you…" he started.

Alwynn and Liutmann brought food, three portions from the cookshop.

"What are you scratching down," Alwynn asked, "and why?"

"His words," she said, "his thoughts. I've heard so much about him from Megana, but those have just been stories, told by someone second hand. When I hear him speak himself, it's like I'm living there with him."

Alwynn shook his head. "All this is beyond me. Priestess stuff," he grunted. "Take some food before it gets cold."

"Then you answer me, why are you and Liutmann here," she said, spearing a chunk of roasted pork with her knife, "guarding him, feeding him like a baby, when any moment the king's guards could burst in and put you to the sword?"

Alwynn placed his bowl on the ground and wrapped his arms around his knees, staring into the far corner of the yard.

"We swore an oath, years ago, when we were young, when times looked good, when this king" – he waved his arm vaguely in the direction of the rest of the world – "when this king was a mere, what, hopeful, pretender, usurper, Drusus called him. He offered us gold, an armband" – he stuck out his forearm – "me and my cousin, here, and a few other boys from our tract. And in return, we swore loyalty. We became his men."

He chuckled to himself. "You remember," he said, "me and Liutmann, sitting at the high table in Oswulf's hall. Not bad for a couple of village boys, and you" – he laughed a little louder – "we thought you were some sort of princess."

"So I was," she said, "then."

"Yeah, well," he said, "so life has its ups and downs, and you have to take the good with the bad."

"And once you've sworn, you've sworn," said Liutmann. "If word gets around you've broken your oath, let your master down, then your life's not worth living."

"Even when he's in this state?"

"Till death, and he isn't dead yet."

"Nor any reason why he should be."

"No, and we depend on that," sighed Alwynn. "So long as he's alive, there are people in Gaul, in Francia, Belgica, as it used to be, who owe him, and the memory of his father and brother. It doesn't cost them a lot to keep us in bread and meat, but we're keeping our oath, and putting food into the mouths of our women and children, and a roof over their heads."

"It doesn't cost them a lot," added Liutmann, "to stir up trouble for your king. So long as they still bear a grudge against him."

"And if Drusus dies?"

Alwynn shrugged. "Then we'll just have to become robbers, like so many others, take what we can, have no mercy because our own lives are at stake."

"So as long as Drusus is alive, you can live in peace, and trouble no one."

"You could put it that way, because *he* certainly isn't going to cause any trouble the way he is now."

She lifted her hand to her shoulder and slipped her dress aside.

"Remember, Alwynn," she said, and turned to Liutmann so he could see the tattoo above her left breast. "The oath you swore to Drusus Astrebanus. So long as I keep him alive, you owe that same loyalty to me."

"I never got a chance to tell you about my trip to Rome, you were so angry with me when we met that last time," Drusus said, almost as soon as she sat by his bed. It was the fourth day she had sat beside him, taking notes. She wondered if he was still deluded that she was Xancha, or whether his mind had cleared sufficiently that it was just enough relief to talk. His ravings had become more coherent, though they still jumped from one time in his life to another in a seemingly disordered manner. It was all she had been able to do to transcribe them from the wax tablet to sheets of vellum in the quiet of her cottage and put them into some sort of order. She wrote each episode on a single sheet and reordered the sheets into a chronological system. That way she had managed to obtain an almost complete record of some periods in his life, and selected anecdotes from others. Each evening, after she had finished and the ink had time to dry, she had bundled up all the sheets and hidden them in the bottom of a chest. She did not know what she was going to do with them, whether, even, they had any use.

What a wild goose chase he had had in Rome, at least according to his telling, and she felt he must be telling the truth, because the story was hardly in his favour. She closed up the wax tablet and slid it into her basket.

"Now, my darling," she said, "take this draught, and you'll sleep again and rest, and tomorrow perhaps you'll be well enough to travel."

He was well enough now to sit up, to observe her as she held the beaker to his lips. His eyes were clearer, more focussed. "You're not Xancha," he said, although there was no surprise or fear in his voice, "though you sound so much like her. Who are you?"

She hesitated. Should she tell him the truth?

"Signy," came a voice behind her, a voice she had not heard for years, but which she recognised immediately, "you're Signy, Thorgill's woman."

She whirled around and there he was, his cold grey eyes fastened on her, visible even in the half-light of the sick room. What a fool she had been! In the excitement of treating Drusus, in listening to his stories, she had neglected to consider his nephew. Alwynn and Liutmann had never mentioned him, and where were they now she needed them?

"Constantinus?" she muttered.

He continued to look down at her.

"Yes, and you've been taking care of my uncle, how very thoughtful!"

"It's been my duty…no more or less. Your uncle was injured, don't you know?"

"You remember me." Constantinus smiled, reaching out towards her. "You remember Laurentius told me to keep my hands off you, you remember he told Uncle Drusus your price was too high for him…for me."

"That was long ago, in a different place."

"Exactly, but not so long ago I've stopped thinking about you. And now Fortuna has brought us back together. What's your price now, little girl, now when there's no Laurentius to guard you? When no one knows you're here in this house?"

Still crouching, she stretched out for her basket, where the dagger was hidden, but he noticed her movement and kicked it away.

"You've taken care of my uncle. Now you can take care of me."

He unclipped his belt and dropped it to one side. Even in the dim light of the stable, it was clear what he had in mind.

She stood up, backed away, but he stepped towards her, pushing her into the corner. She could retreat no further. His hands clutched at her dress, lifting it up her thighs. She beat him with her fists, but it made no difference. His hands were under the dress, clawing at the undershorts she had started to wear, Roman style, dragging them over her hips. She tried to kick, but he was too close. She closed her eyes. She could feel him against her, his hand fumbling between her legs. In a moment…

Then he was gone, stumbling backward. Alwynn half turned him, punched him once, twice, in the gut and in the head, and his knee drove into his groin. Constantinus doubled up and was met with another blow in the face. He staggered, now pushed up against Signy. Alwynn's knee drove home again, and he slipped to the floor. Alwynn's boot crashed into his head, his chest, down onto his neck, until a hand gripped the Frisian and drew him back.

"Enough, cousin. You'll kill the man."

"I'll kill him. I'll kill the bastard."

"No, cousin." Liutmann pulled him away, and all at once Alwynn crumpled himself, crouching weeping on the floor of the stable.

Liutmann's gaze turned towards Signy, who had not uttered a sound during the whole assault. Slowly, she bent down and reached for her underwear, and as she did her torn dress fell open. Oh, what the hell did it matter now if Liutmann saw her nakedness, was all she could think as she tried to adjust her tattered clothing.

"Did he…?" asked Liutmann.

"No," she said.

"I'm sorry," said Liutmann.

"It's my own fault," she said at last.

"No," said Liutmann, "but he wasn't with us."

"Then he found you?"

She looked down at Constantinus' crumpled form. He was unconscious, unmoving, breathing, though not dead. She did not care if he died or lived, but her instincts told her he would live.

Alwynn was on his feet again, wiping a hand across his face.

"Let me go," she said, picking up her basket.

She stepped past them, out into the cool twilight. Alwynn was behind her.

"Just let me go," she said.

"Is that all?"

Then she thought again, turning towards him. "Let me go now. Meet me tomorrow, by the butcher's stall in Sheep Street. You, and you alone."

How she managed to reach her house, clutching her basket to her to hold the remains of her dress in place, without crossing paths with anyone she knew, she could never explain. By some miracle, Maria was not at home. Signy tore off the remains of her dress and the tatters of her underwear, rolled them into a ball and threw them into the fire. Then she managed to draw a bucket of water from the well, and, in a secluded corner of her yard, she emptied the bucket of water over herself, letting it run down her head, her face, her body. For a moment, she stood shivering in the evening breeze, taking deep breaths of the fresh air, as if she needed cleaning inside as well as out.

She found the jug of elderberry wine that she had intended to share with Silke, took a beaker and climbed the ladder to her sleeping loft under the eaves. She sat on the floor, back to the wall, and poured herself a beaker of wine. In a couple of gulps, the beaker was emptied, and she poured herself another, but she put the cup to one side, pulled up her knees and wrapped her arms around them.

I have lost my way, she thought, like a person wandering in the forest. But a real forest dweller was never truly lost. A real forest dweller knew the signs that would lead her to safety…eventually. A real forest dweller kept her eyes and ears open for dangerous beasts, knew how to avoid them, pacify them if necessary. She had turned her eyes away, let her ears be filled with words, and the beast had found her, had her in its grasp. What were the signs, where were the signs, that she could follow out of this forest?

For the first, she thought, I'm alive. I'm whole, unviolated, and that makes me a great deal luckier than many other women. I don't need to look farther than Martha and Leema. I just have to remember the wives and bed partners of Thorgill's neighbours and their memories of their old homes. Every one of them had been taken against her will and forced to submit to the man who now called himself her master, or husband if she was lucky. And they could laugh and joke at the feasts, and love their children, and have pride in who they were, most of them, at least. She took up the beaker and swigged the wine. I can only leave myself off that list because Thorgill never had to force himself on me. I was always quite willing. And that's the difference, isn't it? One of attitude of mind, though I might not be so philosophical if Constantinus had got six thumbs further on.

She took another swig from the beaker. It was almost empty, so she filled it once again. She noticed the contours of the room were beginning to lose a little sharpness.

And his uncle, what am I going to do about him? Everything has got so horribly tangled. I had no real motive to help him, beyond dealing with the emergency. Then I let myself get curious, curious to see if I could keep him alive, curious to hear his stories, to hear his side of the tales I've heard from Megana and Deacon Baxter. And look where that curiosity has got me!

She took another pull from the beaker. Some of the wine dribbled down onto her bare breasts. A good thing I never put on a clean tunic, she thought.

Alwynn and Liutmann owe me, she thought, so long as I keep Drusus alive. I think I can trust Alwynn. He obviously remembers the night we had together, probably would like a repeat. Liutmann and Drusus' other followers, wherever they are, I can believe they'll follow Alwynn's lead. Through Alwynn I can keep Drusus' followers quiet, peaceful, no threat to the kingdom, no threat to Marcus. Everything I'm doing is for the good, she consoled herself.

The room seemed to be rocking, as if she was back on Thorgill's boat. She took another slurp of wine to steady herself, but the waves must be rough, she thought, as this time a good quantity splashed out, trickling down her chest and belly.

What about Drusus himself? She laughed to herself. I have him in my power, his life or his death. His body will walk and talk and eat and sleep so long as I choose. But his soul, his *hugr*, the entity that makes him who he is, is in my hands, scribbled down on my tablet, copied onto my parchment sheets, bound together and closed up in the casket under my bed.

She reached out to touch the casket, but her hand didn't seem to want to go where she ordered it.

Once, she remembered, Irmengaard threatened me before we became friends. Dear Irmengaard, she said she would steal my *hugr* and keep my body alive. Signy laughed out loud. But she didn't know if such a curse was possible…Well, now I know. Now I've succeeded! I'm the best! Better than Irmengaard! Better than Ornfrid! I have a man's *hugr* locked up in my box, and his life is mine, and through his life I can control his people, make them do what I want. Fuck those people who think I'm a witch! I *am* a witch, and a really, really good one.

The beaker was empty once more. She reached for the jug. It was curiously light. She lifted it to her lips. The last few drops landed on her chin, slid off her face, and she did not care where they went.

That wine was strong, she concluded. No wonder civilised people generally drink wine diluted with water. *I swear I'll stick to ale, starting tomorrow. But before then I have to get up from the floor and onto the bed.*

She was seated on a horse, in the open air, on a flat plain which stretched out into an interminable distance. She turned and saw that Marcus was beside her. When he looked towards her, his face was distorted by anger.

"Don't you see what you have done with your foolish talk?"

His Saxon was perfect. He sounded just like the chief in her home village.

"What do you mean?" she asked, filled with dismay.

"Look!" he said, and pointed behind them.

She turned awkwardly on the horse. All across the plain, warriors were fighting, two together, here and there a group in a melee, in another place two long lines of warriors, pushing and heaving at each other. And there were bodies, dead bodies and living bodies, and she could hear the screams and cries as they were being picked at by crows and ravens.

"Don't you see what you have done by speaking out of turn?" growled the king, now wearing his crown, a ring of bronze with an eagle sticking up at the front. "Have you forgotten what I told you, how you will pay for this treachery?"

He drew his sword with a long scraping sound.

"No!" she begged. "Please! I was only trying to help!"

He lifted the sword above his head and moved his horse closer to hers.

"For this you must die!"

"No!" she screamed, trying to back her own horse away. "I didn't mean any harm."

But her horse would not move, standing stubbornly in the same place despite her efforts.

"No!" she cried. "I love you. Have mercy on me! I only did it because I love you!"

She felt a hand grasp her shoulder, a glimpse of Gisla behind her, and then the sword came swinging down and all she could do was whimper.

"Mistress, Mistress," came a voice, and the hand on her shoulder was Maria's, shaking her awake. "Wake up, in God's and Jesus' name, wake up! You were screaming. I was frightened."

Signy shook herself, rubbed her hand across her face. Her stomach clenched, and she felt as if she might vomit.

"I was dreaming, Maria," she whispered, "a horrible dream."

She could not see the girl's expression in the dark, only hear the worry in her voice.

She felt awful. Her eyes burned and her mouth was dry, and she felt frightened herself, that if she fell asleep again she would return to the same dream. She reached out and took hold of her maid's arm.

"Maria, my dear, will you lie down beside me, just so I can hold you and you can hold me. Something horrible happened today, and I feel so bad."

The girl tentatively eased herself onto the cot and stretched out. Signy felt her arm reach over and pull them together. She leaned her head against Maria's breast and fell fast asleep.

When Signy awoke, light was pouring in through the window hole since she had not thought to close the shutters the night before. Maria was still asleep, curled up like a puppy. Suddenly, their cat's head appeared above the edge of the bed, and it mewed reproachfully.

Signy slid off the bed, taking care not to wake the sleeping maid. She got to her feet, and all at once, the floor felt like it was tilting beneath her, and she had to grab at one of the rafters to stop herself falling. Her head was thumping like someone was shoeing a horse inside it. The cat scampered away, disappearing down the ladder to the room below. Signy looked down at the girl. Sometimes, she felt that Maria was like a younger sister, a sister she had never had, and sometimes she seemed so small and fragile that she was more like a daughter. Signy did not know how old her maid was in years, only that her mother had died and her father could not keep her, so Signy had taken her in. She can sleep where she is, thought Signy. She deserves a place on the bed instead of her usual spot on the bench in the kitchen after the comfort she provided during the night.

Signy carefully descended the ladder. The world, at least, had steadied, and in the kitchen would be small beer or, better still, some nettle tea to calm the disturbance in her head and the aches in her limbs.

Alwynn was waiting at the appointed time.

"You look awful," was the first he said.

"So would you if you nearly got raped and then got completely drunk," she muttered.

He took her by the elbow and steered her away from the stall.

"Not so fast, Alwynn," she said. "Sometimes hiding in plain sight works better."

"I don't know," he began, "how Constantinus turned up. Drusus had sent him to the mainland, to a city there, Remis, where he has friends, to keep him out of the way. He must have come back, heard his uncle had come to Corinium, spotted us and followed us."

"It doesn't matter where he *was*," she replied, "or how he got here. I don't want to discuss this any longer. If you want me to continue treating your master, you must make sure his nephew doesn't cross my path again. And take care of your own back. You once had a thing he wants for himself and was frenzied enough to try to take yesterday."

She looked up at the tall Frisian. "That's my price, Alwynn. Peace of mind."

"I can't…kill him, if that's what you mean," said Alwynn. "He's still my master's nephew."

"I didn't ask you to kill him, just to keep him away. It's your master's life that's in danger. If your master isn't given the medication, his illness, his madness, will return."

"I understand."

"I can't come to you anymore," she said. "It isn't safe so long as Constantinus is close by."

"He's not capable of doing anything. He's in nearly as bad state as Dr…my master."

"That doesn't matter. I don't want to see him or hear him again, ever. Here's the medication for today. Your master has healed sufficiently to move, if you're careful with him. Tomorrow, I'll give you enough of the remedy for one cycle of the moon, and then you're to return to me, not in town, that's too dangerous, but by the tombs…by Hypatia Ursina's tomb, do you know it?"

The Frisian nodded. "I do."

"Then understand this, Alwynn. You've only one chance. If I see Constantinus again, you'll not receive a drop more. Take him with you, and make sure he never returns. The means you use you can choose yourself."

"Very well, my lady," said Alwynn. "I'm sorry this has happened. I didn't know…"

She shook her head, and immediately regretted having done so.

"Until tomorrow." And she hurried away, watching from the corner of her eye until she could see him no more.

How long did she dare to wait, to be sure that they had really taken Constantinus? She had no desire to hide in the Fabiansson house, and she wouldn't dare to visit the deserted tavern again. She would just have to lie low, keep quiet for one month until Alwynn returned and confirmed Constantinus had gone.

ℭ Chapter 27 ℬ

She had chosen a good night, by chance, for the rendezvous. There was little moon, and that was obscured by passing clouds.

Signy had spent most of the month in her cottage, readying the garden for the spring, making up medications with the assistance of Maria – powder, creams and infusions, and little bags with dried herbs and beads, and the tedious job of drilling holes in some badger claws she had found in the woods. A couple of patients had called in, and she had ridden out to visit a couple more, but otherwise she had kept herself to herself.

There was a rustle from among the bushes, and for a moment, she was on the alert, her hand reaching for the handle of her dagger. She had swapped the small knife she had previously carried for the lethal weapon that Drusus had dropped. That, too, she had exercised with, Maria holding up a sack tightly stuffed with dead grass, mounted on a stick, while she drew the dagger and plunged it into the heart she had drawn on the cloth…up under the rib cage and into the beating source of life where death would be instantaneous. Another skill she had learned from Thorgill.

The shadow that emerged from the edge of the wood was reassuringly that of Alwynn. He touched his forehead as he approached.

"My lady."

"Is your master well?"

The Frisian grunted. "Alive, at least, and talking now and then. He's convinced he was snatched from death by a witch."

Signy laughed softly. "So he was," she replied, reaching down into the basket and drawing up a stoppered bottle. "Enough to cover your small fingernail, morning and evening. No more, no less. I'm not a mere figure of fear. I've tested the strength and calculated the quantity."

He took the bottle, tested the stopper and dropped it into the bag at his side.

"And Constantinus?"

"He's still alive, if that's what you mean," replied Alwynn. "But it'll be a while before he's interested in women again."

She gave him a firm look, rather than asking the obvious question.

"Two of the lads carried him down to Dubris. He couldn't ride, not with his arms and legs bound. They took him back to the mainland, back to his friends in Remis."

"He's away, far away."

"I promise, my lady."

She felt a surge of relief, a great wave of warmth spreading over her body. She felt like she had been given her freedom once more.

"Thank you, Alwynn," she said, wrapping her arms around him.

"I have to leave," he answered. "I have to be well away before dawn."

She watched him vanish into the woods, heard the sounds of a man mounting a horse, and then he was gone. She sat down with her back against Hypatia Ursina's tomb.

"What should I do, Hypatia?" she asked aloud. "Come to me in a dream and tell me, you who were the daughter of the mightiest man in the land, and Marcus' wife and mother to his children. What should I do?"

"Where the hell have you been?" were the first words Megana uttered when Signy walked into her workroom.

"The weather was awful, and I was sick," she replied.

"Well, why didn't you say so?" said Megana, glancing up from the stack of sheets and scrolls and tablets heaped on her writing table.

"It wasn't that kind of sickness. I…" Signy quickly interrupted.

"Ah…" Megana said by way of reply, and began searching among the documents. "Well, for once I think I have the cure," she continued, withdrawing a tattered piece of parchment from the heap. "Uncle Marcus is back in town."

"I saw him. He had a bit of a limp, but Bryna must have done a good enough job."

"He summoned me…to the basilica, and can you guess why?"

"He's decided to marry you after all, now you're no longer a little girl."

Megana's brow furrowed, as if she was going to make a biting comment, but instead she held out the parchment.

"He wants to build a church…as thanks for being saved. He should call it St Signy's."

Signy took the sheet. She knew enough now to make out the form of a box-like structure.

"He wanted a miniature version of the church we have in town," Megana went on, "and had the brilliant idea it could be constructed of stones salvaged from the amphitheatre. Stack up a lot of blocks, and lay some heavy timbers across the top, and I think we would rid this town of all its Christians in one go, with an instant burial to boot."

"That's not a very nice thing to say."

Megana pursed her lips in defiance. "Whatever, Signy, my dear. I don't have time for it. Can't you go and see what can be done? Have a chat with Father Felix and Mistress Mathilda…and my stepmother. They like you and I only annoy them."

"But I'm not even a Christian."

"No, but you're religious…in your own way. You have a feeling for all that stuff, and you know I don't."

Signy tapped the half-folded parchment with one hand against the other.

"And then," Megana spoke again, "when you've consulted the religious people, you could go and hear what Uncle Marcus has to say and try to make him see sense."

"It could be built in wood," Signy suggested.

"You see, as usual you're already halfway to a solution," said Megana, and bent over her documents again.

"Hm," Signy grunted, feeling that the whole conversation had been diverted in a way she had not intended, and with a suspicion it was deliberate.

Megana was obviously upset. Her first thought was that her friend must have an inkling what she had managed to get herself involved in, though even Megana was not all-knowing. More likely it was just that she had been away from the Fabiansson house without any explanation for nearly a month. Or maybe Megana was irritated because she had neglected to show up at the Minerva House either and jumped to the conclusion she wasn't taking her studies seriously. Not that it was so easy to find time with Deacon Baxter anymore, after Marcus had asked him to take charge of a group of boys, sons of various provincial notables, who had been sent to Corinium to polish their learning and obtain experience of what passed for a court.

I can't disturb Baxter, Signy thought, shrugging, and Megana doesn't seem to be in the mood to listen, so perhaps it's better that I go and talk to the priest, and after that I'll go round to the school, and…and I'll help make dinner for the girls. Maybe then I'll feel more myself again.

"I did mention a church to Marcus," Father Felix explained, "because I had thought that a church by the King's Hall would show he meant to rule in a Christian manner."

"It would offer a chance to bring God's word to the Saxons," added Mistress Mathilda. "We so seldom see them at the church in the town."

Signy supposed she was included in that category.

"It's true," she said. "I think the Saxons find the town church a little intimidating. It is so unlike what they are used to."

Mathilda barely suppressed a glare, as if to ask what exactly she meant by that.

"I mean," Signy stammered, "it's a stone building and right in the middle of town." And besides, she felt like adding, you worship in Latin which they can't understand, but she held her tongue.

"We need to bring these heathens to the Lord," insisted Mistress Mathilda. "It's for the good of their souls, their everlasting souls."

Signy doubted that the heathens considered the matter in quite the same way, but she recognised that Father Felix and his friend were sincere, the deacon, too, and she trusted his judgement.

"Perhaps you have some idea of how a church should look to appeal to Saxons," the priest suggested.

"Well, I *was* born in the Saxon lands," she replied quickly, "but we weren't followers of Christ, of course."

"I'm aware of that, my child," said the priest. "It's why I thought you might know how to attract your…"

Signy smiled and reached out to give him a hug. No need to force him to concede that she had never been baptised and so was among the pariahs herself.

"I thought my goddaughter was taking on this project," Marcus said, almost as soon as Signy appeared bearing a roll of parchment in his workroom in the basilica.

"She asked me to hear your ideas."

"But I already told her – a building like the church we have in town. It's a pity it'll have to be smaller, but we simply can't do things now the way we once could."

"We should build in wood," Signy said, "and use the carpenters who have proved their skill by constructing your hall."

The king grunted, as if he was not entirely convinced.

Signy unrolled the parchment and straightened it out on his worktable. Marcus surveyed the inked outline, scratching his beard, and then stabbed a finger on the diagram.

"Would that be it?" he asked, glowering. "It looks like a cow byre!"

"I've sketched out the shape based on our church here in Corinium," Signy explained. "Megana did explain that's what you wanted."

Marcus frowned, evidently caught between criticising her drafting or admitting his own suggestion might be at fault.

"I'm not sure," he said at last. "Couldn't you – we – come up with a better idea."

"I do have another idea," Signy said with a slight smile, "or at least Mistress Mathilda put the idea into my mind."

She began to scratch at the parchment with a scraper she had fortuitously placed in the bag attached to her belt.

"May I borrow a pen?" she asked, fixing a hopeful look on her face.

"Of course," he replied, waving towards his inkstand.

She sketched a few lines, hoping that he did not notice the marks she had made earlier as an aid to her drawing.

"You must attract the heathen to the church, not frighten them off," she said, as she dashed off a line here, another line there. "I thought of the temples in the Saxon lands. I thought if you built a church which resembled a temple, then it would be natural for the unbaptised to find their way there."

"A heathen temple? This is supposed to be a Christian church," he said, peering down at the tracery of lines.

"A place of worship, Master, a holy place, but for the Christian God now."

She added a few flourishes to represent carving around the door and stood back. The king rounded the worktable to see it from the same direction as she did.

"I still don't see the likeness," he muttered, turning to her.

Shit, she said under her breath. Suppose he doesn't understand. This is never going to work. What am I going to do?

"Do you think you could arrange a little carving in wood," he said, placing his hand in a fatherly manner on her shoulder, "the way Megana did with the hall?"

She glanced up at him, feeling the weight of his hand as if it was placed directly on her heart.

"I'll do my best," she said.

"I'll be away at Verdaris for a while," he went on.

"Of course," she said, tensing involuntarily.

"Fourteen days, can you do it by then?"

"I'll do my best," she responded.

Of course she did her best. She did nothing else, dashing back to the Fabiansson house to find Hrasmus, the whittler, and ask, no, tell him to find a chunk of wood and start chipping out the shape of a temple.

"Which temple?" he asked.

"Any temple," she said. "Just get it done!"

"The one by Oswulf's hall?"

"If you remember it…that's the point. You have fourteen, no, thirteen days. I need to take a look at the result before I go back to him. You're excused all other duties!"

It had to look remarkable, not just because she wanted to impress the king, but because she wanted the building to be recognisably her idea.

Signy unfolded the parchment on the table, and Marcus leaned over. Fourteen days had dragged past. She had felt every hour.

"Hm," he said to himself, running his finger over the outline. "I think I see it, but…"

"I had some help," she said, reaching into her bag, "with the carving. One of my…the prisoners, Hrasmus, he's rather good with a knife."

Marcus took the model from her, twisting it this way and that in his hands.

"The temple by Chief Oswulf's hall, it looked a little like this," she said.

He stood still, holding the model.

"But, my dear, we can't build a church which is a copy of a pirate's temple." He tapped his finger on the central portion which was higher than the rest. "Can't we move this a bit towards one end, make more room for the worshippers?"

"How far would you say?" she said, taking his hand and drawing it gently across the model. "Could we go this far?"

"I don't see why not," he said, leaving his hand where it was, in hers. "And then we could make this…tower…higher."

He freed himself from her grip and raised his hand five or six thumbs above the top of the tower.

She looked from him to the model and back. "Then the tower would stick up quite…out of proportion," she said, catching his eye. "We'd have to raise the whole roof, add a second tier, perhaps."

"You mean about here," he said, now waving his hand above the model until it met hers again.

"I'd have to consult Wulfthere, but I'm sure we could do it."

"Do it," he said. "I'm going to have this built, and I want it to be an extraordinary building, admired by Christians and heathens alike."

"To bring them together, Master, I hope," she said.

"Just send him a note and tell him you'll do exactly whatever he desires," was Megana's suggestion. "Then he'll have to come and see for himself."

◌ Chapter 28 ◌

"Take a look at this." Megana pointed to a set of numbers, neatly written down one side of a parchment.

Signy had carried jugs of water and wine to Megana's workroom.

"Your mother's worried about you," Signy said, placing them on a side table, filling a glass, watering it, and handing it to her friend, "sitting alone in this room, burning the lamp halfway through the night."

She pulled up a stool and sat beside her friend. She had a wooden beaker of ale for herself.

"I'm not the one she should be worried about," said Megana. "Do you know what this is?"

Signy shook her head. There were no words to explain the number series, though it was clear that the numbers at the foot of the column were smaller than the ones at the top.

"This," said Megana, "shows how much we have bought from other merchants and how much we have received in kind from farmers and craftsmen for each of the last ten years. I've been going through the accounts and converted everything into silver weight. It's taken me for ever."

"And what does it show?" asked Signy, although she had an uneasy feeling that she knew the answer.

"It shows, my dear, that trade is going down the cloaca, if we had a cloaca that still functioned."

She took a sip from the glass.

"We've been distracted, misled, by all this work on the King's Hall. I'm not saying it hasn't helped to keep us in our daily meat and bread, though your Jute friends consume most of that. But it's been a distraction, a mask, you might say, the sort of thing an old lady might wear when she's begun to look all wrinkly and sour and seen her better days. If you look at the goods that have always been our staples, the picture's the same: corn – almost nothing after the military cuts; salt – they have their own supply on the mainland; hides – still some trading; lead – there's no mining anymore; we're ripping it off buildings and digging up pipes, and so it goes on. Olive oil – I think Marcus is the only one using it anymore; garum – stinks!"

"What does all this mean?" asked Signy, putting her arm round Megana's waist.

"Have you noticed the changes?" Megana looked up at her friend. "Have you ever wondered why so many of the shops in town are shuttered? Maybe not, because you don't remember the old days."

"I don't understand."

"Lady Bryna is weaving her own cloth, making her own beer and wine, and Marcus is feasting on his own swine and sheep. Edwulf and Merwyn and all these others are drinking from wooden beakers and eating from trenchers of bread, instead of importing fine pottery from Gaul. You see, you're doing it yourself!"

Signy gave an uneasy glance at the beaker she had in her hand.

"Once, we even had our own pottery in the south of the province, on Marcellus' land," Megana continued. "His father sent pots and plates all over Britannia, to the legions, to the officers' families, and now, there's none of that left. And my own grandfather brought in plates and dishes from Gaul, vases and so on all the way from Africa, Egypt, even."

"We always brewed our own beer and made our own clothes," Signy said. "I don't mean only the farm, but in Juteland, too. What's wrong with that?"

"But what sort of towns are the Danborg, Puttby – a conglomeration of wooden shacks." Megana answered her own question. "And what sort of merchants – Laurentius, who passes through twice a year, and a few robbers like the ones who stole you away."

"Factor Titus?"

"Factor Titus lives off plunder, you should know that, and if the plunder dries up, when the remittances from the warriors who've travelled south to serve the Romans stop arriving, Titus will go under."

She tapped once again at the tablet. "If this continues, there isn't going to be any trade in Britannia worth doing. A few jewels, a jar of wine here and there, maybe some spices. Not enough to keep our ships, our wagons, your men, perhaps even this house." Megana sipped her wine again before continuing. "There are still opportunities to trade, of course, just not here in Britannia."

"So where, if not in Britannia, not in Puttby?"

"In the south lands, by the middle sea, where the Empire still clings on, that's what Lanius has written, that there are new masters, 'Our Men' they call themselves…"

"Gutar?"

"You've heard the name?"

Now she was almost caught out, suddenly remembering it was Drusus who had told a story about the Goths, as he called them, all mixed up in his tale about the journey to Rome and the dancer, Xancha, he had fallen in love with.

"Our chief's younger brother in my home village," she hurriedly invented a source on the spot, "told tales around the fire at midwinter. Gutar, 'Our Men', he said, are taking over the Empire."

"Yes, and not just the farms and towns, but the habits and customs, and that means good days for merchants in the south lands, now the newcomers prefer the easy life to fighting and robbing."

Signy got to her feet abruptly. "My beaker is empty. I'll be back in a moment."

She did not want Megana to feel her sudden surge of worry. Her friend had not said it straight out, but Megana almost sounded as if she was considering giving up on Britannia, as her brother had done so many years before. And why not? Her mother had come across the middle sea. And Drusus – when she could follow his meanderings – she had the impression he regretted coming back to Britannia, the fruitless pursuit of his family's former honour, that he wished he had remained in the south lands with his dancer.

As she refilled her beaker in the kitchen, she could not stop herself looking at the scar on her thumb. She had promised to be a sister, a sister on the road, a sister in war, with Megana, and if her sister took the battle to the south lands, what choice did she have but to follow?

By the time Signy returned to the workroom, Megana had tilted her stool onto two legs and lifted her feet onto the desk, her dress slipping to her knees. The wine jug was on the floor beside her; the shade of the wine in her glass seemed darker.

"Are you thinking of leaving for the south lands?" There was no point avoiding the issue.

Megana swayed dangerously back against the shelving which held her records.

"I don't know," she said, then looked hard at Signy. "We'll see. I know my promise to you, too."

"Do you think I should give up on Marcus?"

Megana sat up suddenly. The stool swayed and then all four legs crashed against the tiles. For a moment, she looked as if she was going to lose hold of the glass, but instead, she placed it deftly on the table. How many hours had she spent, leaning back against that shelf, thought Signy, contemplating the future?

"No. There's one thing I've learned as a merchant. The harvest isn't in until the last sheaf is cut. Until then, you have to keep on, keep on as if nothing is going to change. If you don't, a disaster's unavoidable."

Megana's calculation was correct, not just on the declining state of trade, but regarding Marcus' curiosity. Every time he was in Corinium, he paid a visit to the church site, often before Grunwald could send a message to Signy that he was in town.

This time, however, the needs of administration had constrained his movements, and Signy made sure she was at the growing structure of the church as her master strolled up the hill.

A greeting, called out by one of the labourers working high on the roof, alerted her where she was waiting inside the building.

Just as she saw him come in through the door, a beam of sunshine pierced the gloom through an opening where the roof had not been completed.

"Like the illustration in the holy book I have at home," Marcus said, as he gazed up into the tower.

"I know the story," she replied. "Father Felix has a similar picture. Wasn't the light shining on a bird?"

"Yes, the symbol of the Holy Spirit. If we had a bird carved and hung it where the light shines through, it would look just like the picture," he said, taking her by the arm and pointing.

"I could encourage Hrasmus to make a bird," she said, her eyes meeting his. "I'm so proud of what we've done with this church," she added, sidling up against him.

"What you've done," he answered, placing his hand on her waist.

"What we've done together," she said, swivelling towards him. If I stood on tiptoes, my lips would be just an inch from his, she thought.

He held her still, as if…but something made him draw back.

"We should tell them to leave out that shingle," she said, pulling away, not wanting to show her disappointment.

They hurried outside.

"Leave that last place open. Find a small sheet of glass you can fix instead of a shingle," she called up to the workers on the roof. "Not horn, that's not clear enough." But they did not seem to hear.

"I'm sorry, Marcus," she said, letting go of his arm, "but I'll have to climb up and tell them." And with that, she hauled herself up onto the first of a series of poles sticking out from the wall that served as a ladder. A second and a third and her feet were level with his head.

"Take care!" he shouted, clearly alarmed at her sudden ascent.

"I was born in a forest," she called back. "I was climbing trees as soon as I could walk."

It wasn't very ladylike, she thought, or subtle.

"I've been sorting through my clothes," said Megana.

Signy, sitting in the atrium, trying to decode one of the books the deacon had borrowed from Marcus, looked up. Megana's mood seemed to have improved. She was carrying a bundle of folded cloth. "Guess what I found? Something Alexander, my brother, sent me a year or two back. I don't know when he thought I would wear it."

Signy put the book to one side. She didn't understand a word of Plato, even in Cicero's Latin translation. Did anybody, she had already been wondering, even before Megana appeared.

Megana shook the bundle, and a cascade of birds and flowers appeared to fall from her hands.

"Oh, the coat of many colours!" Signy said without thinking.

"And that spelled how much trouble?" said Megana. "What do you think? Do you think it suits me?"

Signy hesitated to answer. It seemed a rhetorical question — isn't that what the deacon called a question where the speaker already knows the answer? Instead, she stood up and held out her hand to feel the lustrous material.

"Silk," said Megana, "from Serica, made up into a gown in Constantinople."

"It is a bit garish for Britannia," said Signy cautiously. It would have gone down well in Oswulf's hall, she thought. How his wives would have gaped if I had shown up dressed like that!

"My mother said that many ladies with excellent reputations in Constantinople wear dresses like this. I'm not sure she was being complimentary." She held up the cloth against herself. "It was made for someone twice my size, and I'm not the smallest, not anymore."

"You could have it trimmed down to your size," Signy suggested.

"That's exactly what I'm planning to do, have it trimmed," said Megana, "but not for me, for you."

"What? You can't! That's too much!"

"Feel it and imagine this against your skin. Imagine it sitting snugly, showing off your figure."

Signy ran the lustrous material through her fingers, almost transparent if not for the images sewn onto the fabric.

"But when would I wear it?"

"Didn't you say you thought he was going to kiss you?"

"Oh?"

"Just imagine…We'll have this sewn so it fits you like a glove, and leave enough for a nice jewelled belt and…You almost had him! You just have to get him close enough. Come on, try it on."

Signy hesitated.

"Come on, take your dress off and slip this one on. I'll call for Delia, and she can mark where to make the alterations."

Signy cautiously undid the brooch holding her dress in place, and let it drop to the tiles. She took the silk from Megana and slid it over her head.

For an instant, she was almost naked, and then the silk fell around her, and she was still scarcely clothed.

Hrasmus carved the bird. It had more than a passing resemblance to a raven, but no one would notice when it was hanging in the tower. At the right time of the day, the bird almost shone with a dazzling light, the very image of the Holy Spirit appearing in before their eyes. Father Felix had immediately named the little church the Church of the Holy Spirit.

The other wonder that Signy had arranged was the golden cross at the very highest point. This had been a terrible trouble to obtain, but Megana had finally found an artist in Francia who covered a wooden cross with gold leaf. It was carried to the peak of the pyramid, and firmly fastened in place. When the sun was setting, the dying rays caught the golden cross while the church below and the rest of the buildings were sinking into darkness, so it looked like the holy symbol was floating in the evening light. That was what she wanted Marcus to see, to see how they *had* succeeded in creating something remarkable.

Signy still did not think of herself as Christian, but all the reading and the construction of the church had had an impact on her. Grunwald had told her Marcus was in town, and on that day she kneeled before the altar of the little church she had conceived and prayed that he would come.

The Christian God must have heard my prayer, she noted in gratitude. As she stood waiting for the sun to slip towards the horizon, a familiar figure, wrapped in a plain grey cloak, came climbing the slope towards the church. First, they went inside and admired the bird, and then they went outside and stood together looking towards the church, as the hall, the barns and stables slipped into shadow, until one last ray of the dying sun caught the golden cross, blazing against the darkening sky. She placed her hand on his arm.

"Will you come and share a glass of wine with me," she asked, "to celebrate this success?"

They walked together towards her home, chatting about this and that, like old friends who had not seen each other for a long time.

"Why did you move out of town," he asked, "when you're such a friend of Megana's?"

"She's like a sister to me," she said, "but this place, the barns, the stables, the cluster of wooden buildings around the longhouse and the church, it reminds me of my old home, the village where I grew up."

He followed her into her house, an open room, partitioned at one end. Maria emerged from the rear section. Signy whispered in her ear, and the girl scuttled away with a half-hidden smile.

The two of them were alone. Signy poured the wine into a pair of glasses, antiques carefully brought over from Francia.

"Interesting," he said, whether of the glasses or the wine was not clear.

She laughed, seeing the wine relaxing him, watching, judging her moment.

If you have patience, I'll show you something more interesting, she thought, but not just yet.

She told him about her old life, growing up on a farm, not so different from his own childhood, so it seemed, though his father had been incomparably richer and more important than hers.

"I had to huddle with the animals for warmth and sometimes went hungry at the end of winter," she said.

"I never had to do that, thank the gods," he replied, "but my mother and my sister spun wool, as all countrywomen have to." He chuckled at the memories of his boyhood. "I had to shovel out the barns and turn the soil with my father, just as your brothers must have done."

"You must be proud of what you have become," she said. "I know I'm proud of my little home and proud of what I've learned while I've been in Britannia. I'm allowed to be proud of myself, aren't I?" She'd kept away from wine ever since the encounter with Constantinus, and it was going to her head a little.

"Of course," he said, placing his hand on her knee. "I'm proud of you. We're all proud of you."

"Wait," she said, sliding his hand away. She jumped to her feet and lightly skipped up the stairs to the chamber above, leaving him alone with the cat and his thoughts. The silk gown was already laid out on her bed. She quickly stripped and slipped her arms through the sleeves. Delia had done a master work, and now the material fitted her form like a second skin. The coloured decorations hid a good deal, but not everything. The belt rested on her hips, sloping suggestively downward. A jewelled clasp at one shoulder held the garment in place. She slid her feet into a pair of slippers of the same material that the industrious servant had also sewn.

I can't put up with this any longer, she thought. If this doesn't work, then the situation is hopeless. I'll give myself to Alwynn next time he's here, and after that…

"Do you like it?" she asked, as she turned at the foot of the ladder. "It's silk. It came from the east. Megana's brother sent it for her, but it fits me much better. She said it must once have belonged to a wealthy lady from Rome."

"It's certainly come a long way," he said. His eyes were like plates. "Perhaps it once clothed a princess!"

She stepped nearer. "Feel how shiny and smooth it is," she said. "Just like skin."

I've come a long way too, she thought. Once I was a dirty slave, a captive, crouching fearful in a swine fold, and now, my lord, now I'm wearing the gown of a princess, and…

He reached out to touch the material. She stepped forward, close up to him, placed her arms around him. His arms were around her, and then, with a little shake of her shoulders, the clasp slipped open, and the gown fell down, falling over his arms as he held her. Just as Megana had instructed, she was naked underneath. Her breasts squeezed against his chest. She reached up her face towards his.

"My master, I love you. I've waited so long. Let me be *your* princess."

She raised her lips to his and kissed him. She could feel him respond, and she whispered in his ear, "Come, come with me," and she led him towards the stairs leading up to the chamber, and he followed after her.

He left in the morning, just as the first streak of grey crept above the horizon. Signy lay in the bed. She was happy, so happy. She had waited and waited and been patient. Her prayers had been answered, whichever god it was who had finally answered them. And he had acknowledged, admitted that he had fallen in love with her that day in front of the Jute camp, that he remembered what he had said, that she was a gift from the gods, and he had fought against it, fought against fate, against the thread that the sisters had woven which brought their two lives together. She knew she could not expect more of him, that she would have to wait again, until the next time circumstances allowed him to slip away, but she could be patient. She knew he would come again. She lived through the next days as if in a dream, until slowly, slowly, reality set in again, and she came back down to earth.

❧ Chapter 29 ☙

The summer passed all too quickly, it seemed to Signy, the autumn, too, but the winter seemed endless. Not just because Marcus took refuge at Verdaris with his family, but because the weather was terrible. First snow had fallen, blown into huge drifts by howling winds, and then it had started raining. When the snow had melted, the rivers had run over their banks, and the rain had only made matters worse. The land resembled a marsh. The seeds that had been sown in the autumn had been drowned, and no one could get out into the fields to plant the spring crop.

Signy's cottage had become unattractively damp and cold, so she and Maria retreated to the shelter and warmth of the Fabiansson house. The cat was given the option to join them but chose to stay on its familiar territory. No one called for Signy's services, even if they needed them. The roads were impassable, rutted and washed away in spots, and the tracks were more like muddy streams than ways to get from one place to another. Only Alwynn seemed to be able to navigate the countryside, but then he used neither roads nor tracks.

It seemed like the deluge would never stop, and it was raining once again. The baths were the warmest place in the house. Signy and Megana sat on the bench in the caldarium. Maria threw some water onto the hot stones.

"Stop," shrieked Signy, "you'll steam us alive."

Maria retreated to a colder part, laughing.

"Well might she laugh," said Megana, "young and no worries."

"She has her worries," said Signy.

"Not while she has you to take care of her."

"And not while we have you to take care of both of us," said Signy.

"But for how much longer? How much longer will it be worth living in town?" Megana commented. "The shopkeepers are leaving. Soon there'll be no reason to come to town, nothing to buy, then the taverns'll close and the market'll wither away."

"Surely there's something we can do, like when a body becomes sick?" Signy added.

"But where's the woman who knows the medicine for our city?"

"Not a woman, Megana. What about Marcus?"

"Marcus?" said Megana. "What can he do? He's like a man playing *latrones*, moving his pieces here and there, while all the time the board is fading away."

"But I can tell him, at least. Why is he the king if he can't do anything?"

"Explain to him, Signy, and see what he says, but he can't bring the legions back. He doesn't need another new hall. He can hardly build a wall round West Britain, like the old emperor did with Pictland. He can't force Saxons and the Welsh to buy silk and garum and olive oil! He can't order people to hold feasts and exhibit their status by impressing their friends with exotic foods! Those days have gone. Now it's just pork and gruel, and if this rain doesn't stop, we'll be lucky to have that by the end of the year."

"Is that what's been upsetting you?"

Megana stood up. "Let's skip the cold room," she said. "If we want to rinse off in cold water, we just need to run through the atrium."

"Naked?"

"Why not? Grab a wrapping if you want, but I'm going to dance in the rain. Maria, we're going to my study! Can you tell cook to send some warm mead?"

They ran, almost slipping on the wet stones of the atrium, where water was cascading down from the roof and into the central pool. Signy, in a foolish fit of enthusiasm, seeing the rain-dappled surface, stepped up on to the surround, then threw herself in.

"Oh, by the gods, it's cold," she gasped. "Help me out."

They dodged back into the shelter of the overhanging roof, wrapping themselves in the sheets they had brought from the baths.

"Now I can show you what has been upsetting me."

Megana pulled the wrap tight around herself, towelling off the worst of the water from her hair, before lifting down a tablet from a shelf above her desk.

Maria appeared, properly clothed, bearing three beakers of steaming honeyed mead. She placed two on Megana's table and retreated to the furthest corner of the room.

Megana took a sip from her beaker, then untied the ribbon around the tablet.

"I've been checking our treasury, the silver my father has always kept in case of hard times."

More numbers, Signy saw, but the arrangement still meant nothing to her.

"Tell me," she asked.

"It should be full, given the work we've been doing for Uncle Marcus, but instead…I went and confronted Father, asked him what's going on."

She cast a worried glance at Signy.

"He's been lending, first to one, then to another, and they've been making promises to pay back, and when they don't, he's lent to them all over again."

She turned to Signy, a look of misery on her face.

"He can't remember anymore how much he has loaned and to who. He doesn't know where the silver's gone. And they'll be back, taking advantage of a sick man."

The rain stopped at last, but within days it was replaced by blazing sun, and the mud that covered the land quickly hardened into a substance resembling brick.

"Thank the gods I'm not a farmer," said Alwynn, appearing from the foetid brush that now surrounded the tombs by the north gate of Corinium. He took an empty vial from the bag slung over his shoulder and held it out to the waiting Signy.

"Thank the gods I made a good stock of this medicine," she replied. "I'm not sure that my herbs have survived the winter."

"And if they haven't?" Alwynn's voice took on a worried tone.

"We'll get by a little longer."

She dropped the empty vial into her own bag and extracted its replacement, carefully stoppered and sealed with resin.

He took it but, turning to leave, was held by the look on her face.

"What is it?"

"I need your help."

"How?" Now he sounded hopeful.

She took out a thin sliver of wood from her bag, reflecting that it was a pity that Alwynn could not read. She would have to rely on his memory.

"Next time you come, I want you to call in on this man, Patronus of White Horse Down, you know who I mean?"

"I know the name."

"He borrowed money from my sister's father, and now he's unwilling to repay what he owes. He needs a little encouragement. The sort of encouragement I'm sure you can provide, Alwynn."

"Your sister…ah, you mean Megana."

"Take this message with you. He'll understand what's written here. You're to demand he pays the debt, to you, and immediately."

Alwynn scrutinised the scribbles. "And if he doesn't or can't?"

"Then take whatever's the equivalent. I'll leave it to your judgement, but no slaves or animals. They're too much trouble. The debt must be paid – in full – at once."

Alwynn looked thoughtful for a moment. "You know who this man is, don't you?"

She shook her head. She had selected Patronus from the list she had found in Megana's workroom only because she knew his villa lay between Corinium and the hiding place of Drusus and his gang. Megana was so organised – names, amounts, where they lived and the nearest town. She had explained she was planning to take them before the tribunal, though she had little hope of finding justice that way. She would lose everything if the debtors could find witnesses who would swear the loan had already been repaid, or claim that the silver was a gift, or the loan was never made in the first place, or…whatever they wanted. Signy had not recognised all the names but was sure they must be powerful men. Otherwise, they would not dare to behave in such an insolent manner. But even powerful men would feel fear with a knife at their throat. She had heard enough of Thorgill's stories to know that truth. She had not told Megana what she was planning to do. Megana would only have tried to stop her.

"He's Counsellor Aurelius' cousin," said Alwynn. "He has friends…in high places."

"He refuses to repay his debt to my sister, that's all that matters."

It was Alwynn's turn to shake his head. "I can always escape, Mistress, back over the border into bandit country, but you…"

"In that case, I don't know you, Alwynn, and you don't know me. You're simply Drusus Astrebanus' man, a rebel, an impoverished traitor. No wonder you've turned to robbery."

"Supposing I rob you?"

"But you won't, will you? You're my sworn man, as long as Drusus remains alive, and besides, Alwynn, I have others who could come after you."

The Frisian chuckled bitterly.

"I'd better not go alone, then. I'm going to need Liutmann and a couple more of the lads."

"You choose, just don't bring them here to our meeting."

"And if Patronus resists?"

"I'll leave that to you, Alwynn."

"So I'm to act a robber." He shook his head.

"Act, Alwynn," she said, reaching out and placing her hand on his arm, "but remember, Patronus is the robber. You're on the side of justice."

"That's what Drusus has been telling me for years," he sighed.

She reached up and kissed him. "I hope I'm a more attractive than Drusus, at least."

The house had baked for days in the hot sunshine. Neither Signy nor Megana could stop sweating, even though they were in the frigidarium. One of the housemen had pulled up a bucket of water from the bottom of the well where it was still chilly and left it for them. Signy emptied a ladle over her head and took a deep breath. Megana let her eyes run down Signy's naked body and pursed her lips.

"You're carrying, aren't you? A child?"

Signy turned to her, a modest smile on her face. "Yes."

"His? An accident? I thought you knew how to prevent them?"

"Yes, and I chose to keep the child."

Once she had been ready to have Thorgill's child, and the feeling that she could be a mother had never entirely left her. She had taken no precautions when she lay with Marcus. She had not checked the calendar, carefully counting the days. That would have been impossible anyway, with his sudden appearances and long absences from Corinium. And she had not purged herself after they had lain together. She had just allowed nature to take its course. And for a long time, nothing had happened, and she had started to worry. Supposing she could not have a child? Supposing she had polluted her womb with all the herbs and concoctions she had taken during the time she had been with Thorgill, or even afterwards, that night she had spent with Alwynn? How she had suffered for that one night, half-poisoned and apprehensive for days afterwards. Or because she had the habit of testing the potions she prepared by sampling them herself. Supposing no seed would grow in her womb, as nothing could grow in the poisoned soil around the mines where she had been held prisoner, a dead and barren land.

And then she had almost missed the signs, like one of her own foolish patients, like some girl who had been out frolicking at midsummer, and by Christmas found herself with a swelling belly.

"Does he know?"

Signy shook her head. "He's been out on his circuit, visiting the north. You know how worried they are about the harvest."

"I know that very well," said Megana, "but don't try to change the subject. Soon there won't be any hiding your belly from anyone. There'll be questions, curiosity. And Marcus won't be able to acknowledge the child."

"As long as I know he's the father, I don't care what other people think," said Signy. "And besides, there are plenty of girls who get pregnant without being married or with someone other than their husband as the father. Believe me, I've heard all the stories."

"You'll never become his wife, you know, not like you did with your bandit chief. It's against our customs, and Bryna…she'd never allow it even if it was."

"I've never said I wanted to be his wife."

"Sometimes I wonder…" said Megana, a sour tone entering her voice.

"What?"

"Whether your feelings are really love, or…"

"Or what?"

"…or a desire for confirmation?"

"That's not a nice thing to say." Signy was angry, hurt. "I'm proud I'm to be mother. I might never be Marcus' wife, but I can be the mother of his child. It's easy enough for you to make a comment like that, with your wealth and comfort. You don't need confirmation!"

"I'm sorry, Signy. Perhaps I'm just jealous that you've found your man, that he's fallen for you. Perhaps it's me who needs confirmation that I'm a woman who can be desired and loved. For myself, I mean, not just for what I represent. Sometimes I wish I could find a man who would love me, who I could take to my bed, without the obligation to give up my freedom."

Megana reached out and placed her hand on the small bump of Signy's belly. Her brown eyes filled with tears and large droplets rolled down her face, mixing with the dribbling water. Signy was taken aback. She had never expected such a reaction.

Megana wiped the back of her hand across her face. "Congratulations!"

"Let's get out of here," said Signy. "Dry off, and I'll cover up. It's not nice to see you so bothered."

"I was never meant to be an old maid, Signy," said Megana, wrapping a gown around herself, faintly smelling of lavender, as they left the bathhouse. "And with Father…is the family going to die out with me?"

"There's your brother, your half-brother?"

"Alexander? He'll never come back to Britannia. Why should he? He lives happily in the Narbonensis with his family. He takes after his mother – writes poetry. He was never interested in being a merchant. It's his wife who manages everything."

They padded, barefoot, still damp, along the passages towards the atrium, where the baking sun and a cool drink should be waiting for them.

"I had a visit," Megana continued, "from Pontius."

"Your father's cousin? The one who trades with Hibernia?"

"Yes," she frowned. "He has a son, Carassus."

"Can I guess, he's pushing for you and Carassus to marry?"

"Luckily Father didn't even recognise him, called him Marius, thought he was Priscilla's father, but that might make matters worse. If Father dies, then Pontius could claim that he has a right to take over the business as the closest surviving male relative."

"But Alexander, surely?"

Megana shook her head. "A marriage would obviate the need for a lawsuit. How very convenient," she added.

"But you don't plan to marry…that man?"

"Of course not," spat Megana, "but still…seeing you. Sometimes, I feel like I'm putting in all this effort for nothing,

Signy. For someone else to steal when my back is turned, Pontius or the men that Father keeps lending to. I'm frightened those thoughts will turn me into some kind of bitter dragon, wrapping my scaly tail round my hoard, seeing everyone as an enemy. I know what it's like to be with a man, to have someone you really want in your bed to touch you, to hold you and…I could be a mother, too. You make me want that, just seeing you as you are now."

Alwynn dumped a sack at Signy's feet. He had expressed his regrets the previous month, but promised he was working on the matter, and he would deliver.

"What's in it?"

"Silver, mostly good coins, and a few jewels. It took him a while to round them up, but as I said, he's got connections."

"Why in hell didn't he just pay Megana without this fuss?"

"That's not how people like him get rich or stay rich."

"Did you have to threaten much?"

Alwynn hesitated.

"Tell me, Alwynn, I need to know."

"We had to kill his best horse – and then kidnap his wife."

"Did you do anything…with her?"

"You'd better ask Liutmann."

"Wasn't she," Signy hesitated, "an old lady? I mean, Aurelius retired. His cousin must be the same age."

"His second wife, apparently. Another privilege of wealth. And congratulations, by the way. You've made a good try with the loose gown, but it's beginning to show since I know to look."

"You know to look?"

"One of the farms I lie up in. The old grandmother was so pleased for you. Just a pity…"

"Why?"

"I always had in the back of my mind I might be the lucky father," he chuckled.

"Well, you're not, you rogue. If you want more children, fuck your own woman, or go and kidnap Patronus' wife again, if she's worth it."

Signy placed Alwynn's sack on Megana's desk. "You can cross Patronus off your list!"

"What? Where did this come from?"

"The man's repaid his debt, but it cost him his best horse, and his new young wife is going to have nightmares of…of a friend of mine."

Megana sat back, examining her. "Signy, what have you done?"

Signy held up her thumb. "A debt owed to you, sister, is a debt owed to me. I wasn't married to a Jutish raider without learning a few tricks of the trade."

Megana looked aghast. "You can't…I mean…you can't go round extorting people."

"Isn't that what they're doing to you, but hiding behind their manhood, their status, the law? You know that in Juteland there are women who take up arms and join the warbands."

"You didn't?"

"No, not like that. What I meant was that in their world, manhood is what a man does, not what a man has between his legs. A woman can show manhood if she fights, fights bravely and dies with her sword in her hand. And a man, a cowardly weakling, can be called for a woman, if he hides from his obligations."

Megana stood up and came round the desk, taking Signy in her arms. "Signy, I love you. If you were a man in *our* way, I would marry you in an instant."

As the year progressed, it became increasingly clear that the harvest would be a disaster for many farmers, especially those who relied on growing wheat and oats and barley. There would be no grain for their own bread and beer, and nothing to sell or exchange for food and fodder from their luckier neighbours. Landowners who had invested in a wider range of crops were better placed to survive.

Signy was grateful for her garden plot, though her produce would be far from adequate to feed herself and Maria, and the maid was fearful that hungry strangers would come during the night and steal their hard-earned crop.

"If they steal my nightshade and foxglove," she said, "we'll survive like the people of the Antipodes, as cannibals."

"That won't be necessary. We'll survive, even you, who is eating for two," said Megana, showing Signy the well-stocked storehouses around Fabiansson's yard. "The prices are high, but the south lands have avoided the worst of the weather. I heard the bishops are taking the credit."

"Are the bishops in Gaul farmers as well as holy men?" asked Signy.

Megana laughed. "Prayer, Signy, prayer and righteous behaviour, that's what's got them through, so they say, unlike in Britannia, where greed, ambition and licentiousness have brought curses on all our heads."

"I never heard Father Felix say that."

"Well, there's the problem. It's the priests who are at fault."

Megana soon had reason to regret her frivolity, though Father Felix was not the cause.

"Uncle Marcus was here," she reported, "and he wasn't happy. He's worried that people will blame him for the poor harvest. He rode all the way down to Litorina to consult with some of the sea captains."

"Oh, yes, he told me he was going! What did they say?"

"The same as I would have said, if he had considered coming and speaking to me before riding around 'fact-finding', as he called it. There's corn to be had – for a price – if he or anyone else is willing to pay."

"And what did he want from you?"

"He wanted me to be the one who would pay. Goddammit, I told him, this is not the Empire where the ruler could order folks about, sail here, invade there, I'm bored, so jump in the arena with some lions." Her voice was almost breaking. "That's what I wish I had said. But actually, I pointed out that the sailing season was almost over for the year, and no one would be bringing grain from the south until spring. And then the price would be even higher, because they'd know we were on the verge of famine."

"And what did he say?"

"He said that's enough of these merchant's excuses. Make sure there's grain here for those who need it in the spring. I'm not speaking as your godfather, but as your king. I don't care how you do it, but you'll do it or else I'll throw *you* to the lions."

"Can you do it?"

"Of course I can do it, for a price, but I'll have to call in some favours, and put myself under an obligation to others. I already rode over to Porta Siluria."

"Oh, that's where you were…to talk to your father's cousin?"

"Yes. His boats are beached there during the winter. If I'm to send a message with Uncle Marcus', I mean the king's, orders to Burdigala, then one of the captains, perhaps Pontius himself, will have to brave the autumn storms and make the trip. It'll cost me big, Signy."

Signy saw the look of gloom on Megana's face, despite her brave words.

"Did he bring up the subject of marriage?"

Her friend merely nodded.

"Did you agree?"

"I asked if we could wait until the crisis is over, and he generously agreed."

Megana spun on her heels and stood with her back to Signy, head bowed, face in her hands. Then she wiped her face and turned back.

"I feel like leaving, Signy. I feel like leaving Britannia altogether. Uncle Marcus is driving me to it. We'll never get back what we'll have to spend for this aid, whatever promises he makes, whatever promises the other landowners make. They won't keep their word to Father, so why would they keep their word to me? I'm not going to marry Carassus. I have to find a way out. I just need to put aside enough for Father in his dying years, and then, who knows? Maybe I'll find a rich barbarian. There are some left, aren't there?"

Signy held her friend, felt her sobbing. She was on the verge of tears herself. How could Megana's life be ruined like this? Someone who worked so hard, who provided a living, food and shelter for so many others, who would keep them safe and full during the coming winter, thanks to her foresight and planning. And who Marcus now thought could do the same for the entire kingdom, or at least the most foolish and undeserving parts of it. Much as she cared for Marcus, she cared for Megana, too, and this was not fair. She thought of the list she had copied, the men who owed Fabiansson for loans they had taken in the past years. She thought of Alwynn and Liutmann. She thought of the Jute boys, Ferland and Hrasmus and Asser and the others. Winter would normally be a quiet time for people like that, a time to sit by the hearth and contemplate. Not this winter! She would say nothing to Megana, but now those greedy bastards would pay up, no matter who they were.

❧ Chapter 30 ❧

"You what?" wailed Signy. "Him of all people!" She was horrified by what Megana had just told her. Not that her friend was expecting a child, but who the father was. "How could you! Don't you know that he tried to rape me?"

"But you never said anything!"

"No," said Signy, stopping in her tracks, her voice falling. "How could you know, when I never said anything?"

She turned to her friend, tears now welling from her eyes.

"I haven't been honest with you, dear Megana, and now my silence has been repaid. The gods see everything, I suppose, and unfailingly pick the most appropriate way to punish a deceiver."

Megana tapped the bench beside her.

"It looks like confession time," she said. "Sit down, right here, and listen to me, because it was you who gave me the idea. And then you can tell me why I did wrong."

Ferland rode into the courtyard asking for me, she began. *When I came out to meet him, he dumped a sack at my feet.*

"Silver," he said. "Your father's loan to Apostoles repaid in full."

An uneasy feeling seeped down my spine, and I couldn't think what to say for a moment.

"You've been so careful to shield me, Signy," Megana said as an aside, "from being confronted directly with a payment."

"I said you would get your silver back. I already gave you the first instalment."

"Yes, but you didn't say how. I thought you were working on Uncle Marcus. Anyway…" Megana held up her hand to keep Signy quiet.

"Voluntarily?" I asked.

"Eventually," he replied.

I gave Ferland a look which must have exposed my feelings of doubt. His eyes wandered everywhere except to meet mine. He evidently did not want to explain.

"Was it you who collected the silver from Patronus?"

He shook his head. "She has others to the east. Hrasmus and I, she sent down to Aquae Sulis where no one knows us."

Of course, I'd heard rumours, the servants talking of mysterious raiders, two here, four there, dressed in black, in the middle of the night, but Apostoles of Aquae Sulis, he was almost a neighbour.

"Beltrice thinks they're Hibernians." Signy almost laughed, then she was reminded of who was growing in Megana's belly. She also felt a tinge of guilt. She had never revealed that after Megana's reaction the first time she had handed over a bag of silver, she had buried the rest that her boys had collected in her garden.

"We can't keep this here," I said, feeling like a thief forced to dispose of loot. "You must take it to Litorina, to the warehouse. Tell them to bury the silver in the wool bales that will leave with the next ship to Burdigala. I'll write a tablet with instructions. Make sure it goes with that sack."

Ferland nodded unquestioningly, but that didn't stop him speaking.

"I met a man on the road, beyond Old Calleva," he said. "He gave me Mistress Signy's sign." He held up his fist so that his forefinger and little finger stuck up like the ears of an animal, a wolf perhaps.

"A cat," said Signy, holding up her hand in the same way. "A lynx is a sort of big cat. Don't you see? Like my tattoo."

"Oh, of course…whatever. I must have looked confused."

"Just a mark between us, so we know we're serving the same person," Ferland continued. "He promised to be here within seven days, when his errand had been completed."

"Can I ask who and where?"

"I didn't ask his name, my lady, and he didn't offer to tell me. I've never seen him before, and I'm not going to get mixed up in his business."

I needed to talk to you. I sent Henrik up to your cottage, but you seemed to have vanished. Only Maria and your boy were there.

Signy's son, Marcus' son, had been born at midwinter. She had named him Einar.

I couldn't have been far away, thought Signy, since I'm suckling my baby myself. Probably just in the woods above the house looking for places where roots and berries might grow under the protection of the trees. Probably Henrik doesn't know the sign, she conjectured to herself, and Maria just sent him away as I told her to do with nosy people.

The stranger appeared on the evening of the sixth day, Megana continued, *riding a dark horse and leading two pack ponies. One had a pair of leather bags across its back, and a bundle, some sort of roll, was thrown over the second. The man said no one stopped him at the city gate or asked questions. Once in the stable yard, he had asked for me by name.*

"Greetings from my lady Signy, Mistress," he said by way of introduction, touching his forehead.

I smiled, though he probably couldn't see in the light of dusk. "So you're the mysterious man who's been helping my friend," I said, half-aloud. I considered asking him in for some wine or ale to pump him for information. He looked handsome enough to make that a pleasure, but he merely grunted in reply.

"I've completed my mistress's errand. These," he then said, lifting the bags from the first pony, "are yours, less the share that was promised to me and my comrades." He placed the bags on the ground, where there was a soft clink of metal against metal. Then he glanced around the yard in a suspicious manner.

"And having dealt with that," he said, "I have a matter that only you and I can manage. I don't wish my mistress to discover it." He backed away, towards the second horse, which had been waiting patiently for someone to remove its load.

"Is Ferland the Jute here?" he asked, evidently feeling he could rely on Ferland's discretion. "I met him on the road."

"No, he's with his girl," I said, "but my people can do whatever you need."

"Can they take care of this?" he said indicating the roll slung over the second pony.

"That depends on what it is," I answered, uneasily realising the package had the shape of a human body. I turned to the open yard and gave a brief whistle. A dog bounded over, sniffing curiously at the newcomer, and after a

short delay, two men came clattering along the gallery and down the stairs, Henrik and your man, Asser.

"He needs help," I said, "with that bundle."

"Careful," said the stranger, "though if I've judged right, he should still be alive."

The two men grasped the foot end of the bundle, while the stranger eased the head end from the horse. He bent down, untied the ropes which kept the roll tight and pulled away the rough blanket, revealing the figure of a man, apparently sleeping peacefully.

"Who is he?" I asked.

"You don't know him?"

"No."

"Constantinus Astrebanus."

"By Christ…and you've brought him here?"

"I wish I didn't have him on my hands at all," said the man. "He arrived at our camp while I was on my business. He should have stayed on the mainland. He got drunk and argumentative. He was raving, almost as bad as his uncle, complaining of Mistress Signy and her son."

"Jealous, was he?" I said. "Well, I suppose he isn't the only one."

I dropped to my haunches beside the insensible figure.

"I couldn't stand it anymore," the man said. "I had to use the medicine, the medicine the mistress gave us to use in case Chief Drusus becomes uneasy. Three drops, she said. The chief's an old man, and sickly, so I put five drops in Master Constantinus' ale. He should wake in a couple of days. The master always does."

What he was saying struck me as strange, although, I must admit, not just then as strange as having Constantinus Astrebanus' unconscious form deposited in my yard.

"And what do you want me to do with him?" I asked.

"Get rid of him…you have access to shipping, don't you? Get him on board a ship and back to the mainland, to Remis as soon as possible, before Mistress Signy finds out he's here."

"Why's that?"

"Once, more than once, he has threatened her, and she has made threats in return. If she ever sees him again, she'll end the treatment she's been giving the chief. He'll die in madness, so she says, and with his death…" He shook his head.

"You're in luck, my friend," I said. *"I think Mistress Signy is occupied at the moment…with her child."*

"You weren't being very fair," said Signy.

"I'm trying to be honest," said Megana, "explain why I did what I did. Which is more than you have been…honest, I mean. This man, why was he speaking as if Drusus Astrebanus is still alive, and prattling on about potions and medications?"

"It's a long story," Signy replied, "and you'll hear it all before the end of the night, I promise. The man's name is Alwynn. He's Drusus Astrebanus' man, and you remember the night Marcus was acclaimed king?"

"That guy! Why the hell didn't you say so? I would've been more pressing with my invitation if I had known he was in the habit of bedding strangers."

"Wait till you hear the rest of the tale. Believe me, Alwynn and I have paid for our night of pleasure, both of us."

Megana shrugged disbelievingly but continued.

"I guessed as much," Alwynn said, and there was a sad tone in his voice. *"She told me not to visit until after the full moon."*

"Now I know who he is, I know why he felt that way. The man still has a fancy for you."

"He's not the only one," said Signy. "I can't accommodate them all."

"Only the best, right?"

"So we have until then, at the very minimum," I replied. And that's *ten days off, I thought, to keep Constantinus Astrebanus in my custody, before he might become the cause of trouble.*

I stood up and turned to Henrik.

"Carry him into the servants' quarters, the very far end of the rear yard. You're sure he won't wake tonight?" I asked the man Alwynn again.

"Absolutely, Mistress. I'll say this of Mistress Signy, she knows what she's doing with her potions."

"Some sort of compliment, anyway," said Signy.

"Let me go and find some food and refreshment," said Megana, getting to her feet. "I've a feeling it's going to take a while before we straighten things out."

She vanished in the direction of the kitchens, leaving Signy sitting contemplating in the atrium.

She felt betrayed, by Alwynn and by Megana. It would serve Alwynn right if I refuse to give them any more of the medication, she thought. On the other hand, he's not a bad guy, and he's proved very useful, and could be again. And there's no avoiding the fact that I've hidden the whole matter of Drusus from Megana. Who am I to feel betrayed?

Megana plonked herself back down on the bench.

"Small beer, and a slice or two of beef," she said, "will be along in a moment. Where was I?"

"You'd put up Constantinus in a back room."

"As a prisoner, you understand, not as an honoured guest," said Megana. "Let me continue…"

Come with me, I said to Ferland, when the news reached me that Constantinus was awake and had eaten. *"I wish to visit the prisoner. Bring a stool."*

"Ferland?" said Signy. "Why did you drag Ferland into this sordid mess?"

"Henrik's one of my father's servants. He's altogether too respectable. And Ferland can keep his mouth shut. Your man Alwynn's judgement's good."

Constantinus was being held in one of the rooms previously used for houseslaves, at the back of the building, quiet and out of the way. The fixings for a wooden beam had been hastily nailed across the door. Ferland had to slide it back before I could get in.

"Put that stool down," I said, *"and wait outside. I'll call you when I'm done."*

Constantinus was lying on a low bed. He had tilted his head to see who was coming in, and then he swung himself into a sitting position, his hands on his knees.

"Who the hell are you?"

"That's my business," I replied, sitting down on the stool, speaking in Latin to ensure that the eavesdropping Ferland couldn't understand. *"Constantinus Claudius Astrebanus, what a sad situation you're in. Even your uncle's friends have given you over."*

Constantinus said nothing, so I continued.

"We've given you lodging and meals, but how are you going to earn your freedom, when no one knows you're here, and even if I told them, they've no ransom to bail you out? I suppose I'm just going to have to sell you, but what price can I set? Can you sing?"

He looked puzzled.

"Poetry, you mean," he asked, "or the responses?"

"Yes, you were brought up by monks, weren't you?" I said, considering my options. "The responses might be more valuable. King Conal of the Osraige might have a use for you in his church, a more suitable situation for a fine gentleman like you, I can imagine, than, say, as a cowherd. I could strike a deal to soften your life in Hibernia if I mentioned your skills with responses, and I might even gain a little more myself. What do you think?"

Constantinus turned his grey eyes towards me. He said nothing, but his look gave away his thoughts.

"So, you don't relish the prospect of serving the king of Osraige. That's a pity, because the alternative is to have a discussion with my dearest friend. Do you know who that is?"

He shook his head. How could he know, since he obviously had no idea where he was, or who I was?

"I think you may, because she knows you, and she's no friend of yours," I said. "My friend spent some years among the Jutes, Constantinus, with a certain Chief Thorgill, and she picked up some of their habits. How much good fortune do you think she would earn for her newborn son if you were to be cast, bound hand and foot, into the Tamesis? Do you think the gods would send the boy a long and successful life in return for your miserable existence, or should we be satisfied if they merely send us the weather we need for a good harvest?"

Constantinus stared back at me blankly.

"I have friends in Remis," he said at last, "who would pay."

"But they don't know where you are," I said, "and I've no interest in telling them, not yet, anyhow. It's your good fortune that I have an alternative proposal, which is based on interests we have in common — your exalted position as the son of Vitellus Astrebanus and our envy of Mistress Signy and her child. I'll set you free on two conditions. The first is this…"

"You can guess what it was," she said, turning to Signy and laying her hand on her belly.

"…and the second is, once you have fulfilled the first condition, you'll leave Britannia, by means I'll provide, and I'll never see you again. I'm also in need of good fortune, especially from Neptunus. Anyone from Bononia to Burdigala will tell you that I keep my side of deals. What do you think, Constantinus?"

"I…I…"

"Do you wish to have some time to consider the options?"

He looked across at me with a sad expression, nodded and turned his gaze to the floor tiles at his feet.

"Very well," I said. "I'll return tomorrow. Ferland, open the door!"

I picked up the stool and handed it to your Jute.

"I shall be ready," I said, turning to Constantinus, "for you to accept my proposition. I shall be very disappointed if you do not," I made sure to add, sliding my hands down my waist and hips in a suggestive manner.

"Why?" said Signy, gripping the beaker of beer so hard that her knuckles showed white. "Why did you do that? How could you have done such a thing?"

"I already told you it was you who gave me the idea," Megana replied, hiding behind her upturned beaker. "Who's going to marry me if I'm carrying another man's child? Not Carassus, not any time soon, anyway, and that's all I need. Then I'll have an heir, and Pontius won't have a leg to stand on. The problem was always finding a suitable man, somebody who could do the deed but had no claim on me. I had already considered inviting Alwynn in, a handsome stranger – we must have similar tastes – but he obviously had other matters on his mind. Then kindly Fortuna provided an alternative, a much better alternative." She took a long swig at her ale.

"But he's a beast, a nasty—"

"There were no feelings between us, other than…need I say it. It had been a long while since I had lain with a man. It had been a pleasure I had missed, I have to admit, even with a barely eager Constantinus. Well, he was only barely eager at first, since I seemed to grow on him. After all, it took two whole months before I was sure my plan had succeeded."

"But why just Constantinus?"

"He's the perfect choice. He's one of the Astrebani, one of the best families in Britannia, once upon a time, anyway," said Megana. "Supposing Pontius, to take just one example, starts to a kick up a fuss that some whore's bastard isn't going to stop him becoming the top trader in the kingdom. Constantinus' mother is Lady Milesia, our queen's dearest friend."

"An intrigue maker," said Signy, "from all I have heard."

"Perfect…all I have to do is go weeping and wailing that Constantinus took advantage of me, and now Primus or Secondus are casting slurs on her grandchild."

"They're touched, unhinged. The whole family. His father was a megalomaniac. His uncle is a homicidal madman, and the nephew is little better."

"Ah, yes…I'm getting distracted…*Is* a homicidal maniac? I thought Drusus Astrebanus was dead?"

"Constantinus said nothing?"

"His mind was on other matters, and I was too busy to ask him."

"Well, to all intents and purposes, he *is* dead."

"That's not the same. You know something, don't you, something you've been hiding from me, something which has you agitated? I'm beginning to suspect that you're hiding something which makes you feel a great deal more guilty than I am. I just had a fuck with a guy and I got pregnant. What have you been doing?"

Signy sighed. She no longer had any choice. Too much had already been revealed.

"Drusus Astrebanus *is* still alive. I found him, with Alwynn and a friend of his, in the street. The man was on the verge of the grave, but I'm good, Megana, I'm very, very good. I stitched him and kept him calm and still for days while his body healed. His soul has fled…" She still couldn't tell the whole truth, that she had captured his dreams and memories, his hopes and fears, and laid them out neatly on scraps of parchment stored in a casket which she kept beneath her bed. "…but his body's eating, drinking, breathing and going about the day like a living man. So long as he gets the potion, morning and evening, and that's where Alwynn comes in."

Megana's eyes were fixed on her, not moving. Her mouth could merely open and close, barely enough to croak out a few words.

"But it's been years, since before you and Marcus…"

"I wish you hadn't had a child with Constantinus," Signy said. "No good will come of it. Fortuna isn't kind. She plays with us."

"And you're telling *me* that. I'm expecting a child, Signy, perpetuating my line. That's my duty. What sort of duty is it to keep the king's enemy alive, even if he is 'almost dead' as you put it?"

"It's my duty," Signy said, her voice rising. "It's my damned duty, because the goddess gave me the power over life and death – the ability to keep people alive or allow them to die – and the goddess placed this man's life in my hands, gave me power over his body and his soul, and it's my duty to use the power that the goddess has given me. I had no choice when I was led to him in the street…"

"But you had a choice whether to tell Marcus, or me, even?"

"Yes," she sighed, "but…it's too late. It's all far too late and has got far too complicated."

"And where does Constantinus come into this?" Megana pressed her advantage.

"He tried to rape me…while I was caring for Drusus. He was this far, a thumb, from getting his way, when Alwynn dragged him off and nearly killed him. The father of your child is a man who tried to rape me and enjoyed it."

"Signy," said Megana, trying to remain calm. "You know I didn't know Constantinus tried to rape you, because you never uttered a word about any of this stuff. Maybe I would've acted differently. Maybe I would've imprisoned Alwynn and forced him to have sex with me. Would that have been better? If I had bedded a man you *willingly* slept with? Listen to me. You've told me yourself. You were in love at one time, sort of, with Thorgill the Jute, a man who admitted he was a murderer and a rapist."

Signy sat in dumb silence. Megana sighed.

"It was too good an opportunity to miss, dear Signy, and so easy to get rid of him once the deed was done. Constantinus has no claim on me, and if he tries…He won't dare, I'm sure. And now the rest of them will leave me alone."

"There's no accounting for Fortuna, Megana," Signy said quietly. "You've opened Pandora's box, and there's no closing it now. Just look at how stubborn Drusus has been, how many years he has pestered Marcus with his delusions of being denied the governorship."

"I'm sorry. I knew you would be upset, even without…what you've just told me. That's why I had to keep it secret. Until I was sure. You'll forgive me, won't you? You must. You've had your moments of pleasure with the man you love. Just think of me. I haven't had that chance. I had to use the only tool God sent me."

Signy burst into laughter.

"That's one way of looking at it, Megana, I suppose. A tool attached to a body. I suppose you didn't care much whose tool it was, and maybe I shouldn't either. Enough of this beer, I'm going to fetch some wine and skip the water this time. If we're going to act like barbarians, we might as well get roaring drunk as well and boast of our conquests."

"Did he live up to your expectations? Did the fine gentleman perform well in bed?" she asked when she returned.

"As I said, he wasn't too willing at first, but you've seen me in the nude. What man could resist? It was quite fun towards the end."

Megana crossed to her friend, the wine flagon in her hand, filled her glass again, and then bent down and kissed her.

"Wish me well, my dear," Megana murmured. "I won't allow Pontius or Carassus to have my legacy. I have the child now and, God willing, we'll see our business completed. There's no going back."

☙ Chapter 31 ❧

In late spring, it had become obvious that Megana was expecting a child, and shortly after, Signy heard the first rumours.

"Someone's husband, who was visiting you on business, noticed your swelling belly," she said to Megana. "They're wondering who the father is. Different versions of the story name different people."

"They?" Megana frowned.

"I've even heard," said Signy, "that some people are saying that you and I have managed to conceive a child together, through magic. Marcus says they're worried that you've married secretly and your mystery husband will emerge as Fabiansson's successor. You're trouble enough as it is, they say, but a husband would be even more dangerous."

"You haven't told Marcus who the father is?" sighed Megana.

"No, of course not."

"It would be the worst if they thought...if the ever-speculating 'they' thought Constantinus and I were married...properly."

The ill-tongued rumours spurred Signy on. The debt collectors roamed further, appearing at remote villas in the early hours, waking the dogs, pushing past bewildered servants to gain access to the master and his family. There was no system they followed, no guessing who would be next. Signy selected the target by casting sticks. People who had debts to Fabiansson could demand their retainers sleep in the house, even in the passageways and anterooms to the bedchambers, but not all of them, all of the time, and the raiders seemed to know just who was most vulnerable. To owe a debt to a merchant could be laughed at, bragged about even, over a drink in the hall or at council, but to admit to having the debt collected forcibly, and by a woman, would be too great a loss of face. That might lead retainers to think their lord and master was not quite the man he made himself out to be, that there might be another lord, a better lord, worth following, or maybe even no lord at all. Better then to send a furtive, apologetic servant, bag in hand, many concluded. As for the rest, so long as each man sat in his own chamber with his own thoughts, they could be picked off one by one.

That did not stop the spiteful rumours about Megana.

"She's in league with evil spirits, that's what I heard," Ferland reported.

Signy was riding out to a farm a few miles from Corinium, and had asked the Jute to travel with her. Farmer Gallum's mother was sick, near the end of her life, probably, and Signy had been called for advice. Earlier, she would have had no concerns about taking a journey like this alone, her reputation protecting her from harm, but hunger turned many people to banditry that spring, and the activities of the black-coated night-raiders provided useful cover for emulators.

"How else does she always seem to know what's going on in the markets? How else does she always seem to make a profit when others lose?" continued the warrior. "Because she has sold her soul to the devil, and now he has claimed his reward. She's half-black already, so they say. It's only natural the devil would favour one of his own."

"That's nonsense," said Signy. "Megana's no different from you or me. The child has a real flesh-and-blood father, just like mine."

"I know what she did," Ferland answered, "I'm only repeating what people say," he added, giving her a look that Signy suspected meant he had a good idea who was the father of her own child, little Einar, strapped tightly to her back by a swatch of cloth, rocked to sleep by the gentle rhythm of the horse. If Ferland knew, who else knew?

"Ah, forget it, Signy," Ferland grumbled, seeing the anger on her face. "This kind of rumour circulates for a while, and then new gossip will come along, and people's attention will be distracted elsewhere."

"I hope so," said Signy, glancing around. "Isn't this where we turn off the main road for Gallum's farm?"

Gallum's mother will be glad to see little Einar, she thought. Signy remembered that she had last visited the farm for the delivery of Gallum's youngest, just a short while after she had confirmed that she herself was expecting. How excited she had felt assisting a new life into the world, knowing that before long she would become a mother herself.

She followed Ferland along the narrow path leading to the farm. She thought of the legends she had read, legends in which the sons of kings and queens had been given away to farm folk to be brought up far from threats and danger. They had to be just stories, didn't they? Would she be able to give up Einar to a family like Gallum's if he was menaced? She answered her own question with a no, no…she had taken the decision to have the child, and she had chosen the man to be his father. The boy was her responsibility, and she could not shirk her duty, whatever happened.

"I need you to go north," Signy told Alwynn. "There are three landowners who are guilty of failing to repay Megana. They were first in line for the grain she shipped over in the spring and did not pay anything, not a *nummus*."

"Who are they?"

"Atle, Maglorius and a man named Notius, and one at least must be made an example."

"Can't you send the Jutes? There are more of them," Alwynn grumbled.

"The Jutes worked up there, Alwynn, when they were first taken prisoner," she replied. "They would be recognised. Nobody knows you and your comrades. We have to keep up the mystery. That's what's keeping us safe. People have to be unsure if it's Megana or strangers, or just their own rebellious tenants and neighbours." She saw Alwynn's doubtful look. "I can give you Ferland as a guide, but he's not to enter any of the houses."

Alwynn looked thoughtful. "Best we take all at once, by surprise, in the middle of the night, and from different directions. I've a Northman in the band. People might take him for a Pict."

"There'll be a lot to carry by the time you're finished. You'll need packhorses. Ferland can take care of those. But, Alwynn, don't come back here. Ride directly to Litorina. Ferland knows Megana's factor. He'll see that everything's loaded straight on to the boat."

"Very well, my lady."

A hand was shaking her. Signy opened her eyes. It was black, dark, the middle of the night. An urgent voice whispered.

"Mistress, wake up!"

She turned, found herself face to face with Maria, who should have been asleep in the kitchen.

"Captain Alwynn's here."

She was suddenly wide awake. "Tell him I'm coming," she said, sending Maria back down the ladder, while she searched for a shift to cover her nudity. She came down the ladder, still barefoot, and crossed to the door.

"What are you doing here, Alwynn?" she whispered. She was about to give the Frisian a piece of her mind when he held up his hand.

"Peace, for God's sake, my lady, and listen to me. I'm on my way to Litorina, I promise. Ferland has held the packhorses on the Londinium road, but I have to leave someone with you."

"What? Who?" Not Constantinus again, was her immediate worry.

Alwynn turned and beckoned into the darkness, and a woman came stumbling forward.

"Mistress, have mercy, I beg of you," she cried, falling to her knees.

"Silence," hissed Signy. "Who the fuck is she, Alwynn?" she continued, turning to the Frisian. "I said no slaves or animals!"

"She's no slave, my lady. She's Notius' wife."

Signy cursed and glanced down at the woman. She might have seen thirty summers, but she looked older, thin, starved, even.

"I prayed," the woman said. "I prayed the raiders in black would come, my lady, and my prayers were answered. He beat me, my lady, when he was drunk, and he was often drunk, and, my lady, he took all the food for himself and his men. Left nothing for me and the servants, and me carrying another child."

What sort of child, Signy thought, would come from a starving and beaten woman in a time like this?

"I can't keep her here, Alwynn," she said, now switching to Jutish, which she doubted the woman could understand but the Frisian would comprehend. "I've no place, and I don't want to attract any questions. And Marcus could show up! I can't even pretend she's a servant. He's probably met her!"

"I can't take her with me," Alwynn insisted. "She's exhausted and weak, and already nearly falling from the horse."

Signy once again glanced down at the woman. "Do you know who I am?" she asked.

The woman shook her head.

"Do you remember a story, a couple of years ago, about a sorceress in Walcastrum who could raise people from the dead?"

The woman nodded.

"Well, I'm that sorceress," Signy said, drawing aside the neck of the shift, "and here's my mark. Now you know whose house you've been brought to."

The woman nodded vigorously. "I'd rather take my chances with you, my lady sorceress, than that devil Notius," she sobbed. "I'll do anything you want, just don't send me back. I swear on the Bible."

"That won't get you far here," said Signy curtly, and took her firmly by the arm. "Into the house now, and my apprentice will take care of you, and don't step on the cat."

She turned to Alwynn. "What were you thinking of?"

"I couldn't leave her. She begged to come. She's covered in bruises. And that fat old bastard—"

"You didn't kill him?"

Alwynn shook his head. "He'll remember the first blow, but nothing afterwards. Listen, my lady, she clung to me, to my legs. I couldn't get away, and she's clung to me the whole way on the road, riding on my horse behind me. I promised I would leave her with a friend, in safety."

Damnation, thought Signy, this is all getting so entangled.

"Alwynn, she's your responsibility, not mine."

The Frisian shrugged. "My lady, you have my oath, so my responsibilities are also yours."

"You did collect the debts, and not just this bag of bones?"

"Good silver and antique stuff. We had to flatten the plate, but a competent smith'll soon restore it."

Signy sighed. "Very well, clear off now, but be back here, alone, with a spare horse, so you can take this woman to your own encampment."

Alwynn saluted and vanished into the night. Signy turned, and saw the woman crouched on a stool by the remnants of the fire and a lamp that Maria had lit.

"I'm sorry that you've led a hard life," she said, though with little sympathy in her tone, "but you can't stay here more than a few days. People visit for consultations, rituals, sacrifices, and you'll be a disturbance. Tonight and tomorrow you can stay in the loft, in the storage place beside my room. After that you'll sleep in the garden hut. It's clean and sheltered, but don't touch the drying herbs if you value your life."

The woman nodded meekly.

"You'll eat a sorceress's porridge, I suppose?" Maria enquired timidly.

The woman nodded again.

Why should I care whose porridge she imagines she's eating? Signy thought. Let her believe I'm a sorceress if it keeps her quiet and obedient.

✿ Chapter 32 ✿

Signy was annoyed to have been trapped in the Fabiansson house – she would much rather have been out on the highways and byways, meeting patients, or in her garden taking care of her plants – but Megana had travelled to Porta Siluria once more. She had some explaining to do now she was damaged goods.

Signy had been left with Colfax, Fabiansson's old clerk, to take care of the business while she was away, sitting in Megana's workroom, meeting irritated farmers and landowners. Some of her visitors were still desperate to fill the gap before the harvest came in. Others were trying to offload the little that they had managed to save while prices were still high.

"I'm sorry," Signy insisted. "Merchant Fabiansson is not purchasing at the moment."

Megana had instructed her before she left. "The prices are too high now, and soon the new harvest will arrive."

"The mistress recommends you barter with your neighbours," was the advice she gave to both would-be sellers and purchasers.

"Who are you to tell me what to do?"

I grew up on a farm, she thought. We had no silver. We were glad to exchange with neighbours. She kept her opinions to herself.

"I want to see Fabiansson himself!"

"I'm sorry, Master Fabiansson is unwell at present, and is not taking visitors." She tried to keep her voice calm.

"When's the daughter back?"

"The mistress will return in ten days…nine days…eight days…tomorrow."

When Megana did return, Signy could see that the journey to Porta Siluria had taken its toll. Explaining her pregnancy had taken its toll as well, Megana reported, though Cousin Pontius had been understanding.

"The nuptials will still take place, once the child has been born, and a decent interval has passed, he kindly conceded." She shook her head angrily. "Nothing's going stand between that man and Father's wealth, so he thinks."

"You look tired. It's best not to worry about such matters at a time like this."

"I feel fucking awful," Megana admitted, "not just tired, but sick and swollen. But I can't just let things go. Then I just get restless and agitated."

"Mistress is unwell," explained Signy, as a maid showed yet another farmer to the door. "I hope she'll be recovered enough to see you next week." But her answer will be the same as mine, she thought.

She was waiting for Colfax to return from the forum where he had been to the tax collector's office to pick up a document and was ready to close up the office for the last time that day. Maria and Einar were waiting in the kitchen. She planned to take a stroll out of the town and sit for a moment in the ruins of the amphitheatre and let her mind wander, let the fresh air blow away the feelings of being closed in, trapped and annoyed.

Colfax was an old man, and tended to carry out his business slowly, but he seemed to be even slower than usual, Signy reflected.

"I'm sorry it took so long, Mistress," said the clerk when he finally arrived, "but there's some sort of disturbance in the town."

"Let me have the message," Signy insisted. "I need to read it before I leave."

The clerk handed her the document, rolled up and tied with a piece of grey cloth.

"There's smoke rising from the direction of Bakers' Street," the clerk commented as she skimmed down the text, checked the right marks were fixed at the bottom, and rolled it up again.

"Very good, thank you. I think that's all for today," she said, and then looked up at the clerk who was still stooping over her. "Did you say Bakers' Street?"

If there was a fire in Bakers' Street, she thought, that would concern the girls in the Minerva House.

"Yes, Mistress."

A fire in the city could easily turn serious, jumping from one building to the next.

She frowned again.

"Colfax, do me a favour, will you, and take a message to Maria. She should be in the kitchen. Tell her I'm just going to pop out and investigate what's going on for myself. She can take Einar home instead of waiting for me here. Tell her I'll come to the cottage as soon as I can."

When she stepped out of the house, she saw people milling around, more than she expected, and their voices were loud and disputative. The street felt crowded and threatening, so she decided to take a chance and go through the back alley. That way she could avoid the mob and reach the rear entrance of the Minerva House. As she made her way through the back streets behind the buildings, she could see and smell the smoke in the air. This was no small blaze, and there must be a risk of the fire spreading.

As she entered the alley, to her shock and horror she saw that the smoke was coming from the Minerva House itself, but she was also surprised to see a huddle of people standing at the rear of the building. When she came up to them, she saw some of the girls, who ran towards her and hugged her.

"Oh, Miss Signy, it's horrible."

"The boys came and chased us."

"Then they set the books on fire, and now everything's burning!"

Signy looked around to see where the adults were.

"Where are Mistress Fonberga and Cookie?" she asked.

"They went to the classroom to stop the boys."

"They tore Knutta's dress, and then chased us out."

It was only the bravest of the girls who were talking. The others were simply silent or crying. Signy was not sure what to do. Fonberga, the teacher, and the cook must still be in the burning building, and there were some girls missing from the group.

"Come along, girls," she said, "let's get to Mistress Megana's house, then you'll be safe," and began ushering the girls in the direction of Fabiansson's yard.

The older girls set off in the lead, but the younger ones were frightened and kept stopping, looking bewildered. In the end, she had to pick one of them up and carry her, and that encouraged her friends to run along behind. Once she reached Fabiansson's house, she handed the small girl to the housekeeper and turned back.

"The Minerva House is burning, and I couldn't see Cookie and Miss Fonberga. I'm worried there are still some of the children inside the house. Henrik," she called, spotting Fabiansson's groom, "send all the help you can." And then she hurried away again.

As she darted back through the alleys and lanes, she saw two figures running in her direction.

"Ferland, Hrasmus, come with me."

Back in the alley, they saw Fonberga, the cook, and the cook's husband, Berthold, and several of the older girls standing at the rear of the burning building. The cook and her husband were carrying fire irons and appeared to be splashed with blood. Fonberga was weeping, holding her face in her ash-blackened hands. The girls were holding Knutta, wrapped only in a piece of sacking, her breast heaving, and blood on her legs.

"What's going on?" asked Signy, almost screaming.

"They raped her," said the cook, pointing to Knutta. "Five of them, pushed her up against the pulpit and raped her."

"Those bastards got what was coming to them," said her husband.

Signy looked from one to the other.

"Who? What?"

"Boys from the school, those who are always hanging around in the forum," Berthold answered.

"You mean Deacon Baxter's pupils?"

"Exactly."

"And where are they?"

"Who cares?" said the man, glancing towards the house, where flames could now be seen licking from one of the windows.

Signy turned to the Jutes. "Go in and check the building. Get anyone out you can see. I don't care who they are. We'll deal with that later."

As the Jutes hurried in through the rear of the Minerva House, she turned to the girls.

"What's happened?"

"It was the boys, Miss Signy. They ran into the classroom, and started to wreck things, and then they tore Knutta's dress, and…after that we didn't see what happened."

"I think they fucked her," said one of the girls, not sure if that was the right word to use. Their story certainly fit with the torn clothes and the blood.

"Who?"

"We don't know their names, Miss Signy. They were big boys."

"You'll know who they were, Mistress," said Berthold. "We went at them with the fire irons."

Signy held her face in her hands. She could hardly think straight, but one fear broke through her confusion. Baxter's pupils were the sons of landowners and big men, only visiting Corinium for schooling. They were the children of important people, not tradespeople and farmers, like the schoolgirls.

She felt like crying and cursing, but that would not help. "Berthold and Cookie, take the girls to Mistress Megana's. Go the back way, through the yard. Fonberga, go with them, and when you get there, tell the people to lock the gates and shut up all the other doors and bar them."

"What about you, Miss Signy?"

"Don't worry about me. I have my friends here. They'll take care of me."

The cook and her husband hurried off, herding the three girls in front of them, with the teacher trotting behind, seemingly barely aware of what she was doing.

Signy took a deep breath, and ended up coughing, half choked on the smoke.

Ferland appeared, dragging two small boys behind him, spluttering and coughing himself, while Hrasmus carried another.

Signy crouched down. "What happened?"

"Greg set the books on fire, Miss, and the flames went all the way up to the roof."

"Butch said we should go and scare the girls, Miss," said the other. "They said that it was wrong that girls should learn to read and write. That's something just for boys."

"What did they do to Knutta?"

"I don't know," said the boy, looking down at his feet. "They sent us out and told us to wreck the school. We pulled the books down on the floor, Miss. It was an accident, Miss, that they started to burn."

"Master Berthold came and was angry, Miss."

I bet, thought Signy, and then she recognised the boy, stained and dirty, and with his clothes torn: Lucius, Marcus' son.

This was nearly too much, too much for her to take in.

"Take these boys to the school, to Deacon Baxter," she said to the waiting Jutes. "You know where that is? Except this one," she added, seizing Lucius by his tunic, "take him to the Ursinus house, and deliver him to Silke."

The Jutes disappeared down the alley, herding the boys as if they were sheep. Signy looked in through the rear gate of the Minerva House. The roof was now well ablaze and could fall in at any moment. She hoped that no one was still inside. She trusted her men to have done their duty, tore her eyes away and started to walk sorrowfully up the alley. When she came to the end, she turned left, and shortly came to the entrance to Bakers' Street. She saw that the townwatch had organised a chain of people with buckets, throwing water onto the buildings closest to the Minerva House, trying to stop the fire from spreading. Suddenly, there was a tremendous crash, a shower of sparks flew into the air, and a cry went up from the crowd. Now the Minerva House's roof had fallen in.

The street was blocked by gaping townspeople. Signy could do nothing more. It was better that she took care of her own boy, so she turned back into the alley, and by going from lane to lane, she was able to make her way to the city gate, and up the track towards the King's Hall and her cottage. Her heart was pounding. She felt sick and frightened.

With an effort, she reached the row of buildings where the royal guards lived, the last part of the old Roman camp still standing. Grunwald saw her coming and called out in surprise.

"Miss Signy, are you alright?"

"No, Grunwald, I'm not. I feel sick and I could nearly puke."

"We got the boys here, four or five older guys. They said in the town that these boys have done something wrong, I don't know what, but they've been beaten badly. We've put them in our barracks. Will you take a look at them?" Grunwald led her up the steps into the long, low hut.

The boys were laid out on the guards' own beds. One had been obviously beaten on the head with a heavy object, a fire iron, she quickly concluded. The boy was unconscious and bleeding. He might even die, she thought. Another was holding his arm at a strange angle. It was clearly broken. Two others were badly gashed about the face and hands. The fifth only sat groaning. The ones who were conscious looked at her blankly. They looked numb with fear, thought Signy, too numb just now to feel shame at what they've done, too numb to think of anything except how they had been standing around the half-naked girl when blows began to rain down on them, how they had tried to fend them off, until they were beaten to the ground, feet in their faces, their groins, until blissfully they had lost consciousness, and then came to in this strange place.

Signy laid her hand on each of them, checking their heartbeats. No one was in any immediate danger of death, she concluded, and turned to Grunwald.

"I need to go and fetch my medicines and my tools. I'll do my best to treat these boys, though they hardly deserve it," she added.

She ran as fast as she could to her house. Without thinking to check if Maria and Einar were safe, she searched through the chests containing her medication. When she did notice Maria, all she did was order her to find a clean cloth, newly washed, and tear it into strips about a hand wide, and let her have them.

She returned to the guard house and, spotting Grunwald again, called out.

"Fetch some wine so I can mix up a medication to take away the boys' pain."

She cleaned the superficial wounds and bandaged them. She gave a double dose of medication to the boy with the broken arm. As he lay on the bed, his eyes glazed, she pushed the bones back together and bound them tight. Finally, she examined the boy with the broken head. There was little she could do for him except ensure that he rested quietly. She took out a pinch of powder, mixed from the plants she had grown in her own garden, and added it to the wine. She held his head carefully and tipped the drink into his throat. He coughed and spluttered, but she was satisfied enough of the medicine had got into him. She turned to Grunwald.

"Pray that I've got it right."

That was all she could do for now. When she looked out, she could already see that the sun was beginning to sink towards the horizon. The whole afternoon had passed, and she had not noticed.

It was almost dark before Signy returned to Fabiansson's house. Einar had needed feeding, and Maria had insisted that Signy should not leave the cottage before she had eaten, too. She had to thump on the small door and shout for a long time before Henrik let her in. The girls were huddled in the kitchen. Megana's cook had given Knutta a large glass of wine with sleeping herbs in it and placed her in one of the guest rooms. The cook from the Minerva House, Berthold and Fonberga were sitting in silence. The seriousness of what they had done was beginning to sink in. They had beaten five sons of important people. The boys were certainly injured, perhaps even dead. There was only one outcome awaiting them – a matter of when and how they would be punished.

Signy asked for Megana. It seemed so long ago she had left her friend resting in her room. The housekeeper said Megana was out in the town. She had been wakened by the noise. She had come into the kitchen to ask what was going on, and when she heard what had happened, she had turned white, asked for her cloak and then left the house.

"On her own?" asked Signy.

"Yes, ma'am," said the housekeeper.

Signy felt like cursing again at the impetuosity of her friend, but she had so little energy left, she could not utter a word.

"There's porridge here," said the housekeeper, seeing her blank look, "good barley porridge. I made it for them, but they won't eat." It was understandable that Fonberga, Berthold and his wife hardly had an appetite, given the situation.

"Eat!" ordered Signy, suddenly waking to life. "Eat, eat until you are ready to vomit, as if you'll never eat again, because who knows when your next meal will be?" She took a bowl herself, filled it with boiled meal and forced herself to eat. Shamefaced, the others helped themselves and, with varying expressions of distaste, swallowed the gooey mass.

There was a noise in the atrium outside. Megana entered the kitchen and looked around. There were beads of sweat on her face. Signy jumped up and took her friend in her arms. Megana groaned. Please, please, thought Signy, not now. It's too early. She held her friend as Megana gasped.

"It kicked. It just kicked," she said.

"Lie down, right here," ordered Signy, and gently let her friend down onto the floor. The housekeeper ran forward with a bundle of cloth and placed it under her head.

"Breathe," whispered Signy, "breathe gently, dear Megana."

"It's okay, it's passing," Megana muttered. "Baby kicked at the wrong moment and in the wrong place." She clutched at Signy's hand. "I told him," she said, "I told Uncle Marcus to get those boys out of town tomorrow or I would kill them, every single one of them, his precious little Lucius included."

Oh, by the gods, what's she done, thought Signy, but squeezed her friend's hand in reassurance. Megana stared up from where she was lying on the floor. The others looked down at her, their anxious faces forming a ring round their mistress. She stared back, from one face to the other, then took a deep breath.

"Berthold, you're in serious trouble," she said at last, "and Cookie, too. You know who you beat? The boy you beat unconscious, he's the son of Chief Atle, who's married to Chief Questus' sister, and…" She closed her eyes but continued speaking. "No one will care about Knutta. She's just a shoemaker's girl, and those pigs are the sons of lords and warriors. They'll want their justice, but I can't hand you over to them."

She took another breath. "Get Henrik."

By the time the groom came in, Megana had begun to recover a little.

"Henrik, is there a wagon in the yard?"

"Yes, Miss. The little one, that we took to Porta Siluria."

"Good. Fasten the horses, and put Fonberga, Cookie and Berthold in there, and then cover them with a blanket and some hay. Signy, can you be a dear and write a few lines to Captain Marius? I want the captain to raise anchor and carry our friends over to Bononia immediately. Tell him to find them lodging and leave them a little money. I don't care if the crew has to row the whole way, only that Fonberga, Cookie and Berthold are away before the news gets to Atle and the others."

Signy let go of her friend's hand and crossed through the darkened house to the office. She found a blank tablet and scribbled a note to the ship's captain, closing it with Megana's seal. When she returned to the kitchen, Megana was sitting on one of the benches. Fonberga, the cook and her husband were nowhere to be seen.

"They're in the yard."

Signy went out through the scullery to see where the small wagon had been hitched up, seemingly carrying a load of hay. She handed the messages to Asser, sitting on the driver's bench, Hrasmus beside him. The yard gates swung open, the horses trotted out and away into the night. The gates closed and Signy returned inside.

Megana was still sitting where Signy had left her. She smiled weakly when Signy came in, bent down and gave her a hug.

"Oh, Megana, you're in serious trouble, too," said Signy. "They won't let you get away with this."

And me, too, she thought, if I'm not careful, considering the visit that Alwynn and his comrades have just paid to Chief Atle. His precious silver, she thought, might be taking the same boat to the mainland as the fugitive servants.

☙ Chapter 33 ❧

The following day, the smell of smoke and burning hung over the town. The heroic work of the citizens had prevented the fire from spreading, but the Minerva House was a gutted ruin. Groups of townspeople hung around on street corners spreading the story about how the arrogant sons of notables had raped the daughter of one of their friends and burned down the school. Megana had no need to follow up with her threat. Marcus and his court officers hustled the boys out of the town. The threat of further violence from the people died away.

Signy visited the injured boys in the guard barracks during the morning. Only Borno "Butch" Atlesson, the boy with the injured head, was causing her real concern. He was still unconscious. She gave him a second dose of the medication she had concocted. Better to keep him that way, peaceful, still and hopefully healing.

As she dropped the medication between Borno's lips, she noticed the boy with the broken arm watching her.

"Miss," he whispered, "will he get better?"

She tried not to frown. "I hope so."

"Miss, will my arm get better?"

Now she had to force a reasoned smile to her face. "Of course. What's your name?"

"Ymer, Miss."

"Well, Ymer, I've treated many strong warriors, and they've all got better. If you're careful, and leave your arm bound up tight until the new moon, then it will mend properly, and you'll be just as strong as before."

"Thank you, Miss." The boy hesitated, continuing to gaze at her. "Miss, it wasn't our idea."

She turned to him again, with a questioning look.

"We weren't really angry with the girls. My sister can read and write. She has a tutor at home. But the man made it feel unfair, saying the girls got help we didn't get, and that they were learning to cast spells and make potions."

"The man?"

"The man in the forum, the man selling cups and beakers made of silver, at least I think he was."

"What did he look like?"

"It's hard to say. He wore a green cloak and kept the hood up. All you could see were his eyes and nose. His eyes," said the boy thoughtfully, "that's what caught our attention."

Signy left her unconscious patient and sat down beside the boy. "What was so extraordinary about his eyes?"

"They were special, a special sort of grey colour, and…"

Signy sighed. "Thank you, Ymer, for being brave enough to tell me this."

She patted him on his good arm and stood up.

"Just remember when you get home, the girl who was hurt, she's just like your sister, with a mother and a father who love her. Just remember when you grow up and become a man, that all women should be treated the same way you would treat your sister, no matter what others suggest."

The boy looked away, ashamed, she supposed.

She quickly crossed to the door and left the room. The corridor outside leading through the barracks was empty.

"Grunwald. Grunwald," she called.

A figure emerged from the common area at one end.

"Grunwald is not here, Mistress Signy."

"Oh, Beltrice?" she gasped. The guard captain waited until she drew near. She did not like the expression on his face.

"Grunwald is a member of the guard, don't forget that," said the captain. "He follows my orders, not yours."

Signy needed time. She did not want to meet Megana and she most certainly did not want to cross paths with Marcus until she had had a chance to contemplate what the boy had told her.

Instead, she walked along the main street until she reached the forum. There she paused, looked around, seeing guards outside the basilica, outside the buildings occupied by the boys' school. She did not care to look closely, on the chance that Grunwald was among the sentries, doing his duty as ordered by Captain Beltrice. She rounded the forum, staying to the shadows of the arcade, until she reached the Christian church, where she slipped between the buildings and past the back of the basilica.

From there, the shortest route to Fabiansson's yard was down Bakers' Street and past the still-smoking remains of the Minerva House. As she rounded the corner, she noticed someone in the street, standing across from the damaged building, a solitary man, wearing a cloak, his head covered by a hood.

She had taken a dozen paces along the street before an unpleasant thought came to her mind. It could be him, she realised, but could she be sure? Wasn't she giving too much credence to a boy probably trying to alleviate his guilt? And hooded cloaks were common. She was wearing one herself. The man made no move to look in her direction, had not noticed her, she hoped, so she pulled her own hood tighter and wrapped it round her face. Then she started to walk down the street with feigned nonchalance. As she approached, the man glanced up, seeing only a townswoman, she thought, and then returned his stare to the building opposite. She hurried her steps. If she timed them right, she could pass in front of him, get one good look and hurry on before he had a chance to react. Five, four, three steps and she was up to him, glanced to her left, looking full in his face, and then wrenched her eyes back to the street. Her heart took a jump. There was no doubt, the man in the green cloak was Constantinus Astrebanus. She felt her heart beating faster, driven by the thought that Constantinus might have recognised her in return. She listened for steps following her, but it was impossible to hear above the sound of her own feet, and the beating in her ears. She had to…she was forced to look back. As she did so, a voice called out.

"Stop! Stop! Don't walk away. I know your shape, your gait, Signy the Sorceress, too well not to recognise you."

She froze, wanting to break into a run, but fearful that would provoke him into running after her. She could not bear the thought of being chased, of being hunted down, dragged away, where and to what end.

He walked towards her, slowly, tentatively, and when she reflected on his shout she recognised there was as much a plea in his voice as a command.

He came to a halt some ten or a dozen paces away. She took a step back, and he matched her with a step forward.

"I knew it was you," he said, "the moment you came around the corner. If you've lived as a fugitive as long as I have, you know how to watch without anyone realising they are being observed."

He took another step towards her, but her feet refused to obey her will and move her back.

Her mouth, however, was more cooperative. "Did you do that?" she asked, indicating the still lightly smoking buildings.

"You mean did I burn down her precious school for girls? I don't know why you even ask."

"Then why are you standing staring at the ruins?"

"Because I had a hand in seeing that it was destroyed. I've been in the marketplace, in the taverns, asking questions, dropping suggestions, first to one man and then to another, sometimes in the guise of a silversmith, another as a pipe player. I'm quite handy on the pipes. You didn't know that, did you? Sometimes I stayed in town, others I wandered around the villages. Sometimes I gave the impression I was a pagan – Freya has always been my favourite goddess – and sometimes I played a fervent Christian. It's wonderful what you can learn from education among the monks. The Socratic method…it allows you to argue both sides, and see the advantages and the disadvantages of both, until you no longer know which is true, which is right, and which is wrong, and with the life I've lived I no longer care."

"Your life?" she murmured.

She had regained control of her legs, and took a step back, and another, and he followed.

"What about all the lives you've ruined?" she asked.

"You can't provoke me," he replied. "I'm beyond that, except in one way, of course, the way that flashed through my mind when I saw you come round the corner."

"Stay away," she said, understanding his meaning, taking another pace back, and then another. She was still frightened of moving too quickly, of inciting him to attack her, despite what he claimed.

"My life has been such a ruin, I could ruin many lives and still the balance wouldn't be restored."

"It doesn't have to be like that, if you weren't so stubborn, if you'd just let go of everything unreasonable."

"Unreasonable?"

"Like believing you should be governor, like thinking you can get your lands back."

"Like thinking I can have you?"

"Like that, too."

"How can I let go," he said, taking a step towards her, "when all those things are what make me who I am? It would be like cutting off an arm or a leg. I *am* Constantinus Astrebanus, Master of Agridurnum, and those fields, those woods, they belong to me and to my child with her..." He waved an arm vaguely in the direction of the Fabiansson house, and Signy recognised at once that a few more steps would take her to the corner of the street which led to the rear entrance.

"I didn't order them to burn down your little girls' school," he said, "but it'll give the so-called king another headache, another thing to complain about when he—" He stopped abruptly, almost as if he was choking on his words. "I didn't need to tell them what to do; their own swinish spirits led them on. I mean, it's a kind of justice after what she forced me to do, to set the little brutes on her precious girls. How much pride do you think I felt, being locked up in a cellar, and forced to mount her like some livestock, day after day?"

Signy felt a shiver of disgust at the thought. It was odd, she reflected in an instant, that she had nightmares, now and then, that Constantinus succeeded in raping her and she felt fear, woke sweating, with her heart beating much as it was beating now, but she had never felt disgust. Perhaps that was what kept enticing him on, that where there was only fear there was still hope.

She reached the corner and for a moment she was out of his line of sight. She took a few quicker steps, but he must have heard her, because almost at once he was outlined in the lane end.

"If you came with me," he said, "you could be a mother to the child. I know you're her friend. You could love her child, if you were with me."

"No," she said, taking another step and another, towards the safety of Fabiansson's yard gate. He stayed where he was.

"I'm not coming nearer," he said. "I'm not going to take the risk. But I'll be waiting…for you…and for my child. I won't forget. I won't forget who's in bed with you, in my place. I won't forget who's the father of your son. I won't forget who's living in my home, or what little is left of it. I won't forget who's marching around claiming to be the king, when he stole my father's rights and murdered him in cold blood. Revenge may have to wait but it will come. Take that smell of smoke, take the cries of those boys and girls – yes, I was there in the crowd and saw their tears and heard their moans – take them as a warning. Take them as a warning that Constantinus Astrebanus is always watching, always waiting, always looking for an opportunity, and I'm not finished yet, not at all finished. And remember this, my darling, longed-for, dreamed-of little angel, that you must watch out for me all the time, every day, when I only have to have the right moment once, and I'll have you. Today wasn't the day. But tomorrow or the next day, or the next…"

He abruptly turned and strode out of sight, back along Bakers' Street in the direction they had come, and she heard his words, fading like an echo.

"…or the next, or the next, or the next…"

"Let me in! Let me in!" she yelled, banging at the postern frantically.

The bar slid open, the gate swung and she nearly tumbled into the yard. She shoved the door closed behind her, leaning against it with all her weight, sinking slowly to the ground until she was sitting on the cobbles. Her heart was pounding. Sweat poured down her head and neck. Never did she imagine she would be so relieved to find herself locked inside the dark confines of the slave yard.

"Mistress, what is it?" The anxious voice of Henrik broke through her thoughts.

"He was there. He was there," she stuttered, her teeth chattering. She held her head in her hands, barely able to suppress a sob. "Everything…everything's going wrong."

Henrik leaned over her, peering out through the grill set at a man's height into the gate.

"There's no one there, Mistress."

He held out a hand and drew her unsteadily to her feet. "Let me look out into the alley, Mistress."

She braced herself, ready for Constantinus to burst in through the gate.

"No one, Mistress," said the groom, turning back to her.

She tried to take deeper breaths, trying to control herself. She reached out her hand, holding on to Henrik's shoulder.

"I saw him, Henrik, the man who Miss Megana held prisoner here. Constantinus is his name."

"I know who you mean, Miss, but there was no one in the alley."

"Oh, gods, Henrik. He was in Bakers' Street, by the Minerva House. I promise. I spoke to him. He taunted me. He can't be far away. He's responsible…He threatened to cause more trouble. We must send people to scour the town. Where's Asser?"

"Miss, don't you remember? Mistress Megana sent Asser to Litorina with the little cart."

"Where's Ferland, then?"

Henrik avoided her glance, before replying, "He's on the road to Litorina, too. Miss Megana sent him with the girls…while you were out."

"And the rest of the men?" She felt panic taking hold again.

"Mistress, I can go and look in the town with some of the stable boys if that will help?"

"Please, please, dear Henrik, do that, do that for me."

He smiled, obviously trying to calm her.

"Go into the kitchen now, Mistress, and find something for your nerves. Your little boy is in there, and Maria with him. I heard him laughing just before you arrived."

"Oh, thank the gods he's here," she sighed, letting go of Henrik and half running across the yard.

There had been no sign of the green-cloaked man in Bakers' Street when Henrik and the stable boys returned. They had enquired in a couple of taverns and at the butcher's shop. Yes, there had been a stranger trying to sell objects of silver, but no one had seen him today. Then they had fanned out and checked the main streets of the town, and as many byways as they could, but there had still been no sign of a silversmith, no sign of a pipe player.

Megana was lying on her bed when Signy found her.

"My back hurts again," she complained.

Signy sat down on the end of the bed and began to massage her friend's feet.

"Meri was here while you were out," Megana continued. "You know how Pacius uses her on occasions when he wants to keep his distance."

"What did she want?"

"She was on her way to visit Aurelius. The lawyers are reviewing the case. There'll be demands for compensation, according to the law and custom, for the injuries to the boys."

"But Cookie can't pay compensation."

"That's why I got her and Berthold out of the way as quick as possible. No…the claims for compensation will be made against me, or rather Father, as their master."

"And the punishment for the boys?"

"Compensation to Knutta or her father, are you joking?"

"But Meri should understand. Her father was a cowhand."

"She does. Knutta was like a sister to her, but the law's what it is. That's what she came to tell me. And…she urged us to help the girls continue their education, those that want to."

"So you sent them away?"

"There were some who wanted to return to their families, but, yes, those girls who wanted to continue, I sent them south, out of the way."

"And Knutta?"

"I don't think she has a choice. The situation's infected enough. How can she stay? I paid her father the compensation he would never receive under the law and persuaded him to let her leave with the others."

"And will you pay the compensation to the boys' fathers?"

Megana shook her head.

"What are you going to do?" asked Signy. "If you don't pay, you'll be putting yourself above the law. They won't accept that."

"I won't pay. I'm going to delay as long as I can."

The gates of the Fabiansson yard and the front door to the house stayed closed. No visitors came and went, no business was conducted. Traders coming to the door to ask for Megana, and when she refused to answer, for Fabiansson, were turned away.

In the guard barracks, five boys waited for their fathers. When Ymer, the boy with the broken arm, now mending straight and strong, was collected by his father, the older man looked on with surprise as his son held Signy's hand and begged her forgiveness for what he had done. The father evidently could not appreciate why everyone was making such a fuss about a few boys exercising their manhood with a servant girl. Why was his son begging forgiveness for the type of activities young men had always done, and with tears in his eyes, too? What was the world coming to?

A few days later, a wagon drew up outside the barracks. Chief Atle had clearly heard the worst, that his son had been beaten about the head and had lain as dead for a week. The chief was considerably surprised to see his boy sitting up, weak but mobile.

He saw the look in his son's eyes as he gazed up at the woman standing beside him. Was his son simple now, or had he fallen in love, were the questions written on his face. Signy helped the boy to his feet. He took one faltering step and then another until he fell into his father's embrace. Signy smiled at the father, who returned her smile with a bitter grimace. Did he realise his son should have died, she thought. Did he realise she could have helped him to die, and no one would have known, and now instead he had his son in his arms again? The boy turned and looked at her. She could hardly meet his gaze. She came forward to where he was standing propped against his father. She kissed him on the cheek.

"Faith, hope and love. But the greatest of these is love," she whispered into the older man's ear. There was no sign that her words had altered his expression. Mistrust, anger and hate were the only emotions she could observe.

Perhaps he's more honest than I am, she thought. There's precious little room for love in this world.

"He was swearing vengeance when he left," said Grunwald. "He said that you had bewitched the boy. His son had done nothing wrong and that you had used the opportunity to cast a spell on him."

"I saved his son's life," said Signy flatly. She was almost devoid of feelings anymore, one way or the other. She was simply getting through each day.

⊰ Chapter 34 ⊱

The look that Chief Atle had given her as he departed worried Signy, and Grunwald's comment only reinforced her concern. Vengeance – what could a man like Atle mean by that? In her childhood world, among the people of the forest, vengeance might mean a knife in the dark, but then they were poor people. In Thorgill's world, not so different from Atle's, she supposed, vengeance could mean gathering his retainers and riding over to the enemy's home and slaughtering everyone they could find – men, women and children. But here, in West Britain, the customs and laws of the Romans were surely still valid, guaranteed by men like Marcus. Wasn't that what Counsellor Pacius thought he was doing, following the law, demanding compensation?

Why was Megana refusing to consider paying? She had enough silver, after all. Atle could be compensated with his own confiscated treasure, or that of his neighbours, providing it was beaten out of all recognition.

No, Signy reflected, Megana is as stubborn as Atle. She thinks that girls are worth just as much as boys, and that a girl frightened and injured, and with her reputation damaged beyond remedy, is worth just as much as Ymer Caeliodubnus' broken arm or Borno Atlesson beaten insensible. In fact, Signy considered, Megana might go even further, and insist that a girl trying to improve her life was worth far more than a boy misusing his privilege. The law did not agree, of course. Tradition did not agree. The boys' fathers did not agree.

Should I speak to Marcus, Signy wondered, persuade him to mediate, to bring Megana round to seeing that she had no choice, that the alternative, swords and axes and fire in the night, was far, far worse?

She did not have the opportunity. Not long after Borno Atlesson had left with his father, Marcus' housekeeper, Silke, came running, panting up the hill to Signy's cottage.

It took a while for the woman to get her breath back.

"Oh, Signy, my dear, that horrible Chief Atle has come back."

Signy could hardly believe her ears.

"He's brought his followers with him," the housekeeper continued, "and the master shut the city gate to keep them out, but now he's let them all in. They're lodging at the Fox Tavern, and Chief Atle's been given permission to question people in the town, to try to find Cookie and Berthold."

"But he won't, Silke," Signy tried to reassure her. "Mistress Megana sent them far, far away, where Chief Atle will never find them."

"But what will he do when he discovers they've gone, and Mistress Megana's responsible?" Silke gave Signy a doubtful look. "I followed the master to the gate this morning. I was standing in the crowd. I saw Chief Atle when he came into the city. He looks such a nasty man, so angry, and such a bully, and his servants are the same, and Grunwald has been saying…"

"Never mind what Grunwald has been saying," said Signy. "I'm sure everything will be just fine, and the master will take of it."

The housekeeper rose to her feet. "He'll be wanting his dinner," she answered.

Signy assumed the housekeeper's thoughts had returned to Marcus, to her usual daily routine, as a comfort in that disturbing moment.

"I'll tell you what. I'll walk back with you, and then I'll call in and check on Megana. Maria can take care of Einar while I'm out," she said, reaching for her cloak.

Silke was right to be worried, Signy soon discovered. There was a very odd mood in the town. Men standing on street corners, talking in hushed voices. Women hurrying through back alleys, avoiding looking each other in the eye. Youths and girls laughing and shouting, taking the opportunity to run wild.

Signy decided she would take a walk past the Fox Tavern, where Atle and his retainers were lodged, with the hope of assessing them for herself. The inn was not far from the Ursinus townhouse, but before she could enter the street, she heard shouting and cursing, and a couple of men came running. She recognised them – the butcher and one of the blacksmiths. They rushed past and hurried off into the distance.

Signy felt uneasy, disturbed by the uncharacteristic turmoil. Should she turn back and seek shelter in the Ursinus house or walk on to check on Megana as she had intended? Suddenly, there came a burst of shouting from the direction of the forum, and just then Corinium did not feel like a place for a young woman to be wandering around alone. If she left by the north gate, she could take the familiar footpath through the old graves, up the hill behind the town, and from there she could reach her cottage and her child.

There was no sign of the watch by the gate, which stood half-open. Signy was not frightened of the tombs and graves, spirits or ghosts, the wind whistling through the trees, or the risk of stumbling over roots or rocks on the path. She had walked this track so many times on moonless nights to stand among the old memorials waiting for Alwynn. She hesitated for a moment, disturbed by an impression of horses on the breeze, and thought she could hear the chinking of harness. Then she smiled to herself for being foolish and letting her imagination run away with her.

As she reached the highest point on the path, where a track diverged towards the little temple on the scarp above, she looked back towards the town. She could see pinpricks of light bobbing in the streets and – was it her imagination again? – the sound of voices chanting. She shivered despite the warmth of the evening and hurried down the slope to the shelter of her home before the night closed in entirely.

Maria was spinning unconcernedly, little Einar kicking his legs in his cradle at her feet. Signy picked him up and kissed him, and she could have kissed Maria, too, if that would not have tangled her thread.

"There's stew, Mistress," said her maid. "I was sure you would come back, so I made extra."

"You're a darling," she said. "Don't get up, I'll take care of myself."

She had just finished eating when there was a sharp knock on her door which startled her.

"Who's there?"

"Beltrice," came a loud voice from outside.

She put her bowl and spoon to one side, crossed the room and opened the door. The guard captain's customary good humour was nowhere to be seen. Hardly surprising, she thought, given what was going on in town. For a moment, she thought he had come to help her, escort her to safety, but that hope was extinguished in an instant.

"Stand aside, Mistress," said a second man, pushing past her into the cottage. She did not recognise him immediately. Then, as he returned from the kitchen area, her heart began to pound. His name came back to her as he climbed the stairs to the sleeping loft. He was Lady Bryna's man, Jarmi.

Jarmi came clattering down again, nodding to Beltrice.

"It's all clear. Only her and the maid."

"And the child," said Beltrice.

Jarmi took no notice, flung the door open and stepped outside. Signy could hear horses stamping and snorting, several horses, the sound of voices, the jangle as someone dismounted. Then the door opened abruptly wide and Bryna herself walked through.

Marcus' wife looked around the cottage, taking it in. Signy almost expected her to say, *so this is where it has all been happening*, but her silence was even more menacing. Marcus' wife took a couple of steps across the room and glanced down at the still-sleeping boy. She looked up at Signy, but still said nothing to her. Instead, she turned to Beltrice.

"Thank you, Captain, you may go now. I think my husband will need you." Beltrice saluted, turned on his heels and left. "And take this girl with you," she added, waving towards Maria.

"Make yourself scarce," growled Beltrice to the maid. She did not need telling twice, and with an anxious glance towards her mistress, fled into the night.

Bryna again turned to Signy, though still did not address her directly, merely making a small gesture to Jarmi.

"I'll wait outside, my lady," said her servant, needing no more instructions.

Signy had barely moved a muscle all this time, no more than her eyes to follow the comings and goings. At last Bryna spoke to her.

"I think it best that we sit, Mistress. This may take some time." Without any invitation she sat herself, taking the corner of the bench closest to her, the very place that Marcus had sat, anxiously, the first time he had visited her cottage. Signy sighed, and with great difficulty, as if her limbs were made of lead, took a couple of steps to the stool beside the child's bed and sat down.

Bryna said nothing more for a moment, merely examining her. There was no smile on her face, no warmth in the brown eyes. Finally, after what seemed like an interminable interval, she spoke again.

"I've known for a long time," she said, "that you and Marcus have been lovers. I suppose perhaps I should have intervened earlier, before the child was conceived."

She paused, watching Signy.

"The first day I saw you," she went on, "when you rode into Verdaris, I made a mistake. I thought you were just a naive village girl, impressed by a powerful man. I thought it best to send you away. You would be caught up in the life in town, soon find a young man of your own age. I underestimated you. I forgot the old adage 'keep your friends close and your enemies closer'."

"If you had kept me at Verdaris," said Signy, "you're right that I wouldn't be the woman I am today. Then I really was a naive girl, overwhelmed by what had happened. I respected Marcus. I had never met a man like him…No, that's not true — one other man. I wanted to understand him, to understand men like him, so different from my father, from my…former husband. And then, with time, I realised that I had deeper feelings for him." She gave an involuntarily glance towards the now sleeping child. Bryna did not follow her gaze. "You sent me to Mistress Megana, and please believe that I'm grateful. You gave me the chance, my lady. You gave me the opportunity to become a different person. You knew I would take it, even if you couldn't foresee where it would lead. I worked hard to learn what there is to be learned here in Britannia, in Corinium, just as I had worked hard to learn what was to be learned in Juteland. I'm not going to beg for mercy from you. I'm sure you've had plenty of time to decide what to do with me, and my life is in your hands, or perhaps I should say, in your servants' hands." She nodded towards the door.

Bryna allowed the silence to fill the room again. Her face betrayed no emotion.

"I certainly did not foresee where it would lead." Unlike her face, her voice was filled with bitterness. "But it's not because you have slept with my husband a few days a year that I've come. It was almost to be expected, given the path in life you have taken. And that you would bear his child. I suppose that I should be grateful there aren't more such brats, the way that the provincial women and the girls at Verdaris flirt with him. No, Mistress Signy, I've come here because your new-found and exaggerated sense of self-worth has become dangerously threatening, not just to me, but to the Kingdom of West Britain itself."

The sense of dread that Signy had felt when Beltrice had first entered her cottage began to seep back. Had Beltrice discovered Drusus Astrebanus?

But if he had, Marcus' wife chose not to begin with that subject.

"The trouble, now, in town," she said, "I assume you know what's caused that?"

"Chief Atle," replied Signy. "He's angry because Mistress Megana has refused to negotiate compensation for the injuries to his son. And now he's infuriated the townspeople with his bullying attitude and his clumsy search for the people he blames."

Bryna shook her head slowly. "Undoubtedly, the chief is angry that his son has been injured, but that's nothing to the injury suffered to his pride and for that, you, you and none other, are responsible."

"I nursed his son. I saved the boy's life. Why should he be angry with me?"

"The chief himself is unaware that you're the source of his humiliation," said Bryna, with a thin smile. "His son does nothing but praise you, so I've heard. The sick fool refers to you as an angel. But *I* am aware of the part you played."

"I don't understand." Better to play innocent, Signy thought, until I see where this is leading.

"Two months ago," Bryna continued, "four armed men, dressed in black, paid a nighttime visit to Chief Atle. They woke the chief and his wife and forced his daughter from her bed at sword point. What were they doing, invading the home of one of my husband's sworn men?"

Signy had to lower her eyes for an instant to hide her expression.

"They were collecting a debt," she said, now looking up at Bryna. "Chief Atle owed the merchant Fabiansson for silver that he had loaned in years gone by. It was silver that Atle refused to repay, now that Fabiansson is on his death bed, and his daughter is managing the business. What the men took was just exchange for the corn and oil that fed Atle, his wife and daughter, and his servants, during the time of hunger. A mere woman, it seems, my lady, is not deserving of repayment, not only by Chief Atle, but by others of his ilk in this kingdom."

The thin smile remained, distorting Bryna's lips.

"I understand your thoughts exactly, Mistress. And the four raiders who visited Atle – and not just him, Chief Notius and his wife, as well – whose sworn men are they?"

Signy's stomach gave a lurch. She could deny them. They were not, strictly speaking, her sworn men. Drusus Astrebanus was their rightful master.

"An ignorant person might have taken them for Saxons," continued Bryna, "and Chief Atle is such an ignorant person. But

I am not. Those marauders were not Saxons, were they, Mistress Signy? They were men from Juteland, your loyal followers, as Marcus finds so amusing."

Signy felt a frown etch itself on her brow, impossible to hide. Bryna clearly did not know the complete story of who had paid the visit to Atle.

"They were purchased by Merchant Fabiansson," she responded quickly. "They are fed and housed by Mistress Megana. They carry out her errands."

"I didn't ask who houses and feeds them. I asked who their lord and master is, or, to be more precise, their mistress."

Signy felt beads of sweat on her brow, but it would be best to continue down the same path, as if it had been the Jutes who had raided Atle.

"My husband may once have been their lord, but I am not their lord. If they choose to feel a loyalty to me, for old times' sake, that's their own choice. Now they're Mistress Megana's property, and they do as she wishes, including collecting her debts."

Bryna's thin hint of a smile grew perceptibly.

"That may be the case, Mistress, but it's only half the case. I'm not the fool you seem to take me for, and my husband has provided sufficient corroboration. The Jutes do your bidding!"

"It's matterless whose bidding they do, my lady," said Signy, rising to her feet. "Atle and his like should be grateful for the help they received when they and their people were going hungry, not resentful, and they should acknowledge and repay what they owe! That's the law!"

"Enough, Mistress!" Bryna's sharp voice cut her off. "Don't lecture me on the law! Sit down and keep quiet!"

Signy spun as if Bryna had slapped her, caught sight of her sleeping son and sat again.

"It would be sufficient enough that you sleep with my husband, that you plague his followers with armed thugs, but the worst I have not yet spoken of."

"And what is that?" said Signy, although she had a horrible anticipation of what it was. Someone had betrayed her, Beltrice probably. Why? Because he, too, desired her and she had never slept with him?

"A short while ago, my husband was almost assassinated," said Bryna. "He was left bleeding and dying, in his own home."

"I ensured Marcus did not die!" interjected Signy.

Bryna lifted her hand and pointed an accusing finger at her.

"The man responsible was Drusus Astrebanus, a traitor to this kingdom! Thank God and Lord Jesus that my husband's enemy is dead, but his followers still carry on the fight, led, I surmise, by his nephew. And you, Mistress, have been consorting with them, even while my husband was lying in your bed, even when he was…when he fathered your child." Bryna struggled to even say the words. "You have been meeting this traitor's followers, secretly at night, for your own purposes."

Signy could have laughed, laughed right in her face. She could have screamed at her: *Drusus is alive, you fool, he's alive and his men are my men, because I've kept him alive.*

But that would mean her own certain death.

She had to force herself to remain calm. The effort took time, too long a time for Bryna to keep quiet.

"What are your purposes, your aspirations, I have wondered. To sell out my husband to his enemies, despite his care for you and this…infant? Is that what you plan, or do you have more devious ambitions? You seem to have grasped all of the strings of this kingdom into your own delicate little hands. My husband is at your mercy, his chiefs are at your mercy, and you even have his enemies in your pocket. Why? To take my place? To twist my husband to your desires? To fill your chests with the treasures of this kingdom? To force all and one to submit to you? To overthrow the word of Christ, perhaps, and bring back the devils you worship?"

Signy shook her head. "No, that's not right, my lady. I've done no such thing. I've merely tried humbly to help my friends, to practise my art and…"

Now Bryna stood up and started to pace back and forth.

"It's no matter whether I believe you. The facts speak for themselves. It's fortunate that you've not escaped the sight of certain civic-minded persons who have been loyal enough to keep me informed. You've insinuated yourself into the body of this kingdom in such a way that you threaten my husband, that you threaten me, that you threaten all of us, our bodies and souls. It's fortunate that circumstances have provided an opportunity to bring this to an end."

Signy watched her, now startled and confused. Marcus' wife swung round at the end of her pacing and glowered at her. Signy felt the blood drain from her face. Bryna seemed to have misunderstood everything, but that did not make any difference. Her misconstruction would have just as dire consequences as if she knew the whole truth.

"I could," said Bryna, "eliminate you permanently this very night. I've only to call for Jarmi, and you and this infant would trouble me no longer. It would be easy to suggest that someone had thought to take advantage of the tumult in the town to rob you. We could carry you off, you and the child. My husband and Mistress Megana would sorrow you for a while, search for you, even, but they would not find you."

No, thought Signy, her own anger beginning to rise, your own logic proves that you would not dare, because Grunwald and Ferland and Hrasmus and Asser, and maybe even Alwynn and Liutmann, would hunt you down, not tonight, not tomorrow, but one day. Perhaps even Constantinus, with his disguises and trickery, if he thought you'd deprived him of his little angel, on top of all his other grudges. You know that, Mistress Bryna, in your heart, even if you dare not admit it.

"However, I am merciful," Bryna continued unabated, standing in front of Signy, gazing directly into her eyes. "I've been willing to listen to the stories I've heard, even as far away as Verdaris, of the services you've performed for the people of Corinium, how many owe their lives to you, my husband included, perhaps, I admit. And you and Mistress Fab…your friend, in building the King's Hall, the Church of the Holy Spirit, in providing assistance during the famine. And I don't worship your gods, the gods of vengeance and retribution, but Jesus Christ our Lord, who forgives our sins. I am, however, a mere human. *I* can't forgive your sins. I will, rather, give you an opportunity to consider them and perhaps atone for them…elsewhere."

She swung around, took three steps towards the door, and then turned to face Signy once again.

"You have until the next full moon to leave West Britain. You, this child, and anyone whose loyalty lies with you, and if you do not, my husband will learn of your relations with Constantinus Astrebanus and his associates. I'll make sure you are declared a traitor and an outlaw."

She opened the door, and stepped out into the night, saying, "Jarmi, I'm finished here. We must return to Verdaris before Marcus brings the situation in town under control and becomes concerned we're missing."

Signy sat quietly, listening intently to the sound of horses being mounted, being ridden away.

Then she bent down and lifted her sleeping son from his cradle, held him in her arms, pressing him against her.

She was not guilty of Bryna's accusation. She would be happy to play princess to Bryna's queen. Yes, there were men who were willing to act on her behalf, but she was no rebel, no leader of a war band. How could she be, a woman? And Constantinus Astrebanus her ally? If only Bryna knew. But it would be impossible to tell her without revealing what she had actually done. It was fortunate that whoever had been spying on her had not followed the black-clad debt collectors back to their lair. Otherwise Bryna might not have been so courteous as to give her a month to leave.

She would have to go, she concluded. She could not defy the king's wife. She had no choice but to tear up her life and begin again, in yet another foreign land. Was that the fate she had been given, merely for being curious? For having dreamed of what lay beyond the horizon, beyond the forest, she was doomed to keep moving, just like the waters in the river.

Tears welled up in her eyes. The baby shifted, and she bent down and kissed his ear. At least she now had her son for company.

❧ Chapter 35 ☙

Alwynn was waiting, sheltering from the rain in the narrow refuge of the doorway of the Ursinus mausoleum. She squeezed in beside him and came straight to the point.

"We've been discovered, Alwynn. Someone's been spying on us."

"Not here," said Alwynn. "I've always taken a roundabout route, and watched before I came to the meeting place. No one's been following me, or you."

"Somehow they have," said Signy. "Bryna came to me, accusing me of collaborating with Constantinus against Marcus."

"Constantinus!"

"You know it's ridiculous, but she believes it, and he's here – was – in the town…in disguise. I've seen him myself, spoken to him."

Alwynn shook his head. "Signy, I promise, he's been nowhere near us. You don't think I…"

"I believe you, Alwynn," she said, laying her hand against his cheek. "You've done everything I asked, you and Liutmann and the others, but now…"

"And do they know about the chief?"

"I don't think so, but it's only a matter of time, and then…then not even Marcus will be able to save me, even if he wanted to. I have to leave Corinium and Britannia, at least for a while, probably for ever."

A shadow crossed Alwynn's face, a change of expression visible even through the rain-darkened night.

"There's nothing I can do. She warned me that I'll be denounced as a traitor if I don't."

Alwynn appeared to be about to speak, but she held up her hand to stop him.

"It's bigger than us, the gods' wishes, I suppose. Megana, too…"

"Megana, a traitor? That's why we had to take the silver to Litorina?" Alwynn sounded doubtful.

"Megana's not a traitor, any more than I am, but she's been made a – what's the beast in the Bible? – a scapegoat. You heard there was trouble in town, that Chief Atle came to Corinium with his men?"

"The same Atle we raided?"

"The same…demanding compensation for his fool of a son…Never mind, it's a long story and it's got nothing to do with you. There was a scuffle, apparently – Megana's been vague about the whole thing – and Atle tripped and fell into the atrium pool in the Fabiansson house. By the time Hrasmus fished him out he had drowned. And he was upset about his silver, old family heirlooms, and blamed Megana…"

"…for what we did."

Signy nodded.

"Marcus has concluded Megana's been behind all the raids and through that, she was responsible for the trouble in Corinium as well. I think he needs someone to blame, and he's chosen his own goddaughter, so men don't turn against him." Signy sighed. "I thought I was helping my friend, and all I did was to make matters worse. I have to accept the consequences, not Bryna's judgement, not Marcus' judgement, but the judgement of the gods. Megana was already considering leaving, but I don't think she really wanted to."

"But we took the silver to her boat."

"To put it out of the reach of men like Atle, and her greedy relatives, maybe. Now she must be gone one month after her child has been born. Marcus decided. I'm sorry he did. I'll miss him, and he'll never see his son grow up."

"And Drusus, and…"

"…and you and the others. Yes, it's up. We played our luck as well as we could, but the gods spun your fate along with mine. As for Uncle Drusus…there's nothing more I'll be able to do for him. I can leave you the medicine, but it'll only last for a few weeks, and then…then the madness will return, worse, I'm afraid, than before, because we've worked so hard to control it. He'll need caring for, more I think than you and your friends can do."

"Signy," Alwynn whispered, "what am I going to do with the chief? Tell me, will he die?"

"I don't know," she replied. "He's an old man, and his body is weak." She thought for a moment. "Megana's child will be born any day, and then the grace period begins before we must leave."

"Can we follow you?"

"No! I don't know when or where we'll be going, just over the sea and away from this place. Here's my suggestion. There's no point in hiding Drusus any longer. After that I'll be out of reach of anyone who wants to use his survival against me. Carry him down to his brother's wife, to Mistress Milesia. Her people will know how to make him comfortable."

"But he hates her, and she hates him. You've heard what he said."

"She'll take him, sick as he is. And tell her, tell her I sent him, Deacon Baxter's second favourite pupil. That should help her make up her mind. She'll know what you mean. But wait, please, Alwynn, until I've left."

She looked up into his face.

"Of course, my lady," he said, and leaned across and kissed her. She held him to her briefly, and then eased him away.

"And Alwynn, ask her advice on your own behalf. She's close to Lady Bryna, closer than anyone would suspect, and close to Marcus, though he doesn't realise I know. It could save your lives, and those of your friends, your women, your children. Marcus is a good man and he'll soon regret what he's done."

She put up a finger to his mouth to prevent another kiss.

"May the gods be with you, and please pray for me."

With that she turned, pulled up her hood and stepped out into the downpour.

Megana was seething.

"He thinks he's done me a favour, letting me stay until the child is born, and then for the twenty-eight days of seclusion after the birth."

"It's better for you and the baby that you do," said Signy. "At least he's following custom."

"I told him that I'd planned to leave all along, and he didn't need to take his anger out on me!"

"That's what I always feared you were planning, especially after Soraya left for the south."

"I might have grovelled and paid up, if you could have stayed with Marcus…"

"You were never going to marry Carassus."

Signy had not told Megana all the details of Bryna's accusations. She was frightened that they would derange Megana's feelings further, perhaps even prompt her to stir up trouble between her godfather and his wife. She had merely told Megana that Bryna's patience had run out, and that made it easy for her to keep her promise and join Megana in exile.

"I could've wriggled out of that," said Megana, "and it wasn't my decision that my mother left. Mistress Patricia wouldn't allow her near Father after he fell ill. She had only the rain and cold to suffer, and mean-spirited insults."

"And now we have no choice."

The first few days after the birth of Megana's daughter went well. Megana seemed buoyed and without hesitation named her Sophia. Then it was almost as if the troubles of the world came back redoubled. She had difficulty breastfeeding and the baby cried. She began to doubt herself, her abilities as a mother, blame herself for bringing the child into the world in such a disgraceful manner.

"You've done well, Megana, my dear, for a first-time mother," said Signy, trying to convince Megana that she was not a failure. "I've seen many mothers who have had difficulty feeding their first child." But Megana pushed her encouragement away. She tried to force herself to be a mother, but the more she forced herself, the worse it became. Signy had seen many mothers who had felt they could not cope with the small new creature that was so dependent on them. Even those who had a home, a caring husband and a loving family. Sometimes the stars just did not align between the mother and the child.

The days had begun to count down until Megana would have to leave her father, her childhood home, everything she knew, so instead she forced herself up from the child bed, into the yard, giving orders, sending messengers.

It's just as well I've not entirely weaned Einar, Signy thought, as she held tiny Sophia to her own breast.

She could not help counting the days until the time Bryna had given her would run out, but when they did, Marcus' wife took no action. No doubt she knew the conditions that her husband had set on Megana and was willing to wait.

And what did Marcus know? Had Bryna told him that she had ordered Signy to leave? And her reasons why? Signy, herself, had still not had the courage to tell Marcus she had decided to accompany Megana into exile. To her, leaving him felt more like treachery than ever keeping Drusus alive.

"The day after tomorrow," said Megana, finally.

"But there are still three days to go before the deadline runs out."

"I'll choose when I leave," said Megana, "not them. If I'm still here, they'll have to enforce Marcus' judgement in some ostentatious manner, or no one will believe he'd ever keep his word. I'll leave before they take the chance to move against me. This way we both save face."

A whole column of wagons entered through the town gate the following morning, rolling into Fabiansson's yard, before the eyes of the population, and not only wagons, but armed men, sailors from the boats which were waiting for them in Litorina. Megana might have difficulties with the role of mother, but there was no doubting her abilities as an organiser, thought Signy, as she made her way out of the south gate to supervise the packing of her own possessions, past the King's Hall, past the Church of the Holy Spirit, up to her little cottage, for what would surely be the last time.

There is no escaping now, she thought, and sighed to herself. I'll have to go and confront Marcus. There was never any future for us. I was a fool to think otherwise. All Bryna did was make obvious what I should have realised all along. It had to end. I had to leave. It was only up to the Fates to choose the way.

Signy took her grey travelling cloak, pulled the hood over her head and left her house, just as dusk was falling. She trudged through the darkening streets of the town, until she reached the Ursinus house. She had dreaded that Bryna would appear in Corinium. She had dreaded that Marcus would leave for Verdaris without realising they needed to say goodbye.

"Signy, my dear," said Silke, ushering her into the kitchen when she knocked on the rear gate, "I heard they are loading the carts, and that Mistress Megana will be leaving tomorrow."

"News travels fast," Signy replied, and with a sigh, added, "I need to speak to Marcus, this evening, alone."

An expression of horrified surprise filled the housekeeper's face as the implications of Signy's words struck her.

"Will you…will you be leaving with her?"

Signy could not bring herself to answer, but only hugged her friend.

It had been weeks since she had seen Marcus, since before the attack on the Minerva House, since before the visit from Bryna. It had just not seemed right to try to meet him in the circumstances.

"Just say there's someone to see him. Don't tell him it's me."

"I'm sorry," he said when he did see her. "I should have come."

She placed her hands softly on his shoulders.

"I know you have had an awful time," she said, "and Einar and I have been safe. But now I had to come. I've been putting it off, but…" She had to sniff. "I'm leaving, Marcus, leaving with Megana. I don't have a choice. I've been fooling myself that I could avoid going, but no…"

"Why?" His voice was breaking.

Was it so bad, not to tell him the truth when it would only sow discord between the man and his wife?

"I promised, Marcus, promised Megana I would support her through thick or thin." She held up her hand. "I told you we had sworn an oath, blood sisters."

He could see the scar, still faintly etched in her thumb.

"Megana was generous, Marcus. She said that I didn't have to fulfil my promise, but…but I've been threatened. People know we're friends, and if they can't get at Megana, then they might take out their vengeance on me."

"That's nonsense," he said. "You have protection. My word!"

She shook her head.

"No one can protect me, us, me and Einar, all the time, and it only takes one moment, one angry man, like Atle."

It was Marcus' turn to shake his head, as if he did not dare to believe what he was hearing.

"You're angry with me," he said, "because I ordered Megana to leave."

"No." She did not dare tell him she would have had to leave whatever he had done with Megana.

"I had to do something," he said. "Atle was just one of many."

"Exactly, and I'm just as guilty. Hrasmus and Ferland, and the others…they wouldn't have helped Megana if I hadn't told them to. You know I didn't think she had been treated fairly."

"Yes, but it…it all went too far."

"I know, I know," she said, "and that was my fault."

She felt his arms around her and pressed herself against his breast.

"Will you stay, one more night?" he whispered.

She nodded. "But Marcus, I couldn't sleep in Bryna's place."

He had a guestroom made up. They lay in the dark, arms around one another.

"I'm sure I could find a way for you to stay," Marcus tried again, "one of the neighbouring houses, so Beltrice can keep an eye on you."

She could barely suppress a shiver.

"No, Marcus, please, don't try. Don't make this worse than it has to be."

"But I love you."

"And I love you, and I love our son, and it's his future we must think of. I have to keep him safe, give him a life without the worry that someone might see him as a way to get at me, to get at you."

"You're thinking of Constantinus?"

She grasped at the straw he had offered her.

"Yes. I saw him in the town, at the time of the fire in the Minerva House."

"Hmm…that confirms rumours I've heard, but we've not been able to find him."

"That's just what I mean. He's devious and dangerous. I have to get away to somewhere he can't possibly find us. The south, with Megana. We can make a new life."

"Perhaps." He rolled onto his back and stared at the ceiling. "Perhaps you're right after all."

She ran her hand down his chest. "Yes, I'm right. Not always, but this time."

They slept in each other's arms until the first fingers of dawn light crept in through the shutters.

"I have to go," she said. "Maria will wonder where I've been, and they'll be coming to load the wagons."

He watched her dress, wrapped himself in a cloak, and walked with her, barefooted, through the kitchen and across the yard. She lifted the latch of the rear gate, turned and kissed him, and then set off down the alley. She knew he was watching her walk away, but she did not turn back.

Signy could barely keep the tears from her eyes as she wandered through the back streets towards the Fabiansson house.

What a fucking catastrophe, she thought, for everyone, no matter how I try to sound positive. I've no idea where we're going, what I'm going to do there, what sort of life I can lead, how I'm going to raise Einar. I have to trust Megana. I do trust Megana.

Memories of the other journeys she had taken flowed into her mind.

I know, she thought, I'm a free woman, even a modestly wealthy woman, no longer alone in the world, but I still feel that I'm bound, not to a man as a slave or even a wife, but to a fate I can't control and don't understand.

Signs of that fate met her the instant she entered Fabiansson's house. Despite the early hour, there were people everywhere, bearing chests and bags, furniture and food, pots and linens. Like ants carrying leaves and twigs back to an ant heap, a steady stream led from all parts of the house and converged in the yard. Signy could barely face the sight. The hustle and bustle, the people rushing to and fro, brought back memories of those other yards, those other early-morning starts. She had no choice then, and she had no choice now. She made her way through the emptying house to her room. Her own chest was already packed. The bed clothes folded. She made for the kitchen. In a cradle, lay the tiny newborn Sophia, being rocked gently by Megana's Delia. Einar held Maria's hand, watching the bustle with wide eyes. Perhaps he's wiser than I am, she thought, taking the whole as an adventure.

"The cottage is all packed up," Maria informed her. Poor Maria, she thought, your fate is tied to mine now, and what a damned poor piece of luck that is.

It's better just to be curious, she thought, just let events take their course. She hunted down bread, a bowl of porridge, something to drink. Megana appeared, unusually buoyed and determined.

"Has Sophia fed?" Signy asked. She got to her feet before Megana could answer. If she did not give the baby her own breast, then her milk would soon stop flowing, and the child would be entirely dependent on her mother.

She gave her friend a hug, felt Megana's body tighten, as if she was tensing herself for a fight, and Megana pulled herself away. The two women faced each other for a moment.

"Yes."

Then Megana wiped her hand across her eyes, and turned and left the kitchen. Signy took up Sophia and pulled back her tunic.

Megana's trying too hard, Signy thought. If this departure's difficult for me, how can it be for Megana to abandon her childhood home, its memories, its familiarity, its safety, to abandon her father, lying sick and frail in the priest's house?

Megana reappeared. "It's time to leave," she said.

Signy placed the baby back into the cradle and went out into the yard once again. Einar was already standing, his hand firmly gripped by…Grunwald.

"Grunwald, are you coming with us?" Signy could not suppress a cry of surprise.

"Yes, my lady," answered the tall Jute, with a smile. "Your master gave his leave, and he gave me this as a mark of appreciation," he added, holding out a small medallion, hanging from a chain around his neck. "I'll have it made up into a belt buckle when I get a chance."

A string of wagons ran in a half-circle.

Henrik showed her the cart that had been set aside for her and Megana and the children. "There are soft cushions and blankets for the journey," he assured her, "and if it rains, though, thank God, it seems like a fine day, then there's a piece of sail cloth which can be pulled over as a roof."

Delia came with the cradle in her arms.

Henrik assisted her to clamber into the wagon. Grunwald passed up the cradle, before lifting the squealing Einar high into the air, and flying him up into the cart, and into Maria's waiting grasp.

"Take my arm, Mistress," he said, and swung Signy up and over the side.

She watched as Megana moved along the convoy, talking to the drivers, talking to Asser, to Hrasmus, to Henrik. Then Megana was standing by their cart. The three of them took hold of her and, as if she was a delicate sack, lifted her into the air, over the side of the wagon, and settled her onto the cushion.

Signy heard a call, and the gates swung open, and with a gathering sound of hooves on stones, the train of wagons slowly circled the yard and left into the street. As they did so, the black-coated Jutes, Asser, Hrasmus, and the others formed up alongside. Signy could not help but recollect the war bands, the marching soldiers, the day she had watched Thorgill stride away to his doom, and she glanced over at Megana.

Perhaps Bryna was right after all, Signy thought. I've been so caught up in my own problems, my own tasks, my own feelings, but all along we've been waging a war. And now, just like Oswulf, we've been defeated and we have to retreat and, as he was with Oswulf, Marcus has been merciful, and we have our lives and our booty intact.

The townspeople watched the procession. Counsellor Pacius with a contingent of the guards around him stood inside the south gate. Signy tried to keep her eyes away from the group as they came level, but she could not. She looked for Marcus, but she saw only the expressionless face of Beltrice. He can't have dared watch me go, she thought. Then there was only the gaping gate and the road ahead. She put her hands to her face and wept.

Three boats were anchored in the estuary beyond Litorina. Three captains paced the quay, captains who had ferried goods for Fabiansson and his daughter through the years, from port to port, around Britannia, Francia, Frisia and all the way south to where the Visigoths were building their kingdom. The captains were waiting for their crews to return from Corinium. Signy could guess that they, like Megana, would also be worrying where trade would come in the spring if there was no one in West Britain to receive their cargoes.

The townspeople of Litorina must be worried, too, she thought. They would have seen ships coming and going all summer. They would have heard the rumours that the warehouses had been emptied. They would know that the dock-hands had been paid off. And now they could see men with strange accents and hard expressions blocking off the streets to the quayside while sailors transferred the contents of the newly arrived wagons to the waiting boats. She could imagine the talk in the taverns and kitchens. Where would this lead? What would become of them?

"I'm excited," said Megana abruptly as she and Signy watched the bustle along the dockside. Signy was standing, tense, while Megana sat on an upended basket. "I've crossed *Oceanus* to Burdigala to visit, but now, for a new life, and I couldn't imagine travelling with anyone better." She glanced up at Signy. "You've listened to my mother's stories, read my brother's letters, talked to the sea captains when they visited Corinium, and now, at last, we'll travel to the south."

Signy glanced down. "I've read the books, too," she said, "and I've heard Baxter's stories, not so glorious always."

Making a new life might be exciting, even fun at times, but in her own experience it was mostly grim hard work.

She noticed the boat captains, clustered further along the quay, talking and gesticulating. They evidently had more immediate concerns than the future of trading to the island. The group split up, one man jumping down quickly into a skiff as his crew cast off the ropes, while the other two hurried towards the women.

"Mistress," began the older of the two mariners, "Lanric has cast off to take the tide, and I would myself if I had a choice, but the loading's not yet completed. We'll have to wait till the next tide and then…" The captain glanced up at the sky. "I don't like the portents," he continued, a grim look transforming his face. "A day or so off still, I would say, but my gut tells me there's a storm on the way."

"And Captain Lanric?" asked Megana, with a gesture to the departing skiff.

"He thinks he can beat the blow, and if not, he can make for shelter further down the coast. There are several coves where it's safe to lay up and wait out a storm."

"And us, Walfrith, if we can't catch this tide?"

"If I had a free choice, I would shelter here in the bay, until it blows out."

"How long?"

The captain shrugged. "Three days, five, maybe seven and then—"

"We have to leave, Walfrith," said Megana sharply. "I've already waited too long. If we don't leave on the next tide, if we are confined here for a week or more, then my enemies will conclude I've broken my word. Tomorrow, I become an outlaw, quarry for every man, and there are several polishing their swords already. Half our force will have left with Lanric," she observed, as his ship was already twisting in the ebbing tide as the crew drew up the anchors. "In port we're all vulnerable, including you, Captain. No, we must leave with the next tide, and put our fate in the hands of the gods."

The captain was about to argue, exert his authority, before he saw Megana's determined expression.

"Then we may have to run before the storm, to the east, Mistress."

"So be it?"

"Into Bononia, with luck."

Pray to the gods we're not blown all the way to Puttby, thought Signy.

Captain Walfrith was correct. No sooner had they put to sea than the breeze started to blow strongly from the west. There was no possibility of making way against the wind. The two boats had no choice but to head for harbour. Their ship scudded over the growing waves, staying well offshore until the captain recognised the landmarks that signalled he could make for the safety of Bononia. They found lodgings in a hostel in the port, a rough shelter for land-driven sailors. The rain and wind continued for three days and nights, until the storm had blown itself out.

Signy stared out through a gap in the shutters at the raging weather. If anything confirmed that her luck had left her, it was this stinking, damp and overcrowded inn.

"I don't want to take the risk," Captain Walfrith told them, "of trying to round the *finis terrae* in the face of the autumn storms. Just because it's calm today, doesn't give any hint of what might await us if we were to set sail again. The weather we just escaped is only a taste of what we could expect out on *Oceanus*. I only hope our friends made it to harbour."

"I agree," said Megana, "though reluctantly. I've also weighed the pros and cons, but that means we have to wait here the whole winter, until the next sailing season."

"It won't be the first time," said Walfrith. "Better safe on land than in a watery grave."

In that moment, Megana's excitement and energy evaporated. She lost the spark in her eye and turned in on herself. She seemed overcome by lethargy, and Signy was worried that her feelings of inadequacy as a mother had returned, and grief at losing her home had overwhelmed her.

Bononia had not been a town with many luxuries at the best of times. Its prosperity had vanished along with the Roman fleet. Signy had to climb the hill to the new town and find accommodation for them in a vacant building, the past home of some long-gone official. Grunwald and Hrasmus, with the captain and his crew, hauled their belongings up the slope and into rooms which at least got them out of the hostel, and could be dried and warmed by braziers, for a price. The new, upper town might be healthier, built for the wealthier inhabitants away from the marshes, but living there meant endless treks to the lower town for food and fuel, whatever the weather. Walfrith and the sailors chose to remain down in the port, among their fellow seafarers, but the two Jutes, Maria and the maids helped to create a simulacrum of a home for Megana and Signy and their infants.

In contrast to Megana, Signy was restless. She hated the grim town. She hated the ceaseless rain, the cold, and the wet snow that came after it. She was terrified that Einar or Sophia would catch some dreadful disease.

"No south, no new life, no adventure, not now, maybe never," muttered the despondent Megana whenever Signy tried to be optimistic.

There were some fine days when Signy could walk along to the old lighthouse, a tower of brick and stone, built high on the headland above the town, or sit as far out as possible along the quay of the abandoned and decrepit naval harbour, listening to the beat of the waves. Then she could afford to smile to herself at the memories of Thorgill the Jute and Helga, Irmengaard and Ornfrid, Deacon Baxter and the merchant Fabiansson, Silke and Meri, Marcus, of course, and even, with distance, Bryna, challenged as she had been by the recipient of her charity. When the sun dipped to the far-away grey horizon, Signy would scramble to her feet and make her way along the slippery flagstones to the port, avoiding the attentions of the sailors, blocking her ears to their suggestions as to how she could spend her evening, and climb the steep alleys back to the house. There, in the light of the guttering candle, she would open a wax tablet and write, and rewrite, until she had the words exactly as she wanted, and then she would commit them to memory, smooth over the wax and begin again, until the whole story was complete. One day she would find enough parchment and ink to write it all down.

⍥ Epilogue ⍥

Bononia, in the winter

As midwinter passed, the rain and mud gave way to a period of still air, clear skies and biting cold. The weather reminded Signy of the winters of her youth, though that is hardly difficult, she thought ruefully: my childhood's still not far behind me reckoned in years. At least with the cold, the roads became passable, and she could hire a horse and ride out into the surrounding countryside to supplement her walks along the quay and to the lighthouse.

When the weather turned a little milder again due to a wind blowing out of the west, Signy chose the lighthouse as the destination for her walk. There was a fallen stone at the foot, where she could sit and imagine she saw Britannia, far off, as a grey smudge on the horizon.

"Good afternoon, Mistress. May an old man sit beside you?" a stranger asked.

She was irritated that someone would break into her thoughts, but she still sent him a quick smile.

"Of course, if you don't mind the company of misery," she answered. That was one small gain of her enforced isolation: her Latin had improved considerably.

The stranger laughed.

"You're one of the British women, trapped for the winter, aren't you? My captain met yours in the inn."

"I'm hardly British," she said in reply.

"Then we're neither one better than the other," the man commented, "masking ourselves in Latin," he continued in Saxon, and fell silent for a moment. "You're from the east, aren't you? There's a hint in your voice."

She nodded. "From beyond Juteland, from the East Sea, as the Jutes call it."

"And what's a young woman like you doing here? If I had seen you in certain taverns in Remis, or on the arm of a fat trader in Senones, or, better still, Arelate, then I would have been able to place you, with your well-groomed hair and your expensive cloak. But in Bononia, in the winter?"

"Is that what you were hoping, when you sat down beside me?" Signy said, still staring out at the sea. "Perhaps I'm not so different from the girls you were thinking of. I could have ended up like that. Still might."

He followed her gaze out into the grey distance.

"Once, perhaps," he chuckled, "I might have taken a chance, but not any longer."

Now it was her turn to laugh, the first time for a long time, but, catching the old man's eyes, she cut her laughter short. There was a vague familiarity about the twinkling look he gave her.

"Once perhaps," she said, "if my memory's not playing tricks on me, you did have your chance, but you turned it down."

The old man frowned.

"You don't remember," Signy asked, "the factor's shop in Puttby, five – or is it six? – summers ago?"

He shook his head. "I've been in Puttby," he said, "several times in recent years to find farm workers, but I don't remember a young woman like you."

Now it was Signy's turn to frown. My memory can't have failed me. The stranger beside me must be Amalric, she thought.

She wasn't entirely surprised to find him washed up on the same shore as she was once again. That was the way the Fates often worked. You could not escape your past. Has he really forgotten our encounter? she wondered. Probably it wasn't such an important or remarkable occasion to him as it was to me. Perhaps he can't remember so well now, a little like Fabiansson. Perhaps he hasn't changed much since then as he's an old man so I recognise him, whereas I've changed a good deal more, being younger. I know I'm not the person I was in Puttby. Maybe my own parents wouldn't even recognise me now.

Amalric's voice broke through. "You can't have been more than a child then," he said.

She smiled. "Exactly," she replied. "Of course, since then I've moved around and learned many things. I've been married. I have a child of my own. That has to change a person…It must do, mustn't it? But can't you see the same girl, looking at you?"

Amalric patted her knee. His hand was solid enough, not the hand of a vision from her own imagination or a ghost.

"You're a fine young woman," he said, "well hidden by a cloak," he chuckled, "but I remember you." She did not really believe that he did.

"I'm beginning to feel a little cold," she said to cover her discomfort. "Perhaps we should make our way back to the port. Will you walk with me?"

"Of course," said Amalric, and offered his arm.

"I think it'll freeze again tomorrow," she said. "Still air and clear skies."

"A little wind, I hope, for me to continue on my way, now that my business is finished."

When they reached the quayside and parted, Signy walked on to the hostelry where she had rented a horse on earlier occasions. The inns of Bononia were no place for honest women at the best of times, and even less so in the middle of winter. She crossed the yard and pushed open the door to the common hall, as usual occupied only by a few of the type of men who skulked in tavern rooms in the middle of the day in the dead of winter. The noise, the smell and the stuffy warmth were almost overpowering. A dozen pairs of eyes followed her as she entered. She was careful not to meet anyone's gaze. Most of the men probably knew her by sight, and those that did not could see in an instant that she was above their class.

"I'm looking for the ostler," she said to the servant.

"You won't find him here," he replied.

"He's in the yard," said one of the men, "but I'm here if you're looking for a ride." The others laughed at his wit.

"I doubt you would last far up the Ambiani road," called the servant.

"I wasn't planning on riding that far," replied the man, to guffaws from his friends.

"What a pity, because I am," Signy replied in a voice as wintry as the air that was waiting for her as she stepped outside again.

The ostler knew her by now, and that she would take care of his horse. Even so he warned her about the road conditions.

"The weather's going to turn again," he said, "I can feel it in my joints."

"That's what I'm hoping," she said, "but if the road is icy I'll take the field paths, like I used to in Juteland."

The ostler was right. The following day was clear and cold once again, and the places that had been damp were now frozen. There was no question of galloping, no question of giving the horse free rein, though the beast seemed grateful to be out of the stable. She took the road inland, the road that eventually led to Ambiani, and beyond that Remis, a city she had heard was even finer than Corinium. However, she had to heed the ostler's warning. The paving was slippery, and ice filled many of the depressions where stones were displaced or missing. The unpaved tracks of Juteland were a great deal safer in this type of weather.

After riding cautiously along the road for a while, Signy turned off to follow a path across the flat fields. The track was bounded on one side by an ice-covered ditch, and where a drainage channel joined it at a field boundary, she put her heels to the horse and urged the animal over the obstacle. Satisfied by her small daring, she trotted along the path a little while longer before noticing that the sun was beginning to decline, and it would be wise to return home before darkness obscured her way. It was a rash-enough enterprise for a lone woman to ride in daylight, but after dark she would be asking for trouble.

She reached the point where she would have to jump the horse over the drain to return, when she noticed another rider, away in the distance, following the paved road. She focussed on persuading her horse to repeat its bravado and leap over the drain. By the time she looked up again, the rider had left the road and was trotting along the track in her direction. For a moment, she thought it might be Grunwald or Hrasmus come looking for her. She had made no secret of her plan when taking out the horse, and anyone could have told them the direction she planned to take.

She slowed her mount to a halt as the stranger approached, stepping the animal to one side so that the rider could pass. But that was obviously not his intention, at least not immediately, as she saw him rein in his mount until he was blocking the track and preventing her from riding on.

"Sir," she said, "I would be grateful if you would let me past. I've a little way to ride, and I would like to get back to my home before nightfall."

"No hurry, Mistress Signy. There's no need for you to return to that home, this night or any other."

These words would have been threat enough, but with a chill that had nothing to do with the weather, she recognised the voice. The strange rider was none other than Constantinus Astrebanus.

"Let me by, Constantinus," she said, striving to sound calm.

"You had better refer to me as Chief Astrebanus now…now that my uncle has passed over, a little delayed, thanks to you."

"I don't know how or why you came to be here," she said, trying to give herself time to come up with a way to escape.

"It's no secret that Megana, Merchant Fabiansson's daughter, was expelled from West Britain," sneered Constantinus. "And the rumour reached Remis that she's been stranded in Bononia, and where Megana is, you can't be far away, even if nobody has any motivation to spread rumours about Signy the Soothsayer." He paused to gauge the effect of his derision, but Signy was not to be provoked by an insult. "More importantly, where Megana is, so is my daughter, Sophia Astrebana, my heir, the future mistress of Agridurnum."

"Megana and her daughter are no concern of yours," she quickly replied. "You have no business with me, and I have none with you. Kindly get out of my way." She kicked at her horse, so it took a few steps towards Constantinus, but his response was to turn his mount so it stood sideways, across the track.

"You may think you have no business with me, but I certainly have with you. You're coming with me, not back to Bononia, but on to Ambiani."

"No," Signy insisted. "I'm not going with you anywhere."

"You're coming with me, Signy. I've waited long enough. I warned you that I would find you, and now the gods have delivered you into my hands. It was fortunate that I had dealings with that old fool, Amalric, that brought me to Bononia, and I spotted you at the inn. Of course, I still desire you, but I want my daughter, too. Megana'll never be willing to part with her, I realise, but with you in my house, I can lay a trap which will force her to hand her over. She's a trader; she'll be willing to strike a deal."

"You're mad, as mad as your uncle was."

"No, I'm determined, as determined as my father was." And with that, he reached out and grabbed towards her, catching her bridle in his hands. In a moment, she let go of the reins and slid from the horse's back, placing the animal between herself and Constantinus.

"It seems you're going to have to walk, my dear Signy."

"I'd rather walk than go with you."

"Which doesn't suit my plan at all," he said, dismounting heavily, slipping slightly, as his feet touched an icy patch of ground. "We'll ride together to Ambiani. I know a comfortable inn with a warm bed, and we'll send a message to Mistress Megana telling her to bring the children, your son and my daughter."

Signy backed away, trying to keep the horse between them, but she had little space for manoeuvre, trapped between the ditch on one side and the mud of the field on the other.

"She won't come," Signy said. "She wants to stay by the coast, so she can take the first boat away from here."

"I don't care where she wants to stay. I don't want to be unpleasant, but I know where you're living. I know where your son is, Marcus Silvanus' son. If I can't have my child, why should you keep yours? You'll tell her to come!"

He slapped her horse on the rump, and it moved aside, letting him pass behind. He took a step towards her, reaching under his cloak for the hilt of his sword.

"It's a little cold here, and dirty, otherwise I would be tempted to take what I missed last time right now. As it is, we'll just have to wait until we reach the inn I mentioned."

"I've become a bit of a trader myself these days," she said, forcing a smile onto her face. "A warm inn sounds quite an improvement on one that was in ruins. To show I'm considering your offer, a foretaste, perhaps…" She took a step towards him.

He halted, a confused look on his face at her sudden change of tone, and his hand fell away from his weapon.

Signy let her hand slide down the front of her cloak suggestively towards her thigh and took another step towards him. His eyes followed her hand as it slipped inside her cloak. Now they were so close that she could raise her other arm and place it on his. He lifted his head and gazed into her eyes, and at that moment, she pulled her dagger, Drusus' dagger, from her belt and with a twist of her arm, stabbed it into his belly. His eyes froze, his mouth opened, but no sound came out. She stepped back, pulled the knife from his guts, and then with the thrust of her entire weight drove it again through his jerkin and up under his rib cage, a move she had earlier practised a thousand times on the sack of hay. She let go of the handle and he staggered back, looking from her down to the knife protruding from his body. Then he sank to his knees.

"You're never getting me into your bed," she said, taking a quick step forward, aiming the sole of her boot into his face. His head was thrown back, thumping against the frozen surface of the trackway. She stood over him, one foot on his stomach, bracing herself to draw out the dagger. "You've threatened me one time too many."

His eyes seemed unfocussed, as if they were staring into eternity.

"I'm not going to live my life wondering when you're going to appear," she said, pulling out the knife. At once, blood oozed through his clothes. She bent over, cleaned off the worst from her blade on his jerkin. "Now there's only one bed left for you! Your own grave!" she added, and slipped the weapon back into her belt.

Only then did she look around. She was alone. The fields were deserted, the sun low against the horizon. No other sign of life but a few black birds making their way across the grey sky to their roost.

She looked down at Constantinus. He was dying, she was sure, even if he was not yet dead. She could not just leave him on the track. There was always the chance that someone would pass by the next day and find him. Most likely he had been enquiring about her at the inn. It was all too obvious how he had died. Even though the landlord, the ostler, the customers, all men, might find it hard to believe that she, a woman, had killed him in cold blood, suspicion might fall on Grunwald or Hrasmus and that would be just as bad.

Where to hide the body of a man on a flat plain, devoid of convenient bushes and scrub? There was only one place, of course: in the ditch. She took hold of Constantinus' feet and dragged him, slowly, across the frozen ground. The water was covered by a sheet of ice. For a moment, a worrisome thought crossed her mind. What if the ice is solid? What if I tip him into the ditch and he remains on the surface, incriminating evidence obvious to anyone passing by?

Tentatively, she took a step down the bank and placed one foot on the ice. Slowly, she shifted her weight. The ice creaked and sagged, and it was only just in time that she managed to withdraw her foot before there was a crack and it gave way. The last few days of warmth had weakened it. The ice would not bear her weight, so it certainly would not hold his.

She swung Constantinus' body round so his feet were by the bank, and then, taking hold of his shoulders, dragged him alongside the ditch. Just then she remembered the sword that he had revealed as he rounded the horse. Carefully, she crouched over the body and reached under the cloak until she felt the pommel in her hand. She gave it a tug, and it slid free from the scabbard, and she laid the blade on the ground beside the body.

Then she stood up and placed her foot against his side and, with a prayer to the gods, heaved him over the edge. There was a crack, a subdued splash, the ice gave way, and the body, weighted by his winter clothing and metal ornaments, sank below the surface. A telltale pool of water remained, and then the slivers of ice slid together, disguising the place where the body had broken through.

With another cold night, she thought, the surface will refreeze. A dusting of snow, and by morning no one will even know the ice has been broken.

There was one remaining problem: the horse that Constantinus had been riding. She did not recognise it as one of the beasts housed at the inn, but it might remember the comfort of the stables and follow her back. If she had time, she would have led it away, a few miles up the road, tied it to a tree if she could have found one, used it to create a diversion.

A quick thought ran through her mind…If she took the bridle and saddle, it would give the impression of a robbery, but she had to hinder the beast from following her. She remounted and, holding the reins of the loose animal in one hand, and her own in the other, urged her horse once again to make the perilous jump of the drain. Constantinus' horse hopped after her. With a few cuts from her knife, she had freed it from its harness, and before it had overcome its surprise, turned her own horse back over the drainage channel and away down the track at a steady trot. She looked back, once, to see the other animal passively watching them leave. Maybe it would finally decide what it would do, but by then she hoped to be well away.

Once she reached the main road, she did not immediately turn towards town, but instead took another track on the other side, which led to the river. There she threw the spare harness as far as she could. Hopefully, it would sink or be carried by the current sufficiently far that no one, in the short days of winter, in the gloom and cold, would put two and two together. She, of course, would be left with the truth. She had killed a man in cold blood, not just any man, but the father of Megana's child,

Sophia's father. How many times would she have to look that girl in the eyes in the knowledge of what she had done?

She took Constantinus' sword in her hands.

"Freya," she shouted, her eyes on the setting sun, "accept this offering from your servant for everyone who has suffered for the greed and hate of the Astrebani – for Megana, for Sophia, for Marcus, for Einar, for Borno Atlesson, for Thorgill and the children we never had, for Fulvia and all the people who died in Durolanium."

And with that, she swung her arms, and the sword flew out over the river and, with scarcely a splash, vanished beneath the surface.

❧ Bibliography ☙

This is a work of fiction and not a place for detailed academic discussion about controversial subjects, though it is impossible to avoid taking a stance if they form a key part of the story.

While I was preparing the final edits for this volume, I came across an interesting discussion of King Arthur on the podcast "The Rest is History" led by Dominic Sandbrook and Tom Holland (31 January, 2021, Season 1, Ep. 19, King Arthur). In it, the two historians discussed one of the most important unsolved questions concerning the period of British history covered in these stories. Why did eastern Britain become predominantly Anglo-Saxon speaking, and give rise to the Anglo-Saxon kingdoms and eventually the English? The traditional view has been that Germanic warriors invaded Britannia in the wake of the Roman withdrawal, carried out a genocide of the Britons, reducing them to a miserable remnant in Wales, and took the land for themselves. The more modern interpretation, labelled jokingly as "woke" in the podcast, suggests that there was no invasion at all, but that eastern Britannia gradually adopted an Anglo-Saxon identity as compensation to, perhaps even in defiance of, the departing Empire. Only afterwards did the self-styled Anglo-Saxons of the east gradually subsume their neighbours to the west. Sandbrook and Holland suggest the traditional view is partly a revanchist explanation constructed by the Welsh and their court and church intellectuals, and partly a *post-hoc*, just-so story to explain the east–west division of England existing at the time of the writers, several hundred years after the events.

Probably the truth lies somewhere in between these two. Caitlin Green provides evidence for a Romano-British culture surviving in the city of Lincoln long after the departure of the legions, which gradually evolved into an Anglo-Saxon kingdom. She also mentions that even early in this process there were probably pockets of Anglo-Saxon settlement around the periphery of the lands controlled by Lincoln, possibly as trading posts or maybe just because they were a long way from the centre of power.

Another proposed origin for the Germanic population is as a remnant of the Empire. The Roman military recruited a vast number of Germanic/Scandinavian auxiliaries and stationed them all across Western Europe, probably including Britannia. It's not hard to imagine that when the formal legions were moved over to the continent to support various usurpers and would-be emperors, many of the auxiliaries remained behind. Perhaps Romano-British landowners tended to keep control of the civil administration while the Germanic auxiliaries retained a strong influence on the military. As the economy declined, that balance of power may have shifted towards the military, and with that, Germanic (Anglo-Saxon) culture and language began to take over.

The question remains why this happened in Britannia and not in France, Spain and Italy, where we have thorough documentary evidence of Germanic ruling classes dominating the landscape for hundreds of years. Yet these areas continued as Latin-speaking societies, proving that it's possible to have Germanic ruling classes without becoming Germanic. In some places, there appears to have been a fairly strict form of apartheid, forbidding inter-marriage between Goths and Romans, which would probably have left large sections of society continuing to function in an entirely Romanised manner. I wonder also if the influence of the Christian Church played a critical role. The Church was stronger and had an obviously more continuous role in the lay administration. Additionally, the "barbarians" themselves were Christian by the time they formed the ruling class. The Church was never as strong in Britannia, and what influence it had seems to have faded away in southern and eastern England for a long period.

Graveyards containing evidence of contemporaneous Romano-British and Anglo-Saxon burial practices suggest peaceful co-existence. There is no evidence for massacres, with the caveat that absence of evidence is not evidence of absence — some authors suggest genetic markers show evidence of biological genocide, i.e. the offspring of continental fathers predominated, although the degree hypothesised varies from study to study.

As noted above, there is no doubt that Germanic tribes flooded over the frontiers of the Empire, whether as armed invaders or refugees, or both, as circumstances and opportunities shifted. Why would Britannia be spared? Given that there must have been armed conflict, how much of it was systematic and how much opportunistic?

In this book and in the previous volume in this series, *In the Shadow of a Fading Empire*, I have chosen to present the Jutes as a type of proto-Viking, that is, seasonal raiders, whose aim is to collect booty and return home. The inhabitants of southern Scandinavia had adequate boats and most likely did cross the North Sea as traders and probably also as part-time raiders before the Vikings. The Vikings did not appear from nowhere; the first hostilities took place in a context of peaceful relationships between Britain and Scandinavia. However, I'd like to emphasise I have placed this handy fiction in the context of internecine political feuding, and that there are Roman-British and Saxons on both sides in the battles that bring Signy and her friends to Britannia. I have also deliberately left the political environment in eastern Britannia vague. I've avoided laying out who the bullying landlords around Durolanium are (probably the Roman-British rulers of Lincoln, according to Caitlin Green!) or the hostile coastal inhabitants who Thorgill is keen to avoid (Anglians). The area where the Jutes come ashore was a conflict zone at this time, and might have been a good place to raid without encountering entrenched local chiefs.

Also, bear in mind I have presented the story of this raid and its consequences from two different points of view: that of a Roman-British chief (Marcus Ursinus) who would have his own reasons for presenting this incursion as a hostile raid which he successfully beat off, and that of a rural peasant girl attached to the raiders (Signy) who is following her master, and has little or no insight into the raiders' plans, or the geography and politics of

Britannia. She's seen towards the end of this book creating her own memories of her time in Britannia, and she'd only be human to emphasise her own role. What did Chief Oswulf think of the whole matter? Perhaps he had more allies in Britannia than the mysterious "Duke". Perhaps he was thankful to get rid of some awkward potential competitors for power in Juteland (Skalgrim and Thorgill) and maybe even set them up for defeat. We'll never know, because he was illiterate and his point of view died with him.

There is an excellent article summarising much competing evidence at: https://en.wikipedia.org/wiki/Anglo-Saxon_settlement_of_Britain, accessed 21 March, 2023.

I have also used the following books, among others. I think it is interesting to get a point of view from outside of Britain and, since Swedish is my second language, I have consulted several Swedish works aimed at Swedish readers.

Ekero Eriksson, Kristina (2021) *Vikingatidens Vagga*. Natur & Kultur (This book is written in Swedish, unfortunately, but it focusses specifically on the period in the Viking world before the Vikings themselves appeared, known in Sweden as the Vendel Period.)

Green, Caitlin (2020) *Britons and Anglo-Saxons: Lincolnshire AD 400–650*. Second Edition. History of Lincolnshire Committee (Caitlin Green examines the evidence for a gradual transition between the Romano-British society and the Anglo-Saxon immigrants in Lincolnshire.)

Price, Neil (2020) *The Children of Ash and Elm: A History of the Vikings*. Basic Books, New York, USA (While this book primarily describes Viking culture, the author clearly anchors this in the people who preceded them. I've picked a few concepts to project backwards onto the people who lived in the Viking lands before they technically became Vikings.)

Lindström, Jonathan (2022) *Sveriges långa historia*. Norstedts (Another book in Swedish, with interesting material about life in Sweden in the pre-Viking iron age and the relationships between Scandinavia and the Roman Empire.)

C3 Acknowledgements 80

Many thanks to Kahina Necaise, Naomi Munts Cecily Blench for their comments and suggestions during the preparation of this manuscript, all coordinated by the folks at The History Quill (thehistoryquill.com). Thank you, too, to my wife, Marja, and to my mother, for their enthusiastic support.

❧ Previous Volumes in this Series ☙

I
Memories of a Fading Empire

In the year 407 CE the influence of the Roman Empire on the province of Britannia is ebbing away. The imperial administrators and the legions have left, but thousands of people must continue their everyday lives as best they can. The departing governor of Britannia Prima suddenly appoints Marcus Lucullus Silvanus, the son of a regional landowner, as his delegate while he travels to Rome. When the governor disappears without trace, Marcus, his wife, Hypatia, the daughter of the missing governor, his friends and colleagues, struggle to preserve the bankrupt province, opposed by the jealous and determined Astrebanus brothers. The Romans have gone for ever, and a new era has begun, an era of chaos and decay, the era we know as the Dark Ages.

II
Journeys Through a Fading Empire

412 CE: From a dinner party in Verulamium, two journeys begin through the chaos and confusion of the late Roman Empire from Britannia, through Gaul and on to Rome. Ophelia Ursina, daughter of the governor of Britannia Prima, is seeking freedom and security. Drusus Astrebanus, son of the governor's arch enemy, is seeking vengeance for the death of his brother and the return of his family's property and status. In the wake of the failed uprising of General Flavius Claudius Constantinus, the usurper and co-Emperor Constantine III, the risks have only become greater as barbarians from the east infest the fading state. The rule of law no longer applies, and violence becomes the only defence. This is a dangerous world for men and even more so for women.

III
In the Shadow of a Fading Empire

430 CE: In the shadow of the fading empire of Rome, Marcus Lucullus Ursinus is toiling to maintain the peace and prosperity of the former province of Britannia Prima. Raiders from over the eastern sea may be the most obvious threat he faces, but the most dangerous challenge comes from growing tensions within the province, amplified by his deadly enemies, the Astrebani. The progress Marcus has worked for, securing the frontiers, forging alliances with neighbours, providing schooling for girls and boys, building a Christian church to appeal to pagans, employing taxes for the good of the public, and supporting competent and resourceful merchants, all appear to kindle disorder and strife. The cycle of history is turning, civilisation is in retreat and, despite Marcus' efforts, the future seems ever darker.